Praise for

Laurelle Cousins

'This exciting new voice in rural romance brings authentic passion to every page, writing from the heart of the land she calls home with her beloved merino sheep and the menagerie of animals that inspire her storytelling. With an irresistible gift for capturing the raw beauty and emotional depth of country life, Laurelle Cousins crafts heartwarming romances that will have readers wanting more.'
Annie Seaton - Award-winning author

'I first discovered Laurelle Cousins through *Sheep Gully Road*—and I absolutely adored it. I quickly tracked down *The Lonely Paddock* and fell in love with that one too. Laurelle's books are beautifully written, warm and heartfelt, with characters you can't help but connect with. Her storytelling has a way of drawing you in completely—they're the kind of books you don't want to put down. Be warned though . . . you might just fall in love with Monica the sheep and suddenly find yourself wanting one of your own. I'm so excited for her new release! Once you've read Laurelle Cousins, she's guaranteed to earn a spot on your auto-buy list. Cosy, charming and unforgettable—these are stories that stay with you.'

Janene Morgan – Book Reviewer - Reads on the Road

'Laurelle Cousins debut novel *The Lonely Paddock* ticked all the boxes for me. You can tell by reading the book she knows all about the land, farming, horses, animals, and the competitive sport of polocrosse. It was easy for me to create an image in my mind of her wonderful and authentic story. The narrative has great characters, with a strong emphasis on the possibilities and includes themes of forgiveness and acceptance, change and community spirit, animals and the comfort they bring family, and hope, healing and romance, and yummy food, and a bad guy to make it even more interesting. Five stars from me and I can't wait to read more from Laurelle Cousins.'

Karren Sandercock – Book Reviewer - 'Karren's Reading Nook'

'Laurelle writes authentic, heartfelt tales steeped in country grit. *The Reluctant Farm-her* captures the true soul of life on the land. A powerful story of love, resilience, and finding home where the heart already belongs.'

Léonie Kelsall – Bestselling Rural Romance Author

'I have read and loved Laurelle Cousin's stories. They are emotional and moving, her characters are so easy to love and her stories are set in beautiful locations. They are warm-hearted, fun, witty, and very easy to read. They are written with heart, emotion, and are so real, her characters—human and animal—come to life on the pages, and friends will be made. I highly recommend them.'

Helen Sibbritt – Book Reviewer

About the author

Laurelle Cousins is a wool classer who lives the country life, with all its unique vibes, sounds and smells—some of which are more tolerable than others. She loves writing characters with strength and sass, her heroes and heroines always getting their happy ever after, but only after she's put them through the wringer to get there. And there's always a misbehaving animal (or two) colouring the pages of her novels.

Laurelle has been Runner-up for favourite debut author in 2022 with ARRA, for her title The Lonely Paddock and has edited a feature piece for Rural Women's Day magazine titled Childhood Memories. And her novels will now be coming out in Audio, starting in late 2025 with Ulverscroft publishers.

She has a sidekick kelpie named Jazz, loves wrestling sticks ten times her size. Laurelle also loves to stay in touch with her wonderful readers and would be thrilled to hear from you. You can find her at:

Website: https://www.laurellecousins.com/
Email: Laurelle@laurellecousins.com
Instagram: laurellecousins.writes
Facebook: Laurelle Cousins Writes
Pinterest: pinterest.com/laurellecousins

Other books by Laurelle Cousins

Settlers Hill Series:

Book 1: The Reluctant Farm-her

Book 2: Playing For Sheep Stations – coming soon

Book 3: The Lonely Paddock

Book 4: The Accidental Farm-her – coming soon

Forest Gully Series:

Book 1: Sheep Gully Road

Book 2: The Home Paddock – coming soon

Shearer's Arms Series:

Book 1: A Shearer's Run – coming December 2025

Pioneer Ridge Series:

Book 1: Kelpie's Pass – coming soon

LAURELLE
COUSINS

The *Reluctant* Farm-her

LCP

ISBN: 9798298274272
Published by LCP

Cover Design: Laurelle Cousins
Laurelle Cousins Press
Cover Images: Laurelle Cousins Photography
Images: All other images using DeepAI
https://www.laurellecousins.com

For JB: 18/8/1959 to 7/6/2025

Beverley Merino Stud

You said yes to a girl who wanted to learn to class
superfine wool.

You were taken too soon. You will be deeply missed.

CHAPTER 1

Charlotte Redding cringed against the icy wind lashing her hair into her face like a whip. She clutched her jacket tight to her chest and looked about. A loose piece of corrugated iron slapped the side wall of her old tack room. The chill of Pleurisy Plains—as the old-timers of the Western District used to call it—was living up to its formidable reputation, and her heart thudded as memories came shooting back.

Moving from the protection of her car, she leaned into the oncoming gale blowing fiercely from the west as she forced herself towards the shearing shed despite her heart screaming at her to turn back. She'd come home—to what exactly? She had avoided Sheepwash Creek—her family property—set amongst the fragrant blackwood gums and expansive hills below the Grampians for six long years, and she would have stayed away longer. But the farm had other ideas, and she was certain she knew what they were.

Charlotte reached the shed, grabbing the cold metal handle that ran alongside the steps to steady herself, then paused. Oscar the garden gnome—named by a shearer long gone—watched her with his trademark chipped, cheesy smile. 'Stop that now,' Charlotte whispered, pointing at Oscar and sending him a rueful grin, wishing it was her Dad she was lightly chastising instead.

Lifting a foot to the first step, a black and tan blur tore past her side, leaping up the steps three at a time.

'Gah!' Charlotte's eyes bulged as she sucked in an unwelcome mouthful of icy air more brutal than any weather Melbourne could throw her way. Her hand flew to her chest as the dog reached the top of the landing and whirled around, panting at her with a toothy grin while his swaying backside struggled to keep up with his tail. The wind rocked her body, and she lunged for the railing, her hair whipping in her face again.

'Lewie, don't do that. You scared me half to death. And how come you're out of your pen?' Had Mum been leaving him out ever since . . .? The air in her lungs hovered as her eyes locked onto her father's loyal kelpie, his tongue lolling from his mouth which managed to tug a reluctant smile to her lips. Just watching the dog as he drew in his tongue and tipped his head to the side at the sound of his name filled her heart with love. He had to be missing her father too, and his enthusiastic welcome sent a flutter of calm through her—something she desperately wanted to hold on to before it was stolen away.

Gathering her breath, Charlotte tugged herself up the stairs and was about to slide the shed door open when the crunch of tyres on gravel halted her, the sound triggering memories she'd fought to keep buried. Turning towards the sound, a sparkling clean ute with a neat stock crate trailer rolled up next to her in the driveway of their homestead.

'Hey, Char,' the deep, cheerful voice called from the open window as the ute pulled to a stop, the disturbed dust swirling in the wind and stinging her eyes. His lips curved in that familiar soft smile, his voice holding a sensitivity so real, so genuine, her chest tightened. She wished he would stop calling her by that nickname. It only dredged up memories, ones she couldn't afford to revisit.

Fraser Pierce had been in her life forever. She narrowed her eyes as she drew her coat closer. She wanted, no, *needed* to be left alone, so she could wallow in her own despair, grief, and deliberate self-loathing, and he was stopping her from doing that.

'Hey, Fraser.' Her voice was small, wobbly, as she blinked, tugging a handful of her hair to the side of her neck as she looked down at him from the landing, waiting for him to speak.

And then go.

In that ever-so-brief moment, she saw the warm smile that had once been hers before it slipped away, replaced by a flicker of hurt in his eyes. And in that same moment, guilt ground over her as she watched his grip tighten and loosen on the steering wheel. Her mouth twisted in a pathetic apology, and that old familiar ache returned for the days when they'd been so close, *before* the moment when she had been robbed of the future she'd dreamt of.

But those times were in the past. She would do well to remember that. She forced her legs to move down the steps, stopping beside his window.

'Hi, Charlotte,' a cheerful voice chirped from the passenger seat. Maddie Nash leaned forward, smiling—a neighbour who lived further down the road with her mother and two brothers.

What was Maddie doing in Fraser's ute? Charlotte bit down on her bottom lip, scuffing the dirt at her feet to hide her surprise. And why were these . . . feelings being dredged to the forefront of her mind when she'd banished them firmly to the past? They had no business trying to creep up on her.

Charlotte kept her eyes only on Fraser, watching the slow bob of his Adam's apple beneath his still-tanned-from-last-summer neck—the same one she used to snuggle into. Regret swamped her, and her heart skittered inside her chest. She hated this distance that had been forced between them, but it was necessary. If she didn't hold tight, remembering why it had to remain that way while she was back, she might crumble.

'Is there something I can help you with, Fraser?' She tipped her head to the side with a weary stare, wishing she didn't sound as exhausted as she felt.

Lewie bounded up beside her, nudging his wet nose into her hand, coaxing a smile from her. She held the side of his head to her thigh, giving his warm cheek an affectionate rub as she looked down at him.

A deep *baa* bellowed from behind the ute, and Charlotte looked up in surprise, taking stock of five proud rams standing side by side in the crate trailer, staring back at her as though they were expecting a feed, gold service style. Lewie immediately stood to attention, ears pricked, his steadfast focus steadfastly on the rams before Charlotte's puzzled gaze found Fraser's deep brown eyes.

'Ah, I'm returning your rams.' His sheepish expression had her tiredness easing a little, his all-too-familiar lop-sided smile lifting, making her insides flutter more than she believed the action deserved.

'And . . . why exactly have you got them?' She quirked her restless eyebrow. The rivalry between the two families had never been a silent one. Both Charlotte and Fraser understood it was all over the land Fraser's grandfather had gifted her parents—Keith and Jayne—when they'd married, as a gesture of good rivalry and goodwill. It was situated directly across the road from their front gate, and smack bang in the middle of Fraser and his father's land. When John Pierce came to the district of Settlers Hill—in a slightly advantageous way—he tried to buy the small parcel of land from her dad, to complete "his side" of the land. And during Charlotte's parents thirty years of marriage, her dad had refused to sell it to Fraser's father, no matter how often he had asked, or in later years, demanded to buy it.

Fraser's hesitation ignited her curiosity, and the longer she waited for him to answer, the longer she had to take in how he'd grown from the gangly sweet teenager she'd known, into the man who—had their unfortunate tragedy never happened—she was certain would have been in her future. She promptly batted aside the stirrings thrumming inside with a deep swallow.

'I'm, um, sorry, Char, but . . .' His brow tightened, as though he found what he was about to say difficult. 'They're your show rams . . . from the Sheep and Wool Show competition.' His expression held sympathy and sincere sorrow. 'I hope this is a good time to return them?' He grimaced, breaking their eye contact, and she could tell this was hard for him too.

She sucked in a gulp of icy air, the chill a relieving distraction from the reminder of the past. Her father had been competing for the last three years at the show . . . alone. All because she hadn't been able to face the distinct, earthy aroma of sheep amongst the buzzing atmosphere of wool growers and experts. She had deliberately chosen not to be there or to help him. The thought hit her like a full-blown punch in the gut. But how could she have ever considered doing it? After her brother, James, had died, she couldn't bear to have anything to do with the farm. Feigning her good old excuse of too much to do and zero time to spare as the reason she'd remained unavailable throughout her years of study, she let it creep into her work life as well. And it was true. Graduating from uni, she had poured everything into building up her business. Thanks to all that hard work, it was finally beginning to take off.

But she'd come home to clean up the farm. Fresh guilt wound its way deep into her heart and it jolted in response. It was time to face the hard facts. She was done with her once fanciful dream of carrying on the Redding name within the wool industry because, without James and Dad beside her, Sheepwash Creek was . . .

Absolutely nothing.

CHAPTER 2

Fraser ran a hand through his hair, his lips pressed tight as Charlotte stood looking more through him than at him, more alone and lost than he could remember ever noticing before. And she would never have owned up to it, that he knew for sure. But he knew her. Even now, there wasn't much she could hide from him.

A waft of her subtle perfume danced on the wind and wound its way into his cabin, toying with the emotions he'd tried so hard to push aside since she'd left her family station. But he couldn't. It teased him with hope, her elegance and wistfulness weakening him at the knees.

He studied her wide eyes, the ones that so often reminded him of a perfect spring day. Had she changed in the time she'd been gone? Or was the same old Char lurking beneath that brave exterior he was sure she was putting on for him?

Fraser backed the trailer up to the opening of the sheep yard with precision, sensing her keen eye watching him closely.

'You alright?' Fraser hopped out of the ute, moving towards the back of the trailer and opening the gate of the crate.

'I'm fine.' He could tell she was trying to brush him off, but he wanted to stay longer; just be near her. The mere fact that he hadn't returned Keith's rams until now was something he couldn't have planned better given her arrival.

'You sure? You were doing that little wobbling-your-head thing and talking to yourself again.' He tilted his head to the side, hoping she might give him one of her smart retorts. He'd always loved the way she did that.

The sun poked through a small gap in the clouds, making her squint as her mouth gave a hopeful twitch before she reined it in, levelling a glowering eye at him. 'Weren't you supposed to be concentrating on reversing rather than looking at me?'

'Hmm, I did that too.' Fraser's sharpened gaze considered her from beneath his Akubra. It was clear she was fighting to keep her smile at bay and his heart skittered at the thought. 'Some men can do two things at once.'

She turned to the rams, clearly choosing to dismiss his attempt at a bit of light-hearted teasing, or was she ignoring him completely? He chuckled quietly to himself, not minding which it was. It was enough to have her back on their home ground again and he'd take that for as long as he could.

'Ho, ho-ho, come on. Out you get.' Charlotte waved her arms in the air, but the rams only stared back, unmoving, so used to human contact because they'd been hand-fed and handled to be show-worthy. 'Oh, come on. Give me a break,' she growled, before scowling at Fraser as he leaned against the ute, watching her. His chest filled with a delightful warmth. She was as determined as ever. And bossy.

'Well—' She splayed her arms out beside her. 'Are you going to help?'

He pushed himself off the ute, unable to hide his smirk beneath his hat. In one lively stride, he lifted his leg to the wheel arch, the trailer shuddering as he jumped over the top, landing sure-footed inside. Lewie ran back and forth along the side of the trailer, giving a deep bark, and with little more than a 'shoo' from Fraser, the rams began filing down the race, but not before the largest ram slowed, pausing to give Charlotte one last, long stare. Fraser didn't miss the shiver that visibly ran over her whole body.

Brutus. Charlotte stared at the monstrosity of a ram eyeing her with disdain as her body tensed. It had to be him.

The sound of another car coming down their drive broke the stand-off between them, instantly sending relief through Charlotte, and she couldn't help but smile as her mother parked inside the shed next to them. *Perfect timing.* Now Fraser could chuff off with Maddie and she wouldn't need to see him again before she left this place for good.

To her relief, he did hop back into his ute, driving forward far enough for her to close his stock crate and then the yard gate. The rams ambled up the ramp, into the woolshed and she closed the door behind them before turning and offering Fraser an on-your-way wave as she headed towards her mother for a long-awaited hug and to help with the groceries she'd already started unloading.

'G'day, Mrs Redding.' Fraser pulled ahead of Charlotte, stopping near the machinery shed and putting his elbow on the window frame while offering her mother one of his charming smiles that had her searching the sky in despair. Did he have to be so nice? Couldn't he go? *Please?*

Charlotte's eyes widened and she pursed her lips—only to ensure they didn't drop open—as her mother proceeded to walk over to him, her face brimming with irritating delight, all without so much as an acknowledgement or a hello her way. Feet slowing, her chin tucked in towards her neck. What was it with this man? Did he have some damned beacon that had the power to have all the women in the district under his spell? And she had thought spending years away would have broken such a frustrating enchantment. It should have, at least with her. She narrowed frustrated eyes at herself. She hadn't forgiven him and definitely wasn't about to start.

Or to forget.

'Are you coming in for a cuppa, Fraser? I'm sure you and Charlotte have a lot of catching up to do.' Her mother's emphasis on the word "lot" had her internal alarm bells ringing as Jayne beamed once more, and Charlotte was acutely aware that her mother's avoidance of looking at her was a dead giveaway as to what she was up to. The air in her lungs evaporated as Fraser promptly turned the ute off, hopped out and reached for the groceries from her mother before following her towards the house, glancing back at Charlotte, his chuffed smile imprinting his cheeks as Maddie trotted behind.

'Well, don't mind me,' she huffed, trudging to the car boot and retrieving the last of the grocery bags, which happened to be the heaviest. She lugged them towards the house as Fraser, Maddie, and her mother disappeared inside, the screen door clunking shut behind them, leaving her to fight it open on her own.

Charlotte dropped the shopping bags inside the door, then tugged off her city-high boots, as she liked to call them. They were boots that reached to her calves, and she loved them, but her heart stirred at the sight of her father's dusty work boots sitting on the shoe rack next to the door, as though they were waiting for him to put them on at any moment, despite the lone cobweb draped from one boot to the other. She took a settling breath. *Hold it together, Char,* and she summoned the strength to continue, closing her eyes and swallowing away the tightness inside her throat.

As she picked up the bags once more, the sight of her father's Driza-bone hanging on the coat rack next to hers—

and James's—was almost enough to undo her. And she would have let it had Fraser and Maddie not already been inside. The fresh wave of grief pricked at her eyes, the sharp lump in her throat clenching hard and fast once more as she glanced above the coats to the wooden coat hanger where the initials J R and C R were roughly etched. She and James had scribed them into the wood above their coat hooks as kids, much to their father's disapproval, and secret delight. They had sworn, long ago, that they would take on the farm together, keeping the legacy of the Redding name forthright and alive for future generations of superfine wool and noteworthy rams that other farms would look to for strengthening their own bloodlines. That had always been the vision.

It still should be.

Charlotte's eyes stung as she looked down while wrestling with the bags. Hopeful no one was looking, she lifted them onto the kitchen table in the centre of the room. But Fraser had his eyes on her from the same side of the table and he reached to help, brushing her fingers with his hand. They both paused, staring at each other like they didn't know what to do. But a rising irritation surged within her, one so well trained and clinging that she angled her body from his, releasing her grasp and leaving behind his tender warmth that fought to entwine her. How could her mother willingly invite him in like nothing had ever happened? How was fraternising with the enemy in her own house okay?

With their steaming cuppas in hand, the kitchen clock ticked like the throb of her threatening headache as quiet fell over the room. She watched as her mum leaned over the table, offering Fraser a slice of her famous chocolate mud cake, the one Charlotte had for her eighteenth birthday. It had always surpassed any cake she had eaten and nothing in any patisserie in Melbourne had come close. Through a side glance, she saw Fraser reach for a piece, taking a bite and nodding his approval, which was exactly the right reaction for her mother. But when Mum passed a piece towards her, all she could do was shake her head politely, regret raking her. She laid odds her mother had cooked it especially for her arrival, but in that moment, the idea of food only made her woozy. It might be the cake to be rivalled by all the local women, its recipe a closely kept secret by her mother, but Charlotte would have a piece later, when Fraser was far from her mind, and she'd had time to accept she was about to sleep under the Sheepwash Creek roof for the next fourteen days.

So, when Fraser asked her what her plans were, her answer was immediate.

'Tidy up, then sell up.'

CHAPTER 3

She can't leave.

Charlotte's words hit Fraser like a hammer to the chest and he sat up abruptly at the kitchen table, hoping the surprise on his face didn't reveal his true feelings. He'd just got her back. He was sure being here would reignite her love of the farm once more. Then she could run the station like she'd always said she would, regardless of their past and the differences that had grown between them. He swallowed a little harder against the mouthful of cake lodged like a thick clump of mud at the back of his throat and pressed his closed fist to his mouth to excuse himself as he fought to swallow. Reaching for his drink and taking a steadying sip, he waited for the combination of coffee and dark chocolate to put him at ease. It didn't work as he hoped.

He hadn't been surprised at her cool reception when he'd arrived, but the way she'd taken the bait from his teasing—well, it was like old times—as if she'd never been away. Was he kidding himself, or had he seen her eyes light up like they used to, when she'd teased him for watching her? A hopeful smile tweaked his lips, and he looked up, only to be caught red-handed as Charlotte's suspicious eyes zeroed in on him.

'Great cake, Jayne.' He shied away from Charlotte, hoping he'd disguised his smile by giving his full attention to her mum, the woman who had never faltered in accepting him regardless of the past or their families' confronting history. There was only acceptance and genuine neighbourly love in her eyes, and precisely what he needed to help him deal with the grief that, to this day, gripped him savagely by the throat at unexpected times, rendering him vulnerable and thoroughly alone until he worked through it for the umpteenth time. Would he never be free to live his life like any other regular young farmer, running thousands of stock and trying to make a future for himself? It was on those days that he busied himself in the paddock on the quad bike or the tractor, where no one could try to console him or say it had been long enough and it was time for him to move on.

Fraser risked a brief glance in Charlotte's direction. He'd always understood it was a possibility that she might leave for good, her physiotherapy business highly successful if what his mother had told him was correct. But he'd never believed she would stick with it long-term. Her love of the farm was far deeper than the lure of any job in the city. The farm would bring her home to Sheepwash Creek.

And to him. Eventually.

But that was before Keith had died, he reminded himself. Things were vastly different for her now.

So, how could he make her see reason, or at least *his* reason? Didn't she get that if she sold everything, there'd be no going back, no changing her mind at a later date and wishing she'd waited before making such a rash decision? How could he convince her to keep Sheepwash Creek and stay on to run the station? Sure, no other woman in this district of Victoria had done that before, but she could, he was sure of it. What he needed was a way to convince her.

But—Fraser's ever-so-brief wave of hopefulness flittered away—what if it was *because* of him that she was intent on staying away? He couldn't blame her for not being overjoyed at seeing him. He had to live with the inner guilt that he hadn't done enough for his best friend—her brother, James—every day, and regret mixed with an overwhelmingly deep sense of remorse crashed into him like a ram with its head down, horns ready to bulldoze its opposition. But he'd been young, and Will Franklin, another member of the local district, had been even younger. It shouldn't have happened on his watch. He stiffened as he reached for the back of his neck, the sudden shift in mood—thanks to her abrupt statement—creating a uniform silence that no one wished to break.

Fraser's mind raced. To own a station like hers was a once-in-a-lifetime opportunity, no matter how much it cost.

Once word got out, every bloke and his dog would be competing to acquire the stud, or more likely, part of it, all so they could have a chance to make it their own, off the backs of her dad and James and the long-established stud excellence. Surely she wouldn't let it go so easily?

Fraser swallowed the last of his cuppa, unusually turning down the offer of a second slice of her mum's cake as he stood, the chair legs catching against the grouted tiled floor. 'Thanks for inviting us in, Mrs Redding. But we'd best be off.' Shoving a hand deep into his jeans pocket, he felt for his Grandfather Jacob's fob watch, clenching it tight as he dredged up a smile. Nodding her way, and then Charlotte's ever so briefly, he ushered Maddie to the door first. He was keen to get to The Small Store and grab some milk from Frank for his mother. He composed himself with a deep breath of the icy late afternoon air. He wished he knew what he was meant to do with the information Charlotte had landed him with so abruptly. It had unnerved him more than he'd been ready for. But in the meantime, he had to keep a tight lid on it until he could work out a plan. Keeping Charlotte Redding at Sheepwash Creek was not only a challenge.

It was a must.

After tea, Charlotte ventured outside as Lewie appeared silently at her side. Reaching down, she gave him a welcoming pat, a gentle smirk appearing at the edges of her lips as she approached the garden gnome who grinned right back. He had been her dad's ploy to make anyone stepping inside the shed take the opportunity to smile first. Then with a bit of luck, they'd start the job in a good frame of mind. Working with sheep had the potential to be the undoing of many, and her father had seen firsthand what a negative—if not jealous—mindset could do, especially with his neighbour.

Charlotte sensed the slight lift of weight from her shoulders that she'd been carrying around since she'd left to come home as she paused beside the little guy before skipping up the shearing shed steps. Strolling inside, the aroma of lanoline and wool threw itself at her, and she closed her eyes, inhaling the wafts as if they were reaching out to her with the offer of a warm hug. There was no better smell, and a rush of homesickness flittered over her. But she quickly reminded herself why she was here.

She walked deeper into the quiet shed, eyeing the empty wool bins with remnants of wool locks trapped in the corners and cobwebs dangling softly from the high rafters. A daddy longlegs spider sailed down gracefully in front of her, pausing as if to stop and say hello at eye level. She tipped her head to the side, smiling, as he continued his descent to the floorboards, scurrying away.

The shuffle of feet on the running boards behind her piqued her interest, and she walked towards the pen of rams she'd moved into the shed earlier, keen to have a better look at the admirable qualities her father had selected for exhibition.

All five rams looked at her with cautious interest, but it was the one with the biggest wide-set horns that stepped forward, dipping his head and bleating as he watched her with quizzical eyes.

'So, I'm betting you're Brutus.' With her hands on her hips, she cast a guarded eye over the ram as his head bobbed, as if he was agreeing with her, his impressive horns catching her immediate attention. He was an incredible specimen, but she was under no illusion that if he wanted to, he could bail her up in any corner of his choosing . . . and crush her. The thought had her left thigh pinging with twangs of phantom pain associated with a memory she didn't want to recall, and she resisted the urge to press a comforting hand to her leg. She wasn't about to show him any weakness.

As if he could read her mind, Brutus stomped his foot on the grating, the sound echoing within the shed. Each ram was in prime condition, but it took more than lucerne chaff and oats to keep them looking that sharp.

'Okay, okay, you win. I'll get you what you want.' Charlotte headed to the end of the shed where her father had stacked several bales of hay. She ran a hand gently over the tops of the bales, the mere thought of him having stood in the exact spot not so long ago filling her with fresh sorrow. She rested both hands on the bales, closing her eyes while picturing his loving grin beaming down on her. Her eyes prickled with heat, and she squeezed them tight, wiping the tears with the back of her hand before blinking, gathering her composure. She knew none of this was going to be easy, but she had to do her best for her dad.

Grabbing three lucerne biscuits, she returned, tossing them around the pen to minimise the arguments amongst the rams over who got to the food first. They stepped up and began munching, all while keeping a cautious eye on her as she reluctantly hopped into the pen to check that their water was fresh and full, before darting out again in a flurry. While they appeared quiet and content with food in their mouths, Brutus' reputation preceded him. She'd heard all about his antics from both her parents.

She leaned back against the railing of the opposite pen, her hands resting each side of her as she listened to their steady chewing, her body finally relaxing. Contrary to what she'd presumed about returning home, she had to admit it was good to be back, or at least to be surrounded by the familiar smells that filled her with peace and calm.

But she had a timeline keeping her on track, she reminded herself. Then she could return to her patients and her life, the one she loved, even if it was faster-paced than life on the farm.

The inky sky was moonless, making it hard not to trip on the uneven stones scattered throughout the driveway as she made her way back to the house. Steam rose from the kettle as she walked in.

'Cup of tea, love?' Her Mum's gentle voice oozed straight into her heart, and Charlotte gave a weary smile, nodding.

'Yes, please.' She sat with a tired slump. She hadn't been ready for the vast array of emotions threatening to pummel her on her return, including James, her father . . . and

Fraser. But her bed was calling, if she could manage to drink her tea before her head fell onto the kitchen table.

Her mother took a mindful breath before speaking, placing her steaming mug in front of her before she took a seat. 'The farm is in our names now, sweetheart. But it's your decision what to do with it. And whatever you decide, I'll back you one hundred percent.'

Charlotte looked up in surprise, and a good smattering of guilt. She'd come back with one mission in mind, never once contemplating her mother's views on the matter. She frowned in disappointment at herself. Mum had never wanted to interfere with what she, James, and her father had planned so long ago for the future of the farm, and she wearily closed her eyes. Too many thoughts were clamouring for attention, and all she wanted to do was ignore them.

'Mum, I'm so sorry.' She clasped the hot cup in her hands, enjoying the sting as she shook her head. 'I shouldn't have said anything to Fraser before I spoke with you. It . . . just, kinda came out.' She'd wanted to keep Fraser at a distance, her renewed mixed feelings about him dealing her a curveball directly on target, threatening to jeopardise her otherwise well-thought-out plans, and she couldn't let that happen.

'Honey, that doesn't matter one bit,' Jayne said, brushing the air dismissively at Charlotte's concern. 'Fraser can be trusted, and besides, it would be an enormous job for you to do on your own. Goodness knows I'm not the young woman I once was.' She squeezed her fingers into her palms, the arthritic stiffness in them more evident to Charlotte than the last time she'd been home.

On my own. That's exactly what it would be if she changed her mind, and the thought both horrified and, strangely, excited her. No one told her she couldn't do something, and that was precisely why she'd fled the farm to begin with. She ignored the brief nudging from her conscience, which teased her with the realisation that this was all about Fraser and nothing to do with her own choices. Besides, *if* she wanted to keep the farm, she *could.* No outdated mindset stating women in the district couldn't be seen to be running a station, let alone a successful one, could, or would stop her.

The thing was, she didn't want it. That's all.

Or the boy next door she'd once loved.

No. The farm was no longer any friend of hers.

CHAPTER 4

Fraser drummed his fingers on the kitchen table as he sat alone, the occasional croak from a frog in his mother's garden pond below the window keeping him company. Samson the Ginja Ninja waltzed in, his almost aloof expression shifting to one of slight amusement as he spotted Fraser and sashayed over to him, planting his backside at Fraser's feet, his tail agitated as he studied the atmosphere of the room.

'How am I meant to keep her here, hey?' he said as the cat glanced up at him with an air of I-don't-really-care before looking away again.

'Yep. I don't have a clue either,' Fraser said, offering the cat a pat on the head, to which the animal pushed against his hand in a rare act of acceptance. No matter how much he'd tried to convince himself there could never be anything between him and Charlotte, he'd failed, despite throwing himself into life at the farm to help him forget what they'd had, and what might have been. For a while, he had managed to succeed. But the moment he'd seen her at the funeral, it was as though his heart had woken his brain, reminding him of all that he'd dared to hope for.

His own grief over losing Keith, a man he'd come to love as a second father, left him with a hollowness his father would never understand.

And Charlotte's companionship . . . What they had was far too special to forget, and he was confident she hadn't forgotten what it had meant. Their love had been steadfast and loyal beyond all logic. It lingered, solid and unforgettable.

He had to be honest. Receiving her brisk welcome had hurt . . . a lot. But if he could remind her of the connection they had had, he might have a chance with her again. He had to believe it. With elbows on the table, he dropped his head into his hands as the Ginja Ninja lifted a paw to his thigh. Fraser looked down between his arms, reaching a hand to the cat's soft head. 'It has to be worth a try. Right?'

Outside the stillness of the room, footsteps moved down the hallway and his father breezed in. The Ginga Ninja gave a sly glance up before slipping from the room.

'What are you still doing up? It's after midnight,' his father said.

'I could say the same to you.' The condensation from Fraser's breath danced about him as he studied his father with a half-smile before standing to put the kettle on as his father

took a weary seat. He wasn't about to tell him it was
Charlotte his mind was swamped with, along with the feelings
he couldn't manage to resist rekindling, all because she was
back home. Seeing her in the flesh, having grown into such an
incredibly beautiful woman . . . his heart pounded with
anticipation at what they could be, but he urged it to slow
down, in no delusion as to what his father would say about it.
No. It wasn't worth mentioning.

'Couldn't sleep.' His dad studied the table like it held
the key to all his troubles, tapping it the same way Fraser had
done before he sucked in an audible breath. 'Have you heard
about Charlotte's plans to sell?' Looking up steadily, his
father's eyes were full of interest and laced with a touch of
suspicion as they watched Fraser intently.

Fraser passed him his tea as casually as he could
manage, then took his seat again. Letting his focus linger on
the table a little longer as he gripped his hot mug, he wasn't
ready to assume what his father might have heard. From the
way Charlotte had blurted it out, he'd been the first she'd
told, and he'd been glad of it as that gave him the upper hand,
plus some all-important time to find a way to make her
reconsider. He would have to get a wriggle on if he was going
to beat his father at the game he was certain he'd choose to
play.

'She did say something about that, but I'm not sure
how serious she is. That's Char, thinking fast and acting
faster.' Didn't he know it. She hadn't so much as said
goodbye to him when she'd left for Melbourne, breaking his
heart into shards he'd found almost impossible to draw back

together. To be honest, his heart was still in pieces, with little hope it would ever be mended.

'Well, I'm counting on her moving fast,' his father began, breaking his musings. 'I'd be happy to help in any way I could to get things sorted quickly, for Charlotte and Jayne's sake, of course. We could buy out Sheepwash Creek. It's good land and rumour has it there's even a bit of gold tucked away in the back hills somewhere.'

Fraser looked up with a fierce jolt and his neck cricked, making him cringe. He reached to it, rubbing against the sting that reverberated as he stared. His father might have made that statement sound like it was off the cuff, but Fraser wasn't fooled. There was a serious edge to his tone and Fraser had the distinct feeling what time he had to persuade Charlotte to stay was suddenly a whole lot less. When had his father ever wanted to lend Charlotte or the Reddings a hand?

Like never.

'What do we want to do that for, Dad? We've got a big enough overdraft as it is. Taking on more land and stock would only burden our already heavy workload. It's only you and I since you sacked Peter Rabbit.'

Did his dad pick up on the subtle, distinctly frustrated tone he used? They'd had Pete for years as a farm hand, and he'd been fantastic. He was a good friend to Fraser, even though he was the same age as his father. But his dad had always been the one to look for any small niggle to pick on, and when Pete had challenged him about making better use of their land up the back of their property for stock and grazing, his father had snapped. He had sacked him on the spot. It had never made sense to Fraser why he had reacted so spontaneously, and with such harshness.

'And there's no gold there, Dad. It's a myth.' Fraser dismissed the comment with a shake of his head as he stared into his mug of tea. 'And it's not good land, it's great. The natural water springs they have along with the soil quality, well it's some of the best, locally. The price for it will be astronomical, well above anything we could manage.' His father liked the best of everything, but for a rock-bottom price. Showing him Sheepwash Creek was well out of their price range would be enough to put his father off the scent.

'That's exactly why we should buy it.'

Fraser lifted his head in surprise, detecting a flinch of annoyance in his father's voice.

'Imagine what our stock could look like running on grazing land like that. Far better than here. And we'd have a real shot at show time. Our rams would be more sought after, increasing our sales.'

Fraser's gaze hovered over his father, laced with suspicion. Did that comment have anything to do with Keith and his stock no longer being in the running for the Sheep and Wool Show competition? Fraser squashed the annoyance angling to make him open his mouth. He took a calming breath.

'Dad, it has nothing to do with our reputation. This is about Charlotte and Jayne. Doesn't sound much like you're trying to help them. Sounds more like you're helping yourself.' Fraser's focus deepened on his mug, his calloused hands gripping it tighter than necessary. He loved his dad, but sometimes his ambition was a little too much to handle.

His father slurped down the dregs of his tea, then stood, placing his cup in the sink.

'Anyway, give it some thought, son. I reckon it's a move we should make sooner rather than later.' He gave Fraser a pat on the shoulder as he headed back to bed, leaving Fraser stripped of his hope about Charlotte staying, instead replaced by concern she could be gone soon, and that they would be the cause of it. If his father was as serious as he sounded, Fraser had to approach Charlotte within the week, if not the next few days. And he didn't want to dwell on what she might have to say to him when he did.

CHAPTER 5

Fraser woke with the break of day, the clouds moving fast across the dreary sky. A cold shiver rumbled over his body and he wearily ran a hand down his face, sucking in a long breath as he lifted his gaze to the ceiling. How in the blazes was he meant to work on a plan to keep Charlotte here when his father was hell-bent on shipping her out as fast as he could?

His heart flinched as he recalled the day she'd told him she could never love someone who wouldn't protect his own best friend. Swinging his legs to the side of his bed, he stared at the bare floorboards. That was the day she'd thrown, what he had termed at the time, a friendship ring in the puddle at his feet, the one he'd saved up for during the summer school holidays while working alongside his mate, Gus Stevens, and Gus's old uncle Neil, at the stockfeed store in Ballarat.

Early on, Pete had been good enough to listen to his sob story about buying Charlotte a ring. But to Fraser, the ring meant so much more. It was him telling her he'd wait for her no matter how long it took. He might have been fifteen when he had bought it, but he'd meant it, giving it to her that Christmas.

Four years later, she'd thrown it back at him before storming off and leaving. For good.

He recalled, as fresh as this new day, the stab of rejection that smacked him fair in the chest the day it had happened. He'd fled to the machinery shed and grabbed his motorbike, tearing off down the paddock as she'd retreated in the opposite direction on her horse at a flat-out gallop.

Several weeks later, he had searched for the ring as his humiliation was tempered by the guilt of his best friend's recent death. But with so many puddles over the large driveway in front of their homestead, he couldn't recall exactly where they'd been standing when she'd thrown it. Back then, he'd walked away, figuring it was gone for good.

And then, as if it was meant to be, four years on, he'd stumbled across it thanks to the sun glinting on a tiny corner of the small diamond, a month before Keith had passed away. And she'd turned up six weeks later? Had it been the sign he'd been hoping for?

Waiting for?

So many things had changed in the blink of an eye. Too many. What was it going to take for her to see he wasn't the bad guy she'd pegged him to be? Was it so wrong that some of his motives were a smidge selfish? Maybe. But if he had to choose between her or his father, he'd choose a future with her alongside him every damned time.

'Hey, Mum.' Fraser spied a hot coffee sitting on the table as he walked into the kitchen wearing an old T-shirt over the boxer shorts hanging low on his hips. He picked it up, desperate for a hit of the life-giving caffeine, and leaned in to give his mother a quick peck on the cheek before he took a sip.

'Morning,' Rosemary said, smiling, before her gaze sharpened on him. 'Didn't sleep well? You should've tried a spiced chai. Always works for me.' She turned her attention back to the scrambled eggs she was stirring on the stove.

'That'll only ever work for you, Mum,' he said, his mouth cringing at the idea as he took a longer sip this time, relaxing into a chair at the table as the Ginja Ninja sidled over to him in his all too casual way, offering one brief purr as his good morning. But he had to give it to her for knowing him so well and he pulled out a glowing smile to settle her concerns. 'Got a few things I don't want to forget to do today. Gotta go into the produce store and collect some dog food and drench.'

'And *that* kept you awake?' His mother's glance said she didn't believe him for a minute.

'I'll come too.' John walked in with a brisk gait, taking the second coffee on the table and sitting himself in front of the eggs on toast at the seat he always sat in. 'Want to do a few other errands too. Need to see Burt for some ammo. The rabbits in the north paddock are getting out of hand. I'll need you to take a look, Fraser, deal with them ASAP. Their bloody burrows are going to make that damn redgum uproot itself if we get a deluge of water like they say is on the cards for spring.'

Fraser's body stiffened, his stare widening as he fought to focus on his drink. He took another long sip to calm himself, not caring that his tongue was singed for his efforts. All it took was the word *ammo,* and he managed to break out into a cold sweat.

Forcing his eggs on toast down in more of a hurry than he'd first planned, the burnt crusts scratched his throat. He had handled a gun only when necessary since that night, and hardly a day went by that he didn't think of James and how much he missed him. But like it or not, he knew he had little choice this time.

In the produce store, Gus wore a grin like he'd won the lottery.

'Hey there,' Fraser said. 'You look way too happy with yourself.'

'Just got back from the beach. The surf was incredible, man. You should come with me sometime. Uncle Neil's beach hut has a spare bed. It's nothing flash but it doesn't matter when you can take on the waves whenever you want.'

'Doesn't look like you've washed the sand out of your hair yet,' Fraser chuckled, eyeing Gus's long locks that hung at his broad shoulders and strong neck. 'Nah, I'll leave that to you. The last time I was at the beach I was inside a floaty blow-up duck, and Mum had to come rescue me from the shallows because I got sand on my hands.' He gave a rueful grin. It was true. He hated the beach then. And still did. There was something about sand between his toes that sent a shiver over his entire body.

'Well, I'm here when you change your mind. Believe me when I say it, you're missing out.'

'What are you two lads rabbiting on about?' The gruff voice had Fraser looking up with a warm smile as Gus's uncle Neil shuffled into the produce storefront on unsteady feet, his grin mischievous as always. The man looked like he was about to fall over, and Fraser wanted to stand behind him in case he did.

'Where's your bloody walker, Uncle Neil? I've told you not to come in here without it. You'll go for a sixer over the loose grain on the shed floor if you don't watch out. The mice can only clean up so much.' Gus crossed his arms over his chest, shaking his head in disbelief.

'No thanks to you for not sweeping it up. Stop that rubbish talk, both of you.' He eyed Gus first, then Fraser, who held his palms in the air with a don't-look-at-me expression.

'And none of that pretending, young man.' He waved his crooked finger at Fraser, a light smirk rising on his lips. 'I don't need any help. I'm as fit as a mallee bull.' He stood as tall as his body would let him, squaring his shoulders defensively.

'You're right, Neil, and I apologise.' Fraser smiled, and the old man turned away, leaving them with a dismissive wave before grasping the side of the pallet of dog food, pausing to catch his breath. Gus and Fraser didn't miss the way his frail body swayed before he steadied himself and then walked back to the office where his heater was humming and his seat would stop him from losing his balance again.

'And some things will never change,' Gus said, shaking his head in light-hearted dismay as he grabbed the computer mouse to open Trentham Park's account. 'So, what can I get you, mate?'

Fraser drove down the middle of the wide feed shed lined on both sides with all manner of stock supplies from grains to guinea pig and chook feed. With the ute tray full, he went to hop into the cabin when Will Franklin pulled in behind him, offering a friendly wave as he stepped from his ute.

'How goes it, Fraser, Gus?' Will grinned as he strode over to them.

Fraser's smile was easy, all too aware that he was one of the few within the district who treated Will as a friend, despite what had happened and even though it was well recognised as a tragic accident. The kid back then wasn't a patch on the young man currently standing in front of them, and although his face still brought an ever-present reminder of that fateful night, Fraser had worked hard to convey his acceptance, free from judgement or disloyalty.

'G'day, Will. Good to see you.' Fraser stepped forward, shaking his hand as he glanced around for his father, spotting him through the glass window of the office with Neil.

'You too, Fraser. I must say, this rain forecast doesn't look great. Dad's real worried about it.'

'Him and I. But we need it. Only we don't want to have to take a dinghy out to the paddocks to check the stock! Make sure you keep all your stock near high ground, okay? They'll have a fighting chance then.' Will was a sensible young farmer, unlike some in the district who raced around half-cocked until everything fell apart around them during a crisis. 'I might throw a rod in the river this weekend. Wanna come?'

'Yeah, sure. I reckon I'm owed the next win. Haven't managed to hook one in like, forever.' Will chuckled.

'That's true, and I'm not about to let my record slip away,' Fraser said, chuckling good-naturedly. 'They should be biting well so how about we meet at the bridge at 6 a.m. tomorrow? That way we can beat the rain, if it does eventuate.' But he had his doubts it would happen. Peter Rabbit always said: 'Only believe it when you tip it out of the rain gauge.'

'You're on.' Will turned to head for his ute once more but slowed, calling over his shoulder. 'And bring our lunch with you this time. It's bloody well your turn to lose!'

'Hehe, will do.' Fraser waved him off before tooting the horn to get his father's attention and hurry him on, any intention of providing lunch for the fishing challenge dismissed as he shook his head and grinned. He hadn't lost to the young fella yet and wasn't about to start.

'You took long enough,' Fraser said as his father finally hopped in the ute and they drove off. 'Neil was in for a chat, was he?' He side-glanced his father, curious about what was so interesting it had held him up in Neil's office for so long. Normally Neil would have sent him on his way in a jiffy, not being one for small talk.

Fraser pulled into the petrol station and was about to jump out to grab some fishing bait when his father stalled his progress. 'I'd like you to go have a chat with Charlotte today. Offer to buy that small parcel of land opposite their driveway. That'll be a good start for her, tidy things up, and be a bit of a cash flow.'

With one foot out of the ute and his hand resting on the steering wheel, Fraser swivelled towards his father, his gaze sharpening as he replayed the comment in his head. Was that the only land his father wanted from Charlotte now? And hadn't that pocket of ground caused enough tension between the two families for a lifetime? But his father wasn't wrong. It would help her to bring in some money and give her time to make plans. It would also give her time to fall back in love with Sheepwash Creek. Despite hating that his father might be right this time, that was the best angle he had to use because she didn't want anything to do with him. And after he asked her about selling to them, he might as well be kissing all his chances goodbye.

'She's not about to listen to me, Dad. She hasn't since . . .' His voice struck mute, unable to say it out loud. He and

Charlotte had always been able to talk so freely, nothing withheld. But so much had changed.

'If she's sensible, and I know she is,' he said knowingly, 'she'll come 'round. Drop by this afternoon. The sooner we find out where things stand, the better.'

His father stared out of the front of the windscreen, a satisfied smile rising on his lips, irking Fraser in a way he hadn't expected. He tapped the steering wheel lightly with a contemplative finger as he stared at the shop window. Was that all his father wanted? But he shrugged his shoulders, more at himself than anything, fully knowing how long his dad had wanted to complete his property with that land. If Charlotte wanted to sell that sixty acres and end the three-decade-long feud, then it was her decision and he wasn't about to stop her. She might even be heartened to be rid of the tension it had caused between the two stations.

And if she wasn't interested, at least it was another good excuse to see her again, even if he wasn't sure his heart could cope with more rejection from her.

CHAPTER 6

'So let me get this straight.' Charlotte eyed Fraser calmly—definitely too calmly—and he rolled his shoulders, readying himself.

'You're proposing it would be smart of me to sell you *my parents' wedding gift?*' Charlotte planted her hands on her hips, her look incredulous as she leaned away from him. He was glad she'd put down the knife she was using to cut the lamb for tea before he'd mentioned it.

Fraser straightened as his scrambled thoughts clashed with what to say next.

'It would give you a cash flow—'

'Oh, I *need* a cash flow, do I?'

She crossed her arms this time, her weight resting on one leg in a defiant stance as the late afternoon sun shining through the kitchen window warmed the cooling air, highlighting her hair in a golden glow. Couldn't she understand this was a solution that would help her, even if he himself didn't like the sound of it either?

'We all do.' He offered her a you-can't-fool-me face as he shrugged innocently. 'We were of the opinion that if you were open to selling it, we'd be helping you out.' Had he gone and included himself in this whole maddening scheme? He inwardly cringed.

'We?' A lone eyebrow on her face lifted high, hovering as if it was doing some mid-air circus act, and while he hoped he looked calm on the outside, inside he was running like a frightened rabbit.

'Since when has your father ever wanted to *help* us, Fraser? Our families have warred for years over that incy wincy piece of land.' She presented her thumb and index finger in front of her face to emphasise the size. 'Since before we were born. It was enough to stop our father's from talking civilly ever again. Has it been that long you've forgotten? Or has your father got so far inside your head you accept it?'

Fraser swallowed hard, both from her stern glare and because he'd never forgotten. How could he? His father had wanted the two of them to break up the moment they'd got together, all because of it, apparently.

'Maybe just consider it, okay?' He held out both palms at waist level. 'There's no rush.' But he was under no false illusions. That was never going to happen.

'You look tired. Didn't get enough sleep last night?' Charlotte's sudden—definitely smug—change of topic threw him and her chin lifted in what appeared to be genuine curiosity. Was Charlotte Redding acting like she cared? The notion warmed him more than he was ready for, and all he could do was nod. He wasn't about to bring up the fact it was her who had kept him awake for much of the night.

'Try a hot chocolate,' she said lightly, a soft smile lining her lips and confusing him all the more. 'It always helps me get to sleep when my mind's whirring.' She gave a slight shrug, all but dismissing him as she resumed chopping up the cutlets in a manner far calmer than when he'd arrived. 'I've been having a lot of them lately.' Her eyes slipped to his but she gave nothing away with her expression.

Now that was the woman he was more used to. And she hadn't been sleeping either? Was it because of him? He dismissed the hopeful thought as fast as it appeared. Her only priority was her station and getting rid of it, not some has-been farm boy she'd once had a crush on.

'Okay, I might give it a try.' He nodded, grateful she wasn't suggesting a chai, his smile fading as he turned from her to leave. His frown deepened from the weight of his worry for her. If only she was privy to the critical timing he had to work with to get her to stay. And he'd done a class-A job of ticking her off even more. Nice move, Pierce. She'd probably start packing the moment he drove away, prepared to sell to some enterprising developer who'd offer her an astronomical amount of money she wouldn't be able to refuse. His father would love that. And he'd never get another chance with her. If only she could grasp the underlying cost of that decision. Ironically, he realised, his future was in her hands.

With Fraser not twenty metres down their drive, Charlotte thundered down the hallway and into her bedroom, slamming the door behind her so hard that the window panes rattled. What had happened to Fraser since she'd been gone? Clearly he'd lost some of his handsome brain cells. Shame, but that wasn't the point, she reminded herself. How could he forget how much that parcel of land had meant to her parents? John had always been annoyed that there was a piece of Sheepwash Creek on his lay of the land, and now he saw her as the easy way to getting it back? Well, she wasn't someone's easy pushover.

It. Wasn't. Happening.

Not now. Not ever. Her fingernails dug into the skin of her palms.

And, oh, what a good son Fraser was to come over and do his father's dirty work, she seethed. He wasn't the guy she'd left behind, the one who had defied his father's disappointment, refusing to end their relationship. She looked around for something to throw. Anything. But the only thing she could see was her stupid soft toy rabbit, the one her father had won for her at the local show when she was seven. Slowly, she took it in her arms, clasping it to her chest. Did

John truly lack the balls to come and talk to her himself? She'd been around him all her life and he'd never been backward in chasing what he wanted. But it didn't matter which one of them tried; they were both tainted with the same Pierce brush—the one that had always wanted what Sheepwash Creek had: a reputation like no other station within cooee, and the land to make it happen. No. Fraser's visit had only cemented her decision. She'd be selling, make no mistake.

And it was not going to be to Trentham Park.

Charlotte walked over to the French doors, the gloomy clouds foreboding as their icy chill reached for her through the glass. Goosebumps ran down her arms.

How was she going to make this all happen? She was well aware from the planning of her business that it was no good having a goal unless she could do something to make it happen. She turned and sat with a thud on the end of her bed, her eyes settling on a photo sitting opposite her, on her dresser. Her gaze turned sombre, the smiling faces staring back at her, giving her a sense the picture could have been taken yesterday. On her left was James, with Fraser on the other side, the two of them pressing down on her shoulders with their elbows and weight, making sure she looked the dwarf they always teased her she was. Her smile was as generous as the sunshine.

Next to it was a photo with a fourth person, making them the awesome foursome as they'd fondly referred to each other as. Nadine. Her once best friend, and the girlfriend of James, before—

Charlotte swallowed hard.

Where was Nadine these days? Not only had Charlotte run from Fraser when her life fell apart, but she'd also left her best friend high and dry. But she had to. It was hard enough for Nadine to deal with the devastating loss of James—the only man she'd truly loved—the one she'd planned a future with. Hanging around, with all her ugly grief clinging to her every move, would have only made things so much harder for her closest friend. She'd done the right thing by leaving before she could ruin anyone else's life.

Unable to stop herself, she stood and picked up the first photo frame, her thumb running over James's face with love, loss and shadowing sorrow. She gave a sad smile, her head tipping to the side as the joy in his expression threatened to draw her in and take her to a place she was too frightened to go.

Then it happened, her gaze slipping to Fraser as her expression turned introspective. She studied him, all dressed up in a smart shirt tucked into moleskins, his sleeves rolled up to his elbows, revealing his summer-tanned skin at the Sheep and Wool Show they'd all been exhibiting at. She'd always loved the way he did that, his forearm muscles flexing from the slightest of movements. And his eyes . . . they sparkled back at her like they had when the two of them had been so in love. Her heart skipped out of rhythm as she allowed herself a moment, her fingers pressing over her lips. They had had it all, or so they'd believed, convinced it would last forever, defying the odds of his father and their family differences. They were ready for anything life threw at them.

But not now.

Who was this Fraser, the one she'd only minutes ago dismissed from their house, all dusty and bothered from fixing a fence earlier in the afternoon, his five o'clock shadow darkening his jawline, already reigniting her feelings of old? He looked so damned good with his near-to-death Akubra hugging his dark curls, and she took in the photo one final time, her heart committing it to memory despite her brain yelling for her to turn it face down on the dresser. How had she forgotten the way his face lit up so perfectly, his straight teeth beaming her way? What would he look like these days, freshly shaven and dressed, ready to hit The Tavern for a Friday night pub meal? She blinked the image aside, refusing to acknowledge the answer that was itching to surface at the forefront of her mind. Instead, she returned the photo to its place amongst the dust on the dresser, promptly turning her back on it. She didn't need to know so it didn't matter.

'Hey, Mum,' Charlotte said as she breezed through the kitchen. 'I'm going to head out and check on the ewes.' She paused at the laundry door, hopping on one foot and then the other as she tugged on her boots.

'They're due to lamb any day,' Jayne called back. 'Can you check the fence line in Jumbuck paddock too? Last time I looked, it had a lean as though something had pushed against it. Looks like it wouldn't take much to fall over, especially if there was a decent wind gust.'

A twinge of guilt riddled her. With no one else here, it had been left up to her mum to do all the chores around the farm, including checking on the stock and fencing. Charlotte bit down on her upper lip.

'Okay. Won't be long.' Letting the screen door shut with its usual bang on her guilt, she headed for the farm ute. Turning the key resting in the ignition, she backed out of the shed. She'd been home two days and there was so much to reacquaint herself with, including Boots, her dear old gelding.

She slowed, leaving the ute running to warm the engine and cabin, while she jogged to the hay shed. *Thanks, Dad,* she smiled, tugging a biscuit from the large, neatly stacked bales left there as though he'd known she would be home soon, her heart pining with immediate sadness and happiness all at once. Her eyes prickled with the sting of erupting tears, and she blinked feverishly to quell them.

With the biscuit under her arm, she opened his paddock gate, and Boots knickered to her from a distance, clearly not forgetting who she was. Her heart squeezed.

'Hey, beautiful boy. How ya doin'?' She breathed in his horsey smell as he nuzzled his nose to the hay she was holding, and she ran her hand down his long blaze, slowing at his soft muzzle. How had she managed to leave this for so long? The softness of his coat, his gentle eyes, and his rhythmic chewing worked to absorb every last trickle of anxiety from her body. She needed to give him a good brush down. The warmth from the sun was causing some of his thick coat to lift, and with each stroke she made down his neck, it floated into the gentle breeze, dancing in front of her and tickling her nose.

'I'll come back and see you tomorrow, okay?' She gave him one last stroke down his nose before she dropped the hay to the ground and headed back to the ute, not wanting to be caught down the paddocks by the evening creeping in early and fast. Bad things happened on farms at night.

The ewes were fatter than fat, their sides moving with wiggling unborn lambs as Charlotte slowly passed by them in the ute. No one had kicked off the season yet, but with udders looking like they were about to burst, some even dripping with milk, Charlotte wanted to keep a close eye on them. There were many more paddocks of pregnant ewes and she'd have her work cut out for her, doing everything on her own.

As she bounced over an unexpected rock lying hidden in the paddock, a fresh thought dawned. Her staff back at her clinic would have to be informed that she would be away a bit longer than she had first anticipated, but there was no way she didn't want to be around for lambing. The tug of responsibility for her growing practice reminded her that the only way she'd get back there was to finish up here first, regardless of how long that took. And given the rumours she had been hearing about town, she would make sure she had the station as well presented as possible. Then she could make Sheepwash Creek's plans official.

Sure enough, the fence along Jumbuck paddock was severely skew-whiff and Charlotte made a mental note to do something about it sooner rather than later. With bouncing stud lambs due in this paddock, they'd be over it in one leap once they grew strong enough and big enough to go exploring. And if that happened, she'd have to face asking

Fraser for a hand to get them back, their north paddock adjoined to his paddock by that boundary fence. That in itself evoked enough incentive to make fixing it happen ASAP.

She found herself immersed in a sweet sense of peace only their farm could offer as she steadily made her way home, traversing the undulating contours towards each gateway as the sun sank behind the horizon and dusk prepared to overshadow the land. It was a feeling she'd once adored, one so far from her city life reality these days. She had turned to physiotherapy to study as a way to work with her hands. She might have lost the farm, but she'd never lose that tangible experience of helping her clients in pain. Yes, selling the farm was a good thing. It was the right thing to do.

So why couldn't she shake the invisible tug pulling at her as she parked the ute in the shed, turned off the ignition, and stared at the dent on the shed wall in front of her?

CHAPTER 7

Charlotte sprang out of bed at dawn, yawning as she tugged her hair into a messy bun. She was determined not to let the sun get too high in the sky before she got the chores done so she could take Boots out to stretch his legs.

As if he'd read her mind, he lifted his head over the top of the railing as she walked over the driveway towards him after lunch. With a grin, she ducked into the small tack room her father had built for her and grabbed his brush, saddle blanket, saddle, and bridle, her excitement palpable. Lewie sat next to the fence, diligently observing proceedings like a sergeant major.

Once Boots had a thorough brush-down, he stood like a true gentleman as she saddled him, then hopped aboard, keeping his reins loose as they headed for the Home Paddock gate. Lewie started to trot behind, but Charlotte turned in the saddle as Boots continued to walk. 'No, Lewie. Stay.' Deep down, she wanted to take him with her, but she wasn't sure she could trust him not to nick off, chasing some random roo and getting himself all banged up. She wasn't sure she could cope if her dad's best dog got hurt, even if it meant watching his sad puppy-dog eyes begging her to change her mind.

Lewie stopped mid-step, then slowly sat in the middle of the driveway, as if the action might make her rethink her decision. When it came to pleading his case, Charlotte had to admit he was good.

'Good boy. We'll see you soon.' She threw him an apologetic smile before turning back in the saddle, urging Boots to sit trot to the first gate.

Without prompting, Boots walked up to it, turning his body sideways so Charlotte could reach the chain without hopping off and immediately her heart swelled. He hadn't been ridden in years and here he was, doing what she'd always done when she was riding him almost every day. Turning to face the gate, he pushed it open with his strong chest, before repeating the process and closing the gate once more.

'That's my boy,' she said, patting his neck with extra care, loving the sight of looking down over his alert ears. How could she have lost sight of this feeling, her deep love for her horse, and the way she could explore their property? Or had she struck it from her mind, her grief overriding everything good about the farm? Nothing compared to this sight and she sat deep in the saddle, drawing in a slow, calming breath. He would be sore after such a long spell, and as for her, she'd be in a world of wide-legged walking pain, but it would be worth every stiff muscle.

Once in the open paddocks, Charlotte urged Boots into a loping, steady canter, the warmth of the sun on her back easily mistaken for the start of spring rather than the late winter vibes she had experienced when getting out of bed this morning. Easing Boots back into a walk as she neared the edge of one of their many steep hills, she slid her feet from the stirrups, leaving them to dangle beside his belly. The beauty of the majestic gums dotted throughout each paddock lifted her heart, their haphazard placement adding to the beauty of the landscape. Come summer, the heat of the day would allow the eucalyptus oil to seep into the air. A kookaburra sang its territorial laugh in the distance, complementing the tranquil silence. This was everything her father had worked so hard to build. The stock, the continued maintenance of the land, so it produced at its best. She visualised his face at the mention of it, and the words he'd spoken to both James and her not long before James had passed away.

'This is all for you,' her father had said, standing between them and looking at each of them with a level gaze as they overlooked the paddock. 'Because if it wasn't for both of you, there'd be no reason for me to do it.' He then gave his signature grin, the one where his lips were pressed together, but his eyes spoke of his love for them, patting James on the shoulder and leaning in to kiss Charlotte on the forehead, wrapping his arms over their shoulders before appreciating the picture-perfect sunset descending over the graceful hills.

Charlotte hadn't forgotten where they'd been standing when he'd done that, and ironically, she found herself in the same paddock, on the same hill where the sun would lower itself in a matter of hours, casting long, lazy lines of shadows over the land. Her throat tightened against the sudden sadness and deep appreciation for all her father had done to set up a future for them. A smidge of guilt pinched, too.

Easing Boots to a halt at the edge of the hill where they'd stood so long ago, she lowered the reins, letting her hands rest on his withers. She blinked slowly, digesting the beauty and immense scope of the land, their property nestled beneath the grandeur of the Grampians in the distance. This was all hers for the taking, and what did she want to do? Dishonour his devotion and deep-seated loyalty to the land by selling up? Where would she ever get the chance to do what she had always wanted if it wasn't here? Sheepwash Creek was the only place she'd ever contemplated doing that. But doing it on her own? A deflated breath left her lungs as the mournful *caw caw* of a lonely crow echoed deep in the valley.

'I'm bloody well cursed, Boots,' she said softly, shaking her head against the cooling breeze that shimmied over the foot-long tufts of grass. If she stayed and *tried* to run it, disaster would be the only outcome. It would only be a matter of time before the farm claimed them all. No. She was better off getting out of there before she also lost her life to its cruel clutches.

To her left, the glint of movement in a far-off paddock caught her attention, and she sharpened her gaze. It was Fraser in the tractor, preparing to feed out hay, the sound of the ewes baaing in an excited chorus as they and their lambs ran towards him. So, they'd already started lambing and by the size of them, it had been a good month ago. Her eyebrows furrowed with a smidge of annoyance before she looked away, the slight shake of her head revealing what she thought. It was so like John, competitive beyond measure and always determined to be ahead of Sheepwash Creek's plans. If Dad decided to do one thing, John would do it too, only earlier. Her father had never been bothered by his antics, but the pettiness of it rankled her, even after all these years.

A loud bang ripped through the air, and she cowered in the saddle. Slowly, she sat a little taller in her seat, her eyes widening as she searched for the direction it had come from, and even Boots turned to look. The tractor had stopped, surrounded by desperate sheep as Fraser's form descended from the cabin. Putting a hand on the tyre, he bent down to study it. He stood again, scanning the array of peaceful land before removing his Akubra and running a hand through his hair, letting it pause at the base of his neck.

A flat tyre. It had to be. And he was stuck kilometres away from the homestead with no alternative but to walk if he wanted to get home. Charlotte couldn't hold back her childish grin, nor did she try too hard. But should she help? He had no clue she was there. She continued watching, unmoving, as he looked behind the wheel, kicking something solid, and a wave of guilt began to grow inside her. Should she go down and see if he needed a hand? Surely he had his phone and would ring home for help. Maybe if she waited a little longer? Boots shifted his weight from one rear leg to the other, releasing a patient breath.

Charlotte's interest piqued as Fraser climbed back up into the cabin. With the ewes losing hope and meandering away, she could hear voices. It had to be John. He'd come to get Fraser. Relieved, she slid her feet back into the stirrups and reined Boots around to head for home. She needed to ring Charlie Saunders and organise a load of hay, as their stocks were getting low. With little sustenance in the scarce grass while they continued to wait for rain, it was crucial that the stock maintained their good condition.

But as she turned, she couldn't help but glance in the direction of the tractor once more. The sorry sight of him pulled at her heartstrings before he jumped down from the cabin, suddenly waving his arms in the air desperately.

In her direction.

Damn it, she thought, her lips pressed tight. She listened to her name being hollered, the valley between them carrying it easily in a drawn-out echo as she stared, unable to decide what she should do.

But there was no avoiding it, and her shoulders dropped a little as she reined Boots to a halt once more. Every time they had seen each other since she'd been home, it had ended with her regretting she'd ever laid eyes on him. And now was going to be no different. She was sure of it.

Grudgingly reining Boots in his direction, she reassured herself she wasn't going to him because she wanted to. He was calling her—for help. Was it something other than a flat tyre? Did he need a hand to get the tractor going? She'd never been the handyman in the family, preferring the four legs she was astride to transport her rather than anything mechanical, but it'd be rude not to go and find out what he wanted. After all, that's what neighbours did for one another, didn't they?

Even if they are annoying, she muttered under her breath.

Charlotte and Boots moved down the sloping hill and through another adjoining gate dividing the paddocks before she nudged him into an easy canter towards the tractor. Fraser, was pacing with impatience, his hat in his hand by his side as she approached. She watched as his walk, once lanky and slow, strode full of purpose towards her. Her heart quickened as her memories of the love she'd once had for him fought for immediate attention. But just as fast, she squashed them. No way could she entertain any interest in him, regardless of his deep brown eyes searching hers with relief. She needed to remember what he'd done, robbing her of her only sibling.

Fraser stood with his hands by his side, his expression apprehensive as she slowed, relief hidden deep within his gaze. Boots halted directly in front of him, and the way their eyes locked had goosebumps quivering over her skin.

'Did your ride buck you off?' Charlotte couldn't help the smirk as Fraser moved to Boots' side, gazing at her with such gravity, she couldn't look away even if she tried. His strong hand glided gently down her horse's neck, and a pointed memory of him doing the same to her arm one summer's day when she was in a sundress down by the river came rushing back. Alarmed, she recoiled in the saddle before checking herself, hoping he took the slight shade of pink rising on her cheeks as the result of her ride. She might not have pardoned him—and never would—but whatever chemistry they'd had between them continued to linger uninvited, at least with her. As long as she kept her distance and concentrated on why she was here, she'd be fine. There was no going back to what they'd had, and there was no keeping hold of a legacy that wasn't meant to be.

'It did.' The simple sentence stalled her, and she watched as he turned to indicate the sharp rock he had taken on before eyeing the flat front tyre. When he turned back to her, his serious gaze danced over her face.

She ignored the shiver of excitement running through her.

'Any chance I might get a lift home? If I could get the ute and another tyre, I might be able to bring it back and change it over here. And Dad might be home by then to give me a hand.'

'Aren't you forgetting something?' She levelled her gaze at him with secret delighted amazement. 'Last time I checked, you were afraid of riding.' Her playful smirk lifted, so sure he'd recoil at the mere prospect of getting on the back of Boots. And she was counting on it. She did not need him sitting snug behind her all while holding onto her waist for dear life, not that it would mean anything to him.

Or her.

But after her heart had reacted as she'd watched him from afar, could she do it? Theoretically, yes.

Please, say no.

'Ah . . .' He looked about as if he was fighting what he was about to say, finally shrugging. 'I don't have many other helpful options currently.' He turned back to her, his reticent smile threatening to melt her resistance.

C'mon, Charlotte, she growled to herself. The guy needs a hand. How would it look if she made him walk home? It would take him at least two hours from here, given the hills and distance. Never mind that the sun was only an hour off setting. And without a doubt, word would get around in a flash. The Settlers Hill gossip line would be buzzing at the news she'd left him for dead. With utter glee!

'Okay,' she breathed, searching for a place for him to hop on up behind her, still fighting the urge to kick her horse into a full-blown gallop and leave him behind. But Boots had double dinked plenty of times when she and James had checked paddocks together after he'd lost his horse to colic. He'd later replaced it with a two-wheel motor bike which he and Fraser had revved all over their multitude of acres, James claiming he was happier on two wheels rather than four legs with a mind of its own for bucking when it felt the need.

As if reading her thoughts, Fraser moved towards the tractor. 'How about here?' He hopped up the first three steps and spun around, waiting for Boots to come alongside him. Kudos to him, he was doing a good job of hiding his apprehension, and Boots didn't miss a beat, knowing exactly what was expected. And before she could brace herself for the full body contact, Fraser was sitting behind her, the back of the saddle the only thing separating the nearness she suddenly craved. To his credit, he kept his hands away from her but if they were going to get home faster than walking pace, he'd have to hold on at some point. But then again, and a trickle of mischief danced in her mind, maybe she could give him a run for his money. A little bit of payback never hurt anyone, yeah?

Charlotte moved off from the tractor at a steady walk, giving him a chance to adjust to the rhythm of movement beneath him. Maybe she should have put him in the saddle, and she sat behind? She'd be able to keep her balance no problem. But where would the fun be in that? A mischievous grin crossed her lips.

Testing his balance, she moved Boots into a gentle sitting trot, feeling Fraser's body bounce out of rhythm from both her and the horse. But much to her contrite disappointment, he grasped the saddle in front of him with what she imagined was a death grip.

'Um, are you trying to make me fall off?' His words bounced with him, and she was relieved he couldn't see her face, her giddy delight way too evident. He deserved everything he got and then some.

It didn't take long before her mood turned to foreboding, settling on her like a snuggly-fitting glove. Fraser was barely sitting behind her, on *her* horse, needing *her* help, and all she wanted to do was to be left alone to work out how she was going to get back to her business in Melbourne.

'Do you want to get home before midnight?' That was a big stretch of the imagination, but hey, a little over-exaggeration was permissible if it worked for you.

'You may have a point,' he managed to say, his body continuing to slip from side to side, but not enough to have him fall to the ground. And as he did, he resisted taking her waist, much to her relief—and disappointment.

She urged Boots into a faster trot, this time feeling Fraser's body bouncing against her horse's natural gait. It had to be hurting her horse, especially as it was his first ride out for a long time. The gelding hadn't put a foot wrong though, taking it in his stride, and Charlotte leaned forward, rewarding him with a firm rub down his neck.

'That'a boy.'

'Thanks.' Fraser's voice jarred against his body's wayward movements.

'Not you, silly. Boots is going to need a horse physio after this, no thanks to you.' And as they continued to ride, a thought struck her. Could she apply her skills to him if he needed loosening up? There was merit in the concept.

'And . . . here I was . . . believing . . . you . . . were happy to be . . . helping me.' His words were breathless, rushing from his lips, and she smothered a chuckle, relieved he couldn't see her face.

'Hold on!' Charlotte urged Boots into a gentle canter, hoping Fraser could sit rather than bouncing against her poor horse's back. The early afternoon chill in the air began to slink over them. She'd need to rug Boots tonight after such a late, challenging ride and stable him.

On arrival at his house, Fraser slid from Boots, his legs crumpling beneath him as they hit the ground, and he gripped the back of the saddle for stability, letting his head drop between his arms. When he finally managed to look up, his windswept look made her heart race a little more than it already was from the exhilarating ride. Where did he get off looking so damned gorgeous, especially when she'd worked incredibly hard to make his trip home as challenging as possible? Was she that mean? She raised her eyebrows, not wanting to admit the answer.

'Where's your hat?' she said in surprise.

'Lost it.'

'What?' Charlotte turned in the saddle, eyeing the track they'd used to come home, before looking back at him. She could tell he was in pain—lots of it. She tried to ignore the guilt beginning to riddle her.

'Want me to go back and get it?' She turned Boots around, ready to head back out as he stood back, and she smiled in satisfaction at her horse's perfect move. He might be out of practice, but her loyal gelding still had it when he needed to.

'No, it was too far back. I'll look for it tomorrow when I head out to the tractor.'

'Okay,' she said slowly, her fresh shame working to settle in with determination. 'I'll head home then. You might want to take a bath tonight.' Gone was her delight in seeing him struggle. She could only feel remorse, so she offered him a soft smile. 'Maybe some Epsom salts too. Your legs are going to hurt.'

'You think that's all that's gonna be sore? I can't feel my bum.' A wry grin spread across his cheeks, accepting his fate as it steadily morphed into an accusing grin, making her stomach flutter in warm and wonderful ways. She shied from his gaze. 'You can't fool me, Charlotte Redding. You meant to do this. You might have grown up and changed, but the same old Char is still in there.' He pointed towards her heart, his focus deepening on her as she risked looking his way again. 'I always did have a soft spot for that mischievous side of you.' His lopsided grin charmed its way straight to her heart.

No. Don't say that!

Charlotte's pulse quickened, and she threw a cautious glance at him once more, unable to mask her delighted alarm from his attention. Could he hear how loud her heart was beating? If he did, he didn't let on.

Suddenly unsure of herself, Charlotte nodded a swift goodbye, not trusting her voice thanks to the thickness in her throat. Not only had the guy who was once the love of her life held on for dear life, but losing his hat was, well, it was like losing an arm for him. And he hadn't said a word. And all while she had enjoyed making his ride home as treacherous as possible. *Well bloody done, Charlotte.* She was definitely feeling the sharp sting of remorse.

Everything inside her wanted to kick Boots into a full-on gallop to get the heck out of there, but John was coming down the driveway, dust plumes swirling in the chilling air. He pulled up alongside her as Fraser's footsteps approached from behind.

'G'day, Charlotte.' John smiled. 'I was hoping to catch you. Wanted to offer to lease some of your land down the back of your place. It'd be mighty handy, and you're not going to need it, obviously.' He chuckled lightly. 'So, what do you think?'

Obviously? That was a loaded word if ever she'd heard one. Was he saying she couldn't run the farm on her own? The edge of excitement in his voice grated on her.

'We're not planning on doing anything yet. Still got a few things to iron out.' She gave him a deliberate, courteous nod, her eyes levelling with his. 'Have a good night.'

Before he could say another word, or Fraser could come up alongside her, she urged Boots forward, unable to escape Trentham Park fast enough. Selling up meant this overbearing family rivalry would finally end, and she wouldn't be reminded of what a farm could tear away from her any longer.

She had to leave this place. Soon. If she didn't, she may find herself tempted to change her mind, and that was something she couldn't risk doing.

CHAPTER 8

'G'day, Paul. How's things?' Fraser tried his hardest to walk to the front desk of the Settlers Hill Car and Tyre Service without revealing the pain gripping his legs and backside, reaching out to shake hands with the owner. His father followed close behind, doing the same.

Fraser and Paul had been lifelong mates, Paul also having grown up on a nearby farm. He did the odd shearing job here and there when the urge to return to his roots came over him.

'So, you need a new tyre? What did you do this time?' The astonishment in Paul's voice was hard to miss. He'd replaced one tractor tyre two months earlier. That one might have been old, but two in such a short space of time? It dented the pride and hurt Trentham Park's bank balance.

'Ran over a bloody rock sticking out in the paddock. The grass was hiding it, and my mind was elsewhere.' He shook his head at his own clumsiness and regretful distraction. He needed to get better at managing where his head was so things like this wouldn't happen again.

Paul nodded as if it was a more than reasonable explanation, then headed out to the back of the shed where all the tyres were kept, with Fraser and his father following him.

'I hear Charlotte wants to put Sheepwash Creek on the market,' Paul said over his shoulder as he continued walking. Fraser resisted the urge to look behind him at his father, but didn't miss the sound of his quickened steps in response to the topic. What was it with this town wanting to glean everything about Charlotte, probably before her? How was he meant to shut this down when the whole main street was already talking about it? He searched the floor with unseeing eyes.

'She needs to,' John said, following behind. 'That farm can't be run by her. It's too big for one person, let alone a woman. And there's too much prestige attached to that station for it to be carried on by someone who can't handle it. Besides, it's not the "done thing" 'round these parts. A Western District property needs to be run by a man and/or his son.' His father strode up beside Fraser and paused, facing him and giving an approving slap on his back. Fraser's body stiffened as he fought to smother a wince from the pain radiating through to his lower body.

John walked across to Paul, but Fraser hesitated, disbelief in his stare at his father's back. Was that how his father saw Charlotte? She was more capable than a lot of men, especially thanks to what her dad had taught her. She might not have James, but he would always be there if she needed a hand, and that thought sent renewed energy through him, selectively ignoring that she had made it more than clear she wasn't happy he was around. But that smirk on her face last night . . . the memory had him smiling, despite his aching limbs.

Once Paul had loaded the new tyre onto the back of the ute with the front loader, Fraser secured it with rope before heading to Frank's Small Store where his father was picking up the local paper and some pies for their lunch. When he pushed the front door of the shop open, Nancy Stone and Elsie Kent were huddled in the baking section, Nancy holding a packet of icing sugar while Elsie fiddled with a patty pan packet, pretending she was trying to pick the best one. Funny thing was, there was only one variety to choose from.

Stepping inside, Fraser didn't miss the way the two town gossips huddled like a pair of excited rabbits over a garden full of lettuce and corn, their ears acutely tuned to what Frank and his father were discussing. Their heads nodded towards each other over every word. Fraser seethed.

Taking a cathartic breath, he returned his attention to Frank and the way the man's ears were flapping with excitement over his father's words.

'Let it be known, Frank. I intend to buy Sheepwash Creek. It's what's best for everyone.'

'Sounds to me like it's best for you, John. You're not the first to say they want a piece of that station, stock, and land alike. Even Steve Haymes has been in here, spruiking he's interested. If you ask me, I don't like your chances.' Frank quashed a satisfied smile as he placed two dried-out pies into paper bags, tossing in two sauce sachets with them.

'Good thing I'm not asking you then,' John said, with an I-don't-care-what-you-think gaze, before fishing out his wallet to pay for the pies.

Fraser looked to see the women in the corner glancing at one another, eyebrows raised so high they almost reached their hairline. Fraser eased himself towards the front counter. Frank's shop was showing its age by the faded chiko roll poster on the wall, a long-legged model astride a mean-looking Harley. He chuckled lightly, remembering how, as a kid, he had thought she was the best-looking woman he'd ever seen.

But something else was vying for his attention. Was Steve serious about wanting to claim a piece of Sheepwash Creek for himself? How much of it did he want? Both Steve and his father were influential within Settlers Hill, and if they fought between themselves for the station, there was a high probability that it could cause a substantial rift within the community.

'Our property is the closest. And once it's a single consolidation, Fraser and I can make it into a truly enviable enterprise.'

Frank's reedy breath wafted over the counter, reaching Fraser and making him recoil as excited whispers radiated from the far corner. But Fraser had had enough. His legs ached from standing for too long, and his head throbbing thanks to the multitude of speculation amongst way too many opinions. His mother had even taken pity on him, offering a cushion from the lounge and placing it on his seat at breakfast time, stifling a quiet giggle. He hoped the price he'd paid for getting Charlotte to take him home would pay off. Sure, he may have been sore after a long walk, but if Charlotte would consider staying, he'd offer to take many more horse rides to be that close and remind her of what could be in their future, if she chose it.

He turned towards his father, instantly annoyed by his obsessiveness. There was no doubt his dad was intentionally sowing seeds, trying to show the whole community he was going to have Sheepwash Creek. And he'd lay bets his father was counting on the two town gossips to help. Nothing like a well-executed, unplanned bonus, guaranteed to spread the news like wildfire and generate enough speculation to put others off the idea of buying Sheepwash Creek. Then there would be no stopping his father from locking horns with anyone getting in his way to obtain everything Keith had ever laid claim to, as if it was owed to him.

But even Fraser didn't comprehend the full meaning of what his father assumed should have been his.

CHAPTER 9

The Tavern was typically busy for a Friday night as Fraser sipped his beer and waited for his friends to arrive. They were all long overdue for a catch-up.

'How ya doin', Big Nev?' The man mountain sidled over to Fraser, smiling as he took a seat.

'I'm not too bad for an old fella.' He chuckled, taking a well-deserved break and sip of his coke.

The ever-responsible pub owner. Fraser grinned, admiring the way Big Nev always looked after his patrons. But the depth of the man's eyes lingering over him a little longer than necessary had his wariness rising.

'And you?' Big Nev was the local publican for good reason. He had the frame for holding trouble at bay and an uncanny knack for keeping his ear to the ground at all times.

There wasn't much that went on in this small town that Big Nev didn't hear about, a fact that proved handy on occasion.

'I'm doing okay.' Fraser gave him a reserved smile before taking another sip of his beer, hoping the man might cut him some slack. Big Nev had looked out for him over the years, especially since the tragedy, and for that Fraser was indebted. But with Charlotte so fresh in his mind, he didn't need the cunning nouse of the man to pry open the firmly closed doors of his heart.

'Only okay?'

Yeah, that was about the sum of it. But before he could answer, one of his Friday night drinks buddies finally strolled over, cutting him the break he was looking for.

'Hey, man. Good to see you both.' Mark Twigg was in uniform, but he'd officially clocked off as Senior Constable of the district for the evening, keen to relax. Even so, a few shifty looks from a nearby table piqued his interest, and he offered them a courteous I-know-you're-there-fellas nod.

Big Nev picked up on Mark's interest in the table. 'Don't worry 'bout them. They're blow-ins, been here for a couple of days. They'll be off soon enough.' Big Nev stood, moving back to the bar to serve another customer.

'But it looks like you've made them a little uncomfortable,' Fraser said, giving Mark a knowing raised eyebrow as he glanced towards the few drinkers he didn't recognise. Eyes only for Mark, they continued their sneers, before steadily turning back to their own conversation.

'I have that effect in this outfit.' He offered a light-hearted laugh, lifting his drink in thanks to Fraser's shout.

'Should try dressing up as a clown next time. Might make 'em crack a smile.' Mark took a swig of his drink before glancing in their direction once more, and Fraser followed suit. Where had the motley-looking group come from? He didn't make a practice of being judgmental, but non-locals with a look like these fellas had wasn't always good news.

'They look like they're harmless enough,' Mark said as he let his final surmise hang on the men, as though he was committing them to memory, before he focused on Fraser. 'So, what's going on with you? I hear you've taken up horse riding.' His jibe had the desired effect as he took another sip, his smirk unmissable. 'How's the bum?'

'Where the bloody hell did you hear that?' Fraser stretched taller in his seat, immediately regretting the action as a steady ache punched every lower muscle his body owned. 'And sore. Very,' he offered, repositioning himself as best he could on his seat with a grimace.

Ross Harrington—the local vet—strode up to them. 'Sorry I'm late. Dad's heifer was struggling with her first calf, and it was presenting with only one leg. Took a while to locate the second foot before I could let her progress.' He offered a light-hearted chuckle. 'Dad was already stiffening up as he walked back to the house.'

'No different to Fraser, then,' Mark laughed.

'Okay, okay,' Fraser said, sliding Ross's beer in front of him with a and-don't-you-start glare. Ross took a long, slow drink like it was overdue, before putting it down. 'So, how was the double-dinking?' He waggled his eyebrows, and both he and Mark stifled a snort.

Fraser looked from one mate to the other, his lips parted as he worked to hide his own smile. 'How is it that the two best mates I have own the biggest flapping ears this side of Victoria?'

The men all laughed, drawing the attention from the table over the other side of The Tavern once more. Mark kept one eye on them.

'I may or may not have gone into the Small Store this morning and overheard Charlotte telling Janice. Gotta say, mate, Charlotte was having a good giggle at your expense.' Ross chuckled, shaking his head at the memory.

Was she now? Fraser's head tipped to the side with interest. Did that mean Charlotte had enjoyed it? But taking a chance on the back of her horse was worth every bit, despite the absolute fear nearly crippling him beforehand and during the ride. He'd prepared himself several times to bounce off and break the first thing that connected with the ground.

But more than any of that, he hoped it might have reminded her of what they used to have. Forget about convincing her. That was a long way off. But if she could remember, it might give him a little more time to find some way to show her that staying in Settlers Hill might be worthwhile.

But the truth clawed at him like his father's words. Finding a way to keep both his father happy and getting Charlotte to stay was monumentally opposed, and out of the question, especially if his father's suggestion about his own dedication in obtaining the property came under scrutiny again.

Mark looked Fraser up and down. 'So, was it a rendezvous like the old days?'

That damned cheeky grin again, Fraser inwardly grumbled to himself as he looked away, focusing on the condensation dripping down the side of his glass.

'Must've been hard seeing her at the funeral. There was no hiding that look on your face,' Mark continued, sincerity in his voice.

Had it been that obvious? He thought he'd worn a mask that day, determined to be there as a friend—nothing more. Fraser finally mustered the courage to glance Mark's way, unsure of what to say. Anyone and everyone involved in wool, from the locals to the wider community, had been there, celebrating a legend in the industry. He could feel Ross's eyes dissecting him, and Fraser swallowed back the thickness forming in his throat.

'Listen, *we* were a long time ago, and you both know how it ended.' His voice hitched, and he corrected it with a cough, hoping neither of them picked up on it. The last thing he needed was for them to recognise that seeing Charlotte these last couple of days had awakened his heart far more than he thought possible. Did they have any clue how hard it had been not to take her by the waist, to hold onto her for dear life while balancing on the back of her horse, constantly breathing in her subtle rose tones while feeling her silky hair on his cheek as it blew against him? They didn't. They were both single guys, footloose and carefree.

But wasn't he that too?

Besides, the way he was walking was punishment enough. He didn't need their ribbing to add salt to his bruised ego.

'Nah, mate, if she's come back to stay, then this is your chance. No one could hold a grudge against you for what happened. Everyone understands it was out of your control, or anyone's for that matter, and they accept it, tragic as it was.' They all silently nodded, the mood suddenly turning sombre.

'Will still struggles with it. He's done his darndest to avoid Charlotte since she's been back.' Mark nodded at him before he hopped up to buy round two.

'He does?' Fraser said to no one in particular, unable to mask his surprise. Will hadn't mentioned it the other day when they fished, and they'd both gone hungry thanks to not a single bite. But maybe that's exactly where it lay. Not mentioning it may have been his way of saying he needed to steer clear of her. And with her selling up, Will might have the freedom to finally move on, especially if whoever bought Sheepwash Creek renamed the iconic station. And how bad would he feel if he was able to turn around Char's thinking while knowing how Will felt? Would it mean Will would have to move out of the district instead? He'd become like a brother to Fraser. Whichever way he looked at it, he was bound to lose.

It was a good thing there were only three of them in their Friday night drinks' group. More than three rounds and they'd have Mark chasing them on their way home, regardless of the beers being light. They enjoyed a drink together, but they weren't the kind to take risks either. Things happened unexpectedly at the best of times, a fact they knew all too well.

The men stood, smiling and moving towards the door as the dodgy out-of-towners eyed Mark one last time. Fraser brushed their glares aside. It had everything to do with Mark's uniform. Nothing more.

'Hey, Mark, you got any spare time tomorrow?' Fraser slowed, waiting for him to turn around once they were outside.

'Yeah, I'm off for the next couple of days. Why?'

'Wouldn't mind your help drafting the one-and-a-half-year-old ewes and wether hoggets. Dad's going to Ballarat.'

'Yeah, no worries. With the state you're in, you're gonna need all the help you can get.' Mark burst out with a loud laugh, slapping Fraser good-naturedly on the back, making him tense against the jolt of pain his muscles screamed with.

'I can probably drop in for an hour or so, too, if you'd like the extra hand.' Ross had always been the quiet overachiever, having lost a little brother when they were both young. But he'd never confided in either Fraser or Mark about what had happened.

Fraser had to admit he wasn't so different, only his loss was to do with the woman he'd thought he was going to spend the rest of his life with.

'*Baa, baaaa.*' Dust stirred in the yards as Fraser, Mark and Ross moved amongst the sheep, Sampson, the Ginja Ninja, skirting around the outside before hopping up on the fence post to supervise proceedings, his tail flicking from side to side.

'I'll go on the drafting gate,' Fraser announced.

'What? You don't trust me?' Mark laughed, waving his arms in the air, 'ho-hoing' the sheep to move towards the force yard in front of the race. He had moved from Tasmania four years earlier when he'd been offered the job to replace an officer who was about to retire. Unlike his brother, Jase, he only had the basics of sheep handling. Jase was a full-time shearer still living in Tassie.

'In a word, no.' All three men burst into laughter as the sheep ran down the race, being diverted either left or right, depending on their sex. 'You do recall you managed to send nearly a third of our ewe lambs to market, don't you?' Fraser shook his head with a sombre chuckle. 'Wethers don't exactly breed too well.'

'Hey, you got more money though!' Mark had the cheek to offer up a sheepish grin. Fraser shook his head disbelievingly.

'Ross, I've been meaning to ask, how's your buddy, Shaun Knox, doing? You haven't mentioned him in a while. Is he still in Ballarat?' Mark asked.

'No. He got a posting in Launceston and travels to Cradle Mountain regularly. They've got a sanctuary for

Tassie devils there and he's helping with the studies on the facial tumours. He loves it.'

'I'll tell Jase,' Mark said. 'I reckon my little brother could do with a sharp nip from one of them, thanks to the Christmas present he's decided to give me. We're going to Cairns on Boxing Day for a week, and he reckons we're going to do the Giant Swing at Skypark. I'm telling you, that ain't happening.'

'C'mon Mark, you have to conquer your fear of something bigger than a four-step ladder. And you might love it,' Ross said, unable to resist a good belly laugh.

'You reckon it'll be fun falling forty-five metres at one hundred and twenty kilometres per hour, in three-and-a-half seconds?' Mark's face was turning white just talking about it.

'I'm sure there's a trampoline you can land on if you fall out. You might even be able to jump right back into your harness if you're good enough,' Fraser said, laughing so hard he almost mis-drafted a wether.

'Great bloody mates you two are. I'm telling you, I'm not doing it.' He shook his head vehemently.

Their laughter faded as they concentrated on the drafting, finishing up in a couple of hours before they headed inside for a drink.

The kettle was already on, the aroma of both savoury and traditional scones filling the air as the men washed up in the laundry before heading to the kitchen.

'G'day, Mrs Pierce,' Mark and Ross said in unison before taking their seats at the table in the centre of the room.

'Lovely to see you boys again.' She placed steaming coffees in front of them before they dug into the morning smoko with gusto.

His mother left the kitchen, instructing the men to finish off the scones or they wouldn't be welcome back, and headed outside. The room fell silent as they devoured the cooking.

'So, do you reckon Charlotte will hang around?' Mark licked the cream from his fingers before helping himself to another scone.

'*Meow*.' Samson sat at Fraser's feet, looking up with cool expectancy. Fraser blinked at the scone, ignoring the way his cat always wanted things on his terms. If Charlotte did stay, how long would it be for? What he wouldn't give to find that out. 'I'm not sure,' he finally offered, frowning more at himself than anything. 'She's made it pretty clear where she stands.'

'And what's that? Mark asked.

'To sell up.' The room fell quiet.

But could Fraser dare to hope she might move past her inability to forgive one day? Because living with himself was proving harder to accept than all the ultimatums his father could throw his way. Not protecting her brother—his own best friend? That had to be the biggest conceivable sin ever. Why hadn't he triple-checked with Will? The kid had been so excited to be on his first spotlighting night with the boys, his enthusiasm infectious. He'd assured Fraser he had the safety switch on.

But the memory still haunted him.

So in actual fact, he couldn't blame Char for not trusting him. But the bigger question in it all? How he was he going to regain her trust?

CHAPTER 10

How was she supposed to have confidence in the man who'd stood by while her brother had died?

Charlotte's heart skipped a beat as she stared at the hallway ceiling in a wash of sadness and frustration before she took a controlling breath and moved towards the rhythmic ticking of the kitchen clock where her senses told her something amazing was about to come out of the oven. But her mind continued to whir with images of her handsome neighbour. The more she saw Fraser or heard his name mentioned, talked about him, and even laughed good-naturedly over him, the more she wished for what they had had all over again. But she could never forget what her heart was also fighting for: the legacy of her brother and her father, who rightly deserved to be honoured through her memory, and by their community.

Fraser had tried on numerous occasions, before she'd left, to speak to her about the night James had died, but she had cut him off at the sound of James's name every time. And for good reason. If she had listened to him, she feared it could feel even more real that he was never coming back to Sheepwash Creek, or to her. It was enough to accept he was gone, not how that had come about.

But two questions remained for the farm. Could she earn the respect from the locals and beyond if she didn't sell—the kind the station required for its continuing successes that it more than deserved? And if she did sell, would the footprint left by the Redding family for superfine merinos be forgotten forever?

Her teeth pinched at her bottom lip. She needed to talk to her mum.

The homely waft of her mother's mud cake filled the atmosphere, and Charlotte found herself closing her eyes in ecstasy as she drew in the aroma like a prized possession. When she opened them, Jayne was smiling her way.

'It always was your favourite.' Grabbing her oven mitts, her mother opened the oven door, releasing a rush of steam before using a metal cake tester to check it. With a satisfied nod, she removed the cake, setting it on a cooling rack on top of the stove.

Charlotte dragged out a dining chair, its legs scraping along the cool tiles, and took a seat, her face thoughtful. Glancing up, she saw her mother watching her with curiosity.

She drew in a deep breath, unsure how her mother would react to what she was about to say. But without discussing it, she wouldn't be able to forge ahead with any plans at all.

'I'm thinking we might need to sell up.' She'd said it when Fraser had been there, and in that split moment, she'd meant it. But was she having second thoughts? She hoped her mother could clarify her thoughts.

She looked down at her hands in her lap, picking at a rough cuticle thanks to the hands-on work she'd been doing around the farm, which oddly, had begun to ground her. Her muscles had complained at first, then protested as she continued to use them. But that was part of what the farm was, a place to be physically active amid a winter frost or the stifling summer heat. Her heart yearned for those days, working alongside James and their Dad. Things had changed so much. Too much. It was a far cry from working in the big smoke, as her dad had always said, her hands not so long ago soft, thanks to the oils and creams she used on her patients when working their aching ailments.

But one question continued to plague her, regardless of their next steps. What exactly did she want? It had to be getting back to her business. It was what she'd aimed for for so long. But was it what her heart wanted? Regardless, she had to concentrate on what she could wrap her head around. That was all she could make sense of before the farm tried to ensnare her life too.

And then a thought dawned on her, and she looked up at her mother with fresh hope. 'We could sell the cross-bred lambs first. They'd be ready to go if I brought them in. We could whip off their wool in no time and have them ready for sale in a month.'

Jayne nodded, the smallest of smiles indenting the edges of her lips. Charlotte continued, thinking of their wool rep.

'I'll get onto Syd Jones and tell him we want to sell the wool ASAP.' Charlotte let her eyes slide to her mother's, smiling a thanks as she placed a steaming cup of strong tea in front of her. Would her mother pick up that she'd chosen to sell them first because, well, that's what they always did anyway? It had nothing to do with avoiding—at all costs— what John Pierce was angling for her to do.

Or could her mother see right through what her daughter was doing? Stalling. Charlotte was one hundred percent hedging her bets so that if she indeed listened to the incessant whisper niggling in her ears night and day—that she didn't have to sell up if she didn't want to—this was a way to keep things ticking along nicely for a little longer. And with Syd, he'd do his best to make sure it sold successfully. He was practically one of the family.

'Okay,' Jayne said, before placing a delicious wedge of the mud cake on a plate, scooped out from the steaming tin with a spoon before it had rested for at least two hours like it should have. Had her mother been able to tell by the look on her face that she was that desperate for an early piece, her appetite for it back on track after turning it down on her arrival home? Her mother had sent the better half of that cake home with Fraser, a sore point she wasn't ready to think about.

Jayne set the plate down on the table in front of her, taking a seat herself as a glint of experience filled her eyes. 'You'll want to entice those shearers with some good food incentives. They've been hard to come by of late, so I've been told.' Her mother's gentle smirk was hiding behind her mug as she took a sip of her tea, never taking her eyes off Charlotte. The whole district could be enticed by the cooking and baking reputation of Sheepwash Creek for a whole lifetime. They would hardly be able to say no if they thought it might be their last chance at sampling some.

'That's a no brainer,' Charlotte said, chuckling before taking a scoop of the steaming mud cake on a spoon, alongside a swipe of double cream, and lifting it to her lips as the flavours danced on her tongue, making her eyes close and her toes curl. 'Mmmm.' Her toes rapidly tapped the floor as she savoured the flavour.

Charlotte was keen to check on Boots after their bigger-than-anticipated ride, and headed outside, her tummy feeling satisfied and her mood brighter than it had been in days. He looked relaxed in the paddock as she approached the gate, and as he moved towards her, he displayed no lameness, but he was showing some stiffness in his movement.

'How are you, old fella?' Charlotte said with affection, stroking his nose as she moved through the gate and he lowered his head for the headstall she had ready for him. She led him to the fence and flipped the rope over it, leaving it to dangle—she'd never needed to tie him—before she ran her hands over his thick coat. She gently pressed along his back, checking for any indication he was sore, and sure enough, he lifted his head in a quick movement when she hit a tender spot beyond where the saddle sat.

'Okay, buddy. Hang in there, and I'll see what I can do.' With light pressure, she worked his muscles while keeping a close eye on his responses, until they were eased and supple beneath her hands. She took the lead rope once more, walking him around, pleased with what she saw. He was moving more freely, although she'd need to treat him again. Getting her hands back into the game she'd trained for, even if it was remedial work on an animal, gave her a sense of satisfaction, as though she was doing something that could help on the farm, rather than watching it close down in front of her eyes.

'Charlotte. It's good to hear from you.' Syd Jones's tone was buoyant, as though hearing her voice had made his day, and it had her smiling over the phone. Like so many she'd seen but shied away from at her father's funeral, she had dismissed his cautious wave and reluctant smile at the time, the gravity of what she was going through all too much. But there had been comfort in knowing he had acknowledged her, unlike so many others, probably because she had already left the farm. They appeared to be more concerned with her plans for a dispersal sale, promising to be there to support her. Yeah right. It was so much more than that, the glint in their eager eyes expressing their true desires: to get their greedy hands on as much as they could of Dad's success.

'What can I do for you?'

'I'm planning on bringing the cross-bred lambs in over the next couple of days. I want to shear them and sell the wool before I send them to market.'

'Now that's a mighty fine thought. When do you plan on shearing?'

'Next week. The offer of Mum's cooking has had the desired effect, luring in a few of the local boys since Jerry's team isn't available.' Not that Charlotte was sorry about that. Jerry was as shonky as they came, unreliability his forte. She gave a soft giggle into the phone. 'They couldn't get here quick enough!'

'Jayne's cooking would be enough to have me picking up a handpiece too, if I could use one.' They both laughed. 'I'll pop out next week when it's all happening and take a look. We can work out a plan then. I might even score morning smoko if I time it right.'

'Mum wouldn't want it any other way. Thanks Syd.' Charlotte hung up the phone, drawing in a long breath that turned into something of a sigh. Her head was telling her she was only delaying the inevitable, but her heart skipped with a shimmer of excitement. Depending on how many lambs there were in the mob, she might be able to use the money to buy in the hay she needed. And there was more than enough work to be done before she could even consider selling. She needed to stick to her plan, and it'd all work out just fine.

CHAPTER 11

The chilled early morning air circulated inside the shed, sending stray wool locks dancing and swirling along the floorboards below the wool table. Lewie lay amongst it, his eyes closed but his ears pricked and flickering at the various sounds in the shed while the locks layered his back in a blanket of woolly snow as they fell from the fleeces above. A distinct shudder ran over Charlotte as she focused on the wool in front of her, sorting it into two lengths— short and long, with one extra line for the board sweeps, while two other shedhands kept feeding the fleeces to her at the wool table. It was a flurry of activity with penning up, changing full butts of wool and pressing up, but she'd always loved the shearing atmosphere. She had to admit, it was more than a little exciting to be doing it again, but she couldn't shake the eeriness within the shed without her father and his ever-present deep voice directing someone to get on and do something in the no-nonsense, good-natured way he always did. It hurt, not being around his encouraging smile as she pushed the lever down on the press for the umpteenth time, sending more wool into the already tightly packed bale, keeping a diligent eye on the bale weight. Pressing an overweight bale led to extra costs, something she didn't need.

She closed her eyes, drawing on the strength she needed to get through this. The memories weren't even the hardest part for her, and she glanced towards the shearers focused on doing a clean, fast job. They were from the surrounding district, born and bred on farms where they had learned to shear as part of their survival tool kit. And it was great they had because otherwise she wouldn't be shearing, thanks to a high demand for shearers and too few of them to go around.

There was only one problem. Will Franklin was one of them.

Her hands slowed as her eyes hovered over Will's bent-over body, shearing like a pro, having outgrown his teenage gangliness and become "one of the men". He was a shearer, a title these men wore proudly, and she didn't doubt it was any different for him, even if it wasn't his full-time job.

She had managed to avoid him since she'd been home, but Paul had rallied the team together with the speed she needed, and not once did she consider that Will might be one of them.

As if sensing her guarded gaze on him, he lifted his head, looking straight at her. She shot her eyes back to the wool, clutching at the hope she hadn't been caught, despite the heat racing up her cheeks telling her something vastly different. But the truth was there in front of her. She had. She knew it from the small smile he'd offered her, much like an olive branch. And her rejection, despite being well-intended, had to make the poor guy feel pretty miserable. She squeezed her eyes tight, unable to unsee the pain he clearly held close, alongside the shame and a depth of sorrow that threatened to unravel her on the spot.

Charlotte hated herself for quietly questioning whether he should be here or not, but everything in her wished he wasn't. He'd only been a kid when he had shot James. How could he have grasped the devastation he would cause their family?

A fresh wash of anger descended in her mind, peppering her with its pain and taunting her with resentment. Will had hardly been able to accept what he had done that night, let alone how it had happened. But Fraser? He should have seen it coming. He had the experience. And he was a safety freak when it came to guns. She could imagine Will, a bundle of nervous energy and excitement, being out with all the boys for the first time. Fraser was the one who should have been paying attention to what Will was doing. Hell, the others were seasoned shooters, all local boys. They were aware of the rules.

And that night, James's life was over before it had a chance to begin.

Eyes stinging, the rattle of the sliding door on the shed landing drew her back from her melancholy thoughts. The overcast sky outside carried the threat of rain, but its brightness compared to inside the shed blinded her. For a fleeting moment, she kidded herself that the person coming in might be Dad.

Steady footsteps walked towards the wool table and she squinted at the silhouette as her eyes adjusted. She was about to smile, believing it was Syd, when her face fell. She blinked again, staring at the man she'd only moments earlier been thinking about.

'Hey, Char.' His tone was reserved as he focused on the shearing board, avoiding her gaze like he recognised his presence wasn't fully welcome. 'Looks like things are going well.' He nodded before reluctantly turning his attention back to her, holding her so tight with his eyes, she momentarily forgot to breathe.

He squeezed his lips together in that uncertain manner he used whenever he was growing nervous. It might have been a long time since she'd seen him use it, but it was as familiar as if he'd done it yesterday, and she offered a cautious smile, the memories she'd driven away suddenly desperate to reach out. He was, without a doubt, lost for what to say next.

'Yeah, they are.' Charlotte's brow wrinkled as she turned her attention back to the wool mounting up on the table thanks to her distraction. She snatched up a fleece, tossing wool into the appropriate wool butt behind her with a little more gusto than was necessary. Why did he feel the need to visit? Was he checking up on her? Did he think, like his father, that she couldn't do this job?

Her hand movements grew flustered and she began dumping clumps of wool into the butts like she was trying to teach them a lesson.

'Do you need a hand? I've got some time if you—'

'No.' She looked up, hands firmly planted in the wool as she took in his handsome face, his lips looking as soft as the last time she'd kissed them—so long ago. They rose in the sweetest of curves, and frustration curled inside her that he still had the same power over her, no matter how much she wanted to forget him. Hadn't she pushed him from her mind, and her heart, for good? She had believed she had. But the longer they both held one another's eyes, the more her mind began to register that maybe her unsympathetic attitude gave rise to how often she thought of him, like nearly every day since she had left to study, and then work in Melbourne.

But it wasn't meant to work like that, and she reminded herself, recalling how much she hated him for what he'd done, as if it might protect her from loving him ever again.

Credit to him, he committed to offering her a warm smile, the crinkle lines dancing around his eyes, threatening to break down her protective exterior.

'How are the boys going?' He studied the shearers one by one, and she watched him, breathing in the sheer relief of him looking away from her. 'I hear Paul couldn't wait to get here for the smoko. He's a bit partial to Jayne's cakes,' he said with a hint of humour, turning to her once more with that sweet, full smile.

Damn it. His heart-warming eyes began to draw her in all over again, begging her to answer him, and yes, she'd been caught red-handed watching him. Her throat went dry. How was this happening? Couldn't he leave her alone? *Please do, but . . . maybe don't.*

'Too right,' Paul said over the noise of the shearing gear, looking up with a grin that suggested he was more than ready for lunch in five minutes time.

This isn't happening. She fought to concentrate on sorting wool and *not* waste time looking at her gorgeous neighbour like he was the latest poster sensation she needed to put up on her bedroom wall. Since when had she become all teenager-like again? But all she could offer was a guarded nod as the radio fell quiet for the end of the run and the last of the wool was thrown onto the table for her to deal with before the shedhands swept up and left the shed for lunch.

Charlotte's hands rested on the wool in front of her as she watched Fraser move away from the table, listening to his warm, deep voice like it was trying to soothe her in a snuggly hug.

'So, you up for another round of fishing this weekend, Will? Or should I say yet another round of me whipping your butt?' Fraser's genuine laugh grew faint as he walked out of the shed with Will, and Charlotte left the wool behind, receding to the back of the group as everyone headed for the house, removing their boots and stepping inside for lunch. The aroma of roast lamb drifted on the air, but it did little to subdue her wary emotions, her stomach protesting at the thought of food. But if she didn't go inside, it would only make matters worse. What she wouldn't do right now for a good excuse to go and visit her ex-café boss, Clare, in Ballarat.

'Fraser, it's so nice of you to drop by.' Jayne's too-cheerful voice carried to Charlotte in the laundry as she took her time removing her boots, glaring at the wall beside her like it had offended her by being there. How could her mother happily feed two men who had robbed her of her only son, and continue to be civil to them? Did she have some driveway gravel inside her head that stopped her from thinking straight?

There was a knock at the door behind her, and Charlotte turned, finding her lost smile as Syd Jones stepped inside.

'Charlotte, good to see you.' He leaned in to give her a peck on the cheek. 'Hmm, smells like I'm right on time.'

'Impeccable timing, as always, Syd,' she said, chuckling, before following him towards the kitchen, her mood ever so slightly improved, if that were possible. He'd been working for the Reddings since she was in nappies, and there wasn't much about their enterprise he didn't know.

CHAPTER 12

Fraser was pretty sure lunch had only been bearable thanks to Syd's arrival. But he couldn't have timed his visit better, regardless of his frosty welcome from Charlotte. When he caught her staring at him, he couldn't decide if it was in confusion, shock, or both. But Syd was his and Sheepwash Creek's wool agent, and his visit had given Fraser the chance to organise their next sale: their merino crutchings to be sold in Melbourne.

The team headed back to the wool shed after lunch, with Charlotte leading the way. Her prompt exit had made it all too clear he hadn't been welcome. Thanking Jayne, he and Syd exited the house, heading for their utes.

'So, what's Charlotte going to do?' Syd asked him, his tone genuine and curious.

'Dunno. Sounds like she wants to sell up.' The concept still managed to unsettle him, but he was grateful for small mercies. At lunch, he'd learned she was staying on for lambing, knowing she couldn't sell with the uncertainty of that responsibility hanging in the air.

'Good on her,' Syd said, surprising Fraser.

'You mean you'd like her to sell?' Fraser couldn't hide the tightness pulling at his forehead, both at Syd's presumption about when she might leave, and that he would lose a client, and a big one at that, if she did. A lot of his commission came from Sheepwash Creek.

'I reckon after everything she's gone through, she deserves better. Besides, women don't run the stations, not really. They're there to support the men. And who has she got with Keith not here? Even your father supports the move.'

Fraser blinked as he listened, staring at Sheepwash Creek's hills which had grown hazy in the distance thanks to the low-lying cloud. His father? Had he said that to Syd? When?

Fraser said his goodbyes to Syd and headed home, disquieted by their conversation. It was one thing for his father to tell him he didn't believe Charlotte could manage the station on her own, but to tell Syd? While he liked their wool agent, sowing such a seed didn't feel right. And besides, she was more than capable of running the station on her own. He knew it.

Only he didn't want her to. He wanted to run it *with* her, one day. He, James, and Charlotte had always talked candidly about taking on the two stations as a joint venture, repairing the rift between their families, even though in what capacity, they'd never been sure. And if he were honest with himself, he'd wanted her to take on Trentham Park with him when they got married. But those hopes had been decimated.

His father was eating a late lunch when Fraser stepped inside, rubbing his hands to warm them in the heat from the kitchen. He took the kettle, filling it under the tap and flicking it on to boil. What he wouldn't do for an extra strong coffee, but all they had was powdery instant rubbish thanks to running out of the good brew, and he inwardly cringed. It tasted bad enough on a good day, so there was no way he was giving himself that all-indulgent extra shot with the way he was feeling. He had planned on dropping by Frank's to grab one earlier, but thanks to Syd, his mind had been elsewhere and he'd headed home on autopilot.

'So, have you talked to Charlotte?'

Fraser stood over the table, lifting his attention from the newspaper headlines distracting him. How could wool go missing? There were procedures in place that made even the presumption of something like that happening ludicrous. He dismissed the thought with a flick of his brow as he returned his attention to his father.

'About what?'

'Don't be daft, son. The land. Is she going to sell to us?' He gave Fraser an impatient glare as his fork hovered in the air, loaded with cheese and salad and a slippery piece of beetroot.

What did he say to his father? Yeah, sure, she's more than happy about it. He opted for the honest answer. 'Nope.' He wanted to add "fat chance" but thought better of it.

Dad let out a frustrated growl under his breath. 'That woman can't recognise a good deal if she was thrown at it. When is she going to come to her senses?'

'What? Because a woman can't run a station?' Fraser fixed his glare on his father, his disappointment drumming. His father was more than happy for Charlotte to leave, and all he wanted was for her to stay. Contrary to what she displayed to him, the Charlotte of old was lurking deep inside, and her own determination might manage to have the louder say. He was depending on it.

'We both know she won't last six months, even if she tries. She might be selling a bit of wool but it's bloody cross-bred. That's not worth more than a scrap of bread in the current economic climate.'

'The lambs will sell well though. They're in good nick.' Fraser's voice became as defensive as when he'd fought to keep the pet ewe he'd bottle-fed as a youngster. He'd won that round, and was more than impressed that Charlotte was following through with her father's yearly plans. She had the strategies. All she needed was a little help in the right direction, alongside a confidence boost.

'I've always liked that tractor Keith has,' John said thoughtfully. 'It's never given him a spot of trouble, unlike ours. Go over there and tell her we'll be doing her a favour by taking it off her hands. I'll offer her good money for it, enough for her to pay the real-estate agent to get things rolling.'

'If she does that, she won't be able to unload hay, move stuff, I dunno, everything, Dad.' He stared at his father in disbelief. 'I'm not going to ask her to do that.'

'I will, then,' John said breezily. 'She needs to get the message we're only trying to help her.'

Fraser let the air seep from his lungs in a slow, steady stream before drawing in his next breath as a slither of new hope grew. If he let his father do this, his plan might work. And even better, he wouldn't have to look like the bad guy. More than anyone, he understood how obstinate Charlotte could be. But then again . . . she wasn't stupid.

'Let me handle it, okay?' Fraser said, giving his father a level stare. She'd smell a rat if his father approached her, if she hadn't already after he'd offered to buy those damned sixty acres. She never was one for taking any nonsense, and he loved the way her eyes narrowed whenever she suspected he was up to something. It seemed not a lot had changed.

'There's no need to rush this, Dad. Give Keith the respect he deserves.' He crossed his arms, disheartened that he hadn't grabbed that coffee he desperately wanted. And bugger his father, now he couldn't even stomach one.

The thrill of hoping to catch some lunch had the desired effect as Fraser cast his fly-fishing line out over the still morning water. He and Will had already seen a couple of trout jumping. They were in the right spot.

'Do you reckon Charlotte will stay?' The unexpected question hung in the air long after Will's hesitant voice, leaving Fraser second-guessing what he meant by it. Was it too much for Will to cope with now she was back in Settlers Hill? The guy had done an admirable job shearing her lambs, considering everything. But that's who he was, with a heart of gold that had been dented with guilt and shame thanks to the accident. But credit to Will, he always held his head high and had earned the respect of many of the locals for it.

'Wish I knew.' Fraser's voice faded as he absently cast his line again, the flick of the lure hitting the surface of the water lightly.

What he wouldn't give to have Charlotte stay.

What he wouldn't do to have her see him for who he really was.

What he wouldn't do to have her in his arms again.

He turned to Will. 'I hope so.'

His line gave a taught tug, loosening then pulling again, and Fraser clenched his rod a little tighter. 'Good thing I didn't bring lunch,' he said, chuckling while angling a teasing side-glance at Will that he hoped might wind him up as he began to reel in his catch.

'Fair dinkum, Fraser, what is it with you?' Will gave a disbelieving laugh as he dropped his rod on the edge of the creek and begrudgingly snatched up the net, wading further into the water to nab the legal-sized wriggling trout. 'That's three in a bloody row now.'

Fraser laughed, his mood lifted thanks to the knowledge they were going to eat, because neither of them had brought anything for lunch—his own calculated risk that he was sure Will also counted on—and the glimmer of hope he'd managed to seed into his countenance. Yes, Charlotte would stay. He was going to make sure of it.

Would there ever be a day he'd be able to please his father? Fraser scratched his head.

'Where's that bloody ammo we bought from Burt?' His father ferreted around in the ute, but Fraser was unsure why he was even looking there.

'Didn't you put it in the ammo safe after we got home? I'm pretty sure you did.' Fraser folded his arms as his father paused before pulling his head out from behind the driver's seat, accidentally smacking it on the roof of the ute. He gave it a frustrated rub.

'So I did, but I did find this,' he said, holding up his old pocket knife triumphantly. Been bloody missing for a couple of years, I reckon. Must've slipped out of my pocket.' He slid the knife into the pouch on his belt, giving a satisfied nod as he tapped it for good measure. 'Right then, go get that ammo 'cause you need to sort out those rabbits. They're multiplying by the hour, and I'm fed up with their antics.'

Fraser gave a weary nod. He'd avoided the job for too long, probably long enough that there'd be another litter, or three, frolicking around their paddocks by now.

The dusk sky glowed with warm orange and yellow hues as the sun slipped effortlessly behind the hills. He was keen to sort out the problem as quickly as possible, but a shaft of apprehension twisted up his spine. Since the accident, he had managed to avoid any rabbit shooting nights that some of the local lads had held, and the boys involved at the time of the accident had done likewise. But now? Life had to move on, even if the guilt refused to. Only difference was he'd shoot until dark crept in. He wasn't about to put any spotlight on a single rabbit under the stars, even if his life depended on it.

Fraser approached the large red gum quietly, its roots hollowed out and sporting more rabbit entrances than the last time when he'd checked on the lambing ewes. He slowed, keeping his distance, his headlights shining in the direction to indicate any movement. What he didn't see were rabbits. What he did see was the fence line between his paddock and Charlotte's . . . lying nearly flat to the ground.

'Shit.' The word seeped from Fraser's lips as he pulled to a stop, leaving the engine running and his lights shining as he stepped out for a closer look. What could have pushed the fence over like that? Fraser ran a hand over his mouth, searching in the near darkness for any sign of movement other than the lone rabbit that had dared to pop its head up, darted in front of him, then disappeared down the next hole in a panicked flurry.

The sheep must've pushed it over, and it was clear whose sheep were the culprits, thanks to the direction the fence was lying. He had no choice but to visit her. They had a major box-up of sheep that needed to be sorted. Fast. But that would have to wait. And the longer he waited, the more likely his father would get wind of it.

CHAPTER 13

'That's enough out of you, Brutus!'

The ram blinked disarmingly, making Charlotte wary that he was scheming against her. She eyed him back, sizing up his possible motives one final time before she shook the bucket of feed into the long trough, the other rams in the pen hovering well away until Brutus sauntered over and plunged his nose in. His horns clunked the sides of the tin as he angled for the oats, and she unconsciously rubbed at her left thigh, the ache tangible purely from the memory.

Despite her close encounter with the bully ram at the time, it had done little to stop her from pursuing her aspirations back then. She had vowed to work on this farm. But too much sadness and tragedy were wrapped up in it, and her aching thigh was all the reminder she needed to stay focused, get the farm in order, and move on.

'Charlotte?' Mum called from the verandah of the house. 'Can you go to Rob's IGA in Ballarat for me? I told Rosemary I'd help out with the cooking for their shearing and I've got a cake in the oven. I'm short of a few ingredients for the slice I promised her.'

'Sure, Mum.' Charlotte slid the shearing shed door shut with a thud, happy to see the tail end of Brutus and his merry men for another day. She reached down, grateful to pat her newest shadow, Lewie, instead of looking at the gnome she was sure was smothering some less than cathartic cackle at her because of her unpredictable friendship with Brutus, before heading inside for her mother's list. Finally, she was getting her chance to drop in on Clare while she was there.

Charlotte stepped back outside onto the verandah, instinctively reaching for her city-high boots, then paused, her well-worn R.M's catching her eye instead. How long had it been since she'd worn them? She pushed aside her tall boots and grabbed them, immediately feeling the comforting sense that she was home the moment her feet slid inside.

'C'mon, Lewie, let's go for a ride.' The dog's ears pricked with eagerness and he bounded to the ute in front of her, leaping onto the back of it. He reached in for a long slurp up the side of her face as she clipped him onto the chain. 'Eww, Lewie.' She angled her face away, chuckling. Loneliness had clung like a close friend when she'd first arrived, especially with the workload on her shoulders. But Lewie had been the little mate she'd needed when sadness set in unexpectedly, or she needed a big hug. She gave him one last pat on the head before hopping into the ute.

Rumbling over the cattle grid, she looked to her left to check for oncoming traffic, and immediately her shoulders slumped. 'You have got to be kidding me!'

Sheep. Everywhere. Ambling like they didn't have a care in the world as they snatched mouthfuls of the juicy untouched grass at the side of the road. She spun her head to the right, checking for traffic, but all was clear. Where was the person who had let these sheep out to graze? Were they shifting them to another paddock? Or did they—

Oh no. Charlotte's enthusiasm thudded to the footwell of the ute. She glanced over her paddocks. There were no missing sheep on her right and the only paddock she was purposefully resting on her left was empty as she expected.

Trentham Park. She let the name slip between her teeth. Of course they were *their* sheep.

Charlotte sprang from the ute, unclipped Lewie, and ran to the paddock she had been keeping aside for the shorn sheep after their main shearing. The grass was long and fresh, better than the roadside offerings. She didn't have time to walk her next-door neighbour's sheep back to whatever paddock they had escaped from, so with a bit of a nudge and some luck, they would see the grass was indeed greener on her side of the fence and waltz right in.

'Ho. Ho, ho-ho!' She waved her arms in the air, lunging to and fro as the sheep moved away from her. 'Lewie, get back.' The kelpie sprang into action, racing anticlockwise around the sheep, gathering the stray ones and bringing the mob back together. Working them towards the gate, Lewie gave a couple of deep barks as he moved back and forth behind the mob, and they eventually angled themselves into her paddock. Not all the ewes were so obliging—always the stragglers who thought they knew better—breaking behind her to escape, but Lewie had them blocked and they begrudgingly turned, racing after the rest of the mob. With their heads down and Lewie panting beside her as she shut the gate, she gave him a well-deserved pat, then glanced down at her boots, smiling with satisfaction.

Munchies café was alive with fresh coffee, cake, and lunchtime chatter as Charlotte pushed the door open. She beamed as she looked around the building with its exposed bricks and wooden tables with sleek black chairs. Nodding with approval, she glanced at the ceiling. 'Nice.' The place had received a makeover of the industrial kind, with the lights surrounded by rusted barbed wire as shades.

'Charlotte!' A voice bellowed from behind the counter at the side of the building, and before she could open her mouth to return the greeting, Clare ran to her, wrapping her in the biggest, squishiest hug Charlotte had been given in a long time. That's what Clare always did.

'Ooft.' Charlotte sucked in a laugh as her friend squeezed her once more for good measure then stepped back, holding her at arm's length as she studied her.

'It's so good to see you.' Clare suddenly turned serious, placing her hands on her hips. 'Why haven't you been in sooner?' She carefully studied Charlotte. 'I'd heard you were back.'

'I've been working at the farm . . . and—' She looked down at her boots, feeling the pang of pain as she prepared herself to say it. 'Dad passed away, so I'm back to tidy up— and sell the station.' She reluctantly met Clare's sympathetic eyes, offering a sad shrug as the words hovered painfully in the air.

'Oh, Charlotte, no!' Clare reached for her again, this time hugging her with all the sensitivity of love and loss. 'I'm so sorry.'

'That's okay.' For a brief moment, Charlotte feared she wouldn't be able to hold herself together. 'Heart attack.'

Clare's face crumpled with compassion before she snatched Charlotte's hand and tugged on it. 'Come on, we need to sit down and catch up properly.'

For the next hour and a half, they cried and laughed and cried again, reminiscing and enjoying their friendship over one too many lattés and a glut of homemade hedgehog slice Clare was famous for. It was everything Charlotte had needed.

'I'd better head off,' Charlotte finally said, looking at her watch in surprise. 'Mum needs a few things.' She went to stand.

'Wait.' Clare raised a don't-you-dare-move finger in Charlotte's direction, and she glanced about, unsure what Clare was up to. When her friend came back, she handed Charlotte a large paper bag that looked heavy.

'Here, I want you to have these.' She passed the bag over, Charlotte shooting her a questioning glance before taking a peek inside. 'You've been through enough.'

'Oh no, Clare. This is too much.' She was about to continue her protest when Clare shushed her.

'Do as you're told for once.' She winked at Charlotte. 'Besides, I want to.'

'Thank you.' Charlotte could feel her eyes clouding over and reached in for another hug. 'You're one in a million.'

'I know,' Clare beamed, shrugging as if she were pretending to brush off the compliment like she'd been told a thousand times before. They both giggled, waving goodbye, before Charlotte headed for the ute.

IGA had a steady stream of customers, enough to give the impression it was busy, but not so many as to make it hard to get around. But getting out at the cash register was another issue altogether.

Nancy Stone and Elsie Kent were at the twelve-items-or-less checkout, stuck together like Siamese twins. Their lips moved in unison, making Charlotte ponder how they even understood what the other one was saying as they both fought for attention. She checked the other queues, but customers were doing their weekly shop, their trolleys loaded.

Damn it. Where was Rob? If she could catch his eye, he might open a new register she could slip into. But he was nowhere to be seen.

Charlotte turned back, right into the gossiping gaze of both women, whose chatter ramped up a new notch—or three—as they stared accusingly at her. Charlotte couldn't understand a word they were hyperventilating over, but it must have been juicy. With approving nods to one another, they didn't bother to turn their backs on her, no doubt delighted she was the centre of their discussion.

'Yes, yes. It was. Oh, I know. How can she even live with herself?' Nancy narrowed eyes on Charlotte, Elsie nodding with such conviction, Charlotte thought her head might drop off.

Charlotte pressed her tongue to the roof of her mouth, calling on the last thread of patience she had left as she tried to feign interest in the chocolate bars begging to be placed in her basket, before reluctantly allowing her eyes to slide back to the women, thanks to the queue moving forward. What was their problem anyway? And what the heck had she done this time?

'I mean, showing her face after *everything*,' Elsie huffed. 'Does she have no shame?'

'Obviously not.' Nancy gave Charlotte one more scathing up-and-down snarl before lifting her basket to the conveyor belt. But that didn't slow her down. 'Abandoning her father like that, and straight after James, for that matter. Disgraceful, if you ask me.' The two women's noses pinched in unison, their disbelief and disgust clear. Then, like a sudden change in wind direction, they pulled out delightful smiles as the checkout girl with braces began scanning their items while giving them a confused, dubious look.

Disgraceful? The word hit Charlotte like a set of gallows, making her throat clench and her saliva feel sticky inside her mouth. Were the two gossips of Settlers Hill so wrong, though? She'd abandoned the farm, and her father, leaving him to do the best he could. And what had that done to him? Caused him to have a massive heart attack, no doubt thanks to the stress of running the station on his own.

His death was all her fault.

Tears welled in her eyes and she welcomed their sting. She searched for somewhere inconspicuous to dump her basket and flee the shop, regretfully catching Nancy and Elsie's scorching glares, as though they took pleasure in knowing they had made her cry. Turning, they toddled off triumphantly, their heads held high and their opinions way too loud, all while she was left to lift her basket to the countertop and face the poor checkout girl who blinked at her blankly.

But the women had done their job, rather effectively, Charlotte had to admit. Their words had never been truer.

CHAPTER 14

Wool sale day had arrived and the show floor where the wool samples from all the clips to be sold were displayed in the Brooklyn warehouse. It was strangely quiet, the only noise coming from a forklift as it shifted bales behind the "off-limits to the public" area with a steady hum. The shed held a briskness that made both Charlotte and her mother tug their jackets closer to their chests as they followed Syd to where their cross-bred wool samples were on display for the wool buyers.

'Here we go,' Syd said, pausing as he placed a hand on the first of the three sample boxes of their wool. 'Must say, Charlotte, you've done a great job. The lengths look spot on. You should get your Owner Classer's ticket.'

'Hehe, thanks, Syd, but that won't be necessary.' Brushing his comment aside with keenness, her eyes widened. She wasn't hanging around on that farm any longer than she had to, and even that was feeling too long.

Charlotte soaked in the surroundings, memories flooding back of her and James running up and down the long rows displaying wool, their laughter and squeals echoing inside the expansive shed whenever they came down as a family to sell their product. A soft smile lifted on her lips as she longed for those days again.

'Rightio then, we'd better make our way into the auction room. Bidding is about to start.' Syd headed off in front of them, disappearing with speed. Charlotte went to follow, but a high-vis vest to the right of the barricaded area caught her immediate interest. Two men were walking towards several bales stacked on top of one another, and her focus sharpened. She couldn't be sure, but—

Charlotte turned towards the barrier, her curiosity growing. The two men were focused on the bales, deep in discussion. But that was their job, right? So why did one of the guys look like . . . like Mark Twigg? She'd met him at Frank's store in his police uniform, his short, solid stature looking strangely familiar to the guy she was currently watching.

'Charlotte, are you coming?'

Charlotte jumped at Syd's voice right behind her, his questioning eyes studying her intently. 'Yes, yes. On my way.' She turned to follow, resisting the almost overpowering urge to glance over her shoulder one more time as she followed him out of the showroom. It had to be someone who looked like Mark, and that wouldn't be a first for her. She'd been mistaken for her mother often enough.

Bidding was strong, and in a blink their wool was sold, fetching a decent dollar considering cross-bred wool prices had dropped dramatically since the same time last year. But it all helped, Charlotte reminded herself. If the lambs could secure a good price, she'd have what she needed to get the hay, and even possibly extra to leave in the shed for the new owner. That had to be an asset to promote on a For Sale brochure, and she nodded in agreement.

Having said their goodbyes after the sale, both women fell into a contented silence on the drive home. It was only when they were out of the city surrounds that Charlotte pressed her Bluetooth to make a phone call.

'Charlie, how are you?' Thank goodness he answered. She hoped he had enough hay to fill her order.

'Ahh, good thanks, Charlotte. What can I do for you?'

'Is there any chance I could get two semi-loads of hay?' She scrunched her face in anticipation of his answer. It was a tall ask but she had to try. Whispers on the grapevine had said hay was becoming hard to come by. Was she being greedy asking for so much? But if it would help Sheepwash Creek sell, then she'd have to take as much as she could get her hands on.

'I reckon we can organise that for you. How would tomorrow suit?' His cheery voice filled her with relief.

'That'd be perfect.'

'Argh, why didn't I grab lucerne chaff yesterday when we were travelling back through Ballarat?' Charlotte watched Brutus, his eyes brimming with what she was sure was total expectation at her miscalculation as she rummaged for the last of the chaff stuffed in the corners of the bags to make up the rams' feed. Gus had run out of his stock, so she'd need to make a special trip in again once his fresh delivery arrived.

'And don't you go looking at me like that, or you just might go hungry.' She pointed an accusing finger in Brutus' direction.

Brutus blinked with innocence as she stood, putting her hands on her back and stretching out the distinct curve she'd developed from bending over for the last fifteen minutes while mixing up the feed and supplements with a short-handled shovel.

She glanced at her watch. Charlie wasn't due until this afternoon. That meant she had time to catch Clare for lunch while in town, then grab her feed supplies and be back home before he arrived. She liked the sound of her plan.

It was a warmer, sunny day, and the breeze wafted gently, making the giant peppercorn tree outside the shearing shed shimmer in the sun. On a whim, Charlotte let Brutus and his mates out for some fresh air before she headed inside to get ready to leave.

Once again, Munchies café was bustling with activity, and Charlotte thanked Clare for rearranging her schedule to make a quick half hour available. But it wasn't until she was pulling the heavy shop door open to leave that her spirits lifted to a new level. On the opposite side of the road, Charlie and his son, Adam, were in town, their huge semi-trucks parked and loaded with hay—her hay. With a skip, she stepped onto the curb, checking for oncoming traffic before she jogged over the wide road with a grassy island in between. She hoped to catch Charlie and tell him which shed to pull up at when he arrived.

But when she reached their trucks, the men were nowhere in sight. The smell of freshly baked hot pies and pastries wafted in the air, and she gave a knowing smile.

Charlotte swung the bakery door open, the delicious aroma swamping her as she almost bowled an elderly gentleman over in her haste to get inside. 'Oh, I'm so sorry.' She offered him an apologetic smile, holding the door open for him. But as she let the door shut and turned to face the counter, the remaining air in her lungs rushed away the moment she saw Charlie . . . talking to Fraser.

She couldn't talk to him, not with Fraser there, and for once she was grateful for the crowded shop, quickly slipping in amongst the people milling in line until she found a chair a few tables away. Sliding into it, she snatched up the nearest newspaper discarded by the last occupant and pulled it in front of her face.

She blinked a couple of times, the blurred words in front of her the last thing she was concerned about, instead straining to discern Charlie and Fraser's voices amongst the clanks and bangs of bakery trays and rambunctious chatter. Her fingers clenched the paper tightly. Why couldn't she make out what they were saying? She leaned forward some more, hiding behind the paper, suddenly puzzled over why she needed to hide at all. She had as much of a right to be here. But then again . . . she thought of Nancy and Elsie, her eyes searching with hot suspicion as she not so subtly scanned the bakery for any sign of them from around the edge of the newspaper. With the strange stares being thrown her way— which had nothing to do with the ridiculous way she was acting—she placed bets on the two women infiltrating the whole of Ballarat's ears with poisonous barbs about her before the week was out. No wonder the customers were giving her shifty looks. She wouldn't trust her either. She had to give it to the two women; they were good. Her paranoia was healthy and flourishing.

Charlotte pulled herself behind the paper again, the bold headline on the second page catching her attention, and a small crease formed inside her brows as the bakery noise faded into the background. It read:

WOOL BALES GO MISSING

Mr Syd Jones—a well-respected wool rep of Cavanagh Rural Supplies—reported that fifty bales of superfine wool had vanished from the wool stores in Melbourne several weeks ago.

"At this stage it is not known how they were taken, or how their disappearance has remained unnoticed for such a significant time. The property owners involved will be notified as more information comes to light and the police are looking into the matter, filing a report as soon as possible. I have no doubt we will get to the bottom of the matter soon."

'How could that happen?' Charlotte said, louder than she'd intended, managing to gather more semi-curious, less-than patient patrons to her new fan club. She cringed apologetically before turning back to read more of the article, a niggle of discomfort running over her skin. She was so intent on the details inside the column that she missed the handsome face peering over the top of the paper, grinning down at her.

'Charlotte?' His voice was warm, full of friendship and genuineness and . . . well, everything she didn't want to offer him back. She jumped, staring at him. Was he trying to scare her half to death? If he was, he was doing a brilliant job. Maybe she should tell him he should take up stalking as a profession.

Her heart hammered like it always did when he flashed her that drop-dead gorgeous, happy to see her smile. She had to curb her subconscious ruling her reactions towards him when he looked at her that way.

'Sheesh, Fraser, don't do that to me.' She slapped the paper down on the table, yet again earning herself some agitated glances that she chose to ignore with a not-so-subtle eye roll. And where had Charlie gone? She fought to peer around Fraser's broad torso which, as always, looked incredible in a checked shirt, his R.M. Williams leather belt finishing off the look. Did this guy have anything not going for him?

She clenched her jaw, pushing herself to stand and stepping around him in a desperate search for Charlie, but she couldn't see him. How had they disappeared so fast? The crowd lining up to order food was several people deep, too deep for her to push through with any speed. Her only hope was that Charlie and Adam were immersed somewhere in the queue, and thanks to her mother's generous gene pool, she was too short to take a good look.

'So . . . what's happening?' She angled for a casual I'm-in-no-rush tone. Was it working?

'Dad's just ordered some hay off Charlie.' He tossed his head in the direction of the door.

Charlotte's eyes flew open as her head spun towards him in alarm. But they were allowed to order hay too, and she looked away again, dismissing her alarm. She stood on tiptoes, unashamedly not hiding that her thoughts were elsewhere as she fought to see over the crowd, staring towards the exit door. 'Oh, right. Yeah, me too. Gotta head off so I get home before they get there.' Was that casual enough? She hoped so. Glancing back at him, she picked up on the slight look of confusion on his face. 'What? Are you suggesting I'm not capable of ordering hay?'

'No, no, that's not it. It's just—' He cupped his chin, one finger brushing his lips.

'Listen, I've gotta go—' She began pushing through the crowd like a kelpie in a sheep yard, leaving Fraser and his oh-so-good looks behind, for good she hoped. She didn't trust herself to look at him any longer, should her mind betray what she was trying to protect: her pride and her heart. She was developing a nasty habit of allowing him to lure her in and she needed to keep her wits about her. Letting her heart murmurings take precedence was not going to get her farm up and ready to put on the market.

Charlotte drove a little above the speed limit, hoping Mark wasn't out with his speed camera. Thanks to the trucks carrying such heavy loads, plus the well-known fact that Charlie never pushed his truck, or the speed limit, she managed to pass both trucks on her way home, waving as both Charlie and Adam gave her a friendly toot in return.

With a little spare time up her sleeve before they arrived, Charlotte drove into one of their paddocks close to the main road, checking on the commercial ewes and the latest new lambs darting about, before the distant guttural roar of truck engines caught her attention. Her heart sped up. They'd taken a lot longer than expected to arrive, but at a guess, maybe they had blown a tyre and stopped to change it.

Now she could feel it, a palpable awareness that things were going to work out for her as long as she kept her head down and her smarts about her.

With time to get to the shed, she jumped up on the back of the ute tray, excited to watch the trucks slow down and turn into their driveway.

But their engines never slowed. And not only that.

They were empty.

Charlotte's mouth fell open as she stared despondently, her heart pounding inside her chest as the trucks motored on past her driveway in the direction of home. Her head swung back to where they'd come from, the dust hanging heavily in the air from the dirt road beyond their driveway. Had she got their arrangement wrong?

Her mind whirred back to what Fraser had said at the bakery.

'Dad *just* ordered some hay off Charlie.'

Humph. Her face tightened. It seemed she needed to pay her next-door neighbour a quick visit to sort out exactly what that word "just" meant.

Gravel skidded out from beneath the tyres as Charlotte planted her foot on the brakes in front of the suspiciously new-looking stack of hay, the ute sliding as it came to a stop. The Ginja Ninja—who'd never liked her—moseyed along in front of the impeding wall of hay like a feline guard, slowing to glance at her before resuming his sentinel parade, swinging his tail high in the air. She hopped out of the ute and slammed the door shut. That in itself made her feel better, but only a little. She thundered towards Fraser, ignoring the nausea swimming in her stomach.

Stopping at the base of the seven-metre-high shed full of hay, she glared at the Akubra moving about on the top row, his muscled shoulders rippling against his shirt as he moved the small squares into place like a perfectly built brick wall. Was he ignoring her? She hadn't exactly made her entrance discreet. Her mood thickened as she punched out a rushed breath of air. She was getting her hay back, mark her words.

'Would you care to explain where these luscious lucerne bales came from, Fraser?' She'd asked nicely, hadn't she? Her glare said otherwise.

Fraser stopped what he was doing and peered over the edge as if pleasantly surprised she'd stopped by for a neighbourly visit, his heart-stopping smile only infuriating her all the more. Her jaw clenched as she fought against the rising feeling he was enjoying every minute of—whatever this was. A damned negotiating meeting? It felt more like a renounce-your-ownership-immediately-and-hand-everything-over foreclosure with her name, her past hopes, and her future all included in the deal.

He inhaled deeply as he remained perched near the edge, watching her like a hawk with that darned charismatic sparkle she was more than aware resonated unspoken delight. Samson sidled up beside him and looked down, having scaled the enormous wall during their standoff, giving her the impression she was outnumbered. She hated that cat. The miserable feline offered her a particularly spiteful hissing welcome anytime she visited. Clearly the spitball had a good memory.

'Okay, Charlotte, what's this about? I told you at the bakery we were getting a load of hay.' He offered another of his brilliantly dazzling smiles, the kind that both dared her to return it and make her feel the overwhelming urge to wring his neck at the first opportunity possible. If she had to climb this tower to reach him and try, she would, even if she did have to fight off the cat in the process.

'*A* load of hay? Not two?' She fought to keep her voice light despite her folded arms clenched so tightly across her chest, it hurt. 'Are you kidding me?' Charlotte pointed a finger straight at him, the undeniable satisfaction of waving her other arm in the air like the madwoman she was turning into, feeding her confidence.

'You stand there, stacking *my* hay, and that doesn't bother you, not one bit?' The self-control to keep her voice pleasant was almost killing her. If she tried, she might even be able to pull out a death-by-smile. 'Have you got no integrity? Oh, but hang on a minute—' She put her index finger to the air for added effect. 'This *is* like you, isn't it. The Pierces don't care about anyone else until they have everything *first*.' She paused, her lips radiating a smile aimed at luring him in before she made her big strike. 'Is there anything else I can organise for you before I go and *re-order* another load of hay? Never mind that my sheep won't get fed for another week.' If they lost condition before she sold them, she was holding him accountable.

Watching him, she prepared her words as she calmed her outrageously wild blinking, hoping he couldn't see it from the top of his castle of hay, before she experienced a nasty dose of dry eye thanks to the hay dust floating in the air. If she was going to have any chance of getting her hay back, she had to pack a final punch.

'What made you do it, Fraser? Did you pay Charlie more money?' She turned towards their second shed—full of at least four hundred small squares—keeping her focus on them long enough to send out her message before she turned back. 'Didn't have enough?' She smiled sweetly, betraying her sarcasm. 'I can tell you *really* needed mine.' She narrowed her eyes at the cat staring down at her, his tail swishing furiously, before it turned to Fraser as though it was assessing his owner's mood, or waiting for permission to launch himself at her, and scratch her to death.

Her mouth pinched in annoyance.

Fraser's silence ticked by, messing with her stay-calm-and-you'll-win-this plan as her anger rose, begging to be released. And this time she let it.

'Just admit you're wrong, Fraser, for the first time in your bloody life.' The words shot out of her mouth with vengeance, reminding her of what the corellas screeching in summertime sounded like. It may have been uncharacteristic of her, but, boy, was it satisfying.

And what did he do? He waited calmly until she'd finished her rant—because that's what he always did—even leaning his head forward a little in case she decided to continue. His brows rose as though he was inviting her to, before he finally opened that damned sexy mouth of his. Samson's glare didn't miss a beat.

'You've been through hell and back, Char, but I'm not your enemy. I told you about the delivery. I haven't stolen your hay. Oh, and by the way, we're getting a truckload of oats tomorrow. Is that going to be yours too?' His smug smile also hinted at genuineness, holding her like a hand clenched around her throat.

It bloody well should be, she seethed.

'Oh, and by the way, are you missing any sheep, *by chance*?' She paused long enough to see his alluring eyes blinking in confusion. 'Clearly it wasn't enough for you to steal my hay. My rested paddock has been mowed down rather effectively by your mob of gluttonous ewes.'

His puzzled look stayed on her. Maybe he hadn't realised they were his? But she wasn't about to let that calm her storm.

'You can do this to me, Fraser, and I'll forever hate you for it, but how could you do it to Dad?' Tears rolled down her cheeks, but she didn't care. She couldn't stop now. 'After everything he did for you. This isn't over by a long shot.' She turned, marching back to the ute, only to be abruptly stopped by John who was walking towards her from the house, his cheerful countenance threatening to give her a fast acting aneurysm. She swiped angrily at her wet cheeks with both hands.

'Charlotte, glad I caught you. Forget about that leasing offer I mentioned the other day. I wanted to chat to you about buying Sheepwash Creek outright. It'd be a nice and simple transaction, clean so to speak. I'd save you a whole lot of worry and you and Jayne could live at the beach, or wherever you like. Have you got a few minutes?'

His relaxed smile had her feet nailed to the ground.

CHAPTER 15

'What the bloody hell, Dad? She'll never sell to you.' Fraser was mindful not to mention his father's slip in genius had been perfect for his plan to keep Charlotte at the farm.

'Listen, those bloodlines are far too valuable to be wasted on just anyone, especially the try-hards around here who fancy themselves with the unrealistic chance of becoming up-and-coming superfine studs. Besides, she'll come around. All she needs is a little nudge.'

Or two. Fraser picked his father's voice to be a little on edge, but when his father looked up and saw the way he was regarding him, he toned it back quickly. If Fraser hadn't seen it, his internal alarm may have been disarmed. Sure, Dad wanted the land, but that was so he could improve their stud.

Nothing more.

But their ewes in her paddock? Obviously, she'd been good enough to put them in there before someone had ploughed into them with a car or truck, causing damage and losses they could do without, or a nasty accident. But he wasn't about to mention it. He'd deal with that one later himself.

The more Fraser thought about it, the more questions disturbed him. What exactly was his father's agenda for Sheepwash Creek?

'It was you, wasn't it?' Fraser shoved his hands into his pockets as he stepped towards his father, his fists tightening as one clenched his Grandpa Jacob's fob watch for strength, and dare he say it, patience. 'You told Charlie to give us his load of hay. It was Charlotte's, but, you already knew that, didn't you.' How could his father do something so low?

'Look, Charlie was all good about it. All I said was we needed it before her, that's it.' His father turned away, shrugging as if it had been the obvious thing to do.

'Unbelievable.' The word rushed from Fraser's lips, causing his father to spin back to him in a flash.

'Has she told you her plans?' His Dad's cast-iron gaze zeroed in on Fraser.

'No.' Fraser searched the dusty ground, wishing she would. Then he could work out how he could help keep her here or at least encourage her to stay longer. Her sheep lambing was a small relief in itself, but that would be over in six or so weeks. Then what?

'I've heard she plans on selling the sheep off in stages, at market,' his father said. 'We need to put a stop to that quick smart.'

'Who for, Dad? It feels like this is all about you.' And where had he heard such a thing?

'Don't be bloody stupid. I'm doing this for us. Do you want Trentham Park to have its chance of getting on the map or not? I've waited long enough for this.'

What? Did his father see Keith's demise as his moment to get what he'd been wanting all along? His father had always been competitive, but this? It was bordering on insane.

'I'll be buggered if I'm going to let it flit on by.' His father leaned forwards, the warmth of his breath rushing over Fraser. 'Exactly how serious are you about the future of our stud, Fraser?'

His father was fully aware of how much he loved the property that had originally been in his mother's family. He clenched the pocket watch tighter. 'Are you really questioning that?' Fraser glared incredulously at him.

'I am if you can't recognise a gift horse in the mouth when you're looking at it. Having those genetics will put us on the merino map, our stud sought after.' His father lifted his chin.

Fraser reeled from his father's words. They may never have achieved the ram prices that Sheepwash Creek did, or the results on the exhibition floor, but they had loyal buyers who came back year after year to buy their rams. That said they were doing something right.

'Listen, you told me to leave it to you, and I have,' his father said, reining in his harsh tone. 'But mark my words, Fraser. If you don't close in on this deal soon, there's going to be pandemonium.' He stopped, drawing in a deep breath that visibly lifted his chest. 'And that won't be the only thing you'll be left worrying about.'

His father's calculated stare told him what every unspoken word hadn't. That if he didn't make sure Charlotte sold to them outright, his love of Trentham Park might be all he'd have left to hold onto.

CHAPTER 16

'Thanks for this, Charlie. I'll see you in a couple of days.'

Charlotte let the weight of her worries show in her drooping shoulders as she lowered her mobile to her lap and tipped her head towards the darkening clouds closing in from the west, their cold beauty normally so breathtaking, stirring a wayward shiver over her. The far-off hills lit by the morning sun were about to disappear, and the breeze picking up signified a change was about to roll in. She needed to check on the newest lamb arrivals. But first she wanted to put Brutus and the boys back in the shed. After everything that had gone down with the hay debacle, they'd been out overnight, much longer than she'd planned.

'No. No, no-no!' Charlotte clasped her hands to the top of her head as she scanned the yards, then jogged closer, sure her eyes had to be betraying her. But the open gate told her otherwise.

Spinning on the spot, she pushed her hair from her face as a distinct headache began to throb. How had they got out? And where were they? If they'd escaped last night, they could be miles away by now. Her hunch told her they would have headed straight for the driveway.

Charlotte ran to the ute, pushed it into reverse and spun the tyres as she backed out. She took off down their long entrance, certain she would find them congregating at the cattle grate.

And she was right.

She desperately counted. One, two, three, four . . . Charlotte's eyes narrowed, and her heart stopped.

Where is he?

Charlotte jumped from the ute, standing on the running board as she searched the paddocks on either side of her. There was no sign of her own sheep to her right, and she wouldn't expect Brutus to visit them anyway. They were all joined and close to lambing. But the mob she'd moved from off the road into her well-munched-down paddock? She'd seen their ear tags when she'd moved them in. One and a half-year-olds. No ram would have met with them yet, unless—

Charlotte got into the ute again, backing up, and turning towards the gateway. She opened it and drove through. And there he was, her pesky ram liaising with the ladies, some clearly looking interested in his suggestive moves. *No. This can't be happening!* If he'd joined with any of them, and he'd had approximately twenty-four hours to do so, it was with John Pierce's ewes.

Dad, what have I done? Regret, failure, and sadness ground together, drenching her in complete misery. What had she been thinking, pretending like she could run this station even for a short time? And why hadn't Fraser come to collect his sheep before something like this could happen? Hadn't her telling him been the perfect trigger for him to act? But no. The Pierces only did things when they chose to, regardless of the position it put others into. She had a right mind to charge him for agistment, but that wouldn't be what her Dad would have done. He had taught her that you helped out a neighbour when he needed it, not set out to hamstring him, making life harder than it already was.

She eased in a steadying breath, collecting herself. First things first. She'd need to bring the mob back into the yards, draft Brutus out, and end his neighbourly rendezvous. Lewie would help her get them in, but she would need someone else if Brutus decided to play hard to get, and with her mother's arthritis getting noticeably worse, there was only one other person to ask.

Charlotte tipped her head to the side as she lifted the phone to her ear and waited for Fraser to answer, her mind mulling over all the possibilities of how Brutus had escaped. Was it an accident? Or had it been done on purpose? Brutus was an established escapee, which could explain the yards. But jumping the fence to get in with Trentham Park's ewes? She supposed it was possible. But . . . if it had been done intentionally, then who would do something like that?

And as she asked the question, her eyes widened. Had Fraser done it to her, on purpose, to get his ewes in lamb to her best ram? It was no secret he liked Brutus. Would he go to that much trouble to infuse some of Brutus' bloodlines into his stock? Did he have the nerve to not ask her first?

'So, are you happy with yourself?' Charlotte stood in front of the yards, her fingers gripping her hips as the greying skies weren't the only thing sending a shiver over Fraser's skin. Lewie ran over to him, giving him a brief sniff and tail wag before returning to Charlotte's side like some loyal servant ready to dob on him at a moment's notice.

He looked about, confused as to why he was even at Sheepwash Creek. He'd left in the middle of drenching, to come help her with a mob—that was his? He rubbed the side of his face. He'd forgotten all about them.

But one thing was clear. She wasn't happy. He didn't need to stand any closer to pick up on that fact.

'Listen, Char, I'm sorry.' He put his palms up in front of him. 'I've had a lot of things going on and—'

'Notice anything *interesting,* Fraser?' she interrupted, tossing her head to indicate the mob behind her.

Fraser scratched his cheek, searching the mob before his attention settled on . . . a ram. But not just any ram. Brutus.

Oh. So that's what she's got her knickers in a knot over, and he tried to squash the small smile threatening to show. He shouldn't have been appreciating the funnier side of this predicament. It was he who was at fault in the first place. But if it kept her here longer, then he'd be with her, working beside her, like he'd always wanted. Was wanting that so wrong?

'So, why is Brutus in with our ewes?' he said, genuinely confused. It made no sense for her to do something like that.

'Ha! You think *I* did this? Are you for real? How do you explain Brutus escaping our yards to begin with?' She glared at him like she was ready to throw him inside a pit with a cranky brown snake.

'I certainly didn't— Hang on a minute, he escaped?'

'You've got to know it wasn't me who let him out with *your* ewes? Why would I do something so stupid?' Her raised eyebrow hovered dangerously high. How was he meant to defuse this? And why did he feel like this was all his fault?

'It doesn't matter how it happened,' she continued. 'It's too late. So, are you going to help me draft him out?'

Lewie ran to and fro, keeping the sheep collected at the back of the mob as Charlotte stomped about the yards, pushing the sheep towards the force that directed them into the sheep race to be drafted, careful not to let Brutus line her up despite him seemingly watching her every move. She glanced towards Fraser, secretly drinking in his face full of concentration as she stepped back to let the sheep move of their own accord and keep the flow towards the drafting gate happening. But using underhanded methods to steal her bloodlines? This was clearly him contending for her land. He could try as hard as he liked because the more someone pushed her in one direction, the harder she pushed back. He wouldn't get his thieving hands on her land and she wouldn't let the farm stop her at every turn from selling up. And as for the future lambs his ewes were now carrying? She'd leave that problem to another day.

CHAPTER 17

Little white bodies bounced through the tufts of grass, finally giving Charlotte the urge to smile again as she drove towards the main mob of stud ewes next to the Jumbuck paddock. They looked up at her, calling out with enthusiasm, hoping she had some hay or lupins to bestow upon them.

'Sorry gals, you're outta luck.' She pressed her lips tight, the memory of Fraser and *her* hay stacked so beautifully—she hated to admit—all too clear. Was the guy hell-bent on making her life so hard he'd go to any length? It was more than clear he had no other intentions, the misconception he may have wanted her back in his life stinging a little more than she was prepared to admit.

'Where are they hiding, buddy?' Charlotte reached over, giving Lewie, who was sitting diligently on the passenger seat, a loving pat on the head. She glanced around the paddock to the places where the ewes, who, when they were about to lamb, gravitated towards, a good distance away from the main mob. Her windscreen began to blur with a sheen of mist, and she turned the wipers on, leaving a distinct dust smear as she leaned forwards over the steering wheel to spot any ewes that might be having trouble lambing. A large tree with what appeared to be a white form at the base of it caught her eye, and she turned the ute towards it.

Pulling up a short distance away, the moody sky lit up with flashes of white, accompanied by the distant rumble of thunder some way off. The ewe raised her head in alarm, sizing up the incoming threat, but with more important things on her mind, she lay down as the urge to push came over her.

Heavy droplets hit Charlotte's face as she nudged her window down for a better look. The ewe continued to struggle, hopping up and down, unable to progress or find a comfortable position. Charlotte searched the ute, inwardly growling that she hadn't brought a jacket, and she waited a little longer, wishing this lamb would make its entrance into the world before she had to face hopping out and copping a drenching. Her fingers thrummed on the steering wheel. 'Come on, little one,' she said and Lewie pricked his ears, tipping his head towards her. But the longer she wished it, the more certain she was that the ewe wasn't going to lamb without her help.

'You stay there, Lewie.' The dog's wagging tail slowed as the ute door clicked open, alerting the ewe who sprang to her feet with speed, turning with alarm to stare at Charlotte.

'It's okay,' Charlotte whispered, standing stock still but offering a gentle smile to the ewe who instinctively reversed towards the trunk of the tree, her eyes glued to Charlotte. The ewe's foot stomped on the ground, intending to scare Charlotte off. But Charlotte ignored it, waiting patiently, unmoving, despite her clothes becoming drenched.

It worked. The ewe gave one last nervous look her way before answering the call of nature and clumsily dropping to the ground again, pushing with all her might. Charlotte squinted against the pelting rain, a shudder rippling over her body before she quietly crept towards the trunk of the tree, staying out of the ewe's line of sight of the as the next rumble in the air closed in and lightning flashes became more incessant. The icy rain hit her face with force, and she wiped her fingers over her eyes before blinking to clear her vision.

Reaching the tree, she stole a calculated peek around the trunk from behind the ewe, hoping to keep the element of surprise on her side. To her dismay, the ewe wasn't progressing in her labour. She had one chance to help before the ewe might spring to her feet and take off down the paddock to the protection of the mob, possibly dying in labour. It was now or never.

Charlotte stole an icy breath, then lunged, her arms wide like she was about to take flight. The slippery mud had her feet sliding in separate directions as she latched onto the ewe's long wool for dear life, her saving grace the fact she hadn't begun their main shearing. Wrestling the ewe back to the ground, she kept the weight of one knee on her shoulder as she checked the lamb. Its tongue was a soft shade of pinkish-blue. She was running out of time.

Another clap of thunder rumbled as Charlotte eased her hand inside the warmth of the ewe, searching for the second foot. Holding her breath, she found it and gently drew it forward, proceeding to coax the lamb out with each contraction the ewe heaved.

A beautiful ram lamb shook its head as it lay in the mud, its oversized ears flopping as it blinked and drew in its first raw breath. Charlotte's chest buzzed with excitement as she eased herself away, allowing the ewe to hop up and start licking her lamb clean. Nothing beat the thrill of new life, even if it was one of Brutus' lambs, and she grinned. Despite the hard decisions the farm was demanding, she would never tire of this sight.

With the ewe bonding successfully to her lamb, Charlotte left them, arriving back home to the sense something was amiss as she parked in the machinery shed. Sodden, she hopped out of the ute, and a tingle ran down her spine as she looked around, unsure what exactly was making her feel on edge.

Odd. Nothing appeared out of place. If anything, it was too quiet, except for the light rain falling and the far-off thunder steadily moving eastward. All except for the distinct sound of hooves . . . moving *throughout* the shearing shed.

Charlotte narrowed her eyes as she ignored the smiling assassin gnome, taking stealth-like steps up to the landing before pausing, the whole shed immediately turning eerily quiet. Had she been hearing things? Imagining things? Her cheeks twitched in confusion as icy water seeped from her hair and down her face. Mum couldn't be in there. She'd be hearing movement if she was. But could there be someone else lurking about? Rumours were flying faster than fire embers about what she would do with the station, and people weren't shy about telling her their opinions, well-intentioned or not. Adding insult to injury, John Pierce had caught her outside the bakery, offering to buy her stock because he was "just trying to help her out". Then he'd told her he wanted to buy Sheepwash Creek outright? He could take his *help* and go jump because there was no way she'd be selling to them, no matter how hard or bad things became. All his offer had done was make her even more suspicious. Some family principles couldn't be severed, no matter how dire things became, and John Pierce was not going to be the beneficiary of any of her father's hard work, no matter how hard he tried to coerce her.

Charlotte gingerly wrapped her fingers around the long door handle one digit at a time, until she held it with a full grasp, the uncanny feeling that entering the shed wasn't about to be her smartest decision. She forced herself to take a long, steady breath and with swift resolve, squeezed her fingers tight and hauled the heavy sliding door partially ajar.

And in that moment, her eyes flew open.

Brutus stood directly in front of her, his head high. For a moment, neither of them moved.

How on earth? He was out of his pen? Charlotte froze, her mind racing. How was he getting the gates open? Her father had mentioned he liked a bit of a wander, but she hadn't truly believed it. And why was he staring at her? Charlotte's feet were frozen to the landing, her eyes darting in all directions as she tried desperately to decide what to do next. Should she step inside and walk around him? Would he calmly turn and follow, moving straight back to his pen with the other rams who were obviously too cautious to join him? That'd be a good story to tell her kids, the ones she was not about to have any time soon, if she knew this ram. Or would he stay where he was, and watch her? Both of those thoughts she could work with.

Or . . . would he lower his head, take a deep breath and run full pelt in her direction, ploughing through her like a bulldozer? He'd be out of the shed in a flash with her wrapped around his ginormous horns. Then what was she supposed to do?

And she didn't have to wait long to find out. Her thigh muscle shot an instantaneous twang, a shooting pain hitting her senses at the memory of when she, James, Fraser, and Gus had been playing hide and seek, all those years ago.

The boys had been frustrated because they couldn't find her. It was only when they searched every pen in this very shearing shed that they found her on the grating floor, bleeding and barely conscious, that they realised she'd been seriously injured. She had been close to bleeding out, thanks to the ram's horn gouging a deep hole in her leg, tearing open the femoral vein. With surgery, way too many stitches to mention, and lots of physio, she'd come good.

But right now, she was ready to cry.

Beginning to heave the door shut, she gasped as Brutus lurched forward, his head down and his bad temper giving full force to the metal frame of the door. The crash of his head on the door made her jump as she tried desperately to pull harder, faster. An imprint caved into the corrugated iron and Charlotte gulped as she looked down, unable to shut the door any further thanks to one of Brutus' horns poking out through the gap. But as the mammoth ram backed up for round two, she threw her shoulder against the door, yelling out as she heaved it forward.

She leapt backwards as a second thwack crashed into the metal door, leaving another dent in the iron. And in the brief moment before he took one last step back, readying for his next attempt, she gave the door the final push it needed.

Slamming it shut, she flung the outside latch down and jumped back, her feet teetering on the landing ledge. With arms flailing, her balance gave way, and she fell, cringing against the pain that shot up her ankle as she landed on the muddy ground below.

'Damn you, Brutus. What did my father ever see in you?' She eased herself upwards, rubbing at her ankle before wobbling to her feet amidst the puddle of slosh she'd landed in. Half-hopping, half-hobbling, she made her way to the side door of the shed, cautiously nudging it open before peeking in through the small crack, her eyes wide and wary. Brutus was standing like a ram statue, staring at the sliding door, as if willing her to come back for round two, and she allowed herself a wary smile.

Despite the agony of her rapidly swelling ankle driving darts of pain through her, she eased her way inside. Wincing, she stopped as Brutus turned his head at the sound, locking fresh, enthusiastic eyes on her.

With no time to spare, she snatched up a biscuit of lucerne sitting at her side and shuffled towards his pen gate as he turned around and began moving down the walkway towards her. She angled his gate open, the edge pressing against the parallel set of pens as she tossed the hay inside, then hobbled backwards. If she had to, she'd jump the fence, but that would only be plan B if the gate moved from its resting place. She didn't want to have to come up with a plan C.

His walk turned into a speedy trot as he swung around the corner, his sights set on her, his head lowered and his attitude all too ready.

Smell the hay. Please smell the hay. Her heart pounded, threatening to explode as he slowed, studying her before noticing the rams he shared his quarters with eyeing the hay with cautious interest. After one agonisingly long stare-off, his stomach finally called louder than his vendetta, and he waltzed into his pen with swaying hips and a bleat to the other rams, which Charlotte was sure told them he'd have her next time.

Ignoring the stabbing pain her ankle screamed with as she hobbled to the gate before Brutus had time to turn around for another chance to reassess his day's entertainment, she slammed it shut. She double latched the chain around the gate before pulling her hands away as if she was about to touch a redback spider.

'And *stay* there,' she said, giving him one last warning glare, her heart racing and her body a jiggle of nerves. As if in one final act of defiance, Brutus stomped his foot, lowered his head and took one steady step forward, almost daring her to step inside the ring. The lucerne remained untouched by all the rams.

Swivelling around in the shed, she cast her eyes over the other rams she'd recently brought in from the outside paddocks—the ones her father would have ordinarily been readying for a ram sale—with more than forty pairs of big brown eyes watching her with guarded keenness, but it was only Brutus who held the trump card. And as she backed away from the pen, the glint in his eye shone fiery and triumphant.

CHAPTER 18

'This cursed farm!'

Charlotte sat on the lounge, her foot elevated on three cushions and a packet of frozen peas resting over the swollen skin that had doubled in size since she'd come inside. 'It really is going to kill me,' she whispered, more to herself than Lewie who lay beside the couch after he'd weaselled his way in as she'd hobbled inside. She pressed fingers and thumbs against the sting of tears running down her face, wishing she hadn't returned to the farm after all, instead putting it on the market as it was. They could take the lot. She didn't want any of it.

But that wasn't entirely true, and to hear her say that would have crushed her father. He'd never done things by halves so she couldn't do that to him now.

'No, it won't.' The richness in the rounded voice coming from over her shoulder was like a soothing blanket wrapping itself around her body, and it took a moment for her to work out who had spoken. Charlotte twisted in her seat and looked up, cursing the tears effectively blurring her vision for not only making it hard to see, but also robbing her of the chance to watch Fraser's handsome face light up especially for her, even if she did inwardly growl at herself for it.

'Yes it will. It's cursed, Fraser.' She turned back, crossed her arms over her chest and glared at her foot, wishing things could have been so different. 'It's trying to kill me too, I know it.'

Charlotte listened to a shuffle as Fraser took a seat close by, facing her. She cautiously side-eying him, unsure if she was happy he was here or wishing he'd leave, but admitting his cheery face was the thing vying to improve her mood. And his smell, fresh woody soap and shampoo wafting in the air, making a direct beeline for her. Why did he have to be so . . . perfect? She didn't need these kinds of complications in her life.

His attention dropped to her lips before he caught himself, looking up in a flash, a soft blush warming his clean-shaven cheeks as instantaneous excitement bubbled in her chest. She needed to get a better grasp on her feelings and emotions when he was around, and when he wasn't. It seemed that no matter where he was, when she thought of him, her head took her in one direction while her heart fought to take her in another. She bit down on her lip as he spoke.

'So, you're going to let it beat you that easily?'

When Fraser had sat back on his haunches and watched—with a smidgeon of glee—the angry Charlotte over the hay, he'd been delighted by her fire. It not only stirred his ever-increasing attraction for her, it also displayed the determination inside her that meant she wouldn't easily cave to the requests his father was suggesting about selling, or him, as long as she could consider releasing him from his own guilt in the end. But was that a wishful fantasy? She wasn't about to let him forget what had happened to James, and that in his mind, was almost worse than living with the tragedy. He couldn't bear to lose her again.

Fraser's interest piqued as she studied him with deep concentration, her mind obviously whirring with a comeback he was certain would try and smack him down, and he secretly delighted in the anticipation of it. But amongst that look was a fragility so tender he had to push himself back into his seat to stop himself from hopping up and going to her, kissing her head tenderly and taking her hand as he told her everything would be okay.

'I don't need to *let* it. It already has.' Charlotte pursed her lips, her disheartenment loud and clear. 'The sooner I sell, the better off Mum and I will be. And now I've gone and hurt my ankle.' She tossed an infuriated hand in the direction of it, her frustration so evident he fought against the smile teetering on his lips. She was cute when she got all wound up.

'Fat chance I'll be any use around here for a while. Can't even go back to Melbourne and work with my ankle like this.' She looked up at him, defeated. 'What?' She narrowed her eyes his way, suspicion filling them. 'Oh, it's funny, is it? Have you tried being bulldozed by a Brutus lately? It's so much fun. You should try it.'

She huffed, linking her arms over her chest again as she avoided looking at him. The sarcasm in her voice only made it harder for him to resist showing his sheer delight and he didn't even have to say a word. He stifled a chuckle, all the while watching her sky-blue eyes as they danced over him like she knew what he was up to. They deepened, and his breathing slowed as she let her eyes fall to his mouth. Being within arm's reach of her caused an inner fight he hadn't been prepared for, and he pummelled himself for not thinking through his visit better. What had he been thinking, sitting so close? Hell, he could have chosen the seat on the other side of the room. He shied from her penetrating gaze, trying to blink it away as his heart ramped up, and his desire to move even closer argued with his common sense, which screamed at him to stay well away.

And when he caved and looked at her again, there was a smile hovering on her soft lips, the same one he'd never been able to shake from his memory. What he wouldn't do to kiss it away, turning it into tenderness and love and—

He shied away, standing abruptly in the hope he'd made it look like he was trying to channel his thoughts into leaving rather than the ache over long-gone memories, wishful hopes and new possibilities that didn't stand a chance of ever taking off. But he had nothing. He took a sobering breath.

'Listen, I dropped by to take home those ewes you were good enough to keep hold of for us. Thanks for that.'

All she offered in return was a slow nod, her eyes cast to the clouds running across the blue sky like they were being chased.

'I had a look at the farm books the other day,' Charlotte said, as though she hadn't heard a word he'd said. It had saved him from more embarrassment but had him focusing on her with concerned interest as she stared out the loungeroom window. Keith had been a smart operator, and that included how and what he spent his money on. So, why did he get the feeling she was about to drop a bombshell?

'I won't make the next overdraft payment if I don't sell.' Her disheartened voice faded to a whisper. 'And I need money before I can even get the stupid paperwork done for a sale.' Her voice was despondent as she turned to look at him. 'How is that even possible, Fraser?' She blinked, staring right through him and he could tell her mind was catapulting over her scant options. But if she needed to make a bank payment, something needed to happen, fast. Or else something far worse than her selling the farm would take place. It could be taken out of her hands, placed into receivership, and sold for a loss, so that the bank could get their money back. And never mind his father hearing about it. Fraser was more than aware that if she had to live with that happening, she'd not only resent him for an eternity, but she'd also find it near impossible to live with herself.

But what could he do? She'd already been here longer than he, Mark, and Ross had put odds on, wanting to see out the main shearing before selling.

But then what?

His eyes widened as an idea surfaced to the forefront of his mind.

'I could buy last year's lambs from you, keep them at our place . . . for a quick cash flow.' He couldn't read her face but hope filled him so he continued. 'Then when you're in a better financial position you could—'

'Are you serious?' Charlotte sat bolt upright, the death glare aimed his way enough to make him flinch, acutely aware she'd seen his reaction too.

If she'd let him finish, he might have been able to say: 'buy them back for the same price.'

'You're as bad as your father, Fraser Pierce. You won't stop, will you, wanting Sheepwash Creek any way you can get your greasy fingers on it. Thanks, but no thanks.' She slumped back onto the couch with a thud, crossing her arms and frowning, her blonde waves draping over her forehead and around her shoulders in a softness that made him want to gently push them back so he could see her pretty face once more. He'd gone and deftly stepped into his own sinking quagmire, finally recalling why he'd dropped by in the first place. He back peddled as fast as he could because all this was doing was rubbing salt into her open wound. How could he be so stupid?

He swallowed, feeling the pull from his Adam's apple as it bobbed in his throat. 'Listen,' he said desperately, 'I dropped by because I needed to tell you . . .' He watched, her impatience taunting him over what he was about to say next. He pressed his lips tight to smother the small smile once again itching to shine through. He loved that spunk about her.

But it had to be said, and done, soon. He'd left it too long already. How his father hadn't noticed probably had more to do with his preoccupation with getting his hands on Sheepwash Creek rather than from any good luck.

'Your fence between Jumbuck paddock and our north paddock has come down.' She didn't need to be alerted to his suspicions that it was in fact his sheep that had pushed it over. She'd work that out soon enough when she saw the damage for herself. 'We've got a box-up of mobs that we'll need to deal with. And we'll need to fix that fence.' If dealing with the mix-up of sheep wasn't bad enough, it was the complication of how they were meant to work out which lambs were supposed to go with which ewes that was causing him the bigger headache. They were too young to wean. He removed his hat and scruffed his hair as he sifted through the logistics in his mind. He'd need more helping hands than only hers for a job of that size, hoping he could rope Mark and Ross, and maybe Gus into helping, even though he had no experience with livestock. But what he lacked in that space, he more than made up for in fencing skills. Gus was a machine when it came to dead straight fence lines completed with professional wire knots.

'I saw that fence on a tilt the other week.' She sighed a deflated breath. 'I don't think I'll be much help, but I'll try.' She glanced at her foot in dismay, before steadily watching the view outside once more, like she was ready to give up. 'I'm going to the doc's tomorrow, so can we do something about it after that, if it's okay with you?'

All her bite had gone, and in its place lacklustre enthusiasm. She turned his way, not with happiness on her features, but with something more like surrender. She shrugged. Relief filled him that she might be willing to work alongside him. That in itself was a huge achievement. And if he could reassure her everything was going to be okay in that time, he might be able to make her see she had options. Which required being open to them. He let out a disheartened breath.

Baby steps. That was all that was needed.

Charlotte stared at Fraser as she sat on the back of the ute tray, her leg elevated and resting on a cushion. No longer was he the gangly boy she'd loved. The muscles of his forearms flexed as he strained the last of the fence wires with Gus, and his back muscles moved with the best of them. And she should know, having worked on many a good looking back, and then again . . . some not so eye catching. The thought made her smile.

Her job . . . she hadn't given it a great deal of thought other than the once-a-week phone calls to check on how things were holding up without her. And it appeared to be coping perfectly. The other practitioners working with her were taking on new clients alongside some of her own, a fact that should have worried her. But, it didn't.

Charlotte's imagination took off on a rampant ride of its own, as she imagined how leaning into Fraser's strong chest might feel these days, the perfect picture of strength and warmth that she could soak in, offering her the reassurance and endurance she craved. She closed her eyes, finding herself yearning for their days long gone. Now they were both adults with mature feelings, desires, and hopes. Were his anything like hers, wishing that horrendous day had never happened, levitating them to a new plateau both of them could grow into and, dare she hope for, grow old with?

And then her mind finally did it, slipping to the forbidden place she'd so far protected herself from. His kiss. What would it be like to be kissed by Fraser these days? She watched as he worked, the light chatter with Gus occasionally ending with a jovial chuckle between them, making her smile contentedly in return. He had no clue what he was doing to her.

'Char? You okay?'

Charlotte blinked as she sat up, widening her eyes at how she'd let simple daydreams swallow her up without realising she was being watched too. How long had his flawless smile been locked on her? How long had she been looking longingly at him? And why did he have to be so damned frustrating in every conceivable way? She grimaced as heat flushed her cheeks.

But credit to his generous nature and good heart—thank goodness—he hadn't taken it further than the glint of suggestion his look danced over her with, the one that said she'd been caught red-handed. Despite the warmth of the sunshine, goosebumps ran down her arms. And all this after she'd roared at him and made his life generally miserable ever since she'd been home? She had to be kidding herself to hope there was any chance he might want to rekindle what they'd had.

And then there was Maddie. Charlotte knew the nearly eighteen-year-old had a serious crush on Fraser.

'We're all done.' Gus perused the length of the repaired fence, giving it a shake with his hand to check the tension. Fraser gave a satisfied grin as he turned back to Charlotte. 'No thanks to you, Miss Hop-along.'

Had he really called her that? And damn that warm glow that came over her every blasted time he called her Char. She needed to keep her wits about her, not a ridiculously melting heart that wanted to rebel against all her determination and decisions about what her future should look like.

And with a bung foot, no money, and way too much to do, how was she ever meant to get this property sorted?

CHAPTER 19

It was mid-morning the next day, a light smattering of rain settling on the driveway of Sheepwash Creek.

'Keep bringing on those showers, Mother Nature, and I'll be happy,' Charlotte whispered, smiling to herself as she watched Lewie's tail thrash back and forth in her rear-vision mirror, his nose high in the air on the back of the ute as they drove. Mixed with the warm doses of spring sun they were getting, the grass would be shooting and the property would look spectacular in the front of the real estate section of the newspaper or a flyer.

The trees whooshed past as she headed towards Ballarat, keen to see Gus and pick up her wool packs and other bits and pieces in preparation for Sheepwash Creek's main shearing. It was a little way off, but she wanted to be organised. That way, nothing could get missed or go wrong, she hoped. She was hobbling about, but her ankle was feeling freer, and she'd managed to round up Mark and Ross to lend her a hand with the mustering and yard work. Jerry, the local shearing contractor, had the rest in hand, much to her surprise.

Her fingers were lightly tapping to the song on the radio when the glint of a vehicle coming towards her in the distance caught her eye. If it was Fraser or heaven forbid, his father, there was zero chance she was going to slow down to say hello, no matter how "neighbourly" the action was. And as the ute grew closer, its white metallic paint obvious, she gripped the steering wheel tighter, setting her sights on the rural supplies shop. So, when the ute slowed and she reluctantly risked a glance its way, her mouth relaxed into a relieved smile.

Charlotte eased her ute to a stop, not bothering to move off to the side of the quiet road.

'Peter Rabbit, how are you?' She couldn't help but grin, not only at his welcoming smile but at his namesake. For her lifetime, he'd been referred to this way, and it dawned on her that she'd only ever known him by his nickname.

'Hello there, Miss Charlotte. You're exactly the person I was coming to talk to.' He continued to radiate a happy zest for life, and she found herself feeling buoyed by it.

'Oh?' She beamed, and he gave a hearty chuckle.

'I'm hoping to buy a new ram. Do you think you might have something for me to look at?'

Charlotte's mind flew to the rams she'd recently moved into the shed, including several younger rams that Brutus was less than happy about sharing his quarters with. Her father sold his best rams at their on-property sale day, but they always kept some commercial-style rams available for buyers, should they need them at a different time and for a cheaper price.

'I'm sure we could rustle up something for you, Pete. Would you like to come and have a look? I'd be happy to turn around and show you.'

'If it suits you, that'd be grand.'

Charlotte rang Gus on the way back home, organising for him to drop off her order instead. As she headed back to Sheepwash Creek, her enthusiasm was buzzing, and her hopes were pushing to an all-time high. And alongside it came a feeling of, what was it exactly? She couldn't nail it. But it was akin to being excited about something. Was it her future? On Sheepwash Creek? Could it be the kick-start she'd been waiting for?

It didn't take long for Pete to sift through the rams and choose one with the appropriate wool style and big barrel that suited his future breeding needs. He was handing over eight hundred dollars to her when Gus pulled in.

'Well, well, well, if it isn't Gus Stevens. My word, son, you've shot up from the little whippersnapper who tried to pinch the goldfish outta my fishpond all those years ago.' He offered a hearty laugh as he reached out for a shake, placing his other hand on Gus's shoulder.

'Hey, I needed a present for Uncle Neil's birthday, and it wasn't like he was going to part with any money for me to buy one. Some things will never change.' The three of them laughed.

'Ah yes. Never was fond of spending the dollars, was he,' Pete said, warmth in his voice. 'So has he still got that nice beachside property in the Otways?'

'Sure has, and it's great. It's nothing fancy, but the beach is your own, and the rabbits.' Gus shook his head with a rueful laugh. 'Speedy loves giving them a run for their money.'

Gus proceeded to unload the wool packs, drench, and backliner, dropping them off on the shed landing as Pete gave Speedy—Gus's loyal blue heeler—a pat through the open passenger window.

'Doin' a bit of shearin,' are we?' Pete's eyebrows rose as he looked up at Charlotte.

'Yeah, soon.' How she was meant to get through it with a bung ankle, she didn't know.

'Don't look at me,' Gus said, recognising the look on Charlotte's face as she turned to him. 'I don't know one end of a fleece from the other.' He put his hands in the air as if to clear himself of any potential guilt. He wasn't a sheep man and he didn't intend on starting.

With a nod and a sigh, she turned to Pete. 'Do you mind if I ask, would there be any chance you'd be available to give me a hand?' Charlotte glanced at her strapped ankle before turning to him again, her expression hopeful but not expectant. Before he could answer, she hurried on. 'Only thing is, I don't have a lot of money, so . . . maybe we could . . . feed you for payment?' She scrunched up her nose, half-smiling as Pete's face lifted and the lines around his eyes deepened.

'What smart man could turn down an offer like that?' He beamed before his face turned earnest. 'Since losing my wife, I've had a lot of spare time on my hands.' He leaned in a little closer to both of them. 'No thanks to *Squire John* next door.' He stood a little taller again, pushing his hands deep inside his pockets. 'I reckon my little place would be happy to see less of me for a bit.' He grinned, sealing the deal.

'Great! Come on in and have a cuppa. Mum has pulled something out of the oven that I reckon you might enjoy.' Pete's face lit up brighter than a spotlight at night as they headed into the house. Gus followed Pete as he rubbed his hands together in anticipation, his stomach grumbling with glee.

'Nope, I'm sure,' Gus said to Fraser, who absently scratched the side of his neck as he considered his mate. Why had Charlotte asked Peter Rabbit to work there for shearing if she couldn't pay him? Gus must have read his mind.

'He was happy to get a feed and, Fraser, the man needs some fat on his bones. I reckon he's been living off jam and toast for way too long.'

Fraser shook his head with a smile, raising his hand in a goodbye to Gus as he left the produce store. The bags of dog and cat food he'd bought were the last things on his mind as he balanced them over his shoulders before dumping them in the tray of his ute. But his thoughts pressed on. If Pete helped Charlotte—and that was a good thing, especially with her ankle—would she consider staying on longer if he continued to help out around the place? The thought had merit.

Drinks night rolled around again and as usual, Fraser was the first to arrive.

'G'day, Big Nev. How's things?' Fraser looked around the inside of the pub, its original cottage house framework having been converted with a distinctly homely feel—if you didn't include the smell of stale beer in the carpet as authentic. Several original rooms had been renovated into varying-sized dining rooms for different levels of quiet and intimacy, and the bar ran the length of the original lounge and kitchen, with a new cooking facility having been built-on out the back in recent years to service the meals.

'Not bad,' Big Nev nodded, concentrating on pouring the three beers for Fraser. 'Not bad at all.' He expertly set down the drinks and his coke at the table before taking a seat at a stool and lifting the glass to his mouth for a long sip.

'Ahh,' he said, before giving Fraser his full attention again. 'There's been a lot of interest in the goings-on at Sheepwash Creek.' He waggled his eyebrows, causing Fraser to question what exactly had been said.

'Oh?' He'd known it would be a curious topic of interest. But enough for Big Nev to be hearing of it at The Tavern? That meant it was the lead topic of conversation within the district, and probably beyond.

'You don't know?' Big Nev's features creased in disbelief. 'It appears your father has his mind made up . . . if you get my drift.'

Fraser stared at his drink despondently, the weight of both trying to please his father and find another way of keeping Char in Settlers Hill almost proving too much. But the longer Charlotte stayed, the more his urgency grew to ensure his father didn't get his way. But in doing so, was he letting his mother down, given Trentham Park was from her side of the family? He had to tread carefully if he was to keep his father's suspicions about his intentions at bay. Otherwise the consequences could be greater than he might be able to handle.

His mind shifted to Will, who was currently playing a round of snooker in a dedicated games room off to the side with some other local lads, their laughter good to hear. The guy was like clockwork, always here with some mates on a Friday night, no different to Ross, Mark, and himself. He gave a small smile, the irony of zero women around him, his buddies, or Will and his mates, more apparent than ever. And he hadn't missed the fleeting glance of regret, sadness, or possibly both, when Will had seen him walk in earlier. Or maybe it was over his latest fishing loss. That made Fraser smile again. He hoped it was that.

Momentarily forgetting Big Nev sitting beside him, he let his mind drift to Charlotte once more. What was he meant to do—let her go back to the big smoke or fight to see her stay? He'd go to the moon and back for her. But wasn't he doing that already? He'd been to the fiery hearth when James had died, and it irritated him no end that she didn't know the full story, despite how many times he'd done all he could for her to understand. She'd always been angered by his bringing up the subject until ultimately, she'd left without a goodbye, never to return. Until now. Will hadn't been negligent or irresponsible. It had come down to inexperience, and it was something that could happen to anyone given the same or similar circumstances, deeply tragic no matter how it happened.

But Will . . . the kid didn't deserve to feel as though he should leave their small town all because Charlotte was back. Besides, Fraser believed he deserved to have them both stay—a great mate no matter what they had gone through. Didn't he deserve a chance for his own happily ever after with the only woman he'd ever loved? Couldn't he have both?

'Will's a great guy.' Big Nev eyed him as if he'd been predicting every word Fraser had been toying with.

'Yeah, he is. I'd trust him in a heartbeat.' It wasn't fair that the guy hadn't been able to pick up a gun since that night;

that he suffered nightmares regularly, and as a result, couldn't trust himself enough to try for a girlfriend.

Big Nev stood, giving him a hearty pat on the back before greeting Mark and Ross as they slid into their seats. Both men pulled their beers towards themselves with eagerness and Big Nev took his seat again.

Fraser glanced back at Will, giving him the invitation to join them with a slight nod, but Will declined with a small shake of his head. Since the accident, he'd shied from the police, even though he hadn't been charged. Mark hadn't been the attending officer, not having arrived in Settlers Hill at that point. But it was too much for Will to sit with them when Mark wore his uniform. And Fraser got it. He turned his attention back to his mates.

'Charlotte's asked Peter Rabbit to help out with her shearing,' he said, in as carefree a manner as he could, waiting for their reactions.

'Bets are he'll stay on after that,' Mark said, before taking a long draw of his beer.

Fraser watched the froth lacing the insides of his glass, caught up in his own thoughts about what might happen. Could she consider keeping him on? And more than that, would Pete want to?

'I'm with Mark,' Ross said. 'I was over there today, checking on a few ewes and lambs she was concerned about. Nothing serious. But Pete was holding the sheep for me, and he made a comment that he'd be willing to stay on for the long haul if he was asked. Said he couldn't stay away from Jayne's cooking.'

At that, all four men burst out laughing, nodding with complete understanding.

And it was precisely what Fraser wanted to hear.

Fraser hadn't tramped two steps into the kitchen before his father bellowed at him.

'What's this about bloody Peter Rabbit working for Sheepwash Creek?' His voice was agitated and he took a sharp sip of his coffee, burning his tongue and returning the mug to the table with a frustrated thud.

Fraser said the only thing he could. 'Yeah, I heard that too.' He took his time, pouring himself the same, hoping it would wake him up a little after the beers he was currently feeling rather relaxed from.

'Well, bloody put a stop to it. Settlers Hill doesn't need some bloody farm—*her*—who likes the swanky idea of owning a station. And that's the last thing we need her doing, adding complications to our already frustrating matters at hand. Having Peter there will only encourage her to stay longer. It'd be bloody futile.'

Fraser rolled his shoulders to disguise the jarring thud that ripped through his chest. If Pete was planning on helping Charlotte long-term, would she need him? But it'd be a small price to pay to see her stay . . . wouldn't it?

'That's not my call, Dad.' How could his father so effectively make him feel guilty for a decision Charlotte had made on her own, and pressure him to fix or even stop it from happening, as he so keenly put it. 'And it's none of our bloody business what she does. For all we know, she might have changed her mind about selling.' He fought against the hope daring to rise in him.

His father looked up pointedly, his honed gaze glaring at his son. 'What do you mean?'

'Maybe she wants to keep Sheepwash Creek.' He dismissed his comment with a non-committal shrug. Opening his mouth to continue, the flitter of hope in his envisaged words egged him on to say them out loud, that she would have his full support—but his father got in first.

'I'd better bloody hope not. And you'd better hope not too. If she tries to run that station alone, then she's madder than I gave her credit for.' Distracted, Dad took another sip of his coffee. 'Ah, damn it.' He dropped the mug back onto the table as he leaned forward, wiping the scalding drips from his lips before he glared at his son.

'You don't want her to stay, do you?' he said suspiciously. 'She was never good enough for you, Fraser. I told you that then and I'm reminding you again. It was a good thing she left when she did, ending it. No good could come of the two of you together.'

'Why not, Dad? Because you'd never get a piece of Sheepwash Creek for yourself? Is that it?'

But his father didn't answer him. Instead, he held him with a long, well-scrutinised glower.

'You're not still in love with her, are you?'

Fraser's chest thudded so loudly, he was wary his father would hear it. What did he say? The truth, and shoot himself in the foot for his second and possibly only chance he had at keeping Charlotte living next-door to him?

'What Charlotte chooses is none of our business and she can do what she likes. And if it isn't what you want to hear then that's for you to deal with, not me.' Fraser jerked his head away from his father, standing and tipping his untouched coffee down the sink with a haphazard splash.

'Perhaps you've forgotten what it means to be a Pierce, son?'

His father's voice was eerily level, foreboding, telling him loud and clear what his father didn't need to say out loud. Unlike his father, the love of his mother's property— Trentham Park—ran deep inside him, as if it were in his veins. His dad had hinted to him when he and Charlotte were teenagers that if he chose to continue seeing her in a serious manner, there would be repercussions about his future on the family property. At the time, Fraser hadn't viewed it as any real threat, only his father expressing disappointment in him. And when he and Charlotte had broken up? It was never mentioned again.

'Why do you want Sheepwash Creek so badly, Dad?' Hadn't it always been about the competitive rivalry between his father and Keith? There had to be more to it, as if a new agenda was driving his father's motives and decisions.

He didn't need to listen to his father's inflammatory or derogatory answer. What he wanted was to get as far away from him as possible before he took a swing at the man.

CHAPTER 20

Charlotte slowed as the cemetery came into view, its neat rows of headstones in line with the church, no more than fifty metres away. Her throat tightened and a shiver ran over her as she stared at it for a few saddening minutes, unable to make herself stop by either James's or her father's graves. She had left Settlers Hill, planning on never returning, her parents' visits to her in the city the perfect answer to her apprehension of confronting her deep fears.

But here she was, back in the town that had torn her world into shreds and her hopes into nothing more than wishful thoughts. And she was *still* here. Introspection rattled her, the mixed emotions of working on the farm drawing her in closer and yet also reminding her of the hold it had on her, especially if she didn't sell up and leave. She was a mess of conflicting thoughts and despair, nothing offering her the security she desperately sought.

Charlotte pulled into The Tavern car park, relieved to be away from the church that held so many confronting memories. Pushing the door open, she looked around, thankful she'd picked a time when the premises was quiet and she could have some space to retrace her convictions and aspirations—regardless of how far-fetched they were—far away from the farm that both enticed her to keep it and sent her a shrill message: that it wasn't finished with her family.

'Now there's a pretty face we haven't seen in here for a long while.'

Charlotte's pained grimace faded away as she searched the long bar, spying Big Nev as he shined a glass with a tea towel, his rosy cheeks warm and friendly. He'd been her father's best mate, a lifetime of memories shared over the wooden bar she was sliding her hand along as she approached him.

'Hey, Big Nev.' Her eyes grew glassy and his brow crinkled at the sight of her forthcoming tears. He put down the glass, flicked the tea towel over his shoulder and came around the bar, reaching out and taking her in the biggest bear hug, one she could cling to long after she went back to the farm. It was warm and safe and comforting. It was the place she needed to be.

Big Nev gently rested his chin on her head, and she could hear his heartbeat, steady, rhythmic.

'How are you doing, Miss Charlotte?'

'Not so great.' She sniffed, and as if on cue, the tears began to fall a little more precariously, seeping into Big Nev's shirt. She drew in a shaky breath. Had he been waiting for her to call in so that he could express his own grief? She wished she hadn't left it so long to drop in and see him.

'What am I meant to do, Big Nev?' A deep sob released itself from her chest and she reluctantly let one hand slip from his comforting girth, lifting it to her face to roughly swipe the tears aside.

'I don't know, sweetheart.' He pressed his cheek against her hair. 'But I can tell you your father would be pleased with whatever you decide.'

At that, Charlotte leaned back, her brow tightening as she looked him in the eye. 'What?'

'Charlotte, he was in here not long before he . . .' he looked aside, 'died.' She could see the pain in his face as he said it. This was hard for him too. Her throat pinched tight as her eyes clung to his every word. 'He was telling me how happy he was that you'd found your own path; done what you wanted to do, and achieve. He understood that losing James had changed your life, your decisions. He wanted you to make your own choices about your future.'

'He did? I thought he was disappointed in me for up and leaving.' Nancy and Elsie's hurtful comments came to mind.

'Maybe he was a little sad.' Big Nev reached to brush aside the lone tear trailing down his face with a tight smile. 'But never disappointed. You showed a strength that made him the proudest dad in town.'

CHAPTER 21

Boots had a lively skip in his step as Charlotte trotted him towards the Home Paddock gate. She wanted to check on the ewes and lambs early and to see if the decent downpour from a couple of nights ago had offered some runoff that could have made a difference to the dam levels before Pete arrived.

Her mind whirred with fresh hope as she watched the water steadily trickling into one of the several water holdings they had. With the amount of things to do growing at a shocking rate, she'd begun a list on her phone, adding to it regularly as anything she'd forgotten or overlooked came to mind. It was getting longer by the day, but without it, she wouldn't be able to stay on track.

Casually cantering back towards the sheep yards, she eased Boots to a halt when Pete pulled up beside her on the quad bike, leaving the engine running. The big mob with both hers and Fraser's sheep were still woolly, thanks to the box-up. She'd shifted them closer to the house early yesterday and it was their turn to be shorn.

'Morning, Miss Charlotte. Are you ready to do this?' His voice held interest and she didn't have to guess why. It was loaded with "Fraser is about to arrive any minute," vibes and she hadn't exactly been exuberant in showing her enthusiasm about it. At least not outwardly. On the inside, it was the absolute opposite of how she was feeling, and she was pretty sure Boots had picked up on her nervous energy. Curse her betraying heart that was calling her to fall for Fraser again. It was the last thing she needed: a sticky-nosed Pete primed and ready to pick up on one slight eye glance or bright flush from some impromptu embarrassment she hadn't invited. She was not ready to discuss her feelings.

With anyone.

'I am. We've waited two weeks for the sheep to be dry but I'm not complaining. The sooner it's done, the faster we can move on and put this place up for sale,' she said with an intentionally gruff voice she hoped might hide her apprehension, dismissing him like a naughty child who'd dared to ask something he had no right to. And she meant it, turning from him and nudging Boots back into a casual canter as she headed out to bring in the next mob, Lewie running at her side as the first of the shearers drove up to the shed. She had to push her feelings aside because, frankly, they didn't matter. Staying focused on the goal was the objective so she could push this life back to where it needed to stay, far from her mind along with her next-door neighbour.

The rain had been coming in consistent showers at least twice a week of late and the long-range forecast warned heavier falls were due as soon as next week. Charlotte glanced at the foreboding clouds, urging them to hold off until all the sheep were drafted and inside the shed. It was big enough to hold them all, and she'd even consider the idea of not separating the ewes from the lambs if it meant they would get the job completed.

Pete and Charlotte had the sheep moving towards the yards when that oh-so-familiar ute rolled up to the shed and Charlotte's heart gave an unmistakable skip, her eyes betraying her direct instruction not to look at Fraser as he hopped out and waved good-naturedly at them. Even her hand had a mind of its own, waving back before she could stop it and she glowered. She might need to depend on him, but that didn't mean she should like it..

Fraser beamed like he'd laid eyes on diamonds. Charlotte looked gorgeous on her horse, her hair blowing away from her face in the wind that held the sure smell of another shower of rain. And how good was it going to be spending the next two days working alongside her in the shearing shed! He'd work in a pig shed if it meant he'd be able to catch the smallest of wafts of her rose-scented perfume as she walked by him. He might even be able to coax a smile from her if he worked hard enough.

'Quick, shut the gate, Pete. Let's get the lambs drafted off the ewes before . . .'

Soft spits of rain landed on Fraser's face, making him squint towards the sky. It didn't look as though there was anything much in it other than a few spots, but it was enough for him to see Charlotte begin to panic. She leapt from Boots, hanging his reins over a branch of the peppercorn tree near the yards.

'I told you it was going to rain,' she growled at Fraser, her eyes glaring his way. 'But you wouldn't listen.' She put her hands on her hips, making her point.

'There's nothing much in it. We'll get them done.' He grinned at the annoyance glued to her features. It was the cutest grumpy face if ever he'd seen one. He'd need to make sure she didn't cotton on and stop doing it.

'Okay, okay, you two, stop acting like an old married couple. The longer we stand here the more likely Jerry will declare "wet sheep". Let's hurry along and get them drafted.'

Charlotte looked at Pete, then at Fraser, unquestionably over the *old married couple* comment and he smothered the smirk his lips threatened to divulge. And when Pete studied both himself and then Charlotte, the cogs in his brain began to clunk like a wind-up clock. He'd been caught. Pete's grin was unmistakable. The cunning old coot picked something was going on between their interaction, he was sure of it given the raised eyebrows and teasing love-sick smirk he wasn't bothering to keep in check.

But it was the look on Charlotte's face that delighted him more than anything. Her eyes widened as heat rushed up her neck and cheeks, her mouth open as she looked on in disbelief. And when they locked eyes . . . Never had a woman affected him the way she did. He needed to focus on the sheep, or anything other than the sexy woman standing way too close and he moved towards the drafting gate as Pete and Charlotte 'ho hoed' and 'ha haaed' the sheep to move, urging them towards the force.

'Why are they being so bloody stubborn?' Charlotte said as she puffed while flapping her arms in the air, her look of exasperation evident.

'That'll be yours holding up proceedings. Mine are too well-behaved to make life difficult,' he smirked, watching her actions slow as she decided how to respond. But it wasn't the sheep making her life difficult. She'd walked to within arm's reach of him, her loose ponytail cupping the side of her face as she bent down again to nudge a lamb forward. She looked up at him and he caught her eyes, sweet and captivating as they shifted from full-on focus for the job to an intensity that held him captive. He sensed all control slipping away, ignoring the way Pete had stopped working to watch on.

'Is that so?' Her voice was smoother than silk. 'Mine weren't rude enough to trample a fence, trespassing and stealing food.'

The way she held her ground, glaring at him again had a smile pushing at his cheeks. He'd been powerless to look away and he hadn't missed it, that small flicker of a smile dancing on her rosy cheeks, and in his peripheral vision he could see Pete's eyes bouncing from her to him like a dog waiting expectantly for a ball to be tossed.

'They know a good thing when they see it.' His stirring smile radiated in his eyes and he hoped she understood what he was getting at. But instead of giving him an answer, she turned back to the sheep, flapping her arms in the air as she continued urging the sheep to move again.

CHAPTER 22

Charlotte brushed aside the sweat on her forehead with her forearm as Lewie sprang across the sheep's backs, barking as he urged the stubborn ewes into the shearers' catching pens inside the shed. Despite her angst about shearing at such short notice, she was relieved to see Jerry's team were working fast and clean, even if it did put her under the pump.

Someone else she was grateful to was Fraser, who was working on the wool table with the shedhands, skirting and classing the wool—thanks to Jerry's classer being unavailable. With his experience, and his Owner Classer's ticket, leaving him in charge would mean their clip was in safe hands. She could manage basic short and long crossbred lambs' wool, but when it came to merino micron and style in the fibre, she didn't have a clue. It was his job to help make

Trentham Park and Sheepwash Creek the most money and if he did, it'd be music to her ears.

She paused after closing the gate on the pen full of sheep, watching him roll the wool into a big ball, test it for its strength then decide which wool bin it should go into. They'd agreed to go halves in the proceeds for the ewes' wool as it seemed the fairest way to do things after the box-up of mobs. They'd divide the wool weight up equally, stencilling her bales under Sheepwash Creek's own brand. Their wool was so similar thanks to it all being superfine, it would only be splitting hairs to have drafted each mob off separately. Not that John was happy about it, but she wasn't about to waste time worrying over his opinion.

Her eyes looked deeper into the man at work, watching the easy way he moved towards the wool bin he was placing the fleece in. He disappeared inside and when he reappeared, as if he sensed her eyes on him, he looked straight at her, his immediate sunny smile lifting, hitting her fair in the chest as it delivered all the warmth of a summer's day direct to her heart.

Her lips rose without permission, returning the smile with one equally as big before she caught herself, allowing it to drop away gently as she turned a shoulder to him, acutely aware that her inner—private—feelings that were growing every day would show like a neon sign if she watched him any longer. She had to get past this crazy notion niggling in the back of her mind that she might be falling for him again.

She pushed through the remaining sheep Pete had moved towards her and headed for the back of the shed to the rest of the waiting mob, her mouth dry. Who was this man to her anyway? A neighbour . . . yes. A guy she used to go out with . . . yes. The guy she'd once . . .

No. She couldn't say the "L" word, not to describe them back then, and definitely not now. They'd been too young then. And they were only friends now, she assured herself.

That's all.

She attempted to turn her attention back to the sheep hugging her legs like a warm woolly coat. Their '*baas*' as they moved from her, their big brown eyes, and the smell of fresh lanolin combined with that sheepy smell she could pick from down the paddock whenever she rode Boots over their property, should have worked. But it hadn't. Why was Fraser Pierce so inside her head? A rush of fresh emotion stirred within her. Resentment. She hated how he managed to draw her attention back to his broad chest with no clue he'd even done so. And that mouth . . . She gave a low-down growl in her throat, chastising her roaming eyes as the buzz in her stomach palpitated. His flexing biceps and muscular shoulders made him look like he had the body of a damned model—which she decided should be illegal in a shearing shed—his farmwork all he needed to keep in shape.

Tipping her head to the cobwebs floating on the breeze of the shed rafters, she bit down on her lip. Why did this keep happening to her, especially when her vow to never let him forget what he'd robbed her of was meant to be pushing these infuriating feelings aside? Any love she'd had for him was never meant to be. His father had made that all too clear. It was what she needed to remind herself of, to keep her self-perpetuating feelings on a leash—an extremely tight one—so as to not set her heart loose to do as it pleased. Unrealistic excitement built false hope, and that was something she could never indulge in.

Besides, John was doing a good job of making her offers he was sure she wouldn't be able to refuse. What he failed to recognise was how determined she could be, a fact that caused a resolute smile to creep over her cheeks. Until she had the farm sorted out, she wasn't about to divert from what she had to do. And that also included Fraser.

An urgent pang of sadness hit her fair in the chest. Cautiously, Charlotte glanced around, wary that someone might perceive in her face the remorse of everything that had gone down on this unforgiving farm, and how much it had changed the direction in her life.

She blinked, her eyes settling on the only pair of eyes watching her. Pete's. His low smile held sincerity and understanding as he gave her a gentle nod.

'G'day, Syd. It must be nearly lunchtime.' Charlotte smiled as the wool rep licked his lips, the smell of roast beef flowing from the back door.

'And ain't that a shame,' Syd said, his grin overzealous. 'Don't mind meself a bit of Jayne's tucker.' And as he said it, he patted his belly in anticipation.

Charlotte giggled, holding the screen door to the house open for him. All the shearers and shedhands were already hoeing into their lunchtime feed, and as Charlotte glanced around for an available spot to sit at the table—as far away from Fraser as possible—her Mum welcomed Syd, calling him over to the seat at the head of the table.

Thanks, Mum. Charlotte resisted giving her mother a narrow-eyed glare as she clenched her jaw and moved towards the only seat left, the one right next to Fraser. He grinned at her like it was no big deal, chewing with that ridiculous sparkle in his eyes that sent shockwaves rippling inside her stomach. What choice did she have?

None it seemed.

Charlotte huffed as she landed in the seat with a thud, her frustration higher on her act-upon-now list because no one else cared, all drooling over the hot salted-caramel pudding Mum was serving alongside ice cream and double cream. At this rate, they'd never get rid of Jerry's team. Charlotte scowled to herself.

'The wool's looking great.' Fraser gave her one of his pulse-surging smiles, disarming her defences. But oh no, the man was not going to get under her skin that easily. She wasn't about to be swayed by any smooth talk or batting of super-attractive eyelashes. She picked up her fork and stabbed an oversized piece of meat, shoving it into her mouth with some effort as she stared at the table in front of her.

'That's good,' she muttered around the piece of meat that refused to be beaten into submission. She offered a courteous smile, her cheeks bulging as her raised eyebrow agreed, before she concentrated on moving the carrots around her plate for the sixth time. She couldn't keep her distance within their kitchen walls, but she damn well could keep her enthusiasm at bay, despite the extreme effort it was taking to do so.

And for whatever reason, Fraser nodded, then engaged in conversation with the others, leaving her feeling lonelier than ever. Was she so contrary that she was confusing herself about her own feelings? She tried to accept what she decided was his rejection like it meant nothing, but the harder she tried, the more it hurt.

With their stomachs filled, the shearers and shedhands left the table, all keen to take a lunchtime nap and put their feet up before the next run began.

'Charlotte, I come bearing good news.' Syd commanded the attention of the table from her father's old seat, and for a moment, Charlotte pictured him sitting there, his low but adoring smile rising. She forced the image aside.

He smiled, shovelling another mouthful of pudding away while he waited for her attention. Her Mum took a seat next to a more than delighted Pete, and Charlotte forgot about her fork hanging mid-air, drips of her mother's delicious gravy falling to the plate as she waited for him to begin.

'Don't keep us all in suspense,' Pete said, scratching his whiskery face while looking impatiently at Syd. 'We haven't got all day.'

'Okay, then.' Syd's cheeks lifted like he was about to tell them they'd struck gold. 'Your crossy lambs topped the sale this morning!'

The elation in Syd's words had Charlotte's eyes widening, a small buzz of hope skittering in her chest. This would mean she would be able to meet the next bank repayments, hopefully with a little left over. She'd organised for Charlie to deliver more hay at the end of the week, riding on the crossy lambs doing okay, but this was great news she hadn't seen coming.

'Syd, while you're here, I'd like to put up Dad's remaining wool from last year. When could we—'

'Your father's wool has already been sold.' Syd picked up his dessert bowl with a good-natured chuckle, using the spoon to scrape the remaining sticky sauce from its sides, leaving Charlotte feeling a little off-kilter.

'Oh.' She gave a puzzled look towards her mum who could only offer a shrug. That was strange. Maybe her father had shifted the time of year when he sold his best lines. Had he sold it before he had died? Traditionally, he always liked to sell it in early December, in case the market fell away in the new year. Maybe she should take a look at the books, but Syd wouldn't have a detail like that wrong.

'I'd best be off,' Syd said, standing and giving Mum a satisfied smile as he patted his belly in approval. 'I'm heading over to your place, Fraser. Your father wants to sell something. Thanks for the wonderful spread, Jayne. You never disappoint.'

'Hear, hear,' Pete piped up, standing also, and grinning down at Jayne like she was the best thing since the invention of chocolate cake. And as Charlotte stood with them, it struck her that these men in her world were ones she couldn't do without, even if it vexed her to admit Fraser might be included as one of them.

CHAPTER 23

It took the best part of two days, but their shearing was done, and Fraser shut the gate on the last of the boxed-up mob walking into his paddock, a sense of loss filling him as he watched them snatching mouthfuls of grass as they drifted away. He and Charlotte had agreed to keep her ewes and lambs at his place post-shearing because he had a spare paddock nearby. She had carried both mobs on her place for this long, it was the least he could do.

The lambs baaed loudly in protest as they tore about, flippantly running up to any nearby ewe in the hope it was their mother, attempting to snatch a drink. But a swift jump and a kick accompanied by a spin-around glare from an extremely disgruntled ewe told it to try someone else. It had the effect of leaving Fraser with a gaping hole in his emotions.

While it was unintentional how the fence had been mowed down by his sheep, there had been definite advantages to it. Should he dare think of this shearing as the first job they'd done together, with future opportunities for them to join their sheep for the unified purpose of making an income on the farm? Or was this a one-off, and futile to hope for more?

But the way Charlotte had sparred with him, keeping him on his toes . . . it was something he'd been deeply attracted to in their teenage years, and now was no different. Everything inside him wanted to hold onto this moment like it was a treasure he might lose if he released his grip. Trentham Park was about to undertake shearing for the next three weeks, and as much as he wanted Charlotte to be a part of it, the reality was she didn't need to. They weren't her sheep. Only, he wished all three thousand of them were, so he'd have an excuse to be around her all over again. But it didn't take much reminding to realise that with the end of their joint shearing, she would let her grip go. There would be no more working together because, well, she didn't want it.

But he allowed himself a pivotal smile, his thoughts suddenly racing. Since when had that stopped him from trying to change her mind? With fresh hope in his step, he headed back to the shearing shed.

'Right, Fraser, there's going to be a change of plans,' his father said, walking around their dormant woolshed like a bear with a sore head. 'I need to sell our wool, all of it, except

the wethers' wool. That mob can be left until later.
December's sale is when Syd says Italy and China will be
buying. If we give them what they both want, they'll fight
each other for it, giving us more dollars in our pockets.'

'Why then? We can sell a bit earlier, like we usually
do. It won't hurt if—'

'I don't want to sell earlier, Fraser. Especially with
Keith's wool out of the mix. He always managed to sell at the
best time. Don't know why I hadn't seen it before. Damned
stupid of me.' He shook his head in disbelief.

Fraser watched as his father wrestled a woolpack
frame into position with jerky movements, growling under his
breath. Of all the things his father had bothered competing
with Keith over, it had never bothered him to sell earlier,
believing he always achieved better prices even if he did hear
otherwise later on. And suddenly it mattered? But at least
he'd stopped nagging Fraser about pressuring Charlotte to sell
that sixty acres. It might be the upcoming mustering and huge
workload that was distracting him, but his father didn't appear
to be worried about Sheepwash Creek anymore. But he knew
better than to think it was over for good.

Trentham Park was buzzing with activity the moment
Charlotte stepped from the ute. Several familiar cars and utes
were lined up out the front of the yards. Stepping inside the

shed, the bustle of movement—from the bleating of sheep to the shearers and shedhands moving about quickly to keep up—had the air feeling electrified, the distinct smell of sheep washing over her. She had loved being amongst the atmosphere again, especially getting to know the team. That would make it easier when they moved onto her shearing as soon as Fraser's was finished.

'Hey Char, come on in.' Fraser waved in her direction, and she couldn't help but take a deep breath. The smell was the same as at her place, but it had been so long since she'd set foot in this shed. Against her earlier apprehension, she was glad she'd come.

Charlotte strolled over, not risking standing next to Fraser, instead taking the opposite side of the wool table as she began to help skirt the fleece.

'I'm glad you dropped by.' There it was all over again, that oh-so-familiar lopsided grin he shot her way. Her heart pitter-pattered, allowing herself to admire it and so much more. She could commit his muscle structure to memory for those lonely moments when she was back in the city, working at her clinic and helping her patients. But looking at him over the wool table, the thought of not being around him, or his cheery disposition sent a sudden wave of sadness through her that she wasn't ready for.

'Do you miss the city life, Char?' He looked over, that sweet dimple flirting with her—she was one hundred percent sure of it—drawing her eyes towards his lips. Her lips parted to speak, but she wasn't sure what exactly he'd said.

'Um.' This time his smile grazed her lips, followed by a rush of warmth in her chest. 'I do.' She paused, giving herself time to regroup, to think. Why did he have this effect on her? That was from a time so long ago. Her future had nothing to do with the station she'd grown up on. That part of her future was over. For good.

'I miss walks on the beach and a swim on a hot afternoon. The ducks on the dam bank don't exactly match up to the seagulls pinching your chips while you're sitting on the sand.' She smiled softly, looking down at the wool in front of her once more. Could she truthfully say she missed the lights and the restaurants, all the things she'd loved when she'd first moved away from Settlers Hill? Had it been an itch she needed to scratch, all in the name of escaping a farm that had robbed her and was still trying to?

She sensed Fraser's light smile as he pulled a staple of wool between his fingers, his gaze hovering on her, making her insides turn all warm and gooey despite refusing to look his way.

'I—' He paused, as though he was about to tell her something important, then changed his mind. She looked up, catching the slight shake of his head. What had he been about to say? She suddenly wanted to know.

'We're selling our wool later than usual, in December.' He shrugged dismissively before continuing. 'I thought maybe we could sell the wool we shore, on the same day and', he hesitated, 'go down together?'

Charlotte smiled, his sheepish grin making him all the more endearing, and she had to remind herself to stay on topic and think straight. She could sell her wool whenever she chose to, thanks to their separate branding, but—

'I'd like that. I'll ring Syd and book mine in for the same day.' What she wanted to say was she'd more than like it. She'd love to. But showing him that much enthusiasm in the one day could have her tripping over her own feet.

'Great! Dad's talking about selling everything at that sale. All the superfine buyers will be there, apparently.' The fresh sparkle in his eyes lit up his entire face, and again, she wished for the days so long ago when neither of them had a care in the world, other than his father wanting the two of them to stay apart. But back then, that would never have stopped them.

And now? This was a whole new ball game, their futures riding on it. With a brief, shy goodbye this time, she left the shed, her excitement bubbling as she headed for the ute, grabbing the goodies she'd been sent with, then headed over to the homestead. She wanted to drop off the array of cakes, slices and tasty treats her mother had promised, say her goodbye to Rosemary, and get out of there before John turned up like some damned trapdoor spider waiting to pounce on its prey.

She was reaching for the door handle to step outside when John approached from the other side, tugging it open and flinging her grasp aside. She sucked in a dry breath, her eyes meeting his.

'Ah, Charlotte. What brings you here?' His tone was cautionary.

Charlotte couldn't disguise her frown fast enough, all too aware thanks to John's curious yet satisfied expression, that he'd hit the mark exactly where he intended. She wasn't welcome. She swallowed while offering a quivering smile.

'Mum wanted me to drop off some food for your shearing.' She nodded, signalling that this was the end of the conversation. *Now move, please.*

But he didn't.

'Listen, Charlotte, I wanted to have a word with you.' And before she could interrupt, push past him—anything—he continued. 'You'll be making a mistake if you split up the land and sell it to several separate counterparts. It's much better to consolidate it all as a package and, like I've said before, I'd be willing to buy it from you.'

There it was again, that light, almost carefree voice he pulled out when he was trying to disguise how desperately he wanted something. Her jaw clenched as he continued.

'I can have the paperwork drawn up in no time, and you can sign within the fortnight. It's best for everyone if we do it this way and keep it quiet. Don't want anyone getting out of sorts for not having a chance to buy any stock.' He leaned in, whispering close to her ear like he was telling her some secret only a best friend might. 'I'm sure it's what Keith would have wanted in the long run.' He followed it through with a winning smile.

Charlotte froze, her unseeing eyes dancing all over the gravel before her, her mind a tangle as her stomach twisted over the words. Willing to buy it from me? He made it sound so carefree and simple. And in what right mind was he in when he said it's what Dad would have wanted? Was the man drunk? She resisted the urge to breathe in and check. Her father would climb out from his grave and haunt her for the rest of her days if she dared contemplate selling to John Pierce.

'Um, I need to go, John.' She took a wide step to the right, offering an apprehensive you-did-not-just-say-that smile as she slipped past him, moving to the ute quickly, forgetting all about the food.

But not quick enough.

'You'll be making a mistake you'll regret, mark my words,' he called out, the words squeezing inside the cabin with her. 'Sheepwash Creek is too much station for you, Charlotte, and you know it.'

Charlotte slammed her door shut, trapping the words inside with her. It made her want to hit something—if she could guarantee it wouldn't hurt her back—as she replayed his last sentence in her mind. And as she left, her rear vision mirror was filled with Fraser's lean body standing on the landing of the shearing shed, his face pensive as he watched her leave. Had he been aware all along his father was going to ask her, no, *tell* her, she was meant to sell to them? And then she'd proceeded to allow her heart to soak in all the warm fuzzy feels he'd directed at her in the shed, all as some set-up for what John was about to say. How could she be so stupid?

Clenching the steering wheel, Charlotte drove faster than she normally would along the dirt road, fuming the whole way. She'd sell her wool, and after that, the Pierces would play no part in any of her decisions.

Hitting her speed dial for Syd's office number, it began to ring as she drove towards her place. She'd sell her share of the wool from the boxed-up ewes without their help. And then she'd talk to the real estate agent about searching out potential buyers for Sheepwash Creek. Anyone with a surname other than Pierce.

CHAPTER 24

'Are you sure?'

Charlotte's face pinched as she pulled over to the side of the road. Pressing her back into the seat, she stared blankly at the rolling hills of Sheepwash Creek, their grandeur less appealing to her than usual. Syd hadn't been in the office, so she'd spoken to his PA.

'I am,' Cheryl said. 'We have all the remaining bales of your father's best lines listed here on the computer. Forty-five bales. He hasn't sold them.' Charlotte could hear the confusion in the woman's voice.

Had Syd got their wool mixed up with someone else's? He had a lot of clients so it seemed reasonable to think so. But wasn't it his job to know these things?

'Great.' Relief filled her at the positive news. 'Let's book them in, along with my six bales I've sent down with Trentham Park's. I can use all the funds I can lay my hands on.'

'And you've got your main shearing to come, is that correct?' Cheryl said.

'Yes, we're starting soon, but I'll hold onto that wool. Like Dad, I won't sell it until February next year.'

Whoa, hang on a minute. Had she said *next year* out loud to Cheryl? Where had that come from? There wasn't going to be a next year.

'I must say, Charlotte, it's incredibly admirable what you're doing. No one would envy the tough decisions you're having to make. Are you planning to stay on for the long haul?'

Was she?

'I have a business back in the city that needs me.' Her words flew from her mouth, fast and desperate. She couldn't risk losing sight of that fact, or all her plans would fall apart.

'I look forward to seeing you at the sale, then, Charlotte. Take care, won't you?' Cheryl said goodbye and Charlotte ended the call, the PA's last words lingering in the air far longer than she wanted them to. She was taking care of this farm. So why did she get the uncomfortable feeling it wasn't about to return the favour?

'Honestly, that man can drive me towards a plunge in the sheep dip at times,' Rosemary said to Jayne as Charlotte entered the kitchen, offering up a warm smile in greeting.

'G'day, Mrs Pierce.'

'Oh, call me Rosemary, please,' she said, waving a dismissive hand in the air. 'That title makes me feel older than I'd like to admit I am.' Fraser's mother tossed her eyes with a shake of her head and they all chuckled.

'That's why it's a hard habit to break.' Charlotte took a steadying breath, arguing with herself over what to say next. Why did she want to know how their shearing was going? Or was it only Fraser she wanted to know about?

'So, is shearing going smoothly?' Charlotte hoped for casual and a little disinterested as she moved to the kettle, flicking it on. It didn't escape her that she knew Trentham Park was in the final week, and she wouldn't be at all surprised if she heard that John was making some of the shearers' lives uncomfortable with his demanding presumptions for a perfect job done in half the time and at a beaten-down price. How did Fraser put up with the insufferable man? One thing was for sure. He was nothing like his father.

'Yes, although John is complaining about Fraser being in the shed and not out helping with the mustering. But classers are hard to come by. Never mind,' Rosemary said, once again waving her hand in front of her as she smiled. 'Speaking of, I'd better run. I only planned on returning your cake tins, not staying for a long cuppa and indulgent chin-wag, even though I know which one I'd rather. Oh, and your food went down a treat. You saved me a lot of work, so thank you.'

'I'm glad there were no complaints,' Mum said, reaching out and taking the cake containers from the table where Rosemary had sat them.

'And don't forget I'll be returning the favour.' Rosemary smiled a goodbye, but before she could leave, they heard the muffled chatter of voices at the laundry door. Charlotte gave her mother a curious grin as she poured the hot water into her mug, dangling a teabag over the water before dunking it in to steep. Who was here? Then, as the shadow turned into a figure at the kitchen doorway, Charlotte squashed her smirk.

'Looks like I'd better re-boil the kettle for you, Mum. You have another visitor,' she said, tongue-in-cheek. Charlotte took a seat at the table, hiding her smile behind her steaming mug of strong black tea as Peter Rabbit strolled in, all plucky and self-assured, ready for his next round of food. He rubbed his hands together expectantly.

'Ah, my two favourite ladies. How are we today?' He planted his backside on the nearest seat, leaning straight across Charlotte as he snatched up a slice of teacake, warm and falling apart as he guided it to his mouth in a rush. Her Mum placed a cup of tea in front of him, her eyes suggesting she was displeased with his antics, when all along Charlotte could see she was unable to hide her grin, her cake gaining a new admirer.

'Good thanks,' Charlotte said, happy to answer for both of them but struggling to contain her giggle as she looked from him to her mother. 'We weren't expecting you today.'

'I'm doing the neighbourly drop in.' He brushed away the crumbs gluing themselves to his peppery whiskers. 'Just checkin' if anything needs takin' care of.'

Charlotte's eyes widened as she studied him closely. Was he going a slight shade of . . . red? And her mother? She glanced at her next. While nothing was going on between them, Charlotte couldn't ignore the likable interchange between them, and a flood of warmth filled her chest. Her mother had given her the final say on what was going to happen with the farm . . . but, what if she had it wrong? It was her mother's family farm after all, and she knew Mum loved it here.

Added to that, Charlotte had to admit she was settling into life on the station almost as though she had never left. Was she being too rash in thinking she should sell up? Because if she did, what purpose and self-worth would her mother feel she had left? She'd been the farmer's wife, shearer's cook, the housekeeper, the gardener, and all-purpose lackey, anytime she had been required, never afraid to get in amongst the action. It was something Charlotte loved about her mother, and she was certain those traits had been handed down to her, genetically or through her watching her mother. She did it all, without question or the slightest grumble. Mum was the one who had held everything together, even when James had died. But was it their future to be living at

Sheepwash Creek? Or was Charlotte meant to end up in the fast lane of city life, even if she'd started to sense its enticement fading?

'Since you're here, Pete, you can help me clean out the troughs. You'd better do something to earn that piece of cake, and no doubt the lunch you're planning on staying for.' She lifted a lone eyebrow his way, which he suitably ignored.

'What are we waiting for, then? Let's get to it.' Pete slung back the last of his tea as he stood. 'Mighty good cuppa, as always, Jayne.' Before her mum could open her mouth to reply, Pete scooted out through the laundry door, allowing it to slam shut behind him.

'Hmmm,' Charlotte said as she put both mugs in the sink. 'I think someone has a fan.'

Her mother turned away, suddenly busying herself with peeling the potatoes for tea.

Down the paddock, the sun's warmth on Charlotte's back seeped into her skin as she scrubbed the green algae like nobody's business.

'Hey, what did it ever do to you?'

She looked up at Pete, his remark slowing her scrubbing before she stopped, her arm resting on the side of the trough. 'Why is John so hell-bent on buying Sheepwash Creek?'

Pete gave a disgruntled half-chuckle. 'That man has worked for decades to be the king of the biggest dung hill around these parts, and your father always had a way of keeping him in second place. Not that he tried to. It came down to who managed things better, and your father was always the clear winner.'

Charlotte shifted on her knees as a stone dug into her skin, and she rubbed it to ease the pain. 'So, it's the perfect opportunity for him to rise to the top, now Dad's not here?'

'More than ever. Like your father, he married *into* the farm. The only difference was, your father was a local from around these parts. Growing up on his own property alongside his brothers had taught him how to manage this land. He had the right heart, and the right approach. But not our John. He breezed in, no farming experience, no job, no future, and hardly a cent to his name. He needed to marry to make something of himself. And he did that, only he burned a lot of people in the process. It's never easy to be accepted as a dinky-die local, but he would've been, eventually, had he done things the right way.'

'He told me he'd have the paperwork all drawn up for me to sign in a fortnight, to buy Sheepwash Creek outright. I get the feeling he's not going to stop, regardless of what I say.'

'What is it you want then?' Pete rested his dripping scrub brush on the side of the trough as he watched her, waiting for an answer. The knowing old-man glimmer in his eye had her flexing her shoulders. She'd asked herself the same question over and over since she'd been home, but it held more weight as it shot through her heart like a searing arrow.

How *did* she answer that question? By giving him the same response she'd given herself time and again, this time out loud so she would finally stick to the decision she had come here to make happen? To return to her business. But did she have to go? Cara—her second in charge—was running it perfectly. Charlotte fought to hide the shame clawing at her over effectively ignoring her work commitments.

But one fact remained, no matter how she tried to convince herself otherwise. The longer she stayed at Sheepwash Creek, the more she sensed her love for the rolling hills, the bleating of sheep and lambs, the long sunsets on Boots, being rekindled.

'I've been thinking, Pete? How do you feel about a bit more work around here, starting with shearing?'

He beamed instantaneously. 'I reckon that'd suit me real well, Miss Charlotte.'

CHAPTER 25

'The absolute nerve.' Was John Pierce for real? Lewie looked up at Charlotte, his head tipping to one side, then the other. She pressed a hand to her forehead, pulling it away quickly when she smelled the stench of urine stain on her hands from the crutching wool she'd been handling. Trentham Park had finished their shearing, and suddenly the man required Pete to help him, the day before she was to start shearing?

Charlotte stomped about the shearing shed, her pie-in-the-sky goal of getting some semblance of order in the shed before they started tomorrow looking a little more like a soggy start to a football season. She had hundreds of sheep to bring into the yards and nearby paddocks, the shed needed wool bins with the remaining dregs of wool removed, the shearing board needed a serious scrub down, and the whole shed had to be set up, ready for start time at seven-thirty a.m. She needed all hands on deck, even if it was only Pete and herself. Was John that vindictive, determined to make her life harder so she'd cave? She flexed her fingers, drawing on her resolve. He didn't know her so well then, did he.

Firstly, she let out all the rams in the shed into the nearby paddock. They could remain there for the duration of shearing, that was, if she could place her trust in them, or namely Brutus, to stay put and not be enticed by the ewes that would be coming in regularly over the next three weeks. After scoring a little extra fun with Trentham Park's ewes, she did not need the complication of an enthusiastic ram all over again, especially if she was going to be doing this job on her own. She released an overwhelmed sigh at the mere thought of her to-do list. At least she had her woolpacks and gave herself an invisible high-five for that small mercy.

Next she swept the board free of accumulated dust, mouse visitations and stray wool locks that were proving near impossible to gather thanks to the steady breeze blowing up through the shearing chutes, then cleared the wool bins of rogue cobwebs with extra vigour. Credit to him, Pete had asked her if it would be okay to lend Trentham Park a hand. They were "apparently" desperate to get all the mobs back to their paddocks at the end of their shearing. Humph.

Pete had clarified that it was only to help Fraser, not John. But Charlotte couldn't shake the feeling there was something else going on beneath the surface of the request. Why was Fraser always taking what she was depending on? She glanced over at Lewie, who was lying beneath the wool table, his head on his paws and his concentration sharp on her. His tail immediately thumped the floorboards.

Charlotte fought with the idea of randomly "dropping in" to find out exactly why they'd needed Pete, not for one minute buying their mustering excuse. And she wanted to know how long she would be without him. Fraser deserved a bit of a wind-up from her over it, but deep down, that wasn't the real reason she wanted to visit. She wanted to see him, feel the warmth rush inside her from his buoyant smile despite all her reservations and reminders of why it was such a bad idea.

But practicality for the job at hand won out, and she marched towards the ute. She was reversing out of the machinery shed to bring in another mob when she abruptly slid to a stop. Fraser's way-too-clean-for-a-farm ute pulled up next to the house. And there it was again, that cautious "oh, hi, I'm your friendly long-term neighbour you love to hate" wave, the one that filled her with ridiculous giddiness as he moved towards her open window. Her open mouth clamped shut. She needed to find a way to stop that from happening so often.

'How's it going?'

And there you go, Charlotte growled under her breath, resisting the urge to roll her eyes at the suddenly overbearing sunny sky as Fraser flashed that delicious smile she tried to convince herself she was sick of the sight of. And yet, here she was, compelled to reciprocate it. Her lips automatically began to curl in response before she broke off the urge. She was not happy with him. And she'd do well to remember it.

'Gotta go get another mob in, no thanks to you.' She glared at the wall of the shed. Don't look at his discerning brown eyes, or his lips . . . or his unadulterated handsome smile that had her cheeks warming at the mere thought and her tight mouth relaxing without consent. But she failed miserably, her eyes betraying her direct order, instead returning his own in one fateful sweep. This game she was playing with herself of hating him was getting harder and harder.

'In fact,' he said, fully interrupting the way she was studying the soft lines around his eyes as they smiled directly at her. 'That's why I'm here. Would you like a hand?'

What? She blinked. Then blinked again. Suddenly gone were the thoughts of how perfectly his hair tapered around his neck. 'So, let me get this right. Your father sent you over to help me . . . because he stole Pete?' Her eyes narrowed suspiciously.

'Uh, no.' The confusion on Fraser's face appeared genuine, but she wasn't buying it, not for a millisecond.

'Look, as far as I was told, Pete had everything done here. And besides, it's been forever since I caught up with you.'

It had only been three weeks since they'd done their sheep together. Had he missed her as much as she'd missed him, so much so that he'd come over especially? And was she admitting that to herself?

'That sounds a hell of a lot like needing my hay.' Ah, that felt better. Keeping her thinking directed in the present and nothing to do with their past had a way of re-firing her up, and while she could admire his darkening eyes hovering on her—and they were—there was no way she was going to be distracted. Again.

'Listen, I'm not taking no for an answer.'

Before she could form the words to protest, he'd jumped into the passenger seat of her ute, his delightful grin sending butterflies racing inside her. What happened to the steely resolve she'd mustered for all of ten seconds? And where had it run away to?

Charlotte huffed, more to make a show of her not being happy with this little stunt he'd pulled, but in actual fact, it was at herself. How had she, yet again, been ensnared by his charm—damn it—and well-intended—double damn it—offer of help? And how could she say no? She needed him—or at least someone. That it was him? Bonuses happened sometimes, she agreed with herself. But *only* for the sheep, she reiterated in her mind as they drove through several paddocks, the cabin quiet other than for the comforting whir of the diesel engine. Fraser opened each gate they came to, leaving it ajar, ready for the mob they were mustering to move through. And every time he strolled towards another gate, Charlotte swallowed hard before he turned around, catching her eye with his slow-rising smile to which she not-so-inconspicuously bit the insides of her cheeks. She even tried tossing her eyes to the roof of the ute when he was looking to make her message clear. But deep down, the question loomed, dangling in front of her with frustrating effectiveness. The guy was irritatingly good-looking. So why was he single?

'Have you been seeing much of Maddie?' Charlotte broke the silence, keeping her voice as light and carefree as was possible given she couldn't help but keep inhaling the attractive fragrance of shampoo he must have used that morning, his hair kicking up with a little extra bounce around his tanned neck. She narrowly avoided the pothole she was aware was in this paddock but had forgotten about, swerving at the last moment. She gave him a quick side glance, not sure what to expect; not sure what she was hoping to hear. But he gave away nothing.

'Why would you ask that?' His voice was an infuriating blend of seriousness and surprised humour, obviously poking fun because he'd always been able to read right through her. In a split-second decision, she tugged her ponytail loose with her left hand, her hair falling around her face, desperate to hide the rapid heat travelling over her cheeks.

'Remember,' she said breezily, following it with a calming swallow, 'the day you came over when I'd arrived home?' She risked a glance at him, and the way he was concentrating on her . . . she wanted to pull over there and then, and bolt from the ute, purely to keep some distance between them. If he kept looking at her like that, she'd want to lean in and kiss him on the spot, breaking the boundaries she'd put up to safe-guard herself from exactly that.

'She's only a neighbour.' His voice was gentle.

'Oh.' She nodded, watching where she was driving. That's all she was too. Charlotte clenched her jaw, annoyed at herself and her unpredictable feelings getting in the way of everything she'd come here to do. She needed to get a grip on the situation so both she and her mother could be free of the station's deathly clutches, forever.

'Speaking of neighbours,' Fraser said, continuing to watch her.

Charlotte's heart pounded like it wanted to push through her skin. Was she in so deep with her rattling emotions that she was losing the plot when it came to Fraser? Was this the moment when he'd say he wished things had turned out differently? Was he about to say he wanted to give things another go? Was she ready for any of this? Could she possibly say yes? He had to be hearing the tumultuous hammering coming from her chest, and she looked at him, her eyes wide.

'Are you still going to be mine?'

'Yours?' Her heart leapt into her throat and she stopped breathing. That's what she wanted. Wasn't it? Or was it? Could it still be? She swallowed against her drying mouth, unable to look away. It was all she'd ever wanted, if she were brutally truthful. Was this truly the moment she'd need to make a decision about a future with him, like the one she'd always had her heart set on, until—

'My neighbour. Or . . . are you going to sell for certain?'

What, just . . . happened? Charlotte's heart thundered so hard, she expected it to explode, and she turned to the windscreen, staring at the long grass in front of her. So, this wasn't about *them* at all? It was all business and nothing more. Forget about being neighbours. Could it be enough that she was finally recognising what she might want . . . to keep Sheepwash Creek?

'I've booked my wool in to sell,' she said, straining to calm the edginess wavering in her voice and steer the conversation back to something she could handle. 'I'll see how that goes, then make a final decision.' Her grip on the steering wheel ached, but she needed it to give herself some time to think.

'There's so much to do, but I'm managing to meet the repayments.' Just. She let her eyes fall to her lap, curling her lips together, the weight of all her worry making her suddenly weary.

'That sounds like a good plan,' Fraser said gently, breaking the conversation when he hopped out to open the last gate. The mob they needed to muster was gathered ahead of them under the shade of a huge red gum.

Was he saying he was . . . happy to see her go? Or did he mean he thought she could stay? When exactly was she going to know what *she* wanted?

'Um, I'd be more than happy to help you with your shearing,' Fraser said, climbing back into the ute and turning to her, 'if you'd like. Things are winding down thanks to Christmas getting closer.'

What she wanted to say was *Oh, so why are you stealing Pete then?* But he hadn't owned up to that. And if he had, why then would he come over instead? None of this was making any sense to her. But it wasn't like she was in a position to turn down help either.

'I'd like that.' This time she couldn't help but smile as she drove towards the mob. 'It'd be a big help. But we'd need Pete too.' Was that subtle enough? If Fraser did help, he would be able to press-up and pen-up, while she and Pete could keep the sheep coming in for the shearers thanks to Jerry having found a classer for her job. The thought of being near him every day secretly thrilled her.

The ewes moved steadily through the drying grass, making it to the sheep yards as darkening clouds to the west began to build. 'I don't like the look of those,' she said, glancing at Fraser as he looked over his shoulder, nodding in agreement. 'They could slow us down if they turn serious.'

'Yeah, they look ominous. We were bloody lucky to get through our shearing like we did, dodging the showers.'

With the sheep settled in the yards and enough sheep in the shed for the shearers, Charlotte latched the gate shut and they both turned to watch the threatening sky. Charlotte perched herself on the top rail, admiring the shimmer of brilliant hues of orange, the descending sun sneaking in one last splash of light before it disappeared for the night.

'I hope the rain holds off for us too. Last thing we need are more hold-ups. Otherwise, I'll be decorating the shed with a Christmas tree.' Her cheeks drew up and her heart burst with warmth as Fraser laughed, moving closer to her with easy steps.

'Maybe I could hang the ball bags from the lambs on it as baubles. That'd add a touch of authenticity to the theme.'

Charlotte wished her laugh was as carefree as it used to be, but with him close, all she could think about was his lips as he continued to smile her way, just like in days gone by. But instead, she reined her emotions into submission and nodded before looking back at the sky in an attempt to defuse the moment she sensed was building. She couldn't risk kissing him. She hadn't even begun to forgive him.

But he wasn't stopping, drawing closer to her with each slow footstep he took. She could see his dark eyes beneath his Akubra, his relaxed smile steadily slipping away as he looked into her eyes, then at her lips, hesitating for an agonisingly long moment before he broached their distance. So close, she could feel his breath on her face.

Why was he hesitating? She could hardly bear it, her heart thundering wildly. She wanted to kiss him so badly, it hurt. Was he having second thoughts?

CHAPTER 26

Should he kiss her? What would it mean if he did?

She'd hate me even more than she already did, that's what.

But it didn't look like she was about to reject him, or even worse, jump down from the railing and walk away, certain she understood he wanted this like his life depended on it. But . . .

And before he could listen to any more doubts, questions, or what-ifs ravaging his mind, he reached out, taking the side of her face in his hand, drawing her lips to his, their softness exactly what he'd lost himself in six long years ago, as they worked in perfect synchronicity, like it had only been yesterday.

She kissed him back as deeply as he was kissing her and in that moment, he registered the kiss wasn't the same. It was better. As though their time apart had kept a tension wound so tightly between them, it was being released with perfection as she continued to search out his mouth ever so gently.

This. It was exactly what he wanted, what he'd dreamed of. For them to be working alongside each other, filling their days working sheep, shearing, even cleaning out sheep manure from beneath the grating of the shearing shed. It didn't matter what they did, as long as it was together. He wanted her and everything she brought, to share it all . . . in *their* future.

He slowly pulled back, holding her face, searching for any indication he'd overstepped the invisible line they seemed to be dancing around continually. But her eyes were tranquil, like a spring day, and he knew there and then, if he wanted to, he could kiss her again and again. There was nothing he wanted more, but he also didn't want to risk scaring her off.

Again. He'd come over to help her, not to steal a kiss from those soft lips. Was it a one-off? A moment of weakness?

That's exactly what it was. Charlotte had made her situation crystal clear. She was leaving. He had caught her off guard when, truth be told, she didn't want this at all. He reluctantly lowered his hand, never shifting his focus from her beautiful face, guilt wriggling into his desperate thoughts.

What he hadn't told her was that he had seen what his father had done, calling Pete over to help for the day, and his blood had almost boiled. It seemed there were many ways to hang a sheep or at least get someone to do what his father wanted, so there had been no way he was going to stay around, despite the look of disbelief on Pete's face when he had left. His father had used underhanded tactics to make Charlotte's preparation day before shearing much harder than it should have been and Fraser didn't want anything to do with the man.

So instead, he had left his Dad and Pete without so much as a word and headed over to her place. There was no way he was going to leave her in the lurch like that.

And they'd made out, tenderly, deeply, and he wasn't sure he'd done the right thing after all.

'Ah, I'd better head off home.' He reluctantly stepped back, kicking at the dirt with the toe of his boot, lost for what to say next. Should he even chance looking at her in case she was angry with him for what he'd done? 'So, catch you tomorrow?' His cautious look caught hers.

'Yeah, sure. See you then.' Her face looked surprised and dare he think it, disappointed.

And with that, Fraser walked away, his stomach alive with a flutter of hope and excitement and apprehension at spending the next three weeks working alongside her. His dad wouldn't be happy about it, but he didn't care. These days, his father managed to find a way in anything and everything to dish out on Fraser, often for no good reason. And it seemed to Fraser his cheap shots were getting more directed and accurate.

But by grabbing opportunities to help Charlotte, he had a greater chance of encouraging her to stay. And if that was all he got, then he'd make every minute he had count.

Charlotte lay in bed that night, her fingers trailing over her mouth as she relived the warmth of Fraser's lips, the same glow spreading to her chest. Why had he pulled away when she'd begun to lean into his kiss? Hadn't he liked it? Was it so different to what they'd shared before she'd left? Was there something wrong with her?

Maybe he'd come to his senses, accepting he was better off without her, and the truth hit her with a crash. She couldn't rely on him. He frustrated her, and she was right to hate him for what he'd taken from her—a future here on Sheepwash Creek. What she had left because of it was a life living in a high-rise where she couldn't be distracted by animals and fresh air or handsome neighbours she couldn't get out of her mind, no matter how hard she tried. That was the sum of everything waiting for her, so that's what she would go back to.

Charlotte sat bolt upright in bed, her mind suddenly whirring. That's it! Why hadn't she considered that before? When Syd dropped by tomorrow to check how the wool was coming off the sheep, she had a question for him she was certain he'd like to hear.

The freshness of the new day had Charlotte almost skipping as she headed to the shed, more than ready to get underway despite the woeful night's sleep she'd had. Stepping inside the shed, the musty smell of lanolin seeped through the air, adding to her excitement. The clatter of feet in the pens rumbled throughout the shed like a Mexican wave as she walked over to the sheep, their wary eyes wide and cautious.

Lewie pushed in front of Charlotte, nosing the first pen door open and leaping over the railing, moving behind the sheep in readiness for her to swing open the gate. With a commanding bark, the sheep moved off him, skuttling into the catching pen like panicked ants before rain. When the distinct rumble of gravel under tyres outside pulled to a stop, Charlotte smiled. *Right on time.*

'Morning, Pete,' she called, as Lewie jumped onto the backs of the less obliging sheep, urging them into the catching pen so Charlotte could shut the gate behind them.

'Well, well, someone's looking forward to shearing.' Pete grinned, walking into the next pen, and Lewie jumped over the railing to help him.

'So, what do you think of this?' Charlotte said excitedly, pausing to focus on him and forgetting about the sheep in the back pen she was trying to move forward. Before Pete was able to shoot her a questioning look, she blurted out her idea. 'What if we have our annual "On Property Sale" and offer the rams Dad was preparing? They've already been fed up nicely in the shed, and it'd bring in a nice cash flow for us. We could get plans for it underway and run it a week after shearing. All we need to do is contact all our regular buyers, like the Hudsons. We could mail them a catalogue and email them. I'm sure Dad would have all the names and contacts on the computer.' It came out in such a flurry that she wasn't sure Pete had caught a word of it, but when he'd finished shoving the last of the ewe's backside into the pen he was filling, he stood, smiling.

'I can't see why not, although it's going to be a bit of work to get the shindig ready in time with shearing beforehand. We'd have to hope we don't get any wet weather, otherwise that'd push this job out further. Maybe we could rope Fraser into helping with shearing? The more hands, the better.' The early sunrise through the shed window glinted in his dancing eyes.

'Already done,' Charlotte said triumphantly, ignoring the definite match-making smirk Pete's lips were laced with. After all, Fraser had offered. All she'd done was accept. Maybe he'd offer to help with the sale too? And if she knew Pete, he'd drop a small comment to Fraser at some stage, and Bob would be her uncle. 'And Syd's coming this morning, so I'll get him to start the ball rolling. I already have all the ram side-sample test results from Dad's records, so he could catalogue them ASAP.'

'It sounds to me like you've already decided,' he laughed, shaking his head in slight disbelief as he moved to the next empty pen to fill it up as the shearers started lining up in front of each pen, getting their handpieces ready as they caught up on the weekend's news. 'Sure, let's go for it. I reckon your father would love that you were making it happen.'

'I reckon so too. It's great you're on board, Pete. Thanks.' Charlotte sensed the hope building inside her, of her father's farm maintaining its well-deserved reputation alongside a future it could possibly have, if she played her cards right. Who said a girl couldn't run a station in the Western District? Only the pessimists. But she was an optimist, or at least she was going to try to be one moving forward, and she had her sights set on the success of Sheepwash Creek, whether she kept it or not.

CHAPTER 27

The hum of spring was in full swing as the bees buzzed, collecting pollen from her mum's prolific fruit trees for which she had a fierce reputation, her jams and preserves always crowd pleasers. Young magpies squawked on the wooden sides of her veggie beds as their parents fed them with squirming worms they'd scrounged.

It was midway into the last week of shearing, and Charlotte had left the stud mobs of ewes and lambs until last. She hopped down from Boots to shut the gate as Pete hustled them towards the forcing pen. She was relieved to see Pete visibly putting on a few necessary kilos despite all the physical labour he'd been doing with mustering sheep and working so hard. He'd been an absolute gem, never once complaining—except when he grumbled that Mum hadn't put enough cream into her strawberry jam sponge—and she'd need to find a way to thank him, other than the food they'd been filling him with.

'Pete, I'll go on the drafting gate, you push 'em up.' They needed to separate the ewes and lambs before they were all shorn because the lambs' wool was too short, so classed and then sold separately.

The dust swirled in plumes as some ewes were more than happy to say goodbye to their needy lambs, while others caused a ruckus, baaing as if the enforced separation had mortally wounded them.

'Ha! Ha! Get on with ya,' Pete shouted, pushing the sheep through the forcing yard and down the narrow race. As each ewe and lamb passed by, Charlotte sent it to a designated holding yard on either side of her.

They were close to finishing, and Pete chased an uncooperative stud ewe and lamb along the fence line, urging them back towards Charlotte. The well-grown ram lamb slowed, spinning around, stomping his foot and daring Pete to take him on.

'Someone's not happy,' Charlotte said, leaving the gate to help Pete move them into the forcing pen. As she did, she glanced at the ear tag number of the ewe as it darted by her. It was the sheep she had helped to give birth during the storm.

'Ha, it's you!' She stopped and grinned, her arms crossed as she appreciated both the memory of how the lamb had entered the world, and the young ram he was growing into. 'Hey, Pete, take a look at this one.'

Pete came to stand beside Charlotte as the lamb put his nose high in the air, breathing in the world around him with a cocky disposition. He eyeballed Charlotte with disdain, taking another step and thumping his foot on the ground.

'Oh, so that's how it's gonna to be, is it?' Pete said, chuckling. 'You won't wanna mess with this lady.' He thumbed in Charlotte's direction, making her giggle. 'She's real good friends with your father!'

'It looks like he's got his father's charming personality,' Charlotte said, recalling how she'd threatened to hang Brutus up to the shed rafters by his testicles only yesterday.

With Pete pushing the remaining stragglers up, she finished drafting off the ewes from the lambs before she spoke again. 'Hey Pete, have you noticed the bare paddocks and the stock in poor condition over at the Pierces?'

'I surely have.'

'Why do you reckon that is?'

'Squire John is a law unto himself. His dung-hill aspirations include both owning the largest amount of land and stock. That's what he thinks will make him formidable as a landholder in the whole of Victoria. So, it doesn't matter how he does it, so long as he does.' Pete shook his head in disgust.

'But why?'

Pete pushed the last lamb and ewe through the force and down the race, walking up to Charlotte as she shut both gates, latching them behind him.

'That man has one agenda: to get everything for himself. Sure, he's nice enough when you first meet him, and it takes a little while before you begin to see his true colours. He's had a chip on his shoulder that's been there since the day he arrived in this town. The power play he uses on Rosemary and Fraser is shameful. But Fraser is a big boy, so with any luck, he might step up and make the changes needed. Thank the Lord he's nothing like his father.'

Charlotte stared at her dust-covered boots. Why would he want all that so badly? And could that mean Fraser was trying to keep her on Sheepwash Creek after all, sending out mixed messages she'd misread?

With not a whisker of rain to slow them down, Sheepwash Creek's shearing was done and dusted for another year.

All one hundred and seventy-three bales had been trucked down to Melbourne for the standard core and side-sample testing to check for micron and other key indicators of the wool quality, and everything had gone smoothly, all except the obvious discordance Fraser had given Charlotte during the busy weeks. But that only solidified her commitment to finalise the loose ends keeping her on the farm, and she was determined to put all her focus into the ram sale which was only one week away.

'Pete, do we have enough ram pens to assemble, or will we need to get more? We have fifty-two rams available for sale.'

'We're right to go. All that's left to do is put up the posters with the test results above each enclosure and then load the rams into their corresponding pens.'

Nothing could have sounded sweeter to Charlotte, and she gave a satisfied nod.

'Pete, thanks for everything you're doing. If it wasn't for you, this wouldn't be happening.' With him on board, she wouldn't have to hope Fraser might offer to help at the sale. She wouldn't have to depend on him anymore, the thought eliciting both pure relief and a sudden let-down. They'd spent much of their time in the shearing shed, avoiding one another, as though unspoken words floated in the air between them. Was it their kiss making him step away, disappointing her more than she wanted to admit? Her heart had happy-skipped every time they passed in the shed when he'd gone to pen-up or retrieve huge armfuls of wool to shove into the press. He'd smiled pleasantly at her before continuing to work, as though what they'd shared was nothing more than an encounter he wasn't choosing to revisit. But her senses told her there was a sizzle in the air whenever they caught one another's eyes, and her heart hoped he felt it too. Should she allow herself to find time to be with him alone again, and dare she hope it, wait for another kiss? But the closer shearing got to being finished, the more that hope faded. It was as if they'd shifted from being friends to acquaintances, their special moment pushing them further apart from one another rather than drawing them closer together.

Charlotte recoiled from her wandering thoughts as Fraser manoeuvred the trolley to retrieve the latest bale of wool from the press. She had to focus on what was real, not the it-might-happen-one-day hopes she had a nasty habit of letting build up inside her the more she was around Fraser, only to have them shot down to dust in one quick puff.

'I'm happy to help, Miss Charlotte,' Pete said. 'I reckon your father would've wanted you to get every bit of help you deserve. It was no secret he was besotted with the woman his daughter had grown into.'

The intensity of Pete's words made her heart swell and she thought of what Big Nev had said. If her father had been so delighted with her, did that mean he had enough faith in her to take on Sheepwash Creek? Could she consider giving it a go? Charlotte looked over at Pete who was watching her with inquisitive, patient eyes, as though he was trying to read her thoughts. She had to stop this before she said something she couldn't commit to.

'I'm heading into Ballarat to grab the ram catalogues. Is there anything else you think we might need while I'm there?'

'Enough food for everyone. I'd hate to see people go hungry,' he said, his smirk unmissable.

'The only way they're going to go hungry is if you eat it all first. You've been doing so much sampling, Mum's needed to make extra.'

'Quality control, Miss Charlotte. You can never have enough.' He nodded to confirm the importance of the subject.

'More like never enough food,' Charlotte giggled, giving him a dig with her glare before turning to head for the house. She'd need to check what her mother wanted before she left, certain the list had grown since this morning when she'd last glanced over it.

The Ag shop was quiet when Charlotte stepped through the sliding doors thanks to many of the wool and livestock agents being down at the wool sales in Melbourne or the livestock exchange, selling stock. Syd poked his head out from his office door at the sound, smiling.

'Good morning, Charlotte. Come on in. I bet you can't wait to see how the catalogues look.'

'Morning Syd. You're right, I'm pretty keen.'

Syd offered her one from the box sitting on a chair near his desk and she glanced over it. On the front it read:

> Sheepwash Creek
>
> On Property Stud Ram Sale
>
> Friday 1st December, 1 p.m.
>
> Fifty-two rams on offer
>
> Micron Range: 15-19.5 um

A surge of pride swept over her, taking her by surprise. Seeing the catalogue in her hands made it feel more real, reassuring her she was doing the right thing.

'They look great, Syd. Thanks so much for rushing them through.'

'Happy to help, Charlotte. Keith was one of my biggest clients. It's my pleasure to see the farm off with a bang.'

Charlotte paused at Syd's words, not wanting to look at him for fear she'd lose her nerve to follow through with the running of the On Property sale and then selling their wool. Did Syd think she wasn't up to the task, too? There seemed to be more Nitpicking Nigels batting against her, when what she needed were more Positive Petes believing for Sheepwash Creek's success.

In desperate need of sustenance, and if she were honest with herself, a chance to clear her head of all the defeatist thoughts yelling for her attention, Charlotte dropped by Munchies for a quick hello. Fifteen minutes later she was leaving with a latté and steaming house-made sausage roll, courtesy of Clare, in her hands. She'd already had one phone call from Mum asking when she'd be home so there was no more time to waste. When it came to her mother's cooking, you didn't mess with the ingredients arriving in time.

But as she neared Settlers Hill, her mother rang again.

'Oh, Charlotte, thank goodness I caught you. Are you near The Small Store by chance? I need some cinnamon for the scrolls I'm about to make, and I've already rung Frank. He has some ready on the counter for you to pick up.'

Charlotte slowed at the curb, chewing the inside of her lip. What was going on? Cars and utes were lined up all along their normally quiet street, so much so that she had to pull up as far back as Jonno's butcher shop. And that was a good thing, serving as a reminder that she'd forgotten to organise the sausages for the BBQ at the ram sale. She'd duck in there after seeing Frank.

Charlotte looked on as Gus, Mark, and Ross were queuing up outside the door, followed by Mrs Hudson and her son Nicholas, and then Nancy Stone and Elsie Kent, who looked particularly perturbed they were in an allocated position outside the shop rather than at the front of the line.

Big Nev was strolling back from The Small Store, hoeing into what looked like a deliciously creamy vanilla slice, and she chuckled at the look of ecstasy on his face. How long had Frank and Janice been selling them? This was something new.

'That looks good,' she said, her mouth beginning to water as she glanced at the slice in his hands.

'It is. Janice bakes them at undisclosed times, like a random surprise, and everyone in the district spreads the word as soon as the news is out. Although, secretly, Frank sometimes lets me know they're on their way.' He gave her an I'm-in-the-know-club wink. 'They're hard to beat.' He took another bite, its ooziness squeezing out the sides of his mouth.

'So that's why everyone is here. I might have to get some to take home.'

'You'll have to be quick.'

Charlotte opened her mouth to reply but found herself distracted when Fraser's ute pulled up ahead, taking a park recently vacated. Her heart did a schoolgirl skip, the sight of him hopping from the ute and rounding the back of it enough for the butterflies shimmying in her stomach to skip. He looked over to where she and Big Nev were standing, offering a brief wave with that nuisance of a smile she was beginning to get annoyed by, before he followed his father to the queue. Had he been happy to see her? Or was he only being polite?

'Looks like even John might get some sweetening up,' Big Nev said, grinning before he shoved the last of the slice into his mouth, licking his custard-laced fingers enthusiastically.

'He needs some.' She was happy not to hide the scorn in her comment. After the stunt he'd pulled on her with Pete, it'd take more than a finger-licking slice to turn his snarky attitude around.

Charlotte watched a little longer, then turned back to Big Nev as he tracked where she'd been looking. What had she seen on his face not a split second ago? Wariness, maybe mistrust? Whatever it was, it had her shifting her shoulders uncomfortably, and she looked down at the lifeless grass around her feet. Maybe she didn't need a piece of Janice's vanilla slice after all, her appetite peeling away at the thought of standing in line with John and the delightful town gossips.

'Listen, about the ram sale—' Big Nev said, and Charlotte turned to Big Nev's cautionary eyes with renewed interest.

'I reckon I can get someone to run the pub that day if you need me to help. I'd be more than happy to.' His affable smile breathed relief into her inner soul.

'I'd love that. And I have the perfect job for you,' she said, not speaking a moment too soon as she glanced back at the shop entrance to watch John exiting with a tray full of Janice's goodies. But Fraser was nowhere to be seen.

CHAPTER 28

Fraser rocked up to The Tavern, letting out a defeated breath as he offered his mates a droll smile. 'What's going on?' he said, reaching for the beer waiting for him, not missing the way Ross and Mark were looking way too pleased because they'd beaten him there for once. He attempted to hide his smile behind a long sip, appreciating the way it glided down his dry throat, but it wasn't enough to burn away the yip-yabber he'd been caught-up in at The Small Store by Nancy and Elsie as they quizzed him about Charlotte's shearing. He'd played the ever-polite card, only telling them what they didn't want to hear, that it had gone well and was done for another year.

The day had been a warm one, a precursor to the heat of summer on their doorstep, and he'd had enough of feeding sheep, no thanks to the rain they were meant to be getting but hadn't turned up as yet, making him uneasy for how the summer was going to pan out with feed for the stock.

'You boys are never early,' he continued, but his chuckle fell away abruptly as both Ross and Mark looked at each other with unease before turning to Big Nev, the fresh alarm on Mark's face clear as Big Nev called them over with a brisk pull of his hand before warily glancing over his shoulder.

All three men stood, moving to the back of the pub where Big Nev pushed the outside door open quietly, putting a cautionary finger to his lips.

They listened.

'No. Bloody. Way. I'm not doin' that again. I don't wanna get caught. Nup, I'm out.'

All four men glanced with wariness at one another, their faces conveying what their minds were asking. Fraser leaned forward, concentrating to catch more of what they were saying.

'You're a bloody wuss. You ain't never gonna get anywhere if you don't get in and give yourself a leg up. It's your loss, mate.'

Fraser crept closer to the fence palings and crouched, flinching against the crunch his knee uncooperatively cracked with, before peering through a small hole in the wood. All he could see was a set of legs.

'Listen, I'm done re-pressing all that wool. It's bad enough when it's only a few bales, but it ain't no fun pulling all that pressed wool out and double handlin' it. Two hundred-plus bales does nothin' for the enthusiasm.'

'You got well paid, you stupid bugger. Easy cash like that don't come 'round too often. I'd quit complainin' if I were you and get on with the job.'

'Nup. I'm taking my ten grand and jumpin' ship. I'm out.'

'Fine. It's your loss. I'll tell Stinger what you said. He ain't gonna be happy with ya.'

Fraser's mouth fell open as he stood, turning to the others as footsteps retreated into the workshop next door, before two car engines revved out the front.

Mark bolted through the premises, hoping to catch a glimpse of the cars, but was too late, the vehicles long-gone. They met back at the table where their drinks were sitting.

'What did you see through the hole, Fraser?' Mark's easygoing nature had sharply switched into work mode as he urged Fraser to speak.

'Not anything distinguishable. Only a pair of well-worn work jeans. But everyone wears those.'

'I've been hearing whispers around the place,' Big Nev said. 'Something's been going on, but I haven't been able to nail what.' A disappointed sigh escaped his lips before he finally took another sip of his Coke.

'Really?' Mark sat taller, his face pensive.

'Like what?' Fraser directed his question to Mark as he tried to fathom what Big Nev had been hearing, alongside what they'd all witnessed. Re-pressing wool wasn't unheard of, but the amount of money they'd talked about . . . it didn't sound right.

Mark watched Fraser, but he was looking through him, and it gave Fraser an unsettled vibe, as though something was going on that involved him. But that wasn't possible. Mark remained quiet as Big Nev changed the topic.

'I'm hearing a few whispers from unhappy locals,' Big Nev began. 'They reckon John might be trying to pull a swifty on Sheepwash Creek's ram sale.' He glanced at Fraser. 'Sorry, mate.' He gave Fraser an apologetic frown. 'There's a whisper that they're being told not to buy any rams because your father is planning on taking over the property anyway. So, they might as well wait for your sale to buy what they need.'

'What?' Fraser gaped at the men, wishing he could unhear what Big Nev had said. 'That can't be right.' His father would've told him if they'd settled on an agreement with Charlotte. Wouldn't he?

That was, unless his father suspected he'd been trying to get her to stay . . .

CHAPTER 29

It was seven a.m. on the dot when both Pete and Big Nev arrived at Sheepwash Creek, looking oh-so schmick and enthusiastic. Even the resident magpie gave them a half-hearted warning swoop before it settled in the big gum near the house, warbling its displeasure at their presence.

'So, whatcha want us to do, Boss?' Pete strutted up to Charlotte like a rooster sounding his victory call, having not long exited the house where her mother was putting the final touches on the food trays. A crumb clung to the side of his mouth and Charlotte unconsciously wiped at her own.

'Could you and Big Nev move the rams into their individual pens please? I'll set up the table where the sales will be made, and then we can put out the hay bales for everyone to sit on.'

'On it, Boss,' Pete said, giving Big Nev a tap on the arm with the back of his hand as he headed towards the machinery shed where the pens had been stored from last year.

Three-quarters of an hour later, Pete emerged, and Charlotte looked up from where she'd begun to place several small bales near the BBQ as a designated seating area. She stood, her hands on her back as she stretched to iron out her aching muscles, and the burning question that had been pestering her all morning. She walked over to Pete, checking over his shoulder in case Big Nev was following, keen to dive on her chance while the coast was clear.

'Pete, did Fraser see anyone . . . after I left?' She aimed for a casual, little disinterested look, keeping her eyes down despite the heat racing to her cheeks. But in all truth, she wouldn't have to worry. Pete wasn't *that* perceptive.

'There was a lot of interest, I recall, and there were a few girls who didn't give up easily.'

Give up? He paused, and she was acutely aware he was watching her more closely than usual. Unable to help herself, she looked up at him as she blinked, urging him to continue.

'No, there wasn't anyone after you. And I'm doubtful there ever will be.'

So much for Pete not having a perceptive bone in his body. She released an I've-so-been-sprung huff. The guy had her like Brutus, the glint in his eyes intrigued, deceptively trusting, and in the end, a goner. She didn't want to think what else he would do to make it obvious he was acutely aware she was sussing out Fraser's life post-her, for good reason. He'd only nail her to the wall and hold her to ransom, for food, no doubt. Nonetheless, she wasn't about to choke, despite fully regretting her curiosity getting her into a fine pickle.

Charlotte's cheeks heated overtime as her eyes widened with the knowledge of what Pete was saying. Had Fraser never gotten over her? Had his kiss held the sincerity she'd hoped it did after all? Could that one disastrous night so long ago haunt her no matter how much she wanted to hope for a second chance, determining what she could have now? They'd both changed so much.

'Okay, *Director of Traffic*, you'd better go man your post. Looks like some of Syd's people from Cavanagh Rural Supplies are starting to arrive. They can park next to the shed if you like. It'll make it easy for them to unload their gear.'

A number of extra agents from the agricultural supply shop were coming to lend support. Some were spotters for the bidding, others were registering prospective buyers. Later, they'd also take the payments for the rams.

Charlotte giggled as Pete's shoulders broadened with anticipated pride for the job he'd been entrusted to do, and he jogged over to the cars, guiding them to a parking spot. And she was thankful for the break in his scrutiny. It gave her time to think through what he'd said, to see if there was anything she could clutch onto, hope for, or even believe in. But she didn't have time for that as more cars started arriving, and fresh emotions pinched at her heart. She stole a crisp breath of air despite the forecast of a warm day. She needed to get a move on if she was going to be ready for everything to get underway. Any other thoughts would have to keep until later, when the ram sale was over and she knew how much the sale had made.

There was no shortage of enthusiasm from the prospective clients who quickly gravitated towards the magnificent spread both Mum and Rosemary had prepared on two fold-up tables beneath the shade of a large portable gazebo. Scones with Mum's raspberry jam and cream, muffins, Janice's vanilla slice, and jelly slice, all stole centre stage along with mini quiches, egg and bacon pies, and savoury slices, keeping everyone happy until lunch was ready. Gus and Will were manning the barbeque, with Jonno overseeing that his sausages didn't get burnt, and Rob's IGA in Ballarat had kindly donated all the bread.

Will. Charlotte's heart pressed against her ribcage. Despite the enticing smell of smoky snags making her stomach rumble, she was taken aback by the sight of him, and her rampant thoughts of the tragedy he'd been so explicitly involved in. He appeared far more relaxed than her, turning the sausages like a pro. But had he been able to move on from the horror of that night?

He glanced up, catching her eye, then began moving towards her. She froze, unsure how she should react. She couldn't convince herself to turn and leave even though she had a thousand good reasons and excuses to do so. But to do that seemed insincere, bordering on cruel, so she slowed her breathing, calling on the warmest smile she could muster that she hoped wouldn't come across as strained.

'Thanks for putting on the sale, Charlotte,' he said, slowing no more than a metre away from her. 'I'm hoping to get one of your rams today to join with my small fleet. I'd like to think it will bring about great genetics to start the mob.' He held her with a friendly smile, one she read as more cautious and insecure, but she managed to offer a short, approving nod in return, her throat tight and uncomfortable. It might never change what had happened, but everyone deserved to live their lives and move forward. Deep down, she knew he was a good guy, and James would have wanted that for Will, so she needed to approach things that way for him too.

But what about Fraser? Had he moved on? Did he have the right to? He'd been James's best friend. Weren't they meant to be there for one another at any cost?

The cost she had paid for his split-second lapse in concentration had been too high.

Charlotte excused herself from Will by politely giving a wave to Mark as he walked towards the display of rams, relieved by the excuse. While he didn't farm sheep on a large scale, he owned a little over one hundred ewes.

'Thanks so much for coming, Mark.'

'It's a great turnout. I'm keen to get myself a new ram. Wouldn't mind infusing some fresh blood with the ewes I bought from your Dad a while back.'

Hearing her father's name on a day like today made her heart constrict and glow in the same breath. They continued chatting before a small kerfuffle at the snacks table had both Mark and Charlotte instinctively heading towards it, her mother waving cooking tongs toward someone. Charlotte watched on as Pete strolled past the table of goodies, and she paused in the shade of the gum tree, unable to smother her chuckle. Mark came to stand beside her, his police face nowhere to be seen as he grinned.

'Ah, look at all the wonderful members of the Cranky Women's Association,' Pete chimed. 'What would I do without you ladies putting on this fantastic spread especially for me?' He gave a good-natured wink in their direction, before his long arm reached forward. 'I'm famished. Don't mind if I do.' And before her mother had the chance to object, Pete had stuffed not one but two mini pizzas into his mouth.

'Peter Rabbit. You've had more than your fair share,' her mother scolded, putting her hands on her hips and eyeballing him to no avail. 'There won't be any left for the guests. We do want them to *buy* rams.'

Charlotte's hand flew to her mouth as she fought to trap her laughter.

'It's all for a good cause, ladies,' Pete assured them, reaching out again. 'Good quality control is crucial on occasions such as this.' He grinned at them all before shoving a homemade sausage roll into his mouth with a cheeky grin, and promptly removing himself from the queue before he got himself ejected. Permanently.

'What's that? You want me to help you? Well then,' Pete called out, with all authority and no invitation, before proceeding to curl around the table, heading directly for Mum, his lovable grin evidence he was enjoying teasing her mother. And as the scene unfolded, a deep happiness settled over Charlotte, one she hadn't contemplated before, but was thoroughly at peace with. Her father had been gone almost six months, and while it was clear Mum wasn't ready for another relationship, it was a nice reminder that Pete had a knack for bringing friendship and genuine contentment to her mum more often these days. To see her happy filled her with new hope for them both.

'Right, Peter Rabbit. You are required back at your post,' Charlotte said, breaking the mock standoff as she strolled up to him, tapping him on the shoulder and giving him a warning frown that he'd best be on his way.

'Yes, Boss.' He gave her a salute before giving her mother a you've-just-gotta-love-me wink as he sneakily squeezed his arm between two clients standing in the queue one last time, snatching a cheese twist before his mischievous grin about-faced and he disappeared into the crowd.

'That man,' Mum said, shaking her head, and Charlotte pressed her lips together to curb her smile at her mother's put-on frustration.

Big Nev's delegated role as bouncer of proceedings came with good reason. Charlotte had him keeping a close eye on everything, including Mr and Mrs Hudson's greedy ten-year-old son, Nicholas. Within the first fifteen minutes of arriving, the kid had already visited the slices table three times, with his sights set on round number four.

Charlotte was returning from the kitchen with a fresh tray of steaming party pies when she spied Nicholas glancing about him as he tiptoed towards the delectable delights for what she guessed had to be round five. Her steps slowed, her curious gaze casually sliding towards Big Nev.

Nicholas sidled up to the table, using a shady glance behind him before he swiped four pieces of chocolate Mars bar slice into his sticky hands. With a satisfied grin, he spun around to scoot away, only to crash straight into Big Nev's crossed arms.

With wide eyes glued to Big Nev's, Nicholas brought his hands from behind him and, in slow motion, lowered his prized haul back onto the table like it had been his plan all along. Then, with a nervous, toothy grin, he shot away, risking one last peek over his shoulder as Big Nev watched him, his fingers thrumming his forearm.

Charlotte chuckled as she glanced about, a deep appreciation settling over her for everyone who'd turned up to help, and to those she hoped would dig deep into their pockets. So many of the women helping out for the day were farmers' wives, like Mrs Hudson. Their community spirit was well and truly alive. The moment Janice's slices hit the countertop, they were snapped up like yabbies taking the bait, people delighted they were getting a slice for free, even if it was a smaller serving than what she sold at the shop.

It was no surprise that Nancy Stone and Elsie Kent were there, not buying rams, but busy-bodying themselves as they bustled about, not missing an opportunity to soak in the happenings of something so big, and dare Charlotte think it, juicy. Mind you, they fronted with not so much as a single plate to offer between them, helping themselves to all the delights on offer, like food was about to become extinct.

And then she saw Maddie. Even though Charlotte couldn't help it, her heart did a twitchy jolt as she considered her long-time neighbour and friend. Fraser might have said nothing was going on, but how could a single guy look past a girl like her?

Maddie had been their proverbial pest growing up, hunting them down like a pesky little sister. And nearly every time, she'd found them. Whether it was herself and James canoeing down the creek, or her and Fraser eating icy poles while they were perched on the branch of a tree on a hot day above the creek as they watched the fish jump, Maddie had wanted to be included. Charlotte was convinced she liked Fraser more than just a friend. But Fraser? Why did that thought send a strange feeling of, what was it, it couldn't be jealousy, through her, even though she wasn't about to accept it as true? She had nothing to be jealous of because there wasn't anything going on between her and Fraser.

Nothing. At all.

The distinct pang of guilt for brushing Maddie aside so often in the past hit her sharply. All she'd ever wanted back then was some alone time with Fraser, and the girl had been annoying, pure and simple.

If only Charlotte could have realised what she did now. Maddie's father had been a shearer, travelling eleven plus months of the year. It wasn't until one day when Maddie was seven years old, that he'd come home and packed more than he usually needed to take away again, that she'd learned he was leaving them to move in with a young shedhand who he'd met on the contracting run. He'd emptied the bank accounts but left them with the farm, and by some extraordinary feat, her mother, her brothers, and Maddie had worked hard, turning the farm from destitution into a viable property with a stable income. Sadly, it was only in the last few years that Charlotte grasped the full weight of what it meant to lose someone you loved, regardless of how it happened.

And watching Maddie, her smile serene as she mingled, talking to Rosemary and her mother like they were long-time friends, Charlotte made a conscious decision. Regardless of whether Fraser was interested in Maddie or not, the young woman was a friend to her. And if Sheepwash Creek did hold her real future, then she was going to need every one of those she could get.

After the smoky wafts signalled lunchtime was over, patrons and wool reps resumed their walks along the rows of waiting rams, discussing the good and bad traits of each with all the know-how of well-experienced sheep men and women. And amongst them were John Pierce and Steve Haymes, both talking with more apparent authority than anyone else. A prickle of unease wriggled over Charlotte. But that's all it was, right? Misgivings about the possible success or failure of the sale. They were here to buy her rams, like everyone else.

A hush came over the crowd as Syd beckoned Charlotte by calling her name over the loudspeaker, and she stepped up to the microphone as people took seats on the hay bales and others stood behind.

'Thank you, everyone, for coming out to Sheepwash Creek today. I want to dedicate the sale to Dad and James.

They'd be overwhelmed to know you are all here to get behind the farm.' Several heads nodded and soft murmurs danced in the air, filling her with relief, but more than anything, with a thrill of excitement and hope that they would be buying rams they would go home happy with. It's precisely what her dad had always wanted. And if she was going to have a crack at keeping Sheepwash Creek, then everything was riding on this sale.

'And thanks to Mum, Rosemary, Janice and all the wonderful cooks this district has, for the amazing array of food, and to our barbeque chiefs.' Charlotte gave a thumbs up to Jonno and Gus, her soft smile lingering on Will as they nodded in acknowledgement to one another. This time, Charlotte's smile was genuine. 'I hope you all find a ram suitable to your needs.' I'm counting on it, she breathed, as the large crowd clapped and she stepped aside.

Syd took the microphone from Charlotte and the auction began. The sale happened with surprising speed, and Charlotte could scarcely keep up with the sale prices, let alone who was landing the winning bids. She glanced nervously towards Mum, whose smile resembled more of a grimace, following where she was looking. Steve and John were bidding on a lot of their rams.

She took the time to pay attention, noticing fresh hands raising their bidding numbers, only to see their hands fall away, their heads shaking in disappointment as they were outbid every time.

By John and Steve.

What the hell? Fraser narrowed his eyes as he scanned the large group of buyers present. Had Big Nev been right after all? Had his father struck a deal with Charlotte that he didn't know about? Any wonder the man was wearing the appearance of a cat who had scooped the cream off the top of the milk.

Fraser looked across to Mark, more than relieved to recognise the occasional I-know-what's-going-on raised eyebrow being directed his way, and he gave a grateful nod back. Mark might have been buying a ram, but his presence counted for so much more, and if what his father was up to was happening right under their noses, he'd have the backup he needed to make the man rethink his underhanded strategy.

Everything inside Fraser wanted to storm over and tell his father in no uncertain terms to back down. But that would only attract attention to the already growing animosity sitting thickly in the air through the expressions of so many farmers. He looked over at Charlotte, confusion written all over her face as she nudged Pete with a baffled elbow and waited for him to give her some indication of what was going on, hoping for an answer as she shrugged concerned shoulders his way.

But when he looked back at his father, his racing heart steadied a fraction. Big Nev had positioned himself directly behind his father and Steve, and by the look of their hesitation to bid over the top of Mr Hudson's current offer, Fraser was left in no doubt they were aware their ploy had been busted.

'Going, going . . . SOLD.' Syd's gavel smacked the table, and his father's head flinched back, a strange look passing between both he and Syd that Fraser couldn't decipher.

With the sale finished, Fraser approached his father. 'What was that all about?' He waved his arm in the direction of the sale, recognising he wasn't doing a good job of hiding his frustration.

'Good heavens, Fraser. We're allowed to bid on rams.' His father looked at Steve, giving a disbelieving scoff. But when he looked back at Fraser, his emotionless stare had him second-guessing what he'd seen. But after the whispers Big Nev had heard, it appeared that his father and Steve had been trying to take the scoop of the rams, his patience wearing thinner than his favourite teenage T-shirt.

'You bloody well *know* what I mean,' Fraser said, angrier than a hornet protecting its nest at having to explain himself. 'You're planning on breeding with them and selling stud rams and ewes off Sheepwash Creek's bloodlines for your own profit and stud name success.' A deep resentment for how that also made him look settled on him. 'Or were you buying those rams at rock-bottom prices only to sell them as Sheepwash Creek's stud rams at our sale, for an elevated price, surplus to our needs? As if anyone is going to fall for that when they work out what you've done. No one is going to want anything to do with Trentham Park after today.'

'Don't be so melodramatic,' his father laughed darkly. 'We'll use them, build up our bloodlines and the Sheepwash Creek infusion will be a selling point. We had nothing but the best intentions. We're helping Charlotte and Jayne so they can make a fresh start.' Dad nodded at Steve, the two men raising rather satisfied eyebrows at one another.

'No, you did more than that. You made sure others weren't bidding against you. You're an idiot if you think no one else but me saw it. Was that the quiet word I saw you having with so many of the farmers before the sale?' He made no effort to hide his disgust towards his father. 'Or the loss of profits that Charlotte rightfully deserved. It's like you're trying to crush her.'

The last of her rams were loaded onto the various farm utes with stock crates, through to small trucks and trailers. They had all sold, but her best prices had come when John and Steve had backed off from bidding, allowing others to step up. Had Big Nev had something to do with that? Charlotte headed to the house for a well-earned cup of tea, and everyone was sitting at the kitchen table as she walked in. Pete was licking his fingers clean of one of Janice's stashed-away vanilla slices she'd kept hidden in the fridge.

Starving, Charlotte snapped up the next piece Pete was reaching for, his look of indignation almost more satisfying than the slice itself as she watched him look on in horror at her first bite.

'Oi,' Pete said. 'That was mine.'

'Not anymore,' Charlotte giggled as she chomped into the slice again, making a show of the icing gluing to her fingers.

'So, how do you think it went?' Charlotte said to no one in particular through her mouthful, glancing around the table as she took a chair, her feet aching. Mum placed cuppas in front of everyone before finally taking a seat for herself. After such a huge day plus all the cooking her mother had done for the shearing team, Charlotte could see her mother was exhausted too. Mum curled and stretched her fingers, their increasing stiffness making Charlotte deliberate on her options once more. She gave her mother a deep smile and Jayne returned it. Many a stomach had been filled with satisfied contentment thanks to her and Rosemary's hard work, and she doubted the sale would have been as successful if they hadn't been there to help. Gratitude for the two women flooded her with immense warmth.

'I managed to put Nancy and Elsie in their place today. I consider that a win.' Big Nev gave a satisfied grin as everyone looked at him, Charlotte's questioning brows urging him to explain.

'Quite the pair, those two. They were having a field day until I came along.' He looked at Jayne. 'Caught them filling not one but two plates each with food. Interestingly, they both thought it best to leave the second one behind once I asked if they were staying for tea.' He chuckled. 'I didn't bother getting them to remove the plates they'd already stashed inside their oversized bags.' This time he shook his head in disbelief. 'I let them get away with that one. Hopefully their bags will be lined with cream and jam when they get home.'

Everyone giggled, shaking their heads in disbelief.

'So, Syd? You're the expert. How did it go?' For Charlotte, the cash flow would be substantial, meaning she'd be able to improve a few more things around the farm. It would help the property stay in the condition her Dad liked to keep it.

'It went well. Having all the rams sell is always the objective.'

'And what about the prices? Were they good for this current financial climate?' It had been so long since Charlotte had been to a ram sale that she'd forced herself not to get her hopes up, rather than set them high and be disappointed.

'Cavanagh Rural will drop a sizable sum into your bank account once our fees and expenses are deducted.'

'That's awesome news.' But as she took in the mood around the table, Syd was the only one agreeing with her.

CHAPTER 30

It bloody well worked!

Fraser sat up in bed, feeling more refreshed than he had in weeks. Restless thanks to constant thoughts of Charlotte's sale throughout the night, he'd hopped up in the early hours of the morning for a hot drink. Instinctively, he'd reached for a teabag, but after remembering what Charlotte had said, had rifled through the cupboard until he'd found a container of hot chocolate hidden at the back. The powder was crusty, a sure sign it was well past its use-by date, but he didn't care, prepared to scrape the chocolate powder with a knife until he had enough. Four lumpy scoops later, he'd made his hot drink, sipping it slowly . . . until his eyelids began to droop.

Now he'd allow himself to start the day with a coffee and toast before he even dared to contend with the shed full of rams they had bought—and didn't need—ignoring the reality that he had no clue what paddock he was going to put them in.

He ran both hands down his face as he chewed on the last bit of his cheese on toast, then let the coffee do its thing. He was on the verge of considering a second dose when his phone rang in his back pocket. He tugged it out, surprised at the caller ID.

'Char, how are—'

'Fraser, you've got to get over here. It's Brutus.'

Fraser listened to the breathlessness in Charlotte's voice, unable to fathom why she sounded so panicked. 'Slow down. What's wrong?' He forced himself to take a steadying breath, the sheer panic in her voice enough to have his shoulders stiffening.

'He's frothing at the mouth, and he's panting like he's finding it hard to breathe. Please, can you come over?' Now he understood the emotion in her voice as it wavered. She'd been crying. His heart lurched.

'Okay. Let me ring Ross, then I'll be right there. Are you in the shearing shed?'

'Yes.'

'Stay with him. I'll be there soon. Char, it's going to be okay.' Without waiting for her to respond, he hung up and dialled Ross, thinking back on his last words as the phone rang. Should he have said that Brutus would be alright? By the sounds of what she'd told him, it sounded dire. But all he had to hold onto was his belief that Ross would work some miracle.

Ross's voice sucked Fraser's thoughts back to reality. 'Hey, mate. I'm about to head off on rounds.'

'Great. Can you swing by Sheepwash Creek first? It's Brutus. Sounds to me like he's been poisoned.' Fraser regretted the panic in his voice, but the value of that ram was worth more to Charlotte than his virtual worth in dollars. He was the last thing she had as a connection to her dad, and without him, well, it might be enough for her to decide to leave. That ram had to live, no matter how cantankerous he was.

Fraser skidded on the driveway gravel, his ute travelling another metre before it finally came to a stop on Sheepwash Creek's driveway. He leapt from the vehicle, barely managing to shut the door as he ran towards the shed. He'd beaten Ross, and hoped he could do something if the vet was waylaid.

The sliding door was open and he went inside, running down the central walkway as his sight adjusted to the dim light between the pens until he reached Charlotte hunched over a lifeless Brutus, his massive head and horns resting on her lap like a puppy.

She looked up at him, her face strewn with salty smears and Fraser slowed, his heart missing a tangible beat as he fought to see if the ram was breathing. Was he too late? He jumped inside the pen with them.

Charlotte's flushed face stared up at him, full of concern and sadness and fear as he knelt in front of them. He reached for a hanky from his pocket, passing it to her. What he wanted to do was wipe her eyes for her. But given his father's little stunt at her ram sale a week earlier, his deft mortification over the whole incident cautioned him. She sniffed loudly, blinking at it before she released one hand from Brutus' muzzle and took it, blowing her reddened nose.

'Thank you,' she whispered, wiping her bloodshot eyes. 'I found him like this.'

'How long ago?'

'Just before I rang you.' She let out a loud sob, the kind that had him wanting to take her in his arms and hold her, comfort her, but he held back.

Fraser nodded, worried they might be too late as he watched the ram struggle to breathe through the white froth coming from his nose and mouth.

'He's going to be okay, I promise,' he soothed. Damn it, he growled to himself. Was he doing it again, making her a promise he didn't feel sure he could keep? But the glance she gave him, her eyes filled with trust and belief in him, had to make it worth the risk, right? He wanted that ram to live more than anything he'd ever wanted before.

He *needed* Charlotte to stay.

The sound of another ute pulling up jarred him back to reality, to what the loss of Brutus could mean for him, for them. He stood, running fingers through his hair as he indicated to Ross where they were by a quick pull of his hand.

Ross reached them with an unnerving calmness that managed to grate on Fraser despite knowing his mate was one of the best in the business.

'Hey, Char. Ross is here. You might want to stand up so he—'

'I'm not leaving him,' Charlotte snapped, her glower stern as she looked up, blinking through her pain with determination and strength, and Fraser breathed in the relief it spoke to him. Right there and then, he could see in her exactly what he needed to. Attitude. It's what would take Charlotte Redding from city dweller to station owner and manager, if she could only see the potential of it.

'Charlotte, it'd help me if you could step aside so I can take a look at him.' Ross's voice was kind, and he looked the way he always did around concerned clients, with a professional look and understanding smile that conveyed the message he'd look after their animal with the utmost care. And it worked. Nodding, she carefully slid away from Brutus as Ross held the ram's head, laying it gently on the grating floor.

Charlotte stood over Ross's shoulder, and Fraser's heart suffered another bout of worry as a slow tear fell from her face, splotching the vet's shoulder. But he didn't dare reach out to shift her away, more than sure he'd receive a less-than-impressed glare for his well-intentioned efforts.

Ross took the ram's temperature and looked in his mouth before listening to his breathing with the stethoscope. Brutus' eyes were dull and vacant as he pried them open one by one, and he sat back on his haunches with his hands on his thighs before looking up at them both.

'I'm thinking he could've been poisoned. I'll take a couple of blood samples to learn what we're dealing with.

It'll be touch and go for the next couple of days, Charlotte. Is there anything he may have eaten that could have been toxic?' As he waited for an answer, he took his battery-operated clippers and removed a patch of wool above a vein in the ram's leg, taking the syringe and drawing blood in two separate vials before naming and dating them, and placing them in a cooler bag he always carried with him.

Charlotte's eyes widened before she blinked at Ross. 'I mix all their food in the trough over there. If there's anything poisonous, shouldn't they all be unwell?'

Ross nodded, thoughts clearly running through his mind at the possible scenarios before he looked up. 'Has he escaped again recently?'

This brought a reluctant but hopeful smile to Charlotte's face, and to Fraser, nothing could have been better. 'He manages to do that at least twice a week.' She gave a reluctant half-smile.

Ross stood, looking around the shed. 'Nothing looks out of place. I might grab a sample from each of those unopened chaff bags, and the minerals and salts bag too. If the manufacturer has suffered some form of contamination, they'll want to learn about it. I may have more sick sheep to treat in the next few days around the district too. You'd better not feed your rams any more of that feed, and Fraser, don't feed yours either. You've probably got the same batch from Gus. Stick to some good old-fashioned lucerne hay for the time being, at least until we're sure what it is we're dealing with.'

'Sure,' Fraser said, as Charlotte kneeled down to Brutus once more. He lay a gentle hand on her shoulder, giving it a heartfelt squeeze, wishing he could make everything marshmallows and sunshine for her. He'd expected nothing more from the gesture than the desire to show her his uttermost support, but when she reached over the top of his hand with hers, covering it and squeezing back, his chest warmed with an unexpected flush and his stomach tightened. Since their kiss, this was the first sign she'd given him that he might mean more to her than a friend. Or was she purely emotional and caught up in the moment? Over the last week, he hadn't helped the situation, backing off so as not to put any untoward pressure or expectation on her.

No, he wasn't about to count his chickens just yet.

Charlotte eventually released Fraser's hand, instead stroking Brutus' soft muzzle and running her fingers down the creases of skin so indicative to a merino ram. How was it that Brutus found himself in such dire straits he couldn't catapult his body at her, his head instead laying helpless on her lap like a loving pet rather than an adversary desperate to avenge all his grievances by trying to send her into the air with his horns?

'Hang in there, Brutus. You have to fight. You won't do it for me, so do it for yourself. I can't lose you.' Charlotte let out a solitary sob, her chest heaving with effort. Her father's ram was the key to Sheepwash Creek's success. He'd told her so during their last phone call before— The tears she'd managed to keep at bay welled fiercely and exposed once more.

'Char, we should leave him for a bit. Let's get ourselves a cup of tea. You need one.'

She nodded reluctantly, setting Brutus' head to the grating floor before she stood. Turning around, she stared at Fraser with eyes that begged him to tell her Brutus would pull through. But reality told her he might not. Fraser reached for her hand, gripping it tight, the sensation spreading immediate tenderness and comfort through her.

'How many rams live through something like this, Fraser?' She'd never heard of a ram being poisoned before. She'd be letting her father down if she allowed this ram to die on her watch.

'He's tough. If any ram can survive, he will.'

He'd avoided answering her, probably for good reason, she mused. But he was right. If it had to be any ram that needed to put up a fight to the death, then Brutus was the right one to give it a shot.

And in that moment, Charlotte stepped into Fraser, wrapping her arms around his strong torso, desperately soaking in his warmth, his strength; everything she had none of. She closed her eyes as his comforting arms enveloped her, the action of his breathing against her cheek acting like a soothing tonic. He seemed cautious at first, but she sensed him relax, holding her so close, so gently, it was as if he was scared she might break. But how could she, her memories of the days of old when he'd comforted her—or held her because he'd wanted to—feeling all too real again? Was that even possible? Back then, he was all the security she'd ever needed. But it was even better, as if his adult form fitting against her so snugly gave her mind permission to rest from the worries of the farm, and from the hard decisions she needed to make. She'd counted on it from him back then.

It was what she needed now.

Charlotte found herself nodding at his suggestion. There was nothing more they could do, and she was wrung out. A cuppa was exactly what they all needed.

Mum was away at a CWA meeting, but true to form, tasty cheese twists were sitting on a plate along with a still-warm brownie slice laced with oozy chocolate pieces on the kitchen table. The smell pulled all three of them towards it the moment they opened the back door.

As Charlotte boiled the kettle, Fraser edged past her, tugging out a seat and eying her with determination as he stood behind it.

'C'mon, sit down. I'll do that.'

Thank goodness Ross was there, Charlotte thought to herself, because otherwise it may have been her complete undoing, her eyes puffy and haggard as she took the seat and he placed a mug of steaming tea in front of her, and a coffee for Ross and himself.

They sat in compatible silence as they sipped and ate, the chocolate the warm hug from home she needed. There was nothing else to say after the morning they'd had. The next few hours were going to be critical for her ram.

'Char.' Fraser broke their agreeable silence, and the way he said her name threatened to carry a weight that made her suddenly nervous. She looked at him on the opposite side of the table, allowing herself permission to soak in his kind eyes and tender lips with more depth, her heart picking up speed, despite the pained expression creeping over his features, raising fresh alarm inside her. Did he fear Brutus would die? He took in such a long breath, she found herself holding hers also.

'I told Will to put the safety latch on the .22, and he assured me he had.' Fraser looked her way, a sadness lacing his eyes so deeply, Charlotte found herself unable to protest at him continuing. She didn't want him to speak about *that* night, but her voice was stuffed somewhere deep inside her throat. She blinked rapidly, begging him to stop. Why wasn't Ross doing something, anything, to stop him?

'But he'd shot his first rabbit, and he was excited. Couldn't stop telling us.' Fraser stared at the mug he was clutching tight with both hands. She didn't want to listen to any of this, ever. She'd pushed him away all those years ago because of this reason.

Shut up, Fraser—

Unmoving, her eyes bulged, and nausea suddenly whooshed through Fraser. She was listening to him? That had to be a first in like, forever. He had to get this out before she could change her mind or find her words again. It might be the one chance to find peace within himself, and he tugged Grandpa Jacob's fob watch from his pocket, turning it in his hand beneath the table to muster the courage as the kitchen clock's loud ticking fought to scramble his thoughts.

'I was in the back of the ute with Will when James jumped out from the cabin to go and retrieve the rabbit. Everyone had put their guns down.' He swallowed hard, thankful to Ross for staying with him while he did this, his guilt-filled grimace shying from her disbelieving gaze. 'The spotlight was on James, showing him where the rabbit was, and I didn't take my eyes off him, not for one second, Char.'

Recollections came flooding back and he pressed firm fingers to his eyelids, as if that might blot out some of the memory of what happened next. But it never had before.

'Will had lowered his gun onto the roof when I heard Gus speak to him from the other side of the ute, asking him to put the gun down in the tray of the ute instead, facing away from everyone.' Fraser's eyes welled up like they so often did when he allowed himself to dwell on the full pain of that frightful night, and he pressed his thumb and fingers to them, urging the threatening tears to subside. But they refused, the reality of this moment so close and so real. He was finally telling Charlotte what had happened, after all these years. It had been a moment he'd both wanted and at the same time, desperately hoped to avoid. But Char deserved to know. If she heard it, maybe they could find a way to step forward, together? Or maybe it would only be him with a chance to move on, on his own . . .

'The next thing I heard was a boom from the gun beside me—as I watched James— falling.' A gut-wrenching sob came from his mouth, and he turned from them, barely able to see the tiles on the kitchen floor. He let his lungs empty, slowly and unsteadily.

'Char, I ran to him. I held him to me.' A deep sob reverberated through his body. 'I begged him to come back.' Fraser pressed the back of his hand to his nose, sniffing then wiping it as he worked to compose himself. Where had all his calm and determination gone? He'd practised telling her for so long, he'd been sure he wouldn't fall apart in front of her when the moment arrived. He'd thought all his tears were behind him.

'Will swore black and blue that the safety switch had been on before he moved the gun. I dunno, maybe in the excitement of shooting his first rabbit, he'd imagined he'd done it.' He drew in another long breath, holding it for what felt like forever, before letting it seep through tight lips. 'But it wasn't,' he whispered, shaking his head painstakingly.

The memory was so raw and so close, and Fraser had no clue Charlotte was looking at him with her hands wrapped around her mouth, her eyes full of despair and dread.

'I had no idea there was a bullet loaded in the barrel.'

Fraser hid his face in his hand, hiding all the guilt and shame and remorse he'd carried so closely for too long as he sobbed—deeply, exhaustedly. Ross reached to him, placing a hand on his shoulder in a stance of sorrow, mateship, and solidarity. But feeling the full brunt of the pain, even after all these years . . . it was what he deserved. It would do him well not to forget it.

CHAPTER 31

How was it possible to slip from never feeling safer in Fraser's arms to wanting to run to the bathroom and violently throw up? But one thing was for sure. It was a good reminder that the farm wanted to chew her up if she stayed. And if the farm didn't get her, Fraser would, if she let her heart fall for him a second time. After what he'd just told her, forgetting him had to happen. It was time to nip those pesky feelings getting in the way of her future—off this farm—in the bud, for good. She didn't need them swaying her decisions, and she wouldn't let him weasel his way back into her heart, even if he was the only man she'd ever loved.

What she needed was to rely on herself. That meant the best thing for her and her mother, was to leave.

'Fraser, you need to go, pleeease,' Charlotte begged, unable to swallow the sharp tightness in her throat as she stood on shaky legs, her hands steadying her body as she gripped the kitchen table, ready to bolt for the bathroom if the nausea became too much. She couldn't look at him, pressing her lips together so tightly, she could feel the blood draining from them.

To her left, Ross's chair scraped against the tiled floor. Then through her blurred peripheral vision, she watched as Fraser stood slowly, as though he might collapse at any moment, inching his way out behind Ross. Behind them, the verandah screen door shut with its usual thud, making her jump despite fully expecting it.

Only after the sound of their utes retreating down the driveway did she gasp for air, unaware she'd been holding her breath the entire time.

The milder atmosphere the following morning was damp and dewy as Charlotte hesitated in front of the sliding woolshed door. But this time it wasn't because Brutus might have escaped his pen. Sadness hit her that he might never pull that beastly stunt on her again, and her face pinched tight at the painful thought. Had the craziness of yesterday messed with her brain?

Her mind trailed to Fraser, failing dismally at unhearing what he'd said, despite trying to for much of the night. Even the hot chocolate she'd forced down at three a.m. hadn't worked its usual charm. He might have needed to get what happened off his chest, but had he thought about what it would do to her? Thanks to him, she'd have to live with that vivid image of Will blindly lining up James before the gun fired. More than ever, this was the fateful reason she needed to get off Sheepwash Creek. Staying would only keep her remembering.

A thumping of horns against the wooden railing of the pens sounded from inside the shed and thoughts rushed back. Was it another ram letting it be known they hadn't been fed, thanks to her finally falling asleep at six a.m. and not waking until mid-morning? It couldn't be Brutus. Had he even made it through the night? Her heart skittered out of rhythm at the notion. She'd checked on him before going to bed, his condition unchanged, although she had managed to assure herself that his breathing had steadied. Even after midnight when she'd been lying awake, worrying, she'd hopped up to check on him, and he had looked no different, so she rounded her shoulders in readiness to open the door . . . and face what greeted her.

Blinking into the dark cavity of the shed, she edged down the long walkway, her eyes hovering over where the ram would be lying down as she approached the pen. He was probably dead she told herself, more so to help her accept the inevitable, but as she looked into the pen, her eyes widened.

Charlotte took a guarded step forward, Brutus' strangely tranquil disposition threatening to disarm her. She tugged her head back, blinking with disbelief. He was standing, his ears pinned forward, looking at her with his signature unrivalled discontent that warned her he was displeased she hadn't come with food.

'But . . . How?' She covered her mouth with a shaking hand, unable to stop the heat forming behind her eyes. After everything that had happened in the last twenty-four hours, this was not the outcome she had been anticipating.

Brutus lifted his nose to the air, as if signalling she was more than welcome to get his food any time she liked, and she smiled the same way her mother had done when she'd received an A-plus on a school report, as tears continued to stream. The ram might not be stomping his foot at her, but give him time, and she was sure he'd make his miracle comeback apparent.

'Okay, okay, I'll go get you something.' As she headed for the lucerne hay, the sound of a diesel motor pulling up slowed her. She poked her head out into the vivid sunlight to see Ross grabbing his work bag from the back of his ute.

'Ross, quick. You've got to see this. Brutus is standing up. He's even demanding I feed him.' Charlotte didn't miss the slow smile forming on the vet's lips.

'For real? That's . . . remarkable. He was down for the count and thought I might have to euthanise him this morning.'

Ross's resolute words combined with the cautious look of doubt written on his face hit Charlotte so squarely, a protective instinct rose up inside her. She pushed her hands to the air, pressing frantically. 'No, he's going to be fine. I was about to give him a biscuit of lucerne.'

'Hold off on that. Let me take a look at him first.' He gave her a reassuring nod, jogging up the shed steps two at a time.

The defiant ram might have sized Ross up like a trophy he wanted to add to his collection, but as the vet lifted his legs over the pen railing, both of them could see Brutus' sting of aggression was nowhere near his usual heightened level. Instead of stepping forward to challenge Ross, he retreated a step, his hind quarters wobbling. The ram stopped, steadying himself, but his wary eyes never left the vet.

'Easy does it, big fella.' In a neat side-step Charlotte could have seen him doing in some fancy dance class, Ross positioned himself at the ram's side, taking his horns and gently tipping his head away from his own leg, towards the ram's body, allowing the massive animal to gently bend his legs and drop to the pen floor without a fight.

'He's definitely lost some of his snarky attitude,' Charlotte giggled. 'I'm beginning to like him after all. Any chance we can keep him this way?'

'I'm a fan of this calmer attitude too,' Ross chuckled, looking up at her. 'Can you pass me my bag? I'm flabbergasted he's this good already.' Ross took the thermometer from its cylinder, giving it a vigorous flick before taking the ram's temperature without so much as a flinch from him, regardless of where it had been inserted.

'Ha! You put that where you did and he didn't object?' Charlotte slowly shook her head. Where had the Brutus she knew so well gone?

'Well, I don't like your chances of him staying like this for too long.' Ross removed the thermometer, glancing at it. Putting it back inside his bag, he checked inside Brutus' mouth, then listened to his heart before sitting back on his haunches. 'He's doing extraordinarily well considering—'

'Considering what?' Fraser's question hung in the air heavier than the condensation dripping from the rafters, thanks to the sun on the roof as he ventured inside the shed. The look of surprise, and dare he admit it, annoyance, on Charlotte's face, was a sure sign she wasn't the least bit happy about his arrival. And he couldn't blame her after what he'd told her last night. The hardest part about it was he'd hoped it would give him the peace he'd been so desperate for.

But it hadn't. Not even Charlotte's hot chocolate hack had managed to help him catch a wink of sleep.

Ross paused, looking up at him, and Fraser could see it was making Charlotte second guess the vet's thoughts. The sun's warmth had the effect of making the atmosphere clammy, and he watched as she laced her hands together, probably to induce some form of calm into herself thanks to him turning up. He'd done it again, thrusting angst into her already uneasy mind. It was the last thing he'd wanted to do, but at every turn, instead of feeling like he was finding ways for her to stay, all he was managing to do was drive her further away. His chest tightened as her face caved with worry. All it would take was one too many nudges and she'd up and leave without a second glance. And he'd only have himself to blame.

Ross looked back down at the ram. 'The test results of the samples I took came back. There were traces of Boric Acid in his blood, but not enough to cause an overdose.' He stroked the ram's muzzle affectionately before continuing. 'Is there any chance Keith kept rat poison in the shed?' Ross's concerned gaze turned to Charlotte.

'We've always had rats and mice around the place.' Charlotte shrugged. 'It's a possibility.' She walked to where she mixed up the feed, scanning the noggins of the shed frame for anything more than the old can of fly spray and a chalk raddle her Dad had left there after using it to mark the rams he wanted to identify.

'Oh no—'

Her voice shuddered, making Fraser take quick steps to meet her before she turned to face them. On a lower noggin, hardly noticeable, was a chewed-open pack of Ratsak pellets. Fraser's body stiffened. The pack looked old and chewed into. 'Maybe Brutus took a nibble on one of his night raids?'

'Maybe. But I've never noticed it there before. It makes sense, given the rest of the rams are fine.'

'Or, could someone have poisoned him deliberately?' Ross spoke the words with caution, having finished giving Brutus the once-over before nudging him, helping him to find his feet again.

'But why would anyone do that?' Charlotte stared at Ross, perplexed.

Fraser answered Charlotte's question. 'Because he's a valuable ram.'

CHAPTER 32

Charlotte bounced over the corrugations of one of their back roads in the ute, her elbow resting on the open window frame. The few paddocks that the road gave access to, hardly got used thanks to being so far away from the hub of the station. The only sheep Dad kept there were the wethers, so the lizard country was perfect for them to grow superfine micron wool.

On the back tray she had a round bale—just in case they looked like they needed a feed—and Lewie, tail wagging, he was doing all the sheep spotting by standing at the lookout above the ute roof.

While checking on these sheep was necessary, it wasn't the real reason she'd taken the hour-long drive. What she'd needed was an excuse to leave the farm and regroup her thoughts.

Ross's last words this morning were haunting her, and as much as she didn't wish to entertain the idea that someone may have purposefully fed Brutus the pellets in his feed, she couldn't shake the worrying nuance from her mind.

She thought back to the ram sale held in the machinery shed. There had been no reason for anyone to go into the shearing shed. She'd already rung Big Nev, hopeful he might have heard something, but that was a dead end too. Besides, this wasn't something you planned to take measures against happening. Who would want to do something so cruel to an animal?

But Fraser was right about one thing. There was no doubt that Brutus was a valuable ram. Her father had paid twenty-eight thousand dollars for him outright, no syndicates involved. His bloodlines were infused in the progeny running around the paddocks since lambing, as well as in many of the rams she'd sold. That's why so many buyers and agents had turned up for her sale, wanting their future breeding to reflect some of his many desirable attributes.

Names rifled through her mind, none of which stood out to her as remotely alarming. Even though John and Steve had bought fourteen of her rams, everyone who had wanted a ram didn't go home empty-handed. So why was Fraser acting so terse towards his father? She didn't care how many they had bought. What mattered was the money in her bank account.

And from what people had said to her, they were over the moon that she had run the sale. Mr Hudson had even gone so far as to tell her he hoped this meant she'd take up the mantle, and his words had ignited a small yet lingering thought. Could she do this?

The truer question was, did she want to?

Rising dust swirled ahead of her on the road and she shuffled in her seat, waking her tired muscles as they objected. Why would anyone be using this road? There was nothing out here but dust and goannas this time of year, and a bit of dry pick for the sheep to haggle over, except for next to the creek where the grass stayed lush all year round.

Charlotte eased her foot off the accelerator as the ute approaching her moved off to the side of the road, slowing to get her attention. It was John, and she eyed his pursed lips. Was he unhappy with what he'd purchased? There was one rule her father had always taught her about selling stock, and that was to return their money or find them an equal or better replacement if they weren't happy. But she didn't have any replacements left, the only remaining rams in the shed were the ones she was planning to use herself come breeding time, if she stayed that was. She called them her insurance policy. Her heart hammered against her ribs as she gave a hesitant nod in his direction.

'Afternoon, John.' She dug deep, pulling out her brightest smile even though her stomach churned at the way his invested focus rested on her.

'You've got a bit of trouble, Charlotte.'

I knew it. He'd bought fourteen of her rams, and it was impossible to keep the man happy. How had she thought he wouldn't come complaining to her the moment a ram he'd bought suddenly didn't look as appealing in his own shed?

Returning his money was going to hurt. A lot. She opened her mouth to speak but he cut her off.

'There's a fence down near the creek, although there are no fallen tree branches to suggest it's been broken by force. And it appears it's been that way for a while. The sheep were helping themselves to the green feed on the other side of the creek. They've done a good job of making a track for themselves. You might want to get it fixed quick smart.' His slow smile held a hint of glee.

Why was she continually disarmed by his presumptuous approach and his detestable ability to keep her on her back foot? Something in his tone sent a shiver down her spine despite the radiance from the sun. She wanted to ask him why he was even on their road, but he beat her to it.

'It dawned on me the other night that you might have forgotten about those sheep Keith had tucked up there, but clearly not.' He nodded a smile at her, sizing up the hay she was carrying. 'Wouldn't want any of them to go missing.'

What was he suggesting? Or was it his tone that had her narrowing her eyes? A niggle dug deep inside her stomach. It had to be everything, and she impatiently tapped her foot on the floor of the ute.

'Thanks, John. I'll take a look and see what I can do.' That was another expense she didn't want to fork out for, but at least he wasn't unhappy with the rams he'd bought.

'Oh,' he said, almost as though it was an afterthought. But she didn't believe it for a second. 'Those papers are ready any time you'd like to have a look at them. In fact, they're right beside me.' He leaned over to the passenger seat, grabbing something before hopping out of his ute, his light-footed steps a little too enthusiastic as he reached her window. He passed her a large envelope, which she took without thinking, giving her a so-great-to-have-run-into-you nod, before getting back into his ute like it had been the expected thing for a farmer to do.

'Good luck.' Without even a goodbye, the obnoxious man drove away, leaving her surrounded in his dust wake, and with the uncanny feeling he was rather satisfied with what he'd done.

Charlotte couldn't move, the light-headedness swirling inside her, swamping what was left of her clear thinking. Had John been carrying the papers with him *in case* he came across her? Who did that? But it didn't matter. His chances of ever owning Sheepwash Creek were precisely Buckleys, and she snatched up the envelope, tearing it in half, then half again, before tossing one of the small squares straight out the window. Much to her delight, it caught in the light breeze, tumbling along the road behind her.

Take that, Mr Pierce. As far as she was concerned, if she didn't have part of the contract she was expected to be "oh so" thrilled about, then she had nothing to sign.

Fraser came to mind, and the amount of time she'd spent with him since she'd been back home. Being honest with herself, she had loved hanging out with him again, like in the old times. And his kiss, even though it was so long ago, continued to stir her heart and conjure up belly flip-flops she wouldn't admit to delighting in out loud, not even to Lewie.

But had his kiss been meant for something else? The sporadic thought had her pausing as she stared through the windscreen. She'd pushed him away ever since, but who knew her better than anyone?

Only him.

So, had it been in his plan all along to kiss her, compelling her to leave the station for good? Had he guessed she'd respond by doing the opposite of what he was suggesting, all because he knew her moves so well? Had it been a ploy to make her decide to sell to him?

Logic and what she knew of his genuine, kind heart told her none of that was true. He was too good a man for that. But the reasoning in this chance meeting she'd had with his father moments ago? She gritted her teeth. There had to be more to it.

CHAPTER 33

Annoyingly true to John's word, the wethers had made a merry old path to the other side of the patchy, dry creek, grazing and laying about like they were dukes amongst the tall green grass. And Charlotte *had* forgotten about them at shearing time. She recoiled at the realisation. That would be another phone call to get Jerry's boys to come back especially, but she counted on them not minding too much. Mum would be on the job.

Well, there goes my "money bale" hopes, Charlotte growled beneath her breath, the wether's wool probably blown out by a good micron or two thanks to the lush feed they had been partying on. She tipped her head back in disappointment before forging on towards the cut fence, the wires lying sprawled in all directions. A weary breath left her lungs. There was nothing she could do to fix the fence at the moment. This was a job she would need Pete's help with.

The wethers looked up at the sound of the ute and sprang to their feet, bolting in the opposite direction, spooked by the rumble of the engine.

The ute bounced as she made her way closer to their camp—the worn patch where the sheep regularly gathered—and her brow furrowed as she studied the number of hardened humps of dirt scattered over the ground, some as tall as a metre or two. They reminded her of the mullock heaps she'd seen at Sovereign Hill back in her school days. Her father had told her and James years ago that when her great-grandparents on her mother's side took claim of this land, they had hoped to mine it. But farming soon turned out to be far more profitable, and the gold fever was brushed aside as a waste of time in the district, thanks to insignificant findings.

Charlotte turned the ute around so the tray faced the sheep, and when she killed the ignition, it worked a treat. Steadily, the sheep slowed, turning back towards her in curiosity as she moved to the back of the ute and climbed up. She'd purposefully parked on a slight downward hill. The bale gently rolled off, landing on the ground with a thump.

With her pocketknife, she cut the plastic mesh wrapping it together, then rolled the bale out by pushing and kicking it with her foot. The natural leaders of the mob inched closer to the smell of fresh hay, baaing with infectious enthusiasm.

Charlotte stood back as they closed in, grabbing quick mouthfuls while dubiously looking about as if danger could pounce at any moment, and she frowned. These sheep were toeyer than any of their other mobs, even the more cautious ones. Was there a fox around? Or a stray dog? She scanned the lay of the land for any indication their hesitancy was justified but couldn't find any.

Happy enough with how they looked, and that they were tucking into the oaten hay, she turned for home. 'Take this, *Mr Pierce.*' Grabbing the torn envelope, she tossed another square of John's paperwork out the window, grinning as it soared on the breeze, landing in one of the shallow pools of water in the creek.

'How did that happen?' Fraser rubbed his chin as he replayed in his mind what his father had said. Charlotte's back fence had been cut? That didn't make sense. No one ever went up there other than to get Sheepwash Creek's wethers out for shearing, which immediately reminded him they'd forgotten about them.

With Friday night here again, Fraser quickly changed before heading to The Tavern, keen to talk to Mark. When he arrived, both Ross and Mark had beaten him for a record second time and he resisted raising surprised eyebrows. Those boys might have beaten him again but it would be the last time they did.

'Look what the cat dragged in,' Mark chimed, and both men laughed as he took his stool and pulled his beer towards him, a pretend scowl on his face.

Even Big Nev chuckled as he took his seat, taking a steady sip of his Coke before letting out a tired sigh. 'So, what's been happening, lads?' He looked to each of them with a curious grin before settling on Mark. No doubt he was curious if more information had come to light given what they had heard from behind the wooden fence.

'Not a lot. No leads on those two shady characters we listened in on.'

To Fraser, Mark's face reflected more disappointment than he thought necessary over the strange conversation they'd heard and he stared at his mate. Was there something he wasn't saying?

Big Nev nodded absently. 'I'll continue to keep my ear to the ground.'

'That'd be good, thanks.' Mark lifted his beer towards Big Nev in a "cheers" before downing a decent gulp.

The conversation fell quiet and Fraser's eyes wandered all over the table. Was this the right time to mention Charlotte's fence to Mark? From what his father had said, she hadn't shown the same suspicion that was growing in him at an all-too-rapid rate, thanks to the odd things happening around her. And she had no clue about the little stunt his father had pulled on the locals at the ram sale, or that she'd done some serious money in the process, something he was mortified at his father for. But if he was to tell her, fireworks were certain to erupt.

'Mark, has Charlotte spoken to you?'

'No, why?' Mark looked as cautious as Fraser was about bringing the topic up. But he cared more than anything about her, and whether she was staying or not, he was doing this because he was looking out for her.

'One of her fences was cut, possibly intentionally. But she probably doesn't fully understand how odd that is 'round here. It's right up the back of her property.' He shrugged, hoping he sounded more laid-back when everything inside him screamed. 'Thought you might like to know.'

Mark crossed his arms as he sat back, watching Fraser thoughtfully. 'Has she mentioned any disturbances, like motorbikes?'

Big Nev cut in. 'There's been a couple of kids on dirt bikes doing monos down the main street here. Usually late at night. Bloody nuisances have been keeping me awake all hours.'

'Not that I'm aware of,' Fraser said, looking to Big Nev, then back at Mark. 'She hasn't mentioned it.' She wasn't mentioning much at all to him these days. Where, exactly, was Mark going with this?

'There's been some random reports of teens tearing around on their dirt bikes in paddocks that don't get checked too often. Again, I haven't had anything concrete to confirm this, but if she can keep a lookout, it might help. Big Nev, have you got any idea who they might be?'

The publican shook his head. 'No. But I'll keep trying. They'll slip up sometime soon. They always do.'

'But why would they cut her fence?' Fraser didn't want to let on that there was a more sinister motive floating around in his mind, like his father trying to get Charlotte to sell. But that had to be a far-fetched notion. His father wouldn't stoop that low.

'Probably lazy. Couldn't be bothered finding a gate. It's happened before,' Big Nev suggested, offering an affirming nod.

Fraser agreed, accepting his theory. But still . . .

'I'll give her a call when we leave here, might even pop in on my way home. Jayne might have lasagne in the oven.' Mark jiggled his eyebrows in anticipation, the rest of them laughing at his never-ending enthusiasm for a good feed.

A sharp stab of longing had Fraser wanting to turn up with Mark. But he squashed the thought before it had a chance to grow. No doubt she wouldn't want anything to do with him, thanks to his father giving her the contract and he hated how his name became smeared thanks to his father's actions. He'd only found out about it before he'd left for The Tavern and he was more than sure it would finalise Charlotte's stance to leave. It wouldn't surprise him if she refused to sell to them at all.

Fraser stood to buy round two, and as he waited for Big Nev to fill their glasses, he strained to recall any motorbike noise he might have heard from their farm. They were a long way from the paddock where the fence had been cut, but while it wasn't normal practice, it wasn't unheard of for his father, or Steve for that matter, to check their own paddocks using that road occasionally. He'd have to ask his father if he'd seen any bike tracks when he got home.

Charlotte stepped from the ram shed, her relief palpable now Brutus was showing signs he was on the mend. While he hadn't managed to escape again, he was throwing his head around at her like a true bully. He'd be ready to join with the ewes come the end of January, as long as Ross gave him a clean bill of health. Then there'd be a new drop of stud ram lambs ready to sell the following year if they made the cut. Things were looking on the up. Deciding to join the ewes was a good move. The interest in the rams at auction had clearly shown that. If a buyer came along when she finally advertised, having lambs ready to drop by the time they took ownership was a great incentive.

She slowed as she drew in a long breath, immersing herself in the smell of lasagne in the air. *Mmmm.* Mum hadn't made it in ages, and her stomach growled as she neared the verandah. But as she reached down to remove her boots, the sound of gravel being disturbed had her standing once more, a relieved smile forming on her face.

'That'd be about bloody right,' she chuckled, certain he'd enjoy the ribbing as he hopped from the vehicle. 'How'd you find out what Mum was cooking this time?' Her eyes narrowed on him.

Mark beamed like he'd won the lottery as he lifted his nose to the air. 'Sometimes it's worth taking a chance. I'm a cop, remember. I work on hunches.'

They sat at the table, general farm and local chatter happening before Mark put his knife and fork on his finished plate and sat back, satisfaction spreading over his face. 'Jayne, you've outdone yourself. No one makes a better lasagne than you.'

'Now, Mark, I'm betting your mother can make one equally as well.' Mum's words teased, but Charlotte could hear the appreciation in her mother's voice at the compliment. She'd always said a good cook baked with love.

'That's true, but she's in Tassie and I've eaten yours so that's all that counts,' he said, grinning again. Mum nodded her thanks to him as she began to gather the plates.

'So, there's another reason I dropped by.'

'What? The free feed wasn't your priority?' Charlotte teased.

'It was a bit of both,' he grinned, before his expression turned serious. 'I've heard a suggestion that someone may have cut your back fence on purpose?'

How had he found out about the fence? And so quickly? Charlotte frowned, but not because she was upset at Mark. What annoyed her more than anything was that word had got out so fast. Every damn person in Settlers Hill was privy to someone else's business, sometimes even before they were aware of it themselves.

'Yes, it's been cut. But I'm not sure when. And I don't know about it being done on purpose. That seems a bit ludicrous don't you think? Besides, the sheep have been appreciating the adjoining paddock for a while by the look of their tracks and their condition.' Why was he suspicious? Something in his voice unsettled Charlotte and she tipped her head to the side. 'What do you suppose may have happened?'

'We've had a few complaints about motorbikes. A couple of local teens have apparently been revving up and down the main street, and Frank has complained. Did you see anything that might suggest they've got into that back paddock of yours?'

'No. It's in no man's land. Even on a still day, we wouldn't be able to pick anything going on over there. But Pete and I are going out there tomorrow morning to fix it. Do you want to take a look?'

'Yeah, that might help. I'll catch you here before you go.'

Even at six-thirty a.m. the sun already held a bite Charlotte didn't appreciate, and she shoved her cap firmly onto her head as Mark drove up beside her ute in front of the homestead. 'Morning, Mark. Want to follow us?' He gave a nod and a thumbs-up.

Pete hopped into the driver's seat of the Sheepwash Creek ute, and Charlotte opened the gates that took them to the road at the back of their station.

When they arrived, the wethers were munching on the hay she had dropped off on the correct side of the fence, filling her with relief. If they stayed there, it would make fixing the fence a lot easier.

Charlotte kept a close eye on Mark's ute as he worked his way through the grass, before he stopped and got out, taking photos with his phone as he went. Every so often he'd pause, staring at the ground, and she found herself following as she tried to understand what he was looking for.

'See anything of interest?' Charlotte wanted to give Mark the freedom to work but her inherent lack of patience was killing her. Was this a case of teens being stupid, or was it something more? During the previous night, her mind had traced back to the events of the day. Seeing John on that road, the contract. Was this all a coincidence?

Charlotte stood a little taller as Mark approached her.

'I'm pretty sure the fence was severed on purpose. You can tell by the clean cuts. As for the bikes, it's hard to tell. The sheep have walked over the tracks so often that I can't detect any tyre marks, other than yours from yesterday. But given what you said about the sheep being in the other paddock for a while, if someone had been on bikes, they could have been and gone long ago.'

Charlotte nodded. 'Is it okay for us to go ahead and repair the fence?'

'Yeah. I'll log a report back at the station.'

'Thanks, Mark. Appreciate it.' Charlotte waved goodbye as their Senior Constable left, before she turned to Pete, who was dragging the fence strainer from the ute.

'Do you think John would do something like this, to get me to sell?' She hated that she had said it out loud, but more and more she couldn't shake the sticky hunch.

'Are you considering selling?' Pete watched her as he blinked, avoiding her question. 'Because I get the feeling you're enjoying hanging around here.' His salt-and-pepper whiskers danced around his cheeky little smile, and Charlotte stared back, unsure what to say. Could she say out loud that her heart was falling back in love with Sheepwash Creek? She'd kept her cards so close to her chest for so long, even she was confused. But the twinkle in Pete's eyes glistened as he waited for her answer.

'Possibly. The longer I stay here, the more I understand what Dad was trying to achieve. And I reckon it was good.' She glanced to the hills, the Grampians towering around them and drawing her in with their beauty. The gumtrees rustled in the warm breeze, and it was a melody to her soul. There were no sights like this back in the city. Could she give it all up?

'Well, then. Seems to me it doesn't matter what Squire John might be up to. All that counts is what you want.' He gave her an intentional grin before he lugged the strainer under his arm and headed for the fence.

CHAPTER 34

'That confounded woman!'

Fraser and his mother both jumped in their seats when the back door slammed and his father stormed into the kitchen.

'Look.' His father slapped dishevelled pieces of paper onto the table.

Fraser gave his mum a bemused gaze, then stared at the scraps of paper. It looked suspiciously like—

A contract? Already? Fraser looked up at his dad in disbelief.

'That bloody woman had the nerve to tear up our settlement offer. Who in their right mind would do that?'

So, his father *had* gone ahead and prepared a contract. Fraser forced his jaw to relax, with little success. He wanted, no, needed to keep things chilled. Riling up his father would only arouse suspicion.

'It could have been an accident,' Fraser said innocently, secretly loving the gutsiness of the woman who was constantly shaping and reshaping all he hoped for in his future, even if she didn't know it. He reached for the tatty pieces, curious to see for himself her handiwork rather than the contract itself.

'Not when you find another part of it swimming in the bloody creek! That girl has gone mad. I'll have to get another one drawn up, and if she even contemplates giving it the same treatment, there'll be words. I'll make her sign it in front of me if I have to. Damned woman.'

The creek? Fraser tipped his head to the side as he watched his father walk back and forth in front of the kitchen sink. No longer did it matter that his father had raced ahead and had the papers prepared without his knowledge. He'd once questioned Charlotte's ability to stand up to his father, back when they were going out. His love for her stepped up another notch.

'Which creek?' There were several scattered over their property and Charlotte's. Had Dad delivered the papers to her in person? Had she read the paperwork and then torn it to shreds to spite his father? He smothered the small smile fighting its way towards his lips.

'That doesn't matter. The point is I'll have to go to our solicitor again, and hand over more money, all thanks to her. When is that woman going to realise she can't run that station?' His tone shifted to frustrated fury, and he snatched up the coffee his mother had set in front of him, spilling it as it reached his mouth. 'Ah, bloody hell.' His dad lurched forward, failing to avoid the scalding beverage as it splashed down the front of him, before he dumped the mug in the sink and marched out through the door again.

Fraser shared an unspoken moment of surprise and a twinge of amusement with his mum before she stood, grabbed a cloth and began cleaning up the mess. Fraser looked back to the paper in his hands, staring at them thoughtfully. If Charlotte had torn up the paperwork—an act he was going to need to applaud her for when the time was right—did that mean she was planning on staying at Sheepwash Creek? This was the news he had been waiting so long to hear. And if it was true, then there was no better time than this instant to ring and confirm how she was going to get down to the wool sale next week.

'Strike a light.' Pete lowered the chocolate chip cookie from his mouth in slow motion—a rare feat in itself—and Charlotte's eyes widened expectantly. Pete was staring at the local paper he'd brought with him, and whatever he'd read had to be on the high scale of shocking.

'Jimmy Strybosch from Amber Estate has had his wool nicked.'

'What? How? Did they steal it from his shearing shed?' Charlotte said.

'Nope.'

'How is that even possible? Peter, talk to us,' her mother urged, but he was glued to the writing in front of him.

Pete harrumphed as he shook his head, clearly unable to believe what he had read before finally putting his biscuit down beside him.

'Well, come on. Tell us.' Mum took a seat next to him as she tried to read over his shoulder. She received a peeved glare as Pete pulled the paper to himself. Charlotte muffled a giggle behind her mug.

'Come on, Pete. What's going on?' Charlotte tried her chances, attempting to look over his shoulder from the other side. He tugged the paper tighter to his chest, glaring at her like she was about to steal a lolly from him. 'Well?' She raised her eyebrows.

'Well—' He shook the paper back out in front of him with a serious flap once both of them angled their bodies towards their seats once more. 'It sounds like someone has been rebranding wool and fobbing it off as their own. But they're not saying much else.' He paused, his voice barely a whisper. 'That's real odd.'

'But they'll find it, right?' Charlotte couldn't believe what she was hearing. 'They have to. Someone can't waltz in and *steal* wool. And besides, an agent trying to sell it for them would recognise that their client had accumulated more wool than warranted their sheep numbers.' Charlotte blinked as

Pete laid the paper down carefully on the table like it might bite him, and sat back, stunned.

'It's beyond me how it's happened.' He finally locked eyes with Charlotte. 'At least yours is all good. It's up for sale next week, right?'

'Yeah,' she said, suddenly feeling as though her nod was less convincing than she wanted it to be.

'Are you and Fraser going down together?' Mum asked, and Charlotte found it hard to ignore her innocent tone. Why did everyone want them back together? Hadn't history made it clear there was no way they could try again? Even she couldn't deny the way her heart responded every time she saw him walking towards her. It wasn't fair the way he looked so good in his snug denim jeans that fitted him just right, with his Akubra resting on his head, his dark eyes hidden beneath the brim, making his smile even more breathtaking.

Before she could answer, her phone buzzed in her pocket. Charlotte pulled it out, ready to answer it like any other call, that was until she saw the caller ID beaming in front of her like an over-bright spotlight. Heat instantaneously rose on her cheeks as she stood, hoping her mum and Pete hadn't caught sight of it.

'I'll take this outside.' Before they could question her—which was a certainty they were going to do as soon as she stepped back inside—she headed for the back door.

'Hey, um, Fraser.' Keep it light and cheery . . . and together. He doesn't know you were thinking about him.

'G'day Char. How's things?' His voice was calm, so opposed to hers, which sounded more like a screechy budgerigar. Could she feel any more stupid?

Give it time.

'Um, good.' Was there nothing intelligent she could muster to say? 'I see some wool has gone missing. Jimmy Strybosch has lost some.' There. That'd do it. She tipped her head to the sky, wishing she could take off with one of the birds flying overhead and stop feeling so drawn to her infuriating neighbour.

'Yeah, I saw that. But Syd's helping the police, so here's hoping they'll find it. Listen, about the sale, would you . . . still like to go down with me?'

Whoa. Had he already mentioned something to Mum? 'Um.'

'Nah, it's okay,' he answered for her. 'The three of you are probably going down together.'

Charlotte picked up the disappointment hovering in his voice even though she was sure he was working to hide it. When he'd first suggested it in the shearing shed, she'd loved the idea. But so much had happened since then. She wasn't sure she could sit in a car with him for that long, fearing it could be what might break down the guard she'd worked so hard to keep taller than Fraser's shed full of her hay.

'No, I'd like to.' As the words floated from her mouth, radiance rose to her cheeks. 'Mum and Pete are heading off to a nursery in Hamilton on the same day, so it'll only be me.' She had to admit the company would be nice, especially if their wool sold as well as Syd predicted.

'Great. Pick you up around nine? We could grab a bite to eat on the way.'

'Okay, sounds good.' Charlotte stared at the phone long after Fraser had hung up, her mind a jumble of what-ifs. What if he wanted more than friendship? What if she wanted to say yes to lunch? What if he tried to suggest buying Sheepwash Creek like his father had? She'd put bets on that he was aware of what his father had done, and he'd no doubt take the opportunity to ask if she'd signed those stinking papers while he had her cornered in the car. But, she reminded herself, he was nothing like his father, and a shimmer of guilt wiggled up her spine. How was she meant to tell him she'd torn the paperwork up? If John found out, he'd throw an absolute hissy fit. Besides, if she changed her mind about selling . . . well, all she had to do was ring and tell him she needed another copy because—Brutus ate it? And that *could* happen, she tried to assure herself, scrunching her nose at the far-fetched notion.

But the more she thought about it, the more the concept of selling teased her thoughts. She loved her job, but every time she'd talked to her work partners, they'd assured her it was ticking along nicely. Did that mean they didn't require her to come back? And more than that, did it mean she was happy about it? What was happening to her?

She was going crazy, that's what. Thanks to agreeing to go with Fraser, she'd have to endure agonising hours with a man who made her question her career and her beliefs, all while he tormented her with his good looks and wonderful charm.

How was she meant to do this? Nothing could ever happen between them again because she wasn't hanging around for the farm to finish her off too.

Except, every night when she closed her eyes, she could feel his lips on hers.

Fraser pulled into their driveway at precisely the time he'd said he would, and Charlotte hated herself for feeling giddy with anticipation. She'd tried to trick herself into believing the excitement was all about her anticipation for the wool sale. If it was that simple, then why was she quivering in her skin?

Awkward silence filled the cabin as Charlotte twiddled her thumbs and stared out the window as the open road raced by them, finding it nearly impossible to push the alluring smell of Fraser's soapy goodness from her mind. They drove past the entrance to his farm, the paddocks deathly parched. A whirly-whirly scooted along the ground with hurried vigour, hungrily sucking up the dusty earth.

'How's Will doing?' she said as brightly as she could, looking at Fraser, who in turn glanced towards her before he spoke, his expression guarded. Was he checking to see what giveaway emotions were plastered to her face? Would he not give her an answer, so as to protect her? That singular thought had her heart pounding. He'd always been the guy who cared without reserve, showing how much someone meant to him by the things he did, or didn't do. Her conscience taunted her. How could she refuse to love a guy like that?

'He's doing okay. Bought himself a tinny for us to go fishing in.' A light chuckle floated through his deep voice. 'Reckons it'll be what turns his luck around.' Fraser's smile was brilliant and forthcoming before he turned his focus back to the road. A pang of disappointment flooded her, as though he'd robbed her of what she cherished more than anything in the world. Him. The one thing she couldn't allow herself to have. If she couldn't find a way to forgive him, she shouldn't start something at all. Playing with hearts was the worst thing in the world to do to someone, no matter how much you wanted love.

'That's good.' She nodded, unsure what to say next. His face turned serious as he watched the road in front of him, and she determined not to let the absence of his smile inject a loneliness inside herself that was growing harder to ignore by the day.

'There's not a day goes by that he's not sorry, Char. There are days it traumatises him so deeply he can't get out of bed. But they're steadily getting fewer and farther between, and he's doing his best to make a future for himself. He's a good guy and a good friend.'

Why was he telling her this? Charlotte turned her attention to the side window, staring at the wrung-out landscape. Did she want to believe Will was managing? That's what they were all doing. None of this was fair to any of them.

The cityscape grew closer as the aircon blew inside the cabin, making the trip bearable. But Charlotte hadn't forgotten what the showroom floor was like—an oversized can of sardines on a stifling hot day. And the closer she got to the high-rise buildings of the city, alive with life and action, the more uneasiness wedged itself inside her. She could hardly believe it had been almost six months since she had returned home. Her brows tightened, both because she was beginning to feel claustrophobic by the buildings towering about them, and even more so because she was starting to realise she hadn't missed the city. Not one bit. Was she earnestly missing the freedom and relief the farm gave to her, the further away from it she found herself? Where had her fear and resentment of the place disappeared to? And when had it happened? How had the time gone by so fast from when she'd first arrived to deal with its woes and concerns? And now she couldn't wait to get back to it? What was happening to her?

In all her ponderings, she'd failed to pay attention to where they were as Fraser pulled into a parallel park across from the St Kilda Beach. She wriggled a little taller, looking about her as Fraser's gorgeous smile lit up his whole face, like always.

'What are we doing here?' Curiosity filled her.

'You said you missed the beach, so would you like to have lunch at one of the restaurants?' He shrugged. 'Only if you want to. We can go somewhere else if you'd prefer.'

'No. No, I love it.' With renewed enthusiasm she was more familiar with in the city, she pointed ahead of them.

'See that bend in the road down there. There's a great fish and chip shop.' She turned to him with a smile, her eyes shining. 'We could get lunch and go sit on the beach. The seagulls will be happy to see us.'

Fraser's lips widened in a smile as he watched her, and for a fleeting moment, she watched a flicker of apprehension wash over his face. Brushing it aside, Charlotte stepped to the curb and they headed for the shop.

Fraser carried the fish and chips and they walked to the beach, reaching the sand where Charlotte promptly kicked off her thongs, wrapping her toes in its warmth. 'Here, let me take that.' She took the food from Fraser. 'Take your shoes off. The sand feels incredible.'

'Nah, I'm good, thanks.' The smile he shared with her seemed a little uneasy as he stepped onto the sand.

'Hang on a minute.' Pausing, she reached for his arm, instantly regretting it. A zing of electricity flowed through her fingers, hitting her in the chest with a thwack. But she couldn't leave this alone. 'You don't like the beach?' Who didn't? She stared at him, gobsmacked.

'There's better places to hang out, that's all.' He scrunched his nose against the smell of drying seaweed.

'Are you for real?' She gave him an I-don't-believe-you teasing thump on the upper arm. 'Why are we here then?'

'For you.' Those two words hit her with full force.

Fraser shrugged with all the discernment of a guy who wholeheartedly understood the woman he was with, giving her a smile that held warmth and sunshine and happiness, and she'd gone and thumped him? Her insides were turning to mush and she froze, unable to stop staring. Could this guy get any better? What was stopping her for goodness' sake?

But the time for kidding herself was done. If she allowed her heart to feel the way it wanted to, eventually John would get his scheming fingers on her land. No matter where her emotions were trying to drag her, staying focused on keeping Sheepwash Creek out of John Pierce's hands was a non-negotiable.

CHAPTER 35

What was his father doing at the sale? Fraser removed his Akubra, then ran a hand through his hair as he walked past his father's ute in the carpark. Wasn't he meant to be at a ram sale in Glenthompson?

He slowed as the sliding door scooted open, the twinkle of Christmas tinsel catching his eye thanks to the air-conditioning's teasing. He motioned for Charlotte to go ahead, and she smelt of spring roses and fresh air, her fragrance catapulting his heart with sudden energy. It had almost driven him crazy the entire trip, and he still had to drive home with her. What was a guy supposed to do? The aroma had him wanting to lean in and kiss her before they'd left her house. Then he'd wanted to take her face in his hand and kiss her at the beach, long and slow, despite the cringeworthy sand. And here, even if he found the opportunity, he was out of luck. Syd was walking directly towards them.

'G'day Fraser.' He reached out, shaking Fraser's hand before leaning in to give Charlotte a welcoming peck on the cheek. 'Great to see you both. I've got a few spare minutes before the sale starts. Come and take a look at the wool. If the prices are anything like I'm expecting, things are looking good.' He beckoned them to follow with a tip of his head as he moved towards the door.

They followed him up the stairs to the showroom floor, Fraser grabbing a copy of the sale booklet before they made their way to the sample boxes holding Trentham Park's wool first.

'It all looks stylish and bright, Fraser,' Syd said happily.

'Thanks. Can we take a look at *our* wool too?' Fraser didn't try to hide his enthusiasm as he caught Charlotte's almost surprised look. It might have happened by accident that they'd pooled their wool together, but he was far from sorry. Being with her, here, sharing this day, it was better than anything he could have hoped for.

Syd glanced at his watch. 'I'm real sorry but the sale's about to start. I need to head back into the auction room.'

'That's okay, Syd,' Charlotte offered, fighting to disguise her disappointed smile.

Fraser's heart clenched, and he leaned in close, the move almost unhinging him and he took a swift step back. Was this torture ever going to stop? And when was he going to give up inflicting it on himself? 'We'll take a look after the sale, okay?' He gave her a reassuring nod, fully intending on making good on his suggestion. If she could see what they could do together, then she might consider trying it again.

She gave a little nod, and they headed to the auction room to take a seat in the viewing area behind the glass.

Fraser looked about him, absently scanning for acquaintances or clients who bought rams from them, who were selling on the same day. It often turned out to be a day of catchups. It was also an indicator of times to come. If prices were holding near what they were last week, he might be able to get his father to accept they needed a new tractor. And not Charlotte's. He'd had about enough of theirs, which had also sprung an oil leak, yet another job for him to deal with when he got home.

Not recognising anyone, his soft gaze settled on the one woman who might as well have been the only person in the room, taking in her soft cheek line as she concentrated on the auctioneer. Her sun-bleached hair flowed over her shoulders in soft waves, and the look on her face held subdued excitement. A longing for what they used to have filled his nerve endings, his blood, and his mind so fully, he had to turn away to distract himself and to resist the undeniable urge to slip her hand into his, in front of everyone. And in that moment, he wouldn't even care if his father saw their hands linked. He glanced towards the exit, surprised he wasn't in the viewing room already.

And that's when he saw his dad talking in angry hushed tones to Syd, their bodies angled towards one another.

He managed to make out what they were discussing by his father's pointed finger and not-so-hushed words.

'What's *she* doing here, Syd? You said there'd be no other competition today.'

'No,' Syd said defensively. 'You've got it all wrong. She's only selling the wool from your box-up with her sheep.'

Fraser sharpened his attention on his father, who was leaning away from a rather shaken Syd, the perspiration on his forehead clear. Why was his father worried Charlotte was here? She had as much right as anyone else.

His father gave Syd a curt nod before taking a seat nearby, his focus solely on the auctioneers and the buyers. Trentham Park's wool came up, selling so well it caused ripples of whispered chatter amongst the onlookers. And while Fraser was more than happy with the result, he was more interested in what his and Charlotte's wool was going to make. He wanted—no needed—to see her happy with the prices. It might be the one thing that could sway her to come home. For good.

He'd loved the way she had stepped up since she was back, making the hard decisions her father had always done. His heart swelled. She had never been one to back down. No woman living in Settlers Hill might have taken on the family station before, but she sure as hell could, if that's what she wanted.

And then he'd have to hope she decided he was the man she wanted.

Fraser watched on with irritation as his father stood, beaming as he moved straight to Syd, taking the wool rep's hand in his and shaking it fervently as they stepped from the room. His Dad's voice was loud and celebratory. Sure, the prices they'd received were good. But that good?

In another fast frenzy, Trentham Park's wool from their boxed-up ewes sold, followed by Sheepwash Creek's, both for elevated prices per kilogram that were higher than last week's sale prices. Fraser's fingers taped against his lips. Something wasn't right.

Standing, Fraser turned his attention to Charlotte, pleased they would be able to celebrate their joint success. But instead of the delight he was expecting to see on her face, all he saw was solemn concern. And dare he say it, panic.

'Hey, what's up? The wool did great.' Fraser couldn't stop his hand reaching for her shoulder as he bent down to her, promptly feeling the need to, what was it, console, comfort, maybe . . . commiserate with her? But over what? It didn't make any sense.

'Fraser—' She looked straight at him with eyes wide and confused. 'Where's *my* wool?' Her pleading face had him taking his seat again, and he angled his body towards her.

'You didn't have any more.' In a calculated risk, he took her hands, squeezing them before his thumbs glided over her skin, so soft and warm to his touch. 'There's no more of your wool in the sale booklet. I would have seen it.'

'But . . . that can't be right.' She searched his face as though she was begging him to take back what he'd said. Her voice grew weak.

'I booked it in to coincide with our wool. Today.' Her voice was shaky. 'It's Dad's best lines he'd been holding onto. There were supposed to be forty-five bales.' Her voice faded, exasperated, confused.

'Char, Syd told us your Dad had sold them all. Remember?' He recalled the day they'd all been in her mother's kitchen, their bellies stuffed and their moods uplifted, before they'd headed back to the shed for the third shearing run.

How could I forget? Charlotte rubbed her forehead as she struggled to comprehend what Fraser had said. Why hadn't she checked her father's records like she'd told herself she would? She rubbed at her forehead before suddenly sitting up.

'Cheryl!' Charlotte stood, staring hopefully at Fraser. 'I booked the wool in with Cheryl. Is she here today?' Without waiting for a reply, she reluctantly released his comforting grip before turning towards the offices near the front door.

'Char, wait.'

But Fraser's voice disappeared like her vanishing wool as she pushed through the crowd, slipping past John, and giving Syd a worried glance before she continued. His alarmed look didn't matter. She needed to find out if her wool had been excluded from the sale— Or . . . if it was here at all.

Fraser caught up to her as she halted in front of Cheryl's desk, relieved the woman was there.

'Hey, Cheryl.' Forcing a smile, she pushed through her shortness of breath. 'Would you mind checking if Dad's best lines were meant to be up for sale today? Or did I book it in on a different date?' Charlotte could feel the crease lines pinching her brow, and she blinked to refocus, taking a slow breath to compose her apprehension.

She turned to Fraser as Cheryl tapped at the computer keys. 'There has to be a perfectly reasonable explanation.' Before she allowed herself to be drawn into the darkening chocolate brown eyes currently regarding her, she turned back to Cheryl.

'Um—' Cheryl appeared baffled as she searched the computer screen, before looking up at them.

'What is it?' Charlotte leaned forward, her hands gripping the over-bench as she peered at Cheryl, begging her to tell them.

'I can't explain this, Charlotte, but . . . your wool isn't here.' The disbelief in the woman's voice was clear. 'There is a note attached to your file, stating it left your farm in May this year.'

Charlotte gave a hopeful nod, her heart pounding. That had to be a good thing. So where was her wool?

'Char, who transported your wool for you?' Fraser interjected, his expression focused and serious.

A shimmer of fear trickled over her. 'Adam or Charlie Saunders.'

'Right, get on the phone to them. I'll stay with Cheryl, in case we find something.'

Baffled, Charlotte walked to the front door of the building. As it slid open, the oppressive heat hit her with a sharp slap. Snatching out her phone, she dialled Charlie's number. It went straight to voicemail. She tipped her head to the glaring sky as she waited out his voice message.

Hey Charlie, it's Charlotte Redding here. I wanted to check some details with you about a delivery of wool you did for Dad. Could you ring me back as soon as possible please? It's urgent. Thanks.

Charlotte shook the phone in frustration, begging it to ring as the roar of a car left the driveway of the wool store in a rush. She glanced around the car park once more, an uneasy feeling nibbling at every nerve in her body as another vehicle took off with speed, their engines rumbling into the distance.

Jogging back inside, the relief of the cooler air on her skin was palpable as she swung into Cheryl's office.

'I don't understand it, Fraser. When I booked Charlotte's wool in, the details of all the bales available for sale were right here.' She pointed a finger at her screen. 'Now I can't trace them. And there's a note attached to the account saying, "Returned at seller's request." The log date shows the 11th of December. That's today's date. And there's no consignment note listed, but that's not unusual. We can only assume Adam delivered the clip regardless.'

'I didn't make any such request. Could Adam have stolen it and we haven't realised until now,' Charlotte said, her head lifting in alarming concern. 'But it's been months. It could be anywhere! I wouldn't have found out if I hadn't tried to put it up for sale.' Her hollow gaze landed on the wall behind Cheryl.

'Anything from Charlie?' Fraser's hopeful voice drew her back.

'He's not answering,' she said, desperation lacing her voice. Did Charlie or Adam have something to do with it? She looked down at her phone again, double-checking the volume.

'This doesn't sound like either of them. But until we find out more, let's not assume anything, okay?' Fraser levelled an even look at her.

She held his warm eyes with her own, searching them as she fought off the insistent urge to take the one step keeping them apart and wrap her arms around his waist, holding on for dear life, as if she was being yanked by some universal drawstring, summoning her to take the final step of faith . . . and see for herself what destiny had in store for them on the other side.

But instead, she blinked. Long and slow, staring dumbfounded at her handsome neighbour and the imminent demise of Sheepwash Creek falling apart right in front of her.

Charlotte closed her eyes, releasing an audible breath of air. This couldn't be happening, not to her. So why was it? Was this the farm's sneaky hand dealing its next big blow to destroy her like it promised, readying itself to put her into her own grave?

'Cheryl, is there anything else we can do to track what has happened to Charlotte's wool?' Fraser's rounded voice silenced her crazy thoughts, and with exhausted eyes, she looked to each of them.

Cheryl looked up at him, hopeful. Charlotte stiffened.

'If I can get clearance, we'll be able to go back and check for any deleted records which might tell us something.'

Cheryl directed what was meant to be an encouraging nod at Charlotte. But it did little to dissipate the sense of doom pressing down on her like a ten-tonne tractor. She needed that wool to sell well, and while she hadn't said it to herself earlier, had made a pact that was dawning on her. Selling that wool had become an unspoken sign that things at Sheepwash Creek were going to turn around. It was also the indicator she had been waiting for, as if it was key to giving her the permission she needed to decide to keep Sheepwash Creek for good. Her father had believed in her all those years ago. She had hoped selling his final best clip would be a way she could believe in her own ability to take on a sheep station.

And succeed.

How wrong she'd been.

'Syd Jones is Charlotte's wool rep,' Fraser said. 'Maybe he could shed some light on things?'

'That's perfect,' Cheryl said. 'If I can find Syd, he'll be able to give me clearance.'

'Thanks so much, Cheryl. I appreciate you doing this for me,' Charlotte said, hoping she'd managed to hide the waver in her words. 'Can you inform me as soon as you hear anything, please?' This time she didn't try to hide the desperation in her voice.

Cheryl's gaze softened in an encouraging smile. 'I certainly will, Charlotte. I want to see things work out for you.'

CHAPTER 36

The trees zipped past in a hazy blur as they travelled home, her mind rattling with loud thoughts and several obtrusive misgivings.

Was it a genuine mistake? Could her wool be sitting in the storehouse somewhere, unintentionally missed? Had the computer glitched at some stage, zapping her details? That happened to her more often than she wanted to admit and was why her business always backed up their client details. But what didn't make sense was that her file said the bales were there two days ago. Two. Days. Ago. How could they be *gone*?

But if it wasn't a mistake, who could, or should she say *would have* removed her wool? She unknowingly pressed a hand to her stomach, the pitted feeling climbing up to reach the back of her throat. The only person she could lay immediate blame on was Adam or Charlie. But that idea was as farfetched as her climbing Mt Everest. And out of all this, was it possible the wool could turn up at some stage?

She had to hope so. That hope was all she had.

Charlotte rested her head on the headrest, pressing fingers to her forehead and rubbing against a threatening headache as images of her dwindling bank balance eroded her mind. She had to find out what had happened to her wool or she'd be planning the clearance sale of the decade next week! And the notion that every man and his dog would likely turn up did little to appease her angst. This wasn't how Dad would have wanted it—any of it. She closed her eyes, desperate to push away every mind-numbing thought.

Letting her head roll on the headrest, she turned towards Fraser, prying one eye open to find him staring straight back at her, his mouth lifting in a slow, goofy kind of reassuring smile that always had a way of making her feel like she was the only one he shared it with. Did the guy ever miss a beat? But it was wasted on her in that moment. All she could think about was how she was about to let Sheepwash Creek down.

'Do you think my wool has anything to do with the missing bales they've been talking about in the news?' She was glad of the diversion from his searching eyes as he fixed his thoughtful gaze away from her.

'I hope not. The chances of wool going missing in the wool store is unlikely.'

'So, it's not possible?'

'Nope.'

But his answer did little to convince her. And why hadn't they been able to find Syd after the sale?

Charlotte let her eyes slide back towards Fraser, his tanned hand resting on his knee as his other gripped the top of the steering wheel of the Land Cruiser. In the time she'd been gone, he'd developed muscles so taut and strong it managed to take her by surprise. Her heart tightened, and for a brief moment, she wished things could be different. But that was impossible.

Charlotte turned to the side window, her wishful, happily-ever-after slipping away as fast as the paddocks rushing by. He had a lifetime ahead of him, with a farm, and the support of a father whenever he needed it. What did she have? A farm that had sucked her dry and threw dirt in her face at every turn.

And what could she offer Fraser, if by some ridiculous chance they did find themselves getting back together?

Nothing. To risk loving him meant his life would be in danger. It had happened to two of her family members who'd tried to run this disloyal station, so the curse would only carry on with her if she dared to do it. No, it was safer for him that she kept her distance. That way he could find someone who loved him and give him everything he deserved. If she left, the jinx would end with her. And she wouldn't have to worry about being left with a broken heart.

Charlotte stood back, watching the comings and goings of the main street in Settlers Hill as Pete helped Gus transfer the bags of chaff he had brought from Ballarat into the back of the Sheepwash Creek ute.

'Reckon I might head down to Janice's and grab us some lunch. Feel like anything in particular?' She eyed them both.

'I'll have a latté, thanks,' Gus said with a grin. 'And one of Janice's vanilla slices if there's any left.'

'It's release day?' Pete suddenly stood tall, his eyes boggling at Gus. 'Count me in.' His tickled-pink smirk filled his whiskery cheeks as he spun to face Charlotte.

'That doesn't sound like much of a decent lunch to me,' she said, fighting the urge to choose between the sweet treat or one of the homemade chicken pies Janice was also famous for.

'What are you talking about? It's the best lunch ever,' Gus said, nodding at Pete before offering her a cheeky flick of his eyebrows and continuing to load her supplies.

The Small Store was buzzing with activity as she opened the door, breathing in the delicious aromas of Janice's cooking, immediately understanding where the men's interest came from. But as her stomach grumbled, her face paled. Nancy Stone and Elsie Kent were heading directly for her, their Sunday best hats threatening to droop around their ears.

'Charlotte, how are you today?' they chimed all too sweetly in unison.

'Good, thanks.' Charlotte looked from one woman to the other with a bemused stare, finally remembering to pull out some semblance of a smile as she waited for them to impart on her their premeditated opinions she wasn't ready to hear.

'You've lost some wool. My, my. That's not good, is it?' Their eyes danced with a hint of excitement, instantly gutting Charlotte's enthusiasm for a naughty vanilla slice lunch. Instead, her stomach plummeted in a wave of nausea with such assuredness she glanced at the door in case she needed to rush for it.

'It's only missing. But I'm sure it'll be found,' —some way or another, she breathed, resisting her urge to look away from their conversation and their gleeful faces. So instead, she tugged her smile higher, refusing to give away the level of apprehension that filled her with dread. It *was* going to be found, wasn't it?

'You do know what they say around here.' Nancy spoke with an all-knowing, pompous tone as she waved her hand like a queen. 'Women are best left to the cooking, my dear. My Harold, bless him, depended on me to have a meal on the table every night, and I did.' She leaned in towards Charlotte, pointing a crooked finger at her nose, causing Charlotte to dip her head back. 'Settlers Hill has been grown by the hardworking hands of the men. Don't try and be one of those *modern* women attempting to outdo them. It wouldn't be fitting for you.' The serene smile she gave Charlotte had her blood pressure accelerating. Would these women ever stop deciding what she should be doing, and more so, where her faults lay? Should she allow herself to hope?

'Well, in the house I've grown up in, women are as capable as the men,' Charlotte retorted, her frustration with the women fuelling her words. And if these women dared call her *dear* one more time she wasn't going to be responsible for her actions. Elsie opened her mouth to offer her own two bobs' worth, but Charlotte interjected, reining in her voice to placate the town gossips. 'And I'm sure you are aware my father was going to run Sheepwash Creek as a family venture with James and me.'

Both Nancy's and Elsie's stunned faces gave Charlotte the satisfaction she was counting on. Her words were hitting home, even if it took being forthcoming to do it. 'So that's what I'm going to continue to do.' She gave them a pleasant smile, their speechless faces the last thing she saw as she side-stepped them to reach the counter.

'I do believe that's the first time I've ever seen that pair without another thing to say,' Janice whispered, giggling with delight.

'Let's hope they can keep their wayward tongues in their heads long enough to get them to their cars and go home before the whole district hears I'm the Settlers Hill fool of the century.'

Janice nodded her understanding with a grin. 'Now, what would you like? I have a few extra pieces of vanilla slice stashed under the counter.' Her eyebrows rose and Charlotte grinned.

Charlotte headed towards the door, balancing the box of vanilla slices—minus her pie—and the lattés, ready to push the door open with her hip as her mind reeled. How exactly had she been persuaded to indulge in such a sweet treat for her lunch so easily? She grinned at herself, her joy falling away sharply as she looked up.

Will had grabbed the door and was holding it open for her.

'Hey . . . Will. Thanks.' Her words trailed to a whisper as he offered a hesitant smile, and she hoped he missed the uneasiness that had brushed over her face. She stepped through the opening, at odds with herself because despite the pain they'd both been through, it was good to see him. Had enough years gone by that she'd started to accept things for what they were, not what they might have been? He'd done it so hard, and she hadn't made it any easier with her presence back in town, or her obviously less-than-ecstatic responses towards him every time she saw him. But if she was going to stay—for who knows how long—she'd need to work towards making amends for any hurt she may have caused him, consciously or unconsciously.

And on the spot, she chose to forgive him, not because she had to, but because she wanted to. And in that moment, shards of the cumbersome weight she'd been hauling around for way too long fell away.

As she approached her ute, Pete as good as lunged at her, grabbing his coffee and taking a long sip before he wrangled the box from her hands. Perching himself on top of one of the chaff bags, his fingers wriggled in anticipation as he eyed the box resting on his lap. His tongue whipped around his lips as he peeled the paper bag away, eyeing the district favourite for the biggest slice before snatching it up and biting into it like he hadn't eaten in a week.

'Hang on a minute,' Gus piped up, nudging Pete to get his attention. 'What's this?' Gus aimed a you're-in-trouble smirk towards Charlotte before making a show of counting the slices. 'Pete, look who's having vanilla slice for *lunch*.' He erupted with teasing laughter.

Charlotte took her piece like she didn't know what he was going on about, taking a bite and chewing slowly as she soaked in the creamy sensation. 'Hey, now that I've had it, I'm not going to knock it, okay?' Hiding her shameless grin behind the slice, she took another bite, a little abashed to admit out loud how much better it tasted than a pie right there and then.

The roar of a heavy vehicle sounded down the road, and all three turned as they munched quietly, watching as a heavy bulldozer bounced past in an awkward rhythm. Steve Haymes was behind the wheel, offering not so much as a wave in their direction, his focus solely on the road.

'That'd be bloody right,' Pete said as he washed down his last mouthful with his latté. 'That man is too rude to acknowledge himself.'

'Why is he driving one of those?' Charlotte wiped the corners of her mouth as the machine disappeared from view.

'That's anyone's guess. Probably had a cow he had to bury.'

And not a moment after they'd lost sight of Steve, John rolled by, lifting a disinterested finger of recognition in their direction before he pulled up in front of The Small Store, waltzing inside like he owned the town.

'Hey, Pete. What's your take on the old tales of gold around here?' Charlotte asked, recalling what her Dad had said about her grandparents taking claim of their land . . . and John surprising her when he turned up near her back paddock.

'Only that it's not there. A lot of miners arrived early on, like your great- grandparents, digging for the wretched stuff. All gold did 'round these parts was cause trouble.' He shook his head, and Charlotte couldn't help but think he was holding back on something.

Mark was the last one to arrive for Friday night drinks.

'G'day, mate. You look tired. Everything okay?' Fraser studied his friend as he slid a glass over to him.

'Just the usual,' Mark said, and Ross, Fraser, and Big Nev nodded quietly, taking a long draw of their beers and coke. It wasn't like Mark to let work get to him, ever the jovial guy everyone loved for his loyalty and trustworthiness. Whatever had him uptight must be serious. But Fraser laid odds his mate would deal with it and move on.

Their light chatter continued until The Tavern door was pushed open, and Ross gave Fraser a nudge with a flick of his eyebrows.

Charlotte looked left, then right, as though she were searching for someone. Her soft hair hung in a ponytail, and her cheeks were flushed from the heat lingering from the warm day. He blinked, hoping it would break the trance she was drawing him into. He didn't need the boys egging him on and causing him to sweat. His heart was doing enough of that for him already as their eyes locked.

'Big Nev, boys, how are you?' his father said loudly, arriving from somewhere behind them and striding up to the table. Instantly, it broke Fraser's interlude with Charlotte as his father stepped between their line of sight, offering the publican a friendly slap on the shoulder with a nod.

Fraser stared at his drink, hoping he hadn't hurt Charlotte with his apparent look of disinterest as he used the opportunity to look away, and Dad proceeded to grab a stool and pull it up. It was the last thing he wanted to do to her, but the only safe thing he could, given the array of emotions racing through him.

The mood at the table took an abrupt turn, the conversation stilted rather than relaxed as everyone except his father picked up on the reason why. His father often ignored the social cues around him, more interested in his own agenda. Some things would never change.

'So, is Charlotte going to sell to you?' Big Nev was never afraid to broach the tough subjects, and Fraser didn't mind the publican's forwardness. What he hated was his father's dog-eat-dog approach when it came to getting what he wanted.

Fraser's gaze shot to Charlotte who was now sitting at the table nearby, sipping a glass of water before checking her watch, reassuring him she hadn't overheard. Who was she waiting for? A niggle of unease wriggled over him.

'I'd like it if she did, Nev. But she's a big girl. Might even decide she could run the station on her own. And good luck to her if she does.' Dad gave an assured nod, raising his glass like he was toasting the idea before slugging down his last mouthful of beer.

Was his father going stark-raving mad? Or was he?

'Since when did you decide she could manage the farm, let alone make something of it, Dad?' He tried to keep his voice low, blindsided by his father's new approach, or was it a tactical ploy put on for the benefit of the others—he wished he knew—that it slipped his father's mind Charlotte might overhear their conversation.

And then Fraser saw it, pure shock mixed with sadness, glued to Charlotte's face as he watched her. Aghast, he shook his head, his mouth dry as he caught her gaze and desperately tried to convey to her the meaning behind his words through his expression, all while working not to attract the attention of the others. No doubt she'd think he was writing her off as a lost cause too. His expression begged her to understand. But it was to no avail. She broke his gaze, looking down at the table before standing quietly, leaving the pub and him behind.

What should he do? He wet his lips as he struggled to think. He couldn't try and explain what he'd really meant. If he did that, then she'd learn his father was lying, undoubtedly so she could overhear it. He could also never tell her that his dad was attempting to look like the good guy, under the guise that he was "helping them", all while he believed she was useless. He ran a hand through his hair as he stared in front of him.

And if he ran after her, his father would assume he was trying to protect her, not encourage her to sell to them. How had the pendulum swung so far from what he truly wanted?

He sank deep into the chair, staring at the drips of condensation trailing down the sides of his glass. Maybe he was never meant to get what he'd wanted all along. Had he been hoping for too much, like it was some untouchable goal he'd never had a right to? You could only go so far before you shot yourself in the foot for good, and that's where he was heading . . . if he hadn't done it already.

With their last round of drinks completed, they all stood, his father having left after his second glass because he'd wanted to get to Ballarat and back before dark.

'Listen, mate,' Mark said, nudging Fraser's arm, encouraging him to hang back while Big Nev moved behind the bar and Ross waved goodnight. 'I need to tell you something.'

If Fraser had thought Mark looked solemn when he'd arrived, he currently looked downright miserable, even after their three light beers.

'What's up?' He frowned.

Mark looked about him, then to the floor beside him, before he took a slow breath, as though he was mustering the courage to tell Fraser something he wouldn't want to hear.

'I have a lead on Charlotte's missing wool. Only problem is, Syd's mixed up in it.'

'What?' The word came out louder than he had intended, his eyes boggling, searching his friend with intense focus as he tried to understand.

'But, how?' Syd was one of the most trustworthy men he knew. Mark had to have his wires crossed. He'd vouch for Syd till the cows came home.

'I've been working down at the wool stores since March, after the first lot of wool went missing. It's been hard to track down, but it looks like Syd might be bypassing protocol, slipping bales off to the side as they arrive at the wool store,' his tone hushed, 'from *selected* clients.'

'You've got proof?' Fraser drew his head back.

'I've been undercover as one of the workers. He doesn't know me well enough to recognise me. He paid me off in cash to do it.'

'Oh, wow.' Fraser was momentarily lost for words. 'What's going to happen? Have you arrested him?'

'Not yet.' Mark glanced around the room, making sure no one was listening in on their conversation. He leaned over the table a little closer. 'I need to put a few things in place first, and I might need your help to do it.'

Now this wasn't only about Charlotte. It was about him and his wool too.

'Anything. Tell me what you want me to do.'

CHAPTER 37

The early summer sky was heavy with thick, threatening clouds, the humidity hanging in the air so uncharacteristic for the Western District. Charlotte went about her chores, feeding Boots and giving him an affectionate pat before she moved towards the shearing shed, putting her ear to the door and listening before she entered.

With no sound of runaway hooves, she pushed the sliding door ajar, peeking through the small opening as her eyes adjusted to the darkness inside. Much to her relieved surprise, Brutus was standing at the front of his pen, pawing the grating and demanding his breakfast.

'Okay, okay,' Charlotte said, walking in and dismissing his antics with a turn of her back, heading to the feed trough to fill two buckets. She topped up the feeders at the front of the pens, avoiding Brutus' horns as he enthusiastically dived his nose into the tasty mix.

Charlotte stood back, pleased with the pen of rams she was priming for the joining of her stud ewes. They were looking smart, and she allowed herself the exhilaration of excitement about what their progeny may produce, starting next June, purely for the new owners, she reminded herself.

But as she grabbed a big armful of lucerne, Fraser's words resurfaced despite having pushed them aside during her night of interrupted sleep. She had gone to The Tavern to catch Big Nev, hoping to ask him if he'd heard anything on the low-down about Charlie or Adam being involved in anything shifty. But when she had arrived, he was already sitting with Ross, Mark, and . . . Fraser. She straightened, lifting her chin at the memory of her feet freezing to the spot when she'd locked eyes with him. And then he'd looked away . . . like seeing her carried some distinct distaste in his mouth he couldn't stomach. Had he never believed she could run the station on her own? Was that why he was happy to see her sell up and leave? Was he only being nice to her, when all along, he had an agenda—to drive her away and take Sheepwash Creek for himself? What a fool she'd been. Fraser's intentions had never been honourable. He wanted her land as much as his father did.

But what about the surprise statement of the decade? Did John *approve* of her giving it a shot? At what stage had he turned into her ally, with Fraser becoming her nemesis? She couldn't trust either of them.

She tossed the lucerne into the pens with more gusto than she intended, and some of the rams shied from it before turning back.

Well, I'll show them. 'Once a Pierce, always a bloody Pierce,' she said to Brutus before turning to leave the shed. She was squashing away any last skerrick of attraction for Fraser, fed up that she had let her heart betray her all over again.

Charlotte's phone buzzed in her back pocket and she tugged it out angrily. *If it's Fraser, I'm not answering.* But as she looked at the caller's name, her eyes narrowed.

'G'day, John,' Charlotte said, her voice laced with cautious apprehension. She hoped his ears were burning.

'Ah, Charlotte. Thanks for picking up.' His tone was pleasant. Too pleasant? She couldn't decide.

You're bloody lucky I have was what she wanted to say, but she held her tongue, waiting for him to continue. She leaned her back against the wall of the shed, crossing one leg over the other, fighting off the strong urge to tune out to his words.

'I have a small matter to clear up with you, and since word is you're heading back to the city, I'm sure it won't be any skin off your nose.' That brought on a raised eyebrow as he gave a light chuckle, like what he was about to say held no real significance. Charlotte's hackles rose. She might not be her father or James, with their farming know-how and expertise. But she loved this property enough to fight for *their* legacy, and not to let the farm win. Whichever way she looked at it, it ended with her. Her silence gave him the cue to continue.

'Those ewes and lambs you had here, the ones that got boxed up with ours when your sheep pushed the fence over. They grazed on our property for a good month.'

Whoa, hang on a minute. Her sheep pushed over the fence? She edged herself away from the shed wall, her blood beginning to simmer. The part about her sheep being mixed up was no secret. But had Fraser not told his father it was his sheep that had flattened the fence? The hairs on her forearms bristled as she opened her mouth, but she was abruptly cut off.

'I'm sending you an agistment bill. Two hundred ewes and lambs eat a lot. I know you'll understand what I'm asking is only fair. It'll be in your mailbox this afternoon. I'd appreciate it if you could fix it up ASAP.'

His affable voice fell quiet, leaving her breathless and mute. Could this man get any more assuming, infuriating or self-righteous? No matter his feelings for the man, her father would never have done such a thing to their neighbour given the same situation. Was he playing her for the fool because she was . . . female?

'Oh, and those ewes from that mob that have fallen pregnant to Brutus, well—' he added a soft chuckle as though it would appease her, 'it'd be no good me giving them to you. After all, they are our ewes rearing them. There's not that many looking in lamb, maybe twenty. It's royally botched up our breeding program, but we'll work around it. That's what neighbours do, right? Thanks for understanding.'

Charlotte gawped as John ended the call, leaving her reeling. She dragged her feet to the steps of the verandah, turned, and sat heavily, staring at the gravel like it wasn't even there. This was the paddock *their* sheep had been eating down after she had removed them off the road. How had John Pierce claimed she owed him money, *and* taken ownership of those lambs, especially when Brutus should never have been able to get into the paddock that day to begin with?

So . . . *how* exactly had he?

Charlotte buried her head in her hands, her mind as tangled as her messy bun. He could ask for agistment, but to demand it? She'd bet her last dollar he'd never do that to his bestie, Steve Haymes.

CHAPTER 38

Charlotte woke from yet another restless night's sleep, fuming. John Pierce was an outright jerk. Was equality in their modern world a concept that hadn't reached him yet? Well, she would be more than happy to show him up for who he truly was.

And thrown into the mix was the annoying realisation she had finally gone to sleep thinking of Fraser, then woken up thinking about him, for all the reasons she wasn't happy to admit out loud. At every turn, he was driving her further away, and yet her mind clung to the hope that his actions weren't of his own doing. But she couldn't ignore his words at the pub. She would do well to keep them close to the forefront of her mind.

Throwing the covers aside, she swung her legs out of bed, her toes curling into the rug beneath her feet as she stood up. Regardless of how hopeless things appeared, she needed to get on with what had to be done.

She tied her tangled hair in another bun of sorts, hoping it wasn't a precursor for the day, and headed for the kettle. If nothing else could help her with everything that was going wrong, at least she'd feel better with a coffee inside her.

Her mum plodded in behind her, flexing her fingers like her night had been long too.

'Sit down, Mum. I'll make the coffee.' Charlotte sent her a sympathetic smile.

Mum took a seat, and Charlotte studied her mother's face. What was going on behind it? Was Mum carrying similar concerns about the farm, their future? Had she not given enough consideration to what her mum wanted? Charlotte hadn't asked for her thoughts on the farm's future in months, not since her mother had told her she would be happy with whatever Charlotte chose. Had she neglected picking up on any signs suggesting her mother was revisiting her thoughts?

Charlotte put the steaming coffees down on the table, her face a mess of concern. 'Mum, is everything okay?'

Mum tilted her head to the side, looking Charlotte in the eye. 'It is, sweetheart.' She smiled before taking a tentative sip, the liquid visibly stinging her lips.

'Mum, what's wrong?' Charlotte reached out, putting a hand to her mother's forearm and squeezing. It took a moment before her Mum focused on her.

'I'm concerned about you, sweetheart. You're carrying the difficulties of this farm everywhere you go, and I worry that the weight is so heavy, you'll collapse.'

How did her mother pick up on those things? Hadn't she guarded her concerns, making many of the decisions on her own to ease her mother's grief and shield her from worry?

'I'll be fine.' Charlotte brushed the comment aside with a wave of her hand, despite her throat clenching tight. It wasn't anything she couldn't handle.

This time it was her mother's turn to put a hand on her daughter's arm. 'Listen, you're trying so hard. But you need to adopt a healthy dose of remorse. Otherwise it'll be the death of you.'

What? Hang on. Wasn't her mother supposed to launch into something about keeping the farm or selling it? Charlotte sat back in her seat, staring dumbfoundedly at her mother.

'I don't have anything to be remorseful over. If anyone is supposed to show that, it's Fraser.' She crossed her arms, glaring at the steam circling above her coffee like a genie might appear at any moment. And she wouldn't mind if it did, especially if it told her what she was meant to do.

'You can't fool me, kid,' Mum said lovingly. 'I've known you too long. You're carrying too much bitterness over the death of your brother. Be truthful with yourself, honey. It's increased tenfold since your father—' She paused, brushing aside a crumb on the table, 'Passed away.' Her voice turned whisper soft. 'And if you let it stay, it'll make it impossible for you to run this place with the heart he had.' Her words held a deep sadness. But they also resounded with a calming restfulness that caused Charlotte's despairing eyes to cloud over. How could her mother live without the resentment that filled her continually?

'It wasn't what anyone wanted, but we can't change any of it. You need to let go of your anger at the farm. Give Fraser the peace he deserves, because he's the best thing that ever happened to you back then. And he still can be.'

Charlotte shook her head adamantly. 'No, Mum, you're wrong. What he did has torn our lives apart forever.'

'What he did, he's had to live with for six excruciating years. I've seen a broken man while you've been away, one who has taken Will under his wing, both to help the kid get through this terrible tragedy and to help heal himself.' She reached out, taking Charlotte's hand and squeezing it. 'Since you've been back, I've begun to see the man he used to be again. His smile lights up every time he sees you, Charlotte. Don't miss what's right under your nose.'

Charlotte swallowed hard, took a distracting sip of her coffee, then choked as it went down the wrong way. But was her mother right? She was keeping him at arm's length, yes. But it had been the right thing to do. She put her cup down, her eyes narrowing on it.

'John wants us to pay him a month's agistment for our ewes and lambs that were on his property, *and* he's told me he's keeping Brutus' lambs.' She looked up at her mother.

'What if it was him who let Brutus into the paddock on purpose for that reason, all when I'd done them a favour so *his sheep* wouldn't get run over? None of the other rams were in the paddock with them. Where does the man get off doing something like that?' Why was she bothering to try and find the heart for this place her father had?

'Do what your father would have done. Let it go. Pay the bill, and fight for the things you can, not the things you can't.'

'And what about you?' Charlotte's expression turned softer, sharing her own worry for her mother's health and happiness.

Mum looked at her in surprise. 'I have no clue what you mean.'

But Charlotte watched the subtle creases softly gracing the sides of her mother's mouth. 'Oh yes you do. And it might have something to do with a certain Peter Rabbit that keeps chasing you.'

Her mother's cheeks grew heated and she fanned herself. 'Are you hot?' her mother suddenly asked. 'Must be my hot flushes.'

And that's when Charlotte lay hold of what she had to do. She wasn't going to dwell on stuff that was petty. She'd fallen for the lie that she couldn't make a difference on the station. But the people of the district and beyond were wrong. She might not have had their respect before she had left, but it was about time she proved to them all she could do this.

CHAPTER 39

Charlotte's expression was a muddled mixture of delight and annoyance as Fraser's ute pulled to a stop and he hopped out, striding towards her as she groomed Boots. Despite her standoffish demeanour towards him of late, the smile he wore effortlessly had her stomach buzzing with giddiness as she fought to remind herself he wasn't welcome. Could this man get any more exasperating and bothersome? She'd hate to see him try.

Lewie raced over to him for a pat and Charlotte offered him a blank look before turning away, but not before noticing the way her dog walked alongside him as he neared her. 'Morning, Fraser,' she said curtly, looking his way again and noticing he looked a little sweaty, and too damned sexy. She frowned, working harder to brush Boots.

'Hey, Char. Can I have a chat with you?'

'About the weather? Good thing the rain they predicted is petering away. We don't need flies making life harder in this heat.' She was rather pleased with her diversion. All she had to do was not watch his slow rising smile, and she'd be able to keep it together.

'I might have a theory about what's happened to your wool.'

'What?' Her arm fell away from Boots, her annoyance evaporating into mid-air as her eyes widened. But how could he? Wouldn't Mark be the one contacting her if he had any leads? But she was dying to hear something, anything.

'I can't confirm it, but there's a possibility . . . Syd might be involved.' He had the good grace to look sheepish at his words.

'Syd? How? No, Fraser, that's not possible. He wouldn't do that to us. Besides, you said it was improbable for wool to go missing from the wool store.' She knew she shouldn't have listened to him. She began brushing Boots again with a surge of vigour.

'I know what I said, and I don't have any proof.' He drew in a long breath, as if steadying himself. 'I'm also concerned Dad may have had a small part to play in it all.' His voice turned distant, disappointed. And was there a whisper of "sorry"? That stopped her in her tracks.

'Are you serious?' Charlotte dropped the brush to the ground, leaving Boots to eat his hay in peace as she stepped forward, zeroing in on him for any hint that she may have misunderstood what he'd said. 'What do you mean?' She lengthened her body, taking a smidge of delight in her glare that threatened to shatter glass. Was this another ploy to make her sell Sheepwash Creek to him—to them? She wasn't going to fall for some slimy excuse if it was.

'I'm not saying he is.' He removed his Akubra in that coy boy way he used to do back when—she hit pause on the thought as he raked a hand through his hair, damp from the heat. 'I'm trying to understand why Syd disappeared so mysteriously the day of the sale. He hasn't been contactable since. And I've tried to get hold of him.'

His pained face begged her to listen, but her mind was racing with thoughts that were all beginning to add up. 'You've been trying to get me to sell to you this whole time. Is this the next level of lowness you're prepared to stoop to, for me to hand over my farm to you? When's this going to stop, Fraser?' She crossed her arms over her chest, her glare egging him on to answer.

'No, Char. You don't understand.'

'Oh,' she said, giving a disappointed chuckle, 'I do.' This man! He was calm and composed, the polar opposite to her. But he wasn't the one with anything to lose. Her temper heated up another level, her arms hanging at her sides in sheer disappointment.

'First it was James. And Dad dying was quite the convenience for you, wasn't it?' She gave him a sarcastic smile despite recognising it was a low blow. The sudden hurt in his sincere eyes gutted her like a punch. But this was about saving Sheepwash Creek, and she would do what it took. 'Were they your chess pieces, with you and your dad knocking them off your playing board so it would leave you with the prime chance to snatch away everything good my dad had ever done here?'

Ouch. She should never have said that, and she stepped back, disturbing the dust into angry swirls about her feet. The last time she had been this wild was over the hay they had stolen from her. But she was allowed to be. This was her father's estate, and no one was going to stop her from keeping his dreams for the future of Sheepwash Creek alive, no matter what new or unexpected direction they took.

'Please, Char, that's not true, not at all.'

Oh no, she wasn't going to get sucked into those pleading eyes as his face caved into a crumple of worry and disbelief at what she was saying, and she raised her index finger, shaking her head to hold her composure.

'You can forget about trying to take the farm. I'm never selling it to you.' Her breathing was heavy as she stood her ground. It was the final blow she needed to land, and the instant she did, his body froze.

'And one more thing. Stop. Calling. Me. Char.'

That was the moment she fully comprehended how much she had pushed him away—for good—making her heart plead with her brain to take back her words. But she couldn't. If he continued to call her by that name, it would only shred the last of her resolve, something that was imperative she keep intact.

Fraser was so angry with Charlotte's irrational accusations—which he knew deep down she didn't mean—that all he wanted to do was pull her to him, kiss her until her body melted against his, and hold her until he worked some sense into that infuriating brain of hers. But if he did, she would, without a doubt, pack her things tonight, then head back to her comfy city life, leaving him with zero chance to tell her his true feelings.

And was she considering keeping Sheepwash Creek? He hoped he could think he knew her well enough to know that if she wasn't going to sell to them, then she wasn't going to sell at all. Her stubbornness alone told him that much. But even if she did, she would be back and forth to her growing business. There would be no way she would consider settling down, not when he'd witnessed the excitement in her eyes when they had arrived in the city together. There was no doubt in his mind that she would go back eventually. That lure was too strong for him to fight.

But how could she suggest he was happy that James had died on his watch? It had devastated him beyond belief. There had been days he couldn't get out of bed, his best mate's death entrenched on his conscience alongside the grief that Charlotte had left him, forever.

And to say that Keith's dying was only adding to Trentham Park's cause? He wanted to punch something. The man had been like a father he hadn't found in his own dad. How did she not recognise he had been trying to keep her here on the farm this whole time? Despite his good intentions, even if they were a little selfish, he had been working to keep the peace with two people he loved . . . who wanted such different things.

CHAPTER 40

Fraser walked through The Tavern doorway and grinned, their Friday night drinks table empty, and his reputation secured once more. He had purposefully left the farm a touch earlier than necessary, wanting to have a chat with Paul about the plan he and Mark had hatched.

'Just give me a text when they arrive, okay?'

Paul nodded, the disappointment clear on his face. He had suffered a regretful dose of remorse over employing potential felons who might insult his sound business reputation, but he agreed it needed to be done if they had any chance of catching the men in the act.

Fraser strode over to the bar, his mind sidetracked. Charlotte had told him she wasn't selling to them. That should have been enough to put his concerns aside. Only problem was, it hadn't. He wanted, no needed, to hear she was staying. For all he knew, she might take on a manager permanently, then return to Melbourne. Then where would he be? She would be as good as gone, leaving him with little chance to find out what a future together might look like. He would never love anyone like he loved her.

Fraser pulled out a smile as he reached the bar, grasping the three beers Big Nev had poured, before taking a seat at their table. Big Nev joined him and they chatted lightly before the others arrived.

'What took you both so long?' Fraser raised his beer in the air with a smirk as Ross and Mark strolled over, taking their seats and sliding their beers towards them, their own grins undeniable.

'You have no idea how I've been looking forward to this,' Ross said, taking a long draw from his glass and letting out a loud 'ahh' as he placed it back on the table.

'Long day?' Mark leaned back in the seat and stretched his body down the length of the chair, crossing his legs at his ankles.

'Couldn't pull a foal from one of Malcolm Reeve's polo mares. It was huge. Took the two of us three quarters of an hour to deliver it. Bloody lucky it was alive.'

'All ready, I see.' Fraser raised his brows as he looked at Mark who was sitting in his civvies.

Mark grinned back. 'You bet. I've had enough of these slippery slugs. Chasing them for months has taken it out of me, but it will feel pretty sweet when I catch them. Then they can be put away, but not before we get them to confess.'

Fraser's stomach danced with anticipation. All he had to do was pull off the role. After that, everything was up to Mark. And then he might finally have the evidence to clear his name and prove to Charlotte he didn't want Sheepwash Creek without her. 'So, the plan is all set. Let's hope they turn up like clockwork.'

'Have you got your phone on sound?' Mark pulled himself into an upright position, watching as Fraser checked.

'Sure have.'

Big Nev left the table to retrieve a bowl of beer nuts, placing them on their table, and Mark's hand was the first one in. They continued with light chatter until Fraser's phone dinged with a text notification. Fraser turned serious as he snatched it up, all eyes on him.

Fraser's mouth tightened and for the briefest of moments, he hoped it was Charlotte telling him she had been wrong. But it wasn't, and he couldn't hide the disappointment filling him.

'Was that Paul?' Mark had a sense of impatience in his voice as he leaned in.

'Ah, yeah. Looks like we're a go, fellas.' He gave them a tight smile before standing, and all four men slipped through to the back door where Fraser grabbed the garbage bag Big Nev had set aside for him. He slung it over his shoulder before stealing a deep breath.

Opening the back door, he hesitated, listening for any sound of movement from Paul's side of the fence. Mark stood beside him, glancing to his left, and then right out of habit. They could discern light chatter from over the fence as the men moved about, shifting tyres with the occasional thud as one landed in a trailer.

Mark gave Fraser the nod, taking cover behind the recycling bin while Big Nev hid behind the door frame.

Fraser slowed his breathing to subdue the nerves racing through him before he moved towards the large garbage bin, hoping he sounded something like Big Nev would, to not arouse suspicion. With the rubbish in the bin, he let the lid drop down with a loud clunk before he spoke.

'Listen, with Syd needing to go underground till the dust settles, I'll finish off the job. That wool won't re-press itself. When Syd gives me those contacts, we'll get the job done and be gone before anyone's the wiser.'

Fraser's heart pounded so fast he thought it might explode. He had never done anything like this, and given the way his stomach was twisting, wasn't looking to ever again. How did Mark do this every day?

Ross had remained out in the open with Fraser, in case the pair behind the fence took a confirming look through the peephole, and from Ross's eye glance in that direction, Fraser was sure they had.

'C'mon, let's grab a beer.' They headed back inside, not missing the footsteps next door briskly moving back inside Paul's workshop.

Fraser shut the door behind him and Mark spoke quietly. 'Right, you two go back out there and sip your beers like nothing is out of the ordinary. I'll lay low back here, and Big Nev will remain behind the counter. Got it?'

Everyone nodded, moving with haste. Fraser positioned himself to face the front door at a new table, and as Ross was walking over with their fresh beers, the door opened in a burst, the summer heat rushing in with vengeance. The first guy held onto the door handle as he leaned in, squinting around the room. The second guy peered over his shoulder. And as Ross slid a beer in front of him, Fraser could tell from the corner of his eye that both men were staring in their direction.

Fraser took an uneasy sip, trying for casual, and nodded at Ross even though he had no clue what he had said. With his stomach in his throat and the beer that usually went down a treat ready to fly from his mouth, he took a steadying breath. But he didn't need to carry on the charade for long. The men had seen what they needed to, closing the door before Ross had a chance to take his seat.

It was a good five minutes before Mark surfaced from out back, settling himself beside Fraser.

'Don't you want to go and get a look at them?' Fraser blinked at Mark before looking towards the door once more, hoping the men hadn't changed their minds, ready to barge in and join them for a drink.

'No need. I've been working with them at the wool stores under a pseudonym and in disguise. Their faces are imprinted in my brain.'

Charlotte rode Boots in no particular direction, her mind far from anything on her mammoth to-do list for the day. She could smell the heat from the gums, the heady scent of eucalyptus giving her some peace despite her raging emotions. Never had she contemplated feeling so many sentiments about coming home, but they were all there, shiny and sparkly and in her face.

She had tried to talk herself into believing she hated Fraser, that she would never picture him the way she used to. But contrary to what she wanted, her fondness for him was stronger than ever. Prior to this, no one could have told her she would be arguing with her feelings on a half-hourly basis over the next-door neighbour she had fought to never forgive. She grimaced at the recollection of yesterday, wishing for the umpteenth time that she had never said her father's dying was convenient for him. That was spiteful and cruel, and he was clearly heartbroken. But she was angry, she reminded herself. And rightly so.

But to break him so wholeheartedly? She would understand if he never wanted to lay eyes on her again. It would be tricky, given they were neighbours, and without a doubt, they would run into each other, be it at The Small Store or over the fence. She let the reins hang from Boots' neck, hiding her face in her hands as he quietly continued to walk, his ears flicking back and forth to her like he was understanding her angst.

That sounded so much easier than the humiliation she would face from the locals as soon as they learnt what she had done to the "darling" of Settlers Hill. But so what? They didn't believe she could run the station either. So there really was no difference after all.

She wiped a stray tear from her eye, staring at the towering hills, the shimmer of haze giving the illusion that there was an oasis ahead. Regardless of everything, this was all hers, and she needed to do what was right by the station. She would do it for James and her dad.

And then she would do it for herself.

CHAPTER 41

'Is it all done? I'm more than a little nervous about this, Mark.' Fraser gripped the phone so tightly his hand ached. 'When is it arriving at the shed?' The Ginger Ninja circled his legs, hugging them with his sleek body as he purred on repeat.

'Everything's on track. Your wool should be arriving at the Hudson's shed in the next hour. Les will be there to receive it, and don't worry. The men don't suspect a thing. The little camera I've got hidden on top of the rafters above the press will catch everything.'

A shiver crawled over Fraser's body despite the heat. 'So, I'll need to be there at the same time, right?'

'I'd be getting ready to leave if I were you. The less suspicion on their part, the better.'

Fraser nodded, his mind a jumbled whir. 'Yeah, right.' His voice faded as he took in the scope of Trentham Park from the wool shed steps, catching the movement of his father trailing over the house paddock towards the homestead on the quad bike.

'I'd better head off then.' Beads of sweat trickled down his back beneath his shirt as the bike drew closer. Fraser was in for a world of pain if his father caught a whiff of what he was about to do.

'And Fraser. Thanks for sticking your neck out like this. It's taken some wrangling, but if we can pull it off, your wether's wool will be safe.'

'Then we'd better make it work.' He said goodbye to Mark, ending the call as his father drove through the gateway and pulled up alongside him. Samson leapt from the steps onto the back of the bike, angling for a better spot to score a pat. His Dad gave the cat a shove, sending him back to the ground. Fraser forced his lips into as casual a smile as he could manage, hoping the guilt he was harbouring didn't leak onto his face.

'There's a dead ewe up under the big old gum. You'll need to go get it before the flies make a feast out of her.'

'Sorry, Dad. Gotta go. I'll do it later.' He jogged down the steps, heading towards his ute, but not before his father yelled out after him.

'Do you take this farm seriously or not, Fraser?'

What? Fraser almost skidded to a stop, turning back to face his father. 'You know I do.'

'Well, it doesn't look like it to me. You're shirking your responsibilities too much lately. It's been happening ever since Charlotte Redding turned up.' He raised a discerning eyebrow, holding Fraser's wary look.

Fraser kept his irritation on a tight leash, despite it wanting to leap out. He hated the menacing tone his dad used whenever he mentioned Charlotte's name.

'I may need to make my feelings about this situation a little clearer, since you don't seem to be receiving them, son. I will buy that station, and you won't be having anything more to do with that hair-brained neighbour of ours. Do I make myself clear?'

Irritation dangled from Fraser's words but he kept his voice even. 'No, Dad. You don't. She's not selling. She told me yesterday.' This conversation was getting tedious, and Fraser glanced at his watch, sudden shock hitting him in the gut. He had forty minutes left to get to Les's shed and give himself enough time to get things ready.

'She *will* sell to us, and if you decide, in your infinite wisdom, that you don't want that to happen, then you'd better rethink your position on this farm. That land should have been mine to begin with, and I intend to get it.'

'You can't threaten to disinherit the farm from me.' His words were full of disbelief. Where was this madness coming from? Did his father harbour such hate towards the Reddings, he had finally crossed the line, losing his marbles in the process?

'You continue to see that girl, and you'll give me no choice. I don't want to do it, son, but there are some things you don't want to cross with me.'

Fraser stared at his father like he'd morphed into a man he had never met before and didn't like. Without another word, he stormed towards his ute. Backing out in a rush, he forgot his dad had left the quad bike in the driveway, narrowly missing it. His heart thudded as he checked the clock. He had thirty minutes to get to the shed. He needed thirty-five.

Fraser was speeding, but thankfully he was mates with the town cop. Mark was lying low at Pete's house as he waited for Fraser's text. All he had to do was act confident, hand over half the cash Mark had provided him with to ensure they started the job, and watch his wool get re-pressed—the irony of the idea making his hackles rise. The rest was up to Mark.

Les was pottering inside the stifling shed, thanks to its poor ventilation and the tin absorbing the late afternoon heat, when Fraser arrived.

'Thanks for doing this, Les.' He shook Les's hand.

'Not a problem, Fraser. If we can catch the bastards getting away with stealing the profits from the livelihood we spend twelve months growing, I'm all in. I'll take off before they get here. Don't want them getting suspicious an' all.' He tapped a finger to his nose, letting out a knowing chuckle.

Fraser waved him off before readying the new wool packs beside the press, then pulled out Syd's wool classer's stamp and stencil that Mark had seized, to brand the new bales. The guys who were doing the re-pressing were running late, and he wasn't sure if he was relieved or worried about it. Had they got wind that they were being set up? Or were they not bothering with the final job? One of them had already said they wanted to bail, but Mark was certain the lure of a higher payment would rope him in.

Finally, the sound of tyres on gravel drew closer, and Fraser straightened his shoulders, the stretch of his muscles doing little to put him at ease. Car doors slammed, and he took one more anxious glance about him before the men entered the shed.

'You Spud?' the first of the two men asked as they sized him up like a carcass they were about to carve up. They strutted over, stopping in front of him with their arms crossed over their sizable chests and distinct wariness glued to their faces. Fraser was no slouch, but he wouldn't want to run into these boys down a dark alley.

'I am. Let's not waste time. The packs are ready, as is Syd's stencil. I'll open the bales and you do the rest.'

Fraser's heart thundered as he recalled his last conversation with his father while popping open the first bale near the press, the wool spurting out like shaving foam. If his father was serious about his threat, then he was about to cement his future if his father found out what Fraser was doing. But it had to be a low tactic by his father to get him to do what he wanted, right? Besides, it was mid-December and there was plenty of time after the felony to get the wool back into their own wool packs, then down to the wool store before February when this wool off their wethers would be sold.

Mark had gone to extraordinary lengths to enable this to happen, so it had to go off without a hitch. And his father would be none the wiser.

Fifteen bales later, Fraser stood back, keeping a poker face as he wiped the sweat from his forehead, then took his phone from his pocket. Texting Mark, he glanced up with uncertainty, guilt writhing inside him each time the press lever went down. The men hadn't missed a beat. Matter of fact, they were doing a great job, so there was no reason for them to question his allegiance. He hoped he had allowed enough time for Mark to arrive before they demanded full payment.

Mark's text came back.

Walk out of the shed. If they ask why, say you need a pee. I'm 2 minutes away.

Fraser took the confident approach, which was a good thing since he could feel the nerves in his body buzzing, and the men's eyes on his back as he strode to the door, leaving before they could ask what he was up to.

The sound of gravel being disturbed rumbled, followed by a plume of dust, and Fraser checked out the unfamiliar car from behind the corner of the shed he was standing behind as it approached. Mark was in disguise, and Fraser couldn't help but take a second look. With his moustache, drab work attire, and scrappy wig beneath his cap with sunnies, he was unrecognisable. He looked like a replica of the two men inside the shed.

With a brief wave in the air, he hoped he looked business-like as he approached Mark. They didn't shake hands, and as he watched Mark glancing over his shoulder, giving a firm nod towards the shed, Fraser knew the men had indeed stuck their heads out the door, checking what was going on.

'Go around to the other side of the shed. When they leave, get in your ute and follow me down the driveway,' Mark whispered, keeping their conversation brief as he cautiously watched the shed door, despite picking that the press was whirring once more. 'I'll give them their final payment. My backup is at the gateway behind the tree line. They'll only find out what's hit them when they're intercepted at the bitumen.'

Fraser's sweaty hand clutched his keys in his pocket as he listened intently, frustrated that he couldn't catch the short conversation between Mark and the men. When all three of them stepped out from the shed, he glanced around nervously, sure one of the guys would overhear his heart as it pounded against his rib cage, revealing his hiding spot.

Crunching footsteps moved towards the cars, and Fraser risked a cautious peek around the corner. Mark was nodding to the men like an old mate before they hopped in their V8 panel van, turning around and leaving in a flurry of dust.

Fraser glanced towards his ute, then back at the disappearing car before he walked as calmly as he could, hopping into the vehicle. His hands shook, and he found pressing the start button near impossible with one finger. *C'mon!* he growled. He steadied his hand with a deep breath and the ute finally came to life. He put it in gear, following

Mark down the long entrance, desperate to see this escapade over and done with.

Fraser blinked against the overbearing dust, which was making visibility in front of him near impossible, but when he saw brake lights, followed by flashing red and blue lights both in front of the offending car and behind, his pulse tripled. With Mark blocking their retreat from behind, and a police wagon sealing their exit, their only option was to run on foot.

And they did.

Fraser stepped from his ute, unsure if he should join in the chase or wait it out. But when one of the guys bolted across the paddock in the opposite direction to where Mark was in pursuit, he took off without a second thought.

He ran towards the fence post, letting his hand support his weight as he flicked his legs out to the side and sailed over the fence. The guy glanced back, anger filling his face as he recognised Fraser's betrayal before slowing, turning to him, more than prepared to put an end to his problem.

What was Fraser meant to do? But a memory of James flashed in his mind, of him with a rabbit in his hand. At first, it had Fraser's eyes widening in desperate fear, then it shifted to determination and resolve. Unlike James, his wasn't a guy he wanted to protect, but by hell he didn't want to be the one left staring in disbelief without doing something to change the situation this time, and he slowed as he neared the wool thief.

'Shoulda known you couldn't be trusted. You've got it written all over you,' the man sneered, flexing his hands into fists at his sides.

Fraser approached slowly, stopping a distance away to give himself time to think. He was well aware the guy was also keeping a close eye on what was happening to his buddy in the opposite paddock, beyond Fraser's shoulder, but Fraser couldn't risk a look in case the guy used that as his opportunity to pounce. The midday sun pounded down on them, and he fought against the sting of sweat trickling into his eyes.

'Take it easy, mate. I'm not looking for a fight.' Fraser held up a calming hand. What else did he say to a guy who oozed anger, retaliation, and betrayal? And rightfully so. He'd taken possession of a lot of money and wouldn't be easily persuaded to part with it.

'You bloody stay where you are. This was my last gig. Leave me be and you'll never have to see me again.' His stare narrowed menacingly, his finger jabbing in Fraser's direction.

Fraser wished he could be sure things would play out that way. But even if he did let the guy go, he was certain there would be retribution of some kind for himself in the future, knowing he wouldn't be hard to find. The thought unnerved him.

'It's not that simple. You're an accessory to theft.' Fraser could feel the vein in his neck pulsing. The disrespect for someone else's property, the deceitfulness, and the arrogance this guy used to try and manipulate him had his muscles quivering. It might be different to the circumstance of James's death, but the principle of what was happening remained. He wasn't going to let something dangerous on his watch go down without trying to do something to stop it. These men needed to be brought to justice.

'Bloody let me walk, and you can have half.' The guy took a step towards Fraser, his death stare locked on him with that same sinister snarl as the one he'd seen when they had first arrived. This guy didn't intend on sharing ten bucks, his snarl telling Fraser he wanted him dealt with, then he'd be gone.

Fraser urged the fear swelling in him to settle as he took one steady step at a time, keeping his hand up in front of him. 'Listen, mate, this doesn't have to be hard. Besides, if you cooperate, they'll probably go lighter on you.' Would the guy even consider listening to reason? Fraser didn't think so, but it was all he had, having no clue where Mark or his backup were. All he had was time, and that was fast running out.

'What would a stinkin' farm boy understand about the slammer? Ever been in one?' The man offered him a sly eye, taking a step closer. Fraser stole a steadying breath, unable to hide his deep swallow behind his Adam's apple.

'Humph.' The word came out in a knowing tone. 'So don't tell me to give myself up.' He took yet another step, their bodies a mere metre apart. 'It. Ain't. Happening.' Spittle lightly showered the ground between them as a calculating smile rose on the man's lips, taking Fraser by surprise. 'Tom, help me get this prick outta my face. We've gotta move!'

Tom? This time, Fraser risked a glance over his shoulder. Mark stood off to the side, not three metres away.

And in that moment, the thug lunged.

Fraser turned back in the nick of time, ducking before diving to the side, his agility quick enough to avoid a severe punch to the cheek and gut. The guy spun around, ready to lunge again, when Mark jumped behind him, snatching his left arm and pinning it to his back.

'What the—'

'This *is* your last gig,' Mark said, his face set as the felon tried to glance from behind at him.

This was Fraser's cue, and he leapt forward, snatching the other arm in a fierce grip, wrestling with him and tugging his second arm behind his back. The guy was no slouch, probably thanks to the many hours of pressing he'd done. Mark grabbed his handcuffs, securing him before leading him towards the police wagon where the other felon was already apprehended.

'Good job today, Fraser. I couldn't have done it without you.' Mark gave him a nod and a firm handshake as they watched the police van drive away.

'Well don't go asking me to do something like that again. My heart couldn't take it,' Fraser said, pressing a hand to his chest and giving a relieved chuckle.

'Hopefully I won't ever have to, mate.' Mark gave him a solid pat on the back, then hopped in his ute, offering Fraser a job-well-done wave before heading to the police station to formally charge the two men.

Fraser drove back to the shed, his shoulders drooping at the thought of the task in front of him. He had the mammoth job of repressing his wool, again, before the day was out. He wasn't looking forward to it. Not one bit.

CHAPTER 42

'Where the bloody hell have you been?'

Fraser walked into the kitchen, dehydrated and wrung out, shed dust and lanolin clinging to the dried sweat on his brow and forearms in unnatural lines. He didn't hide the impatient puff of air he let expire from his lungs as he stared blankly at his father in response, before grabbing a can of Coke from the fridge and collapsing on a chair at the table, slugging back half of it before he came up for air. As if he could give his father the truthful answer.

'Helped a mate press his wool.'

'Who?' The word came out sharply from his father's mouth and Fraser caught the surprised look on his father's face.

'No one you've met.' But that was a ridiculous answer. Everyone knew everyone's affairs around here and he quickly corrected himself. 'Only an out-of-towner.' He kept his weary eyes on his father, recognising the flicker that passed over his face at the term he'd used. His father had always been a little reactive when referred to by the term.

Fraser took another long slug, finishing the can. He kept his eyes down, hoping his father would take the hint and have the decency to leave him alone. Les had helped him with the pressing, the bales now on his truck. Fraser would be taking them back to the Melbourne delivery centre tomorrow, where Mark would ensure they were placed back in storage as though nothing had happened.

'I'm bushed. I'll catch you in the morning.' Fraser went to stand, but his father spoke before he could leave the room.

'It wasn't Charlotte you were helping, was it?' His words were cloaked with scorn.

The creases in his father's brow wove a thread of infuriation inside Fraser before he tipped his head, calling on every inch of calm he could muster. He was too tired for this, and besides, why did he need to tell him anyway?

'What? No.' Relief flooded him that he wasn't lying this time. Not unless his father dug deeper.

'That's good to hear. She can't stay.' His Dad looked at him, a hint of intent and accusation dancing in the air between them, only aiding Fraser's building resentment over his father's ruthlessness to get his hands on Sheepwash Creek.

'Everything would only get messy if she did.' Dad finished his cuppa, standing and putting his mug in the sink in a controlled manner. He strolled over to Fraser, giving him a firm slap on the back. Fraser bristled at the touch. There was no denying the intent of his father's hand, and it left him staring at the floor like it might bite him. He was the son who was about to become a huge disappointment. And his father would never believe any different.

'I'm keeping the farm.'

Charlotte didn't have to wait long for her mother to tug the pot full of melting butter she had been stirring with a wooden spoon from the stove and turn to look her way, her eyes bright as her smile widened.

Her mother put the saucepan down, and moved towards Charlotte, cloaking her in a bear hug. The sheer comfort of it had her easing into her mother's arms in utter relief.

But now? She'd come this far, fully invested in both her love for the station, and her desire to do what her dad would have wanted. So, whether their wool was found or not, she was determined to go down with a fight. Not the Pierces, or anyone else would take her farm from her before she had exhausted all her options.

Fraser's mobile distracted him, and he tugged it from his pocket, struggling to refocus from the chill that continued to run over him thanks to his father, until he saw who the caller was.

'Mark. Got any news?' Fraser blurted it out, unable to hide the desperation in his voice.

'Those boys weren't too hard to persuade. They must like their freedom more than they like Syd.' He gave a dry chuckle. 'We've got a lead on him.'

'That's great news. Anything I can do?' Should he even ask that after what Mark had already put him through? But if it meant finding Charlotte's wool . . . It wasn't about her staying anymore. It was about them remaining friends in whatever capacity she chose. That was the best he could hope for, given that she believed he was a traitor. A tightness filled his chest. *Remember, whatever it takes.*

'Yes, there is. But only if you're up for it. Word is, Syd has been lying low. He's planning on catching a plane later tonight. But—'

'But . . . what?' And damn it. Why couldn't he have kept his mouth shut? If his father's suggestion that he might take Trentham Park from him for meddling in Charlotte's business to keep her here wasn't enough, the thought of playing spy had him reaching for the wall to steady himself.

But he'd come this far, and if this was the way he could show Charlotte he was sorry, he would do it.

Fraser glanced about him, heading for the front door as he listened to Mark. He wasn't sure where his father was, but he needed to be careful he didn't get wind of what he was about to be a part of.

'If he recognises me, especially in my uniform, he might bolt. We lost him when he fled the wool sales. We can't afford to let that happen again. Any chance you could pack a bag like you're heading off somewhere, and come down with me? If you can intercept him at the airport, it might give us a better chance to nab him. If he cottons on to someone he doesn't know watching him, he might run. He's slippery, and my boss won't be happy if he gets the slide on us again.'

'So, you want me to pretend I'm catching a plane?' Fraser whispered, glancing behind for his father.

'Yeah, somewhere in the opposite direction to where we think he's going, so it doesn't arouse suspicion or spook him. Maybe Orange in New South Wales to look at some rams? If our intel is correct, he's trying to get to King Island.'

Why was everything he was doing these days based on mistrust and not being noticed, especially by Charlotte? Apprehension danced deep within his gut. Was he about to do this *again*? And what would his father say when he hadn't retrieved that dead sheep?

But more than that, what would Charlotte do if he didn't? She needed that money. This was what you did for love, wasn't it? He might be kidding everyone else, but

Charlotte was his forever love, whether he got his happily ever after with her or not.

'Fraser?' Mark broke all the what-ifs he was thrashing about in his mind, and Fraser bit his bottom lip before he answered.

'Yeah, okay.'

'Great. Meet me at my place in half an hour.'

Mark sped down the freeway, lights flashing, and Fraser was relieved his mate had refrained from using the sirens as well. Mark was no slouch when he was on a mission and they had made it to Essendon airport with an hour to spare before Syd was due to fly out.

The ring tone of the car phone broke Fraser's introspection as Mark spoke to his superior via Bluetooth.

'We've pulled up out of sight at the airport. I have Fraser Pierce with me. He will intercept Syd Jones. If all goes to plan, we'll have him at the station before you leave for home, sir.'

'Good. Mark, I've notified the airport, and they are on standby. As soon as he checks in, I'll send you a text. Then Fraser can meet up with him. And Mark, don't lose him. We've been watching him for too long.'

'I'll do my best.'

Mark released a long sigh, pressing "end" on the call, and Fraser was all too aware this long pursuit had taken a heavy toll on him.

'Have you told Char?' Fraser didn't realise his hands were pressed tightly in his lap.

Mark glanced his way. 'No, not yet. I was hoping I'd be able to ring her with good news.'

The airport was small, but busy. Fraser wove his way through the groups of travellers, trying not to fidget as he glanced around for Syd. Mark had suggested Syd might be disguised, so anyone with a wide-brimmed hat or a Hawaiian shirt was fair game.

'We're good to go, mate.' That was Mark's text message to Fraser, alerting him that the airport had registered Syd's check-in.

The voice over the loudspeaker announced the arrival of a plane from Dubbo, and the imminent boarding call for a departing flight to King Island.

Fraser flinched. No closer to finding Syd, he scanned the area around him. Mark and his partner, Steve McCarthy, were somewhere in the building, no doubt with eyes on him, waiting until they could make the arrest. He had to hope he didn't stuff up the plan when he found Syd.

No sooner had the call-out been made than Fraser spotted Syd looking nervously over his shoulder as he made his way towards the seating area for his flight. With a welcoming smile plastered on his face, Fraser walked towards the same departure gate, resisting the urge to look for Mark. He had never been good at lying, but he had to do this. Syd had to be made accountable for the livelihoods he'd threatened through his wool theft.

'G'day, Syd. How's things?' Fraser's sensed the nervous tones in his voice, so reached his hand out to offer a handshake and a nod, aiming for the casual approach. Syd's eyebrows rose above his sunglasses. His wrinkled brow was the next dead giveaway, as was his sweaty palm in Fraser's hand.

'Fraser?' Scepticism filled Syd's expression, revealing his discomfort as he looked over his shoulder again like he was about to be pounced on. From not being able to look Fraser in the eye to sitting down in a chair, then standing again, he wore guilt like an ill-fitting shirt. 'What are you doing here?'

'Catching a flight to Orange. Want to check out a couple of studs up that way before the sales begin. There are some nice-looking rams with fine microns, and I'd rather look them over myself before I decide to bid online. Wouldn't mind if you could take a look at them for me sometime too. You'll be heading to the sales, right?' Fraser was impressed with himself for the excuse he'd come up with on the spot, knowing full well Syd would know of every superfine ram sale around, although he had to admit that part of his story didn't make a lot of sense given the ridiculous amount of rams his father had recently bought from Charlotte. Diversity in bloodlines, that's what it was about, he assured himself.

He had also been careful not to ask Syd where he was off to. That one was smarter to leave that to Mark, especially given the distinct jitters dancing in his stomach.

'Yeah, um, okay. I'll take a look . . . when I get back.' A soft frown crossed Syd's brow.

Fraser caught sight of Mark, who had positioned himself so that Syd had his back to him. Taking Mark's nod as a sign to say goodbye, Fraser gave Syd a parting smile.

'Well, have a good trip. I'll look forward to discussing the rams with you.' With a parting smile, Fraser walked towards the terminal for his fake destination of Orange, something he'd been careful to check was available as an actual flight, in case Syd kept an eye on where he was heading off to. He turned into the boarding lounge, taking a seat. Not ten minutes later, Syd had been handcuffed and was being escorted to the entrance of the airport by Mark and Steve, leaving Fraser with disappointment so deep he wasn't sure he'd be able to keep his last meal down.

CHAPTER 43

'Your father would be so proud.' Her mum beamed as she held Charlotte at arm's length. 'His daughter taking on the station in the western district? That's sure to get some tongues wagging.' She gave Charlotte a mischievous grin. 'He always liked innovation, whatever the form it came in. That's why he was so excited for you and James to be working alongside him.'

Those words hit Charlotte with an intensity she wasn't ready for, and she took a step back to steady herself, her emotions already on such a rollercoaster she was struggling to keep up. Why hadn't she come home sooner? If she had, she might be working alongside her dad, not alone, without his words of wisdom and support. But it was better than never. It had to be. It was all she had.

'But what about Dad's edge over the competition?' Charlotte sat down at the kitchen table, taking a wedge of freshly made blondie slice her mother had made and absently squishing it between her fingers.

'Don't doubt what your father taught you. And even more than that, don't forget your innovative views and ideas. They carry the future of this place. Start cutting yourself some slack and learn to trust yourself.'

But how much harder was this going to be than running her business in the city? Ten times harder. While she had loved her business growing, starting it from the ground up, it wasn't as rewarding as the loyalty welling inside her for Sheepwash Creek and Settlers Hill, if she wanted to hold tight to the real truth.

Late that afternoon, Pete and Lewie arrived home from down the paddock, having thrown some hay to a few of the mobs of ewes due to be joined in the early new year. They waltzed in for morning smoko, a strand of tinsel around each of their necks and Pete wearing a grin from ear to ear as he took his seat.

'It's starting to feel a lot like Christmas,' he said, a silly grin plastered to his face.

Mum waved his antics away but Charlotte could only blink. 'I reckon you and Lewie need to set up camp in Mum's veggie patch.'

'Oh, why's that?' He snatched up a piece of the blondie and stuck it in his mouth, chewing as he looked at her with interest.

'You can both scare away the blackbirds.' Charlotte laughed at his indignance, her Mum following suit. 'Did the ewes run a mile in the opposite direction when they saw you?'

'Young Charlotte, the way to a woman's heart is through remembering the special occasions.' He gave her a beat-that tip of his head, before sliding his attention to her mother, who currently had decidedly flushed cheeks.

Mum slid a fresh plate of hot sausage rolls in front of him. 'Eat,' she said, keeping her eyes down, no doubt relieved to turn her back on both of them as she fussed unnecessarily with the mugs and re-boiled the kettle.

'Well, Pete, who'd have known? No one has ever done that for me before.' Her cheeks began to ache as she leaned over, making a scene of snatching one of his sausage rolls and taking a bite as he watched on in pretend offence.

'And no one ever bloody will if you steal food from under their noses,' he said, playfully swatting at her hand.

Charlotte was chuckling when a knock at the verandah door caught their attention, and she glanced across at Pete and her mum with curiosity, relieved when it was only Mark who had let himself in. She might have wanted a pitchfork beside the door for a certain next-door neighbour had he tried to enter.

Charlotte studied Mark's expression as he walked towards her . . . with Fraser close behind. Damn that pitchfork, she muttered under her breath, wishing she could boot him out. But that didn't seem so smart given Mark was in his uniform, ruining all her fun.

'That'd be right. Smelled the food, did you?' Charlotte said with an accusatory grin as Mark took a seat, and her mother pulled out more mugs from the overhead cupboard with a smile.

Charlotte gave a sideways glance at Fraser, his warm smile irritatingly genuine and gorgeous. She looked away.

'Don't you go gettin' all hopeful I'll be sharing these with you lads,' Pete said, wrapping his arm protectively around the plate and tugging it close to his chest, half of the sausage rolls already gone. 'There's already been one thief in the room.' He glared at Charlotte as he bit into another with pretend annoyance.

'Too slow,' Fraser chimed, reaching over Pete's shoulder from behind and snatching a handful, tossing two towards Mark before Mum placed a coffee in front of him as he took a seat.

'Cor blimey, Fraser. Get your stinkin' fingers outta my smoko.' He gave a deft swipe at him a moment too late, only to watch as Fraser put one into his mouth, exaggerating his delight in the taste of it. 'What did you ever do to earn it?'

Charlotte found her chest filling with a cosy warmth despite her determination to never be charmed by Fraser again, and her smile rose instantaneously. Fraser glanced her way, and she cursed her cheeks that were burning raspberry red. She left her seat and turned on the aircon, the relief not as immediate as she would have liked. Why were her contrary thoughts messing so thoroughly with her, one minute making her wish Fraser might drop in for a cuppa; to look at the rams, or, even better, to share in a casual chat, and the next wanting to banish him from the house forever? And here he was, his glowing smile directed at her, and she found herself wanting more—for herself, and for *them*. But admitting she had such strong feelings for Fraser, when all he did was torment her in his infuriating, self-assured way while he tried to get her to sell up? She wished she knew what to do.

She turned from him, squashing the feelings stirring within her. She needed to keep them in check. Mark spoke, drawing her back even though the sound of her heart thundered in her ears.

'Jayne, I have to admit, I did time my visit.' He had the good sense to look a tad sheepish as he reached for a piece of slice under the scrutinising eye of Pete.

They laughed, Charlotte feeling the wound-up tension in her stomach easing a smidge. *Keep talking, Mark.* She needed him to. And she needed to stop looking in her neighbour's direction.

'Don't we know it,' Pete chimed, and with only a handful of sausage rolls left on the plate, he relinquished his hold, pushing the plate to the middle of the table with a reluctant grumble.

Mark reached for one, took a bite, then continued.

'But I also came for another reason.'
Uncharacteristically, he scratched the side of his head. 'I have
a bit of news regarding your wool.'

Charlotte sat up immediately, her attention piqued as
she silently urged him to hurry up and finish his mouthful.

'Well, spit it out, lad,' Pete said, giving him an
impatient glare.

'We've caught the perpetrator who acquired your
wool.'

Acquired? What did that mean? Confused, she stared
at Mark.

'And you're not going to like who it is.'

She prepared herself for the blow, wishing she hadn't
had that extra sausage roll after all. What could be worse than
her wool going missing? If they found who had taken it,
surely she'd get it back.

'Syd Jones has been streaming bales of wool from the
wool store to his little side hustle, removing and then re-
pressing them into bales stencilled with his property brand.
He was selling them when either the market was doing well
or suspicion was too much for him to bear. And he's made a
tidy profit.'

Charlotte wanted to run from the room and lose what
she'd eaten. 'But— Why? What possessed him to do it?'

'He'd done it several times before, siphoning bales in
bigger shipments with the help of his thugs. With your wool,
he saw the perfect opportunity when Keith died, never
contemplating that you might take up the mantle with such
diligence. He was building himself a nice-sized nest egg with

the proceeds, and your clip was the last he wanted to risk taking before he went into hiding, or retirement, so to speak.'

'But how did you work it out? I—' She looked over at Mum. 'We trusted him.'

'Everyone did. That's how it was so easy for him. I've been working undercover for months, down at the wool store. Although it took some time, we finally built up enough evidence against him for an arrest. He's sitting in gaol at the moment, waiting for a hearing date.'

Charlotte was floored. How could Syd do something like this to them? She turned to Fraser. 'Did he steal from you too?'

'No, he didn't.' His apologetic frown said he was sincerely sorry this had happened.

'So, how did you find him?' She turned back to Mark, impatient for his answer.

'It was a joint effort. He went into hiding after acquiring your wool, so we had to find another way. I set up his two gofers, who I worked with on my days on duty at the wool store, in a sting to also catch them. We used Fraser's wool to lure them to the job. They are currently in custody. After that, they gave up Syd's plans for a lighter sentence.'

Charlotte blinked repeatedly, her focus blurring in and out. If they used Fraser's wool, did that mean—

Mark must've read her mind, answering her question. 'Fraser allowed me to remove bales from storage especially for it. He met the guys at the Hudson's shed, supervising the whole thing. I couldn't have done it without him.'

With her mouth ajar, Charlotte looked from Mark to Fraser, his kind eyes warm and hopeful as he offered her a reticent smile. Had he really risked so much for her?

'Is everyone okay?' Her gaze locked on him, fearful he had placed himself in a situation where he could have been hurt. And then it struck her. If she couldn't bear to see him in danger, what was that saying about her feelings for the man she'd tried desperately to keep at arm's length?

'We're fine,' Fraser said, and she forced herself not to get up and hug him, her sense of gratitude for what he'd done so full she could burst.

'There's something else,' Mark said, and the ease in his features transformed to concern.

'What the bloody hell now?' Pete said, looking agitated at the patience with which Mark was delivering the news. Charlotte couldn't disagree.

He took a long breath as though what he was about to say could drain him of all his strength. 'It appears that John set Syd's plan into progress, putting pressure on him to ensure Sheepwash Creek's wool didn't make the sale for the same day as Trentham Park's.' Mark looked over at Fraser, as did Charlotte, the revealing news causing his expression to pale.

Now she did want to go to him and hold him tight enough to absorb some of the pain Mark's words were inflicting on him, and she went to stand before forcing herself back into her seat.

'Fraser, your father isn't in any trouble. All he did was accidentally set the wheels in motion and Syd took advantage of the opportunity.'

Accidentally, my bloody foot. Fraser wanted to gag before disappointment set in so hard and fast, he wouldn't be able to move, even if he wanted to. So, his father wanted Sheepwash Creek, Charlotte and Keith's reputation, *and* he was happy to see her left without a cent for a wool clip that was revered within the wider community as one of the best. Who did something like that? He was acting like a possessed madman with a passion to win at any cost. But hadn't that always been what his father did, only not on as grand a scale as this?

He checked Charlotte's expression. Clearly she was in as much shock as himself. After everything he'd done to please his father, all he had managed to do was fail his aspirations, and he'd lost Charlotte for good as well. There was no way they could come back from this.

Fraser stood, his chair scraping against the tiles before he pushed it towards the table, letting his weight rest on the back of it as he studied Pete's pastry crumbs scattered on the table in front of him. He needed some time to process what Mark had told him.

'Thanks for the smoko, Jayne. It's always great to be here.' Inadvertently, his hollow gaze lifted to Charlotte before he gathered the strength to say goodbye, then exited through the laundry as fast as he could.

'Fraser, wait!' Charlotte tried to make herself stay at the table, aware he needed time, but she couldn't let him go without telling him how grateful and how sorry she was for this sudden turn of events. She reached him as he was about to open his ute door, the despair on his face shattering. Lewie raced to her side, nudging her with his nose.

'Fraser, I'm so—' She caught herself mid-sentence and looked down at her feet. What could she say? He was hurting, but, he was listening. She had to find the right words. She looked back up at him, their eyes locking, as if every word she wanted to say was being spoken through them. And then, before she could stop, she stood on her tiptoes as she reached for him, hesitating for the briefest moment before her lips touched his, the spark that had always been there between them, striking alight as his gentle lips melted into hers.

Could this be any more perfect? Her heart was alive, rushing in her chest as he softly returned her kiss, reaching for the side of her neck and holding her to him like they'd never been apart. In this moment, she needed him, and if she read him right, he needed her too.

Slowly, she eased her feet back to the ground, her gaze begging him to understand her torment; that she loved him, and that it didn't matter what his father tried to do to her, or the grudge she'd held onto for so long. She wanted to be with him. But before she could say anything, he spoke.

'Charlotte, can you still picture us growing old together? We swore, even when my father wanted us apart, that we'd make sure it happened.' His throat clenched as he swallowed, his low smile wistful as their gaze met over the shared memory. It reflected their hopes and dreams of so long ago as he continued to hold her face with a caring smile, even if it was hesitant. And he'd called her Charlotte—that didn't feel right.

She nodded, a tear rolling from the edge of her eye as she angled a bright smile. 'I do.' She nodded eagerly. Did this mean he wanted what she had finally comprehended was her dream, to stay on the farm and be with him?

'Not sure that's what we're going to be able to have.' He angled his head away, the hills in the hazy distance holding his attention.

'What? No, no that's not what we have to settle for. Fraser, I need you. Please—' Her throat grew so tight, she struggled to swallow, grasping his forearms like the action might wake him from the trance he had to be in. He was in shock, that was all. He didn't mean what he was saying.

He couldn't.

Fraser eased her away before sliding into the ute seat, keeping his focus on starting the engine rather than on her. She stared at him, rubbing at a sudden twitch on her brow. What was happening? She had all but told him she loved him. What else did she need to do to get him to stay? To be with her?

Fraser drove away, leaving her more hollow and alone than when she'd first arrived back at the farm all those months ago. The isolation deepened when she brushed a finger over her lips and closed her eyes. He had kissed her without reserve, before checking in on his true feelings, then checking out on her. Didn't he want what she wanted? What had she done so wrong?

Or should she be looking at it from another angle? What had he done wrong? Had he only kissed her to complete the mission? It was the ultimate move on his behalf, one that guaranteed he would get what he wanted. The pain of deception jack-knifed her heart.

CHAPTER 44

Fraser took the long way home, unable to clear his mind of the kiss he had shared with Charlotte, and not wanting to face his father, the thought making his gut twist. But what did he have at the end of all this? If he challenged his father over the matter, he would be giving away that he'd allowed the use of their wool to catch Syd and his syndicate. His father didn't like to be shamed at the best of times. Would he be risking his future on Trentham Park if he said something, or was it some hot-winded threat his father had taken to using on him, to get him to back down?

And Charlotte? He'd kissed her with all his heart until the moment his father's involvement resurfaced in his mind. What woman would want a dishonest father-in-law who was relentless in securing Sheepwash Creek for himself? He shook his head despondently. Sheepwash Creek was safer if he and Charlotte stayed apart. That would be his last kiss with the girl he'd always loved.

But wasn't love meant to come in and make the pain less? Fraser tapped the steering wheel with his thumb. Or had he been such a dreamer, it was impossible for him to see clearly when it came to Charlotte Redding?

When Fraser hopped out of the ute and went up the steps to the house verandah, he held the back door handle for the longest time, his breaths shallow as he drew on the strength to go inside. But he didn't have to say anything to his father until news broke of what had happened, so until then, he planned on avoiding him. And where he couldn't, he would give him nothing. If for no other reason, keeping Trentham Park in his future was for his mother. This was her family's heritage and he wasn't about to risk that by saying something so damaging before it was necessary, even if he couldn't understand why.

Rather than head for the kitchen as usual, Fraser took the passageway and slipped into his bedroom, closing the door firmly behind him. What he wanted was to get out on his motorbike, watch the sunset over the Grampians, and think. But before he did, there was something else he needed to check on.

Fraser sat on his bed, staring at his side table for a long minute as memories flashed before him of the times he and Charlotte had swum down at the river, climbed trees, and kissed as they picnicked. But the time most vivid in his memory was the day he'd taken her yabbying down at their dam. It had been a cool autumn day, and they had wanted to cook their lunch by the fire on the dam bank. Fraser had set it up before taking her there, the pot ready, the yabby bait in the nets, and the bread already buttered. She was fourteen and it was the day he had given her a ring as a sign they would be together forever. He'd meant it with all his heart, and she had accepted it like it was the greatest gift she'd ever received.

Until that day, four years later, when she had thrown it back at him in anger, grief, and hostility, declaring she never wanted to catch sight of him again.

Fraser's fingers lingered over the drawer handle before he collected the strength to open it. He reached to the far back where it took him a moment to feel his way, until his fingers closed around a small box. He drew it out from its hiding place, twirling the box over and over between his fingers. She had always been his one and only, and he opened it, staring down at the small ring with an open heart on top. Was it conceivable he could have a forever life with her? She was the one person who made him a better man.

Or was he destined to a life alone? He had backed himself into a hole he couldn't picture himself climbing out of. Up until yesterday, he hadn't been this happy in a long time, his worries from home non-existent whenever he was with Charlotte; holding her; laughing with her . . . kissing her. With her around, he forgot about his father not trusting him enough to make good choices for himself, or the farm.

His father's intentions revolved around acquiring more land. He was blinded by his own ambition, not able to grasp that if Fraser kept Charlotte in his life, it could benefit them all. What was it about Sheepwash Creek that had him acting like an obsessed man?

Whatever it was that his dad was up to, Fraser wanted no further part in it. It was about time he looked to chasing what *he* wanted for his future, his father's warning of disinheritance nothing more than a hollow threat.

Brutus blinked at Charlotte with curious, challenging eyes, an expression on his face she wasn't sure how to read. She glanced about her before studying him again, not trusting his tranquillity, or the calmness of the shed atmosphere hugging her. Had he pre-warned the other rams that he was going to mess with her again? Where was the bully, the ram with so much attitude, she second-guessed, for the quadrillionth time, her plans about joining him to some of the stud girls? She had seen firsthand how his progeny had turned out in that ram lamb, and personally, she didn't need more of it. But if he was good enough for her father, then she needed to believe he was good enough for her.

Charlotte's mind shifted to Fraser like it managed to do so often these days. More and more, she found herself preoccupied with thoughts of him, especially after their kiss yesterday. It had been perfect until he'd pulled away. What if everything she was feeling for him since being back was nothing more than nostalgia? They couldn't make a future together on that.

'You're right, Brutus. It wouldn't work.' Giving the ram a brief smile, she tossed hay into each pen, then headed for Boots. She needed a cuddle.

Boots was in a sprightly mood, trotting up to her, and she slipped through the gate, offering him the carrot she had in her back pocket. He chewed on it contentedly as she ran her honed hands over his body, feeling for any tension within his muscles, and gently working them free. She had taken to doing this regularly, and he appeared to be enjoying it. She'd also ridden him enough that he no longer came home sore after a ride, a bit like her own backside, she chuckled to herself.

As she was brushing out his mane, her phone rang. It was her clinic. When she had first arrived home, her heart would skip with an excited jitter at the sight of seeing her own clinic number on the screen. But that thrill had subsided, and she stared at the number before she finally answered.

'Hey, Cara. Is everything okay?' Why did she always assume something might be wrong? The clinic had been running seamlessly without her, a fact she had accepted rather than been sorry about these days.

'Hi, Charlotte. It's going great. So well, I wanted to ask you something. Have you got time to talk?'

Charlotte shrugged her shoulders to relax the sudden tension forming in them. 'Sure.' She didn't need anything else to go wrong. 'I'm brushing my horse. I've even been giving him some massage treatments. Isn't it great that our techniques can also be applied to animals?'

'Oh, wow. That sounds amazing, and . . . what I kind of wanted to talk to you about.'

Why did Charlotte get the feeling Cara wanted to chat about things other than about appointments, how many clients they'd had that week, or what they needed to order for the coming fortnight? She took a calming breath.

'Would you be open to selling your business? That is, if you're not planning on coming back? Every time we've talked, you chatter on about the ins and outs of the farm with so much excitement, what you plan to do next, and you especially go on about your next-door neighbour. It made me think you could be thinking of staying there. Are you?'

Charlotte could hear the tentative hope in Cara's voice. But was she ready to relinquish everything she'd built from nothing, making a solid name for herself in physiotherapy in such a short space of time? Then again, she'd done that once. What was stopping her from letting her business go, to pave a new career as the stud master of Sheepwash Creek?

'Would you like to make me an offer?' Charlotte smiled into the phone. Out of nowhere, her heart rallied with anticipation of the unknown and nerve-wracking excitement for a new challenge. This might be everything she had been waiting on, to give her the final permission to take a leap of faith into a man's world.

'Only if you're okay with it. I don't want to step in if you want to come back, but if you aren't—'

'I love it, Cara. Let's start talking figures soon.'

Charlotte hung up the phone, her heart bursting with excitement for the farm in a soaring rush.

CHAPTER 45

Charlotte looked up from Boots' water trough, all smiles as Mark's police ute drove in. Settlers Hill was in good hands with a Senior Constable like him.

'Hey, Mark. What brings you here?' She shaded her hand over her eyes from the sun.

'I've got a bit of an update for you. Any chance your Mum has scones on the table?' He grinned, his eyebrows gleaning with hopefulness. Charlotte laughed.

'How did you—? Mark, you're like a food beacon for her cooking. But don't go telling everybody, or we'll never get any work done around here. Pretty soon, you'll be protecting your plate of food like Pete.' They chuckled together before walking inside.

'Mark. How are you? Another timely visit, I see,' her mother said, raising her eyebrows with teasing pleasure. 'C'mon, sit down.'

'What brings you here, lad?' Pete was already vigorously hoeing into the chocolate chip cookies that were gooey and warm.

'Well, I have some good news, and some bad news.'

Jayne, Pete, and Charlotte shared the same surprised look amongst themselves as Mark reached for a cookie.

'Well, don't wait for us to go to sleep, young fella. Out with it,' Pete said.

'Peter Rabbit. That'll be enough out of you,' Mum said, giving him a glare that clearly told him there would be no scones for him if he didn't shut up.

Charlotte giggled as Pete teasingly narrowed his focus on her mother, unable to hide his newfound zest for life since his involvement with their family.

Mum laid out the steaming scones in a basket lined with a clean tea towel, put the butter out with a knife, and Charlotte helped her with the cuppas.

'Right, Mark. Let's get this over with,' Charlotte said. 'Rip the band-aid off, starting with the bad news.'

He nodded before he spoke. Charlotte wished Pete could learn a couple of lessons from him.

'Okay. I hate to tell you this, but your wool is gone.' He said it gently, but his words shocked Charlotte. What would this mean for them?

'But the good news is, we have been tracking Syd's accounts and can recover your money at the time when he sold your wool under his own brand. The wool is long gone, but you were fortunate he sold it during September when the prices were high. That was all thanks to him having the inside information he was privy to. The tricky part is, we can't take back what he stole until he's proven guilty in court. My suggestion is that I help you put in an insurance claim. That way you'll get your money back sooner.'

'That sounds like the best way to go,' Charlotte agreed. With the last of her hay fed out to the stock, Charlie and Adam would need to drop off more, especially with summer on their doorstep. After everything her mum had gone through, plus supporting and believing in her, she wanted to get her something great for Christmas. And if she were truly honest with herself, she needed to thank her next-door neighbour too.

CHAPTER 46

Even though the early heat of the day parched her mouth, Charlotte couldn't contain her anticipation as she headed to The Small Store. She planned to meet up with Fraser, and she'd devised the best way to do it.

'Morning, Janice.' Charlotte radiated happiness as she walked towards the counter, her excitement ramping higher when Janice placed a large paper bag in front of her. Charlotte lifted her basket to the top of the counter and placed the rolls, the coffees, and the slice inside, snatching a bag of raspberry lollies for good measure.

'My, don't you look lovely. Great day for a spot of lunch down the paddock,' Janice said, a tone of enchantment in her voice as she smiled knowingly.

'Indeed it is, Janice.' Paying for her goods and waving goodbye, Charlotte scooted out the door with her walking-on-air smile plastered to her face. Her next stop was to set up the back of the ute in the dappled shade of the peppercorn tree beside the sheep yards, and she was counting on an audience to enjoy the moment with her.

On her way, she texted Fraser, hoping he had reception and would get the message straight away.

Meet me at the sheep yards in half an hour. It's important.

No sooner had she sent it, than a message came back. Okay.

Perfect. She smiled to herself. He had no clue what she was up to. Charlotte's chest squeezed as his response tried to meddle with her mind, thrusting doubt into her heart. Had he continued to reel from their kiss? She was, even though doubts about how they could make things work continued to plague her. Were his feelings going through a grinder like hers? But if she could decide it was worth one more shot then . . . maybe he might too?

Fraser wasn't a second late, his ute slowing, and she kept a close eye on him from the shadows of the yards as he stepped out of the ute, his rolled-up sleeves revealing his tanned arms, one of her favourite things about him.

'Over here.' Charlotte beckoned him with her hand, his Akubra snug on his head, hiding his expression beneath its shadow as Lewie trotted beside him.

As he moved towards her, the look of surprise on his face was worth every lost moment they'd had these past six years. He had come from the sheep yards at home, his jeans dusty and his cheeks ruddy.

'What's up?'

'Come and sit down.'

She smiled and he followed her lead as she moved to the other side of the yards, with Brutus following alongside the fence, his nose in the air as Charlotte waited for Fraser, patting the rug set out on the back of the ute. Taking her seat on the drop-down tray door, he did the same and she reached into the basket, offering him a hot takeaway coffee before setting the brown paper bag down on a plate in between them. She grinned at him as Lewie leaped into the back of the tub, lying dutifully behind them with his head resting on his feet. Brutus gave a throaty *baa*.

'What's in there?' Fraser's inquisitive frown never failed to set her heart racing, and she chirped back.

'Take a look.'

With a questioning frown, Fraser looked down at the bag, glancing at her one more time before he opened it. What could be so special that she needed to make such a fuss? When he'd received her text, the relief that swept over him was sweet. She wanted to see him.

He slipped the bag away from the box which contained a large vanilla slice the size of a small cake. But that wasn't the only surprise. What was written on top was the best thing he could have ever hoped for.

Country girl, now and forever.

His hand slowed, the paper bag waving in the light breeze as he did a double-take. Did this mean—? He fought against his hopes rising faster than the heat of the day.

'I've sold my business and I'm moving back here. For good.' Her face lit up, her beaming smile stirring excitement inside his chest.

Was she saying what he thought she was? How would she cope? When was this happening? His mind boggled with questions, but instead of asking them, he could only watch her, frightened that if he broke this moment, his expectant bubble might burst.

'Fraser.' She reached for his hand, linking fingers with his and holding it tight. 'I'm staying. The sale goes through next month.'

He wanted to smile, but he couldn't fully make sense of what was happening. Did this mean she wanted to give *them* a chance? He'd wanted this for so long. Could he dare to let his heart hope for real this time?

But what if his father found out? He didn't love the prospect of that either. There was no way to hide the time they would be spending together, clearly for more than farm issues alone. What he truly wanted was *their* future from this moment. This was his chance at his forever, and he wasn't about to let it go a second time.

Her excitement was contagious, and he found himself with butterflies swirling in his belly and an all-too-powerful urge to kiss those sweet lips that had tormented him for way too long.

'Charlotte . . . I couldn't be happier for you.'

She put a gentle finger to his lips, quickly shaking her head. 'Call me Char.' And before she could say another word, he covered her mouth with his, their kiss tender, long, and promising a future of forever between them.

Brutus baaed on cue, tossing his head up and down in the air.

Fraser's eyes remained closed when Charlotte sat back, breaking the intimacy between them that, in all the time they'd been together, he had never recognised to be so strong. Opening his eyes, he found her watching him, her gentle smile calling him to kiss her again before she spoke.

'Fraser, I'm sorry I've been so hard on you.' She looked down at her fingers interlaced with his, her expression contemplative. 'It was easier for me to never forgive you. But allowing myself to hold onto that only eats me up. I care so much about you, and I want a future with you.' Her shoulders sagged as she released a relieved breath, grateful she was finally able to tell him everything she felt. 'It was easier for me to make allowances for Will and not you, and for that, I'm so sorry.' She kept her eyes down, her head shaking in regret and despair that was all too real. 'But it doesn't change the fears I have about the station, and what it might take from me.' She glanced back up at him, her eyes wide and concerned.

'What? Why? The farm can't hurt you, Char.' He dipped his head, catching her eyes as she reluctantly lifted them to him.

'Yes, it can. I came back here believing the farm had robbed me of everything I loved, and it had. I was better off hating you and not letting you near, because everything I love gets ripped away from me. Forever. Fraser, I'm scared the farm will steal you from me too, because I love you.'

Fraser's heart swelled, the impact of her words gripping him.

'Char, I've never stopped loving you. There's never been anyone else. Ever.'

Charlotte looked at him, blinking. 'But doesn't it scare you? I'm jinxed.'

'Nothing will ever scare me if I have you.'

'Not even your father? He's not my biggest fan.' This time she managed a small grin.

'I'm not the biggest fan of his either,' he said, reaching out to brush the stray strand of hair behind her ear as every last shred of uncertainty faded away. All that mattered was them. He'd deal with tomorrow and what his father had to say about it when the time came. 'I reckon I'm with the right person. Char, Sheepwash Creek was never the thing trying to take away loved ones from you. That can happen anywhere, anytime. But you allowed yourself to believe it did because that gave you permission to hate it. And run from it. But look at you. You're here.' He squeezed her hands in his, urging her to look at him. 'Now you're so much stronger than that.'

CHAPTER 47

'Peter Rabbit, will you please stop eating and sweep the verandah.' With her hands on her hips, her mother's mood was not one to be messed with as she put down the tray of smoked salmon. Charlotte paused from hanging the fairy lights across the verandah roof, giggling as Pete took one last swipe at the plate before the tea towel her mother was holding flicked his way with a sharp snap.

With the lights up, Charlotte proceeded to hammer a nail into the wood before hanging a Christmas bauble from each. The heat radiating off the tin roof was stifling, but tomorrow was going to be worth the effort, the temperature a much more pleasant twenty-nine degrees.

'Is there anything you need from Ballarat, Mum? I need to do some last-minute shopping.'

'Yes. Can you get me a bottle of cream? Oh, and we'll need custard and brandy. Take a cool box and ice bricks with you or they'll never make it home.'

Charlotte headed out to the verandah, closely followed by her frazzled mother, the meticulous note for Rob's IGA in hand as Pete unenthusiastically cleaned out the junk lumped at one end of the verandah in preparation for the big lunch. No sooner had he finished than a broom was thrust in his direction.

'Oh, no, I wouldn't want to steal your mode of transport from you,' he said, winking at her mother.

'Well, if you sweep down the verandah, I might let you have a turn.' Mum waggled her eyebrows, smiling back, and Charlotte hid her embarrassment by turning away.

Pete gave her a tauntingly dashing smile. 'How about we take a ride together?' His bushy eyebrows danced with glee.

'How about you get the sweeping done, and then I might decide if you deserve feeding or not,' her mother said, chuckling as she spun towards the door and out of his reach.

'What you do to me, woman,' he exclaimed, holding the broom in the air.

Charlotte tried not to encourage Pete, but she couldn't hide her laughter. What was happening to these adults she loved? Shouldn't they be acting more, what was it, mature than this? She was reaching for the handle of the ute when Mum frantically popped her head back out the door.

'Don't forget the extra butter and the maple syrup for the ham. And get extra prawns and a small garlic clove, and more milk, please. Check my list,' she said, waving her hand in the air before disappearing back inside again.

Charlotte dutifully checked the list. From when she'd last looked, it had grown—a lot. She hopped in the ute, closing the door before anything else could be requested. The amount of food already taking pride of place inside the kitchen was about to burst out through the laundry walls, and she didn't want to be party to the explosion when it did.

Charlotte called in at Munchies, giving Clare a bunch of flowers she'd picked from her mother's garden, before she made her way to the country clothing store in the main street. They had everything from leather boots to jeans, shirts, and jumpers. Charlotte had toyed with what to get Fraser, but it wasn't until she stopped in front of the wallets and accessories display cabinet that she found the perfect gift.

She headed for Rob's, her mind racing with Mum's to-do list, not sure if she was going to be able to complete it before tomorrow. But if she could run a farm for a few months, surely she could whip Pete into gear, the two of them getting it all done.

The heat was sending a reflective shimmer over the iron roof by the time Charlotte arrived home, the ice-cream beginning to melt and the tasty cheese turning soft. Pete came out to give her a hand with the groceries.

'Wow, the verandah looks good. Did Mum use the whip on you to do it?'

'No, Miss Charlotte. I did it all by myself. This old bull can clean when he wants to.'

'So how come you never normally offer? I wasn't sure you had it in you.'

'Why, you—'

Charlotte giggled as she ran up the steps and through the back door before he could pick up the broom and chase her with it.

Yes, Christmas was going to be great.

Christmas morning was peaceful up until nine a.m. when Pete flew in, clutching presents which he threw under the tree, before moving over to give Mum a whiskery kiss on the cheek. Her mother went suitably red, and Charlotte marvelled at how different Pete was to her father, yet how perfect he was for her mother, should she decide he was the man for her. Until then, Pete wasn't about to stop trying.

Charlotte escaped to the shearing shed, ignoring the various cars arriving. She needed to feed the rams, and truth be told, she wanted some quiet space of her own.

'Brutus, I'm going to spoil you today.' She tossed him an apple she had cut up. It was one of his favourite things, and she was well aware she was going soft, but hey, it was Christmas.

'Are you going to spoil me too?'

Delighted warmth radiated from the top of her head to the tips of her toes as she straightened her body, unable to resist the one person walking up to her from behind. Fraser wrapped his arms around her in a snuggly hug, nuzzling into her neck before she could turn around.

'Merry Christmas.'

She twisted her body towards him, placing her arms around his neck as she gave him a kiss that sent her toes curling inside her boots. 'And a Merry Christmas to you.'

'I have something for you.' She grinned, removing a small present beautifully wrapped and hidden snugly in her pocket. She wanted to give it to him privately, and this was the perfect moment.

Fraser's endearing smile morphed into surprise and deep curiosity as he took it, unwrapping the small present. His face morphed into surprise as he pulled out a gold fob chain, swallowing hard before he looked at her.

'How . . . did you know?' He reached into his pocket, tugging out his Grandpa Jacob's fob watch, attaching it to the chain. Her heart swelled. She knew it had been the perfect gift.

'When you told me about the accident—' She paused, hoping the mention of it wouldn't upset him today of all days. 'I saw you twisting it over and over in your fingers. I took a chance that you may not have one. I know how much it means to you.'

'You remember that?' Fraser's eyes were damp and her heart lifted to bursting point for him.

'I have something for you too,' he said, swallowing hard before tugging the gift from his pocket and passing it to her.

The rush of blood inside her ears overtook the noise of the rams munching on their hay. It was a box that looked all too familiar. Was he—

'Open it, Char,' he encouraged, and she fought to focus, her love for him ready to spill from her eyes at any moment.

She untied the ribbon, teased the paper away, and as she opened the box, Fraser dropped to one knee.

'Marry me, Char. You're the only woman for me.'

Inside the box was the ring with a small open heart, the one he'd given her when she was fourteen, declaring his love for her.

And he was doing it again.

She turned the case towards him and he removed the ring, placing it on her left ring finger as tears streamed down her face.

He kissed her hand before he stood, brushing away her tears with his thumbs and kissing her with renewed hope, love, and everlasting loyalty.

Charlotte had the table almost set when everyone else began arriving at lunchtime. All manner of food was strewn on the kitchen benchtops, and the air conditioner kept her mother from blowing a gasket as Janice breezed in with a fresh vanilla slice. Rosemary balanced tins of savoury nibbles and a pav in her arms, and Mrs Hudson tottered in with a big fruit salad dressed with lemonade syrup rather than her famous sweet sherry recipe because she didn't need to witness Nicholas attempting to steal mouthfuls of it for the whole afternoon.

The longest Christmas lunch, which the Redding's hosted every year, was set out on three long trestle tables that ran the whole length of the verandah. Gum leaves swathed the hessian table runner, and glass jars dotted the tables, filled with hickory wattle flowers from Dad's summer flowering collection, and some of Mum's summer garden blooms.

Her mother's ham stole centre stage, its golden maple glaze turning heads. Interspersed along the table were plates full of salamis, cheeses, grapes, cherries, and dips, with crisp, parmesan cheese straws Rosemary was making regularly these days. Fresh salads graced the table, and Pete ensured he was well within arm's reach of the choices on offer, having already gathered a considerable sample of everything on his plate. Big Nev sat next to him, shaking his head as Pete asked him to pass the potato salad for the second time.

Jimmy Strybosch and Mr and Mrs Hudson sat opposite. She had removed the bowl of lollies from in front of Nicholas, but that hadn't stopped him leaning over the table and swiping handfuls, hiding his rather large collection in his lap. But with Big Nev keeping a close eye on him from across the table, he hadn't worked up his bravery to slip some into his mouth. John and Gus were making suggestions for the local CFA shed improvements, before Gus worked to convince his uncle Neil to sell his stock feed shop so they could both move down to Forest Gully, where Neil could retire and Gus could surf to his heart's content. Charlotte caught the brief glimpse John tossed her way, as if he was telling her that despite them reaching a stalemate between one another, their differences weren't over yet. She smiled softly as he looked away again. If she could handle the farm on her own for six months, then nothing John threw her way could frighten her.

Rosemary and her mum bounced like yo-yos, attending to all the food, and ensuring everyone had enough, helped along by Janice.

Paul was in a deep discussion about the new choice of tyres that Fraser and Will might like to try out for their utes, as Maddie stared starry-eyed at Will, clearly moving on from Fraser, much to Charlotte's relief. Ross and Mark light-heartedly argued over how many tonnes per acre the recent cropping had achieved thanks to the latest rain. Frank was trying to assure Jonno it would be good for him to sell some of his cuts in his store, gourmet style, which wasn't going down well at all.

Charlotte watched the people she loved. And remembering, sadly, the ones who weren't here to celebrate. Her heart filled with sadness, but as she turned to Fraser sitting next to her, more happiness than she'd ever thought she could hope for immediately replaced it. He turned to her, sharing a loving wink, one that said you are my world, forever, and her chest radiated with deep love. This warmth was the kind she had been looking for ever since leaving

Settlers Hill and here it was, sitting beside her like an unopened gift. It had been here the whole time.

Charlotte's heart skipped as Fraser's hand settled on her knee, her fingers twisting the ring on her hand. He was in deep discussion with Paul, but keenly sensed how she was feeling anyway. The guy couldn't get any better if he tried.

Fraser reached into his pocket and pulled out Grandpa Jacob's pocket watch. He clenched it in his hand before he turned and looked at her, planting a tender kiss on her lips, grinning, then turning back to chat.

It was then that Charlotte recognised how she had been so caught up in her own desperate need to prove herself, she hadn't been able to appreciate this whole time all Fraser had been doing was trying to keep her here against his father's wishes. He cared for her so deeply, unafraid of any consequences his father might throw at him. And she was sure they would come at some point. But they had each other, so it didn't matter what they came up against. It was never going to stop them from being together.

Her mind trailed back to the two people missing from the gathering, and that dreaded day at the Wool Show where Dad had died, and she recognised something that John Pierce had said at his funeral. Something he'd been so wrong about. She might not be the perfect replacement for either her father or James, but she sure as hell would do her best for the farm, her way. She would still be working alongside Dad and James, through their memory. She had discovered she *could* be a woman of the Western District, one who smashed the unspoken tradition of both owning and running a large sheep station. A flicker of pride glowed in her. The farm could throw all it wanted her way, but it wouldn't beat her, *and* it wouldn't kill her.

She wasn't a reluctant farmher anymore.

Now she was a farmher.

JANICE'S FAMOUS VANILLA SLICE

This recipe is "oh so yum", even if I do say so myself! It was given to me by a wonderful woman named Jan, who would sometimes surprise us at smoko, so you can see where my inspiration came for the character's name. Jan used to do the books for the large merino sheep station I work at, and during shearing time, she would always pop up to the shed to say hello. Finely built, she was also a fierce competitor in the Commonwealth Games for shooting, and I admire anyone who has the get-up and go to do something they enjoy, regardless of their gender or what others might think or say.

I hope you love this recipe as much as everyone I share it with does. It's a little ripper, and always a winner.

Enjoy

Love Laurelle xo

INGREDIENTS:
- 2 sheets frozen Puff Pastry, thawed
- 600 ml Thickened Cream
- 100 g packet Instant Vanilla Pudding Mix
- ¼ cup Icing Sugar, plus 2 teaspoons extra for dusting
- ¾ teaspoon Vanilla Extract

METHOD:
1. Preheat oven 220 degrees C (200 fan-forced).
2. Place 1 pastry sheet onto a single tray and prick with a fork. Do the same with the second sheet, only this time scoring it into 4cm squares (or larger if you prefer

bigger vanilla slice pieces).

3. Bake 8-10 minutes until pastry is puffed and golden brown. Remove from oven, then press down on each sheet with a clean tea-towel or oven mitt, to flatten. Allow to cool.

4. In a small bowl, using an electric mixer, beat together cream, pudding mix, icing sugar and vanilla extract for 3-4 minutes, or until thick and creamy. Spread mixture onto unscored sheet of pastry, top with scored pastry sheet. Dust with extra icing sugar.

5. Cut into squares (beware it's super squishy), boil the kettle, and sit back in the sun, ready to indulge your senses with a cup of tea, a yummy, sweet treat, and a great book!

And please remember, I'd love to know what you think.

You can contact me via:
Website: www.laurellecousins.com
Email: laurelle@laurellecousins.com
FB: Laurellecousins.writes
INSTAGRAM: laurellecousins.writes

Acknowledgements

Sometimes I think this is the best part of writing a book! A manuscript doesn't get written all on its own, well not for me anyway. It takes a cheer squad and yes, the all-important peanut gallery (yes you, Ceeny), to get it across the line, and there are so many I'd like to thank.

This book is the first one I ever wrote and has had at least four complete rewrites because, let's face it, you think your first book is perfect (I really did), and then you learn a whole lot more and realise the road to improving this craft is far wider than you ever thought possible. I was inspired to write this story after I started working at Beverley Merino Station, studying wool classing while working there as a farm hand, having given up my teaching career after having our two beautiful girls. Agriculture is in my blood and I love every part of it, except maybe the -3 degree mornings out feeding sheep and marking lambs when my fingers refused to bend.

John Barty. I will forever miss you, and I can't help but think the timing of this book coming out was meant just for you. I've met so many wonderful people in my classing career—Mac, Terry, Kelvin, Mr P and Mr H, Candice, and yes you little Bridie, to name but a few—and even with the lows that inevitably come with every job, I wouldn't change a thing. Thank you for letting me be a part of your lives and learning from you all. I'll always consider you my friends outside of the industry we love.

Annie Seaton, what a treasure you are! You're happy to ride my highs and my lows (both as an editor and a friend) and shape my words with just the right warmth and nuances to make the story shine. My heartfelt thanks.

Tan – Petit Pixel Design – yes, I'm going to plug you! You have the patience of a saint when mine is going down the drain at a million miles an hour! That means you are integral to both my computer illiteracy sanity and my confidence when I think something is beyond my brain to learn. You've been riding this crazy ride with me from the word go and I couldn't do it without you, so please keep hanging around!

Amy Doak, what a legend Young Adult fiction writer and friend you are! From pep talks, the 'In conversation' chat with me at the launch of Sheep Gully Road, to my book teasers and trailers, you are one of the girls in my corner and I wouldn't want it any other way. Hugs!

Marni Pollock, the osteo who keeps me on the straight and narrow when I've been hunched over my keyboard far too long. Thank you for your invaluable input into how muscles behave and what to look for when they misbehave. Boots loves you for it.

Lisa Ireland, it's been a long time now since you mentored me but you still manage to perch yourself on my right shoulder every time I write. I can hear your voice saying: 'We need to feel her emotion,' or 'Don't forget deep point of view.' Your kind yet strong advice has shaped my writing more than you know and I'm so grateful.

Kelli – um, no words. Well maybe just a couple. How do I thank someone who literally tells me almost every day that I am good enough to do this? And asks so many questions I sometimes forget where I live! I've got you too, and I wouldn't want it any other way.

Jeanette, I love the way we do life together, regardless of the business of our lives and family. Let's not change a thing! Xox

My amazing ARC readers! I am so incredibly grateful to have you all in my writing world, and so so glad you're happy to keep hanging around. Helen Sibbritt, Karren Sandercock, Bianca Malyan, Janene Morgan, Leanne Lovegrove, and Happy Valley Booksread, Craig and Phil. Thank you, thank you, thank you! And an extra special thanks to Craig and Phil who drove two hours to celebrate the launch of Sheep Gully Road with me in person. Truly grateful. xox

Merrilyn Kinsman – is there a super fan bigger than you? Absolutely not! And I get to do life with you too. How lucky am I! And to Frank, Lyndsey and Leigh, you are the best, as is all my wonderful immediate and extended family. Mike, you're still hanging in with me despite my computer tantrums (a less regular occurrence these days thankfully and maybe you really are managing to teach me!) and our beautiful girls, Corinne and Breanna, and you too, Jeremy. Love you all to the moon and beyond!

Ida Brady, we've been having a shot at this writing caper right alongside each other for a loooong time. Love our sporadic phone calls (I pinch myself every time that I talk to you when you live in Ireland!) Big squishy hugs and love.

Lois L and Sonn W, where would I be without you girls. Your friendship is second to none, and you're knack for scanning my words for those pesky typos is brilliant. I'm keeping both of you!

Roby Aiken, proofreader extraordinaire. My heartfelt thanks.

If you are ever in Bendigo in the middle of July and feel like taking a look at lots of sheep and stunning woolly products (and a whole lot more), then make the time to visit the Sheep and Wool Show. It's a great day out!

To my wonderful readers who have given me all the love, incredible support and encouragement to keep tapping away and writing the stories of my heart. Your feedback and requests for new stories makes my heart beat faster, so please keep letting me know.

And to all my new readers, let's hang around together some more! I'd love to hear from you. You can find my contact details on my 'About The Author' page at the front of this book.

 Laurelle xox